OUTTAKES FROM THE GRAVE

OUTTAKES FROM THE GRAVE

A Night Huntress Outtakes Collection

JEANIENE FROST

Outtakes from the Grave
Copyright © 2015 by Jeaniene Frost
ISBN: 9781519762429

NYLA Publishing
350 7th Avenue, Suite 2003, NY 10001, New York.
http://www.nyliterary.com

TABLE OF CONTENTS

FOREWORD BY JEANIENE FROST

The Night Huntress series is a *New York Times, USA Today,* and internationally bestselling series that has been published in twenty different countries. Just writing that is humbling, because originally I hadn't intended for it to be a series at all.

Although I had wanted to be a writer since I started fashioning stories out of my dreams at age twelve, I'd never had the fortitude to finish an entire novel. Fast-forward to age twenty-nine when I had a dream about a half-vampire woman arguing with a vampire man about why she'd left him. In the dream, I knew the half-vampire woman still loved her fanged former boyfriend but didn't believe they could make it as a couple. I also knew the man had been looking for her for years and wasn't about to give up now that he'd finally found her. Over the next several days, I couldn't stop thinking about the dream. Who were those people? Why had she left him if she loved him? Why had he kept looking for her even after years of no word? How did they fall in love, and what tore them apart? And how did a *half*-vampire come to be, anyway? Answering those questions eventually became my first novel, *Halfway to the Grave.* Thus, Cat and Bones's story was born.

Much to my surprise, *Halfway to the Grave* didn't finish Cat and Bones's story. In fact, I hadn't even gotten to the scene from my dream yet. So as soon as I finished the first book, I started the second one. When I reached the end of that, I realized I was still nowhere near done with their story, so I started writing the third novel. When I finished that, I immediately started the fourth one.

At this point, my husband suggested that I should see if I could get the *first* novel published before I kept writing more in the same series. I agreed, albeit reluctantly because I wasn't optimistic about my chances. Still, pursuing publication would be a good way to keep writing while also pacifying my husband, so I began looking into how to get published. This was back in 2004, and I knew nothing about the process, nor did I know anyone in the industry. The digital market didn't exist at this point, so self-publishing wasn't a viable option. My chances seemed limited to having a major publisher take a chance on me or never being published at all.

I'll sum up the next two years by saying that I learned about the industry the hard way, such as being scammed by a pay-for-service literary agent. I also learned the hard way that finishing a novel did *not* mean the novel was ready to be shopped for publication. Since I had written *Halfway to the Grave* for my own entertainment, I didn't think about things like pacing, sticking to the main plot instead of exploring side stories, staying within genre constraints, or a host of other things that resulted in many, many cuts and rewrites. In 2006, I signed with a legitimate agent who sold the first two Night Huntress novels to Harper Collins. In late 2007, preorders for *Halfway to the Grave* were strong enough that Harper bought three more novels before the first one was officially released. Their prediction proved correct: *Halfway to the Grave* debuted on both the *New York Times* and the *USA Today* bestseller lists. No one was more surprised about this than me: I made my editor e-mail me a copy of both lists before I believed her.

I ended up being ridiculously blessed by having all seven novels in the Night Huntress series hit those and other best-seller lists. Cat and Bones's story came to its conclusion in *Up from the Grave*, although they have and will continue to appear as side characters in spin-off novels from the Night Huntress series. For all the reasons listed above, a lot of scenes from *Halfway to the Grave, One Foot in the Grave, At Grave's End*, and *Destined for an Early Grave* ended up on the cutting-room floor. Putting them all together made me real-ize that they equated to more than the size of a full-length novel.

As mentioned, when I originally wrote the books, I didn't only write scenes that advanced the main plot forward at the most brisk pace possible. Instead, in those first drafts, I took more time to explore the characters through alter-nate scenarios, multiple side plots, additional backstory, and increased revelations. I also wrote several love scenes that never made it into the final versions of the books. It was very, very hard to take those scenes out and to make a choice between different versions when the time came, which is why I saved those old versions instead of deleting them. Over the years, readers requested that I post some of the deleted scenes and/or alternate versions, and I did release a handful of them. Much to my surprise, the overwhelming response I received was that readers wanted more. That is why I decided to compile the best of the deleted scenes and alternate versions into an anthology of sorts, so that readers could see the untold side of Cat and Bones's story in addi-tion to the official, published novels.

This was a big task. I had several different versions of each of the first four novels spread out across old disks, CDs, and/or backup files on my hard drive. For added amusement, some of the files were password protected, and in the decade-plus since I wrote them, I forgot what the passwords were. That meant I had to comb through over ten years of Sent files on my e-mail to see if I'd e-mailed the story to any friends for feedback (I had, thank God!) Then, once I had versions that I could actually open, I had to comb through them to pull out the scenes and alternate versions that people would hopefully want to read. I also wanted to include commentary as to why a particular scene or version didn't make it into the official version so that readers would get a glimpse into the process. Finally, I sent the entire compilation to be professionally edited and proofread. Needless to say, in its original state, there were grammar and spelling errors galore.

The result is *Outtakes from the Grave*, which includes both previously published as well as never-before-seen deleted scenes and alternate versions with behind-the-scenes commentary and explanations. Where necessary, I've also included bits of scenes that ended up in the published versions to provide context for the deleted/alternate scenes so that they're easier to read. I hope you enjoy getting a chance to explore the adventures of Cat, Bones, and the Night Huntress gang more deeply with these stories and that you enjoy seeing "what might have been" with versions of events that differ from the ones in the books.

The scenes and versions are listed in chronological order according to the series timeline. Each scene or alternate version is broken into its own individual chapter, so you can read them all or skip to the ones you're most interested in. As always, thank you, readers, for taking this journey along with me. I hope you've enjoyed the ride as much as I have.

CHAPTER ONE
ORIGINAL BEGINNING OF
HALFWAY TO THE GRAVE

Author's note: *Beginnings are the bane of my existence. I tend to overwrite them and thus end up cutting a lot from my first draft to my published version.* Halfway to the Grave *was no different. Not only did I overwrite it, I crossed markets because the original beginning shows Cat as a naïve, teenage girl, which would have confused editors and agents into thinking that this was a young adult novel instead of an adult paranormal romance. In addition to that, the former beginning is also very violent as it shows Cat encountering her first vampire, so there wasn't much in it to appeal to an editor or agent even if they did figure out that this was an adult romance. That's why, after several rejections, I cut this from the manuscript after realizing that its innocence-lost, homicidal-tendencies-found theme didn't match with the rest of the novel. The original beginning ends at the first sentence of the published version of* Halfway to the Grave.

One more difference that readers will notice is Cat's age. In this version, she's only nineteen when she first meets Bones. This was a combination of authorial intrusion and lack of knowledge about the publishing industry. I was moved out and married at nineteen, so I didn't think it was too young for my heroine to be involved in a passionate relationship. I also knew that Cat would age several years between the first book and the second one, so I wasn't worried

*about her being that age for the entirety of the storyline. However, the
agent I eventually signed with told me I needed to make Cat older
because she was too young to be a heroine in the traditional adult
market. I compromised by aging her up to twenty and then had to
age her up again to twenty-two when Harper Collins acquired the
novel. I didn't change much else about Cat to match her new age in
the story, so later, some readers correctly pointed out in their reviews
that Cat seemed to read younger than twenty-two. In the original
beginning, however, she's an innocent sixteen-year-old who's about
to go toe-to-toe with her first vampire.*

When I left my house that day, I'd had absolutely no
intention of killing anyone. I'd been looking for my
boyfriend, Danny. I met him a few weeks ago when his car
broke down near my grandparents' orchard. Driving late at
night was one of the ways I escaped from the taunts of other
kids over my illegitimacy. That's how small this town was.
People still cared about things like that.

Of course, if you compared being illegitimate next to
my father being a vampire, it hardly measured up.

Not that my neighbors knew that. Neither did my grandparents, whom my mother and I lived with. People didn't
believe in vampires. Only my mother knew what I was. The
man who raped her almost seventeen years ago had rede-
fined the term "necking." At least that explained her distant, suspicious nature when it came to everyone, especially
me. My mother hated vampires with a pathological passion,
and I was half-vampire whether I wanted to be or not.

Danny hadn't called me all week. I called him Monday
and left a message. Tuesday, I called again. Wednesday, I left
a more worried message. Had he called but my grandparents hadn't told me? They thought I was too young to date,
so that wouldn't have surprised me.

By Thursday, I imagined all sorts of horrible things that might have befallen Danny. He was a victim of a robbery. Or a car accident. Food poisoning. In jail for driving while drinking. My mind was an endless supply of bad possibilities. When Friday came, I was nearly sick with worry. I knew there were other, more terrible things that could have happened to Danny. Things no average police department would know about.

Without telling my mother where I was going, I set off for Danny's apartment. He lived an hour away in Columbus. When I pulled up to his building, I flew out of my truck and pounded on his door. No answer, and his car wasn't there. Okay, no luck here, but someone had to know if he was okay. After a few wrong turns, I found his friend George's frat house where Danny had taken me the previous weekend. I parked out front and pushed my way through the milling college kids.

A guy stopped me on my way to George's room. "Who are you?"

I smiled up at him. "I'm Catherine. I'm looking for George, I was here last week. He, uh, helped me with my license."

George was a counterfeiter in addition to being a college student. Last Saturday he'd made me a license showing I was twenty-one. Danny already had one. That was the point, so I could go to the places Danny went to.

"Wait here. I'll see if George is still around."

A few minutes later George came down, looking confused and slightly irritable. "Cathy, what're you doing here? You didn't lose your ID already, did you?"

"George." My voice cracked a bit from strain. "Have you seen Danny? I haven't been able to get ahold of him all week. Is he all right?"

Something I couldn't name passed over his face. "Yes, Danny's fine. In fact, I think he's at Galaxy, the club the two of you went to last week. You remember where it is?"

"Um, we never made it last weekend." I knew my face was red, but I didn't let it stop me. "Can you give me directions?"

Reluctance was written all over him, but I persisted. When I had the directions, I thanked him and left, so excited to know Danny was okay that I forgot to wonder why he hadn't called me.

Galaxy turned out to be huge. Their doors were open, the sounds of music spilling into the parking lot. I walked up to the entrance hesitantly but with determination, not about to let a thing like nerves stop me. At the door the bouncer gave a hard look at my fake driver's license, holding it under his light and comparing it to my face. I tried to look blasé and smiled as if I didn't have a care in the world. All I needed was to go to jail for possession of false identification, but he finally waved me inside. The music was pounding, and it seemed like hundreds of gyrating bodies were all around me. My plain white T-shirt turned hues of neon in the fluorescent glare of the lights. Pushing through the dancers was like walking through deep water. When I found my way to the nearest bar, I scanned the people around it. No Danny yet.

"Buy you a drink?" a voice behind me asked.

I whirled, smiling, but it wasn't Danny. An unknown guy in a red shirt grinned at me.

"No thanks," I said, and turned back to the crowd.

From my vantage point, I noticed there were several bars in the club. Wading once more through the living barricades, I reached the other side in what seemed like an hour. My head had started to pound along with the music, and my eyes were sore from the flashes of light scoring the room. The second and third bars were no more helpful. Despair began to set in that George had been wrong and Danny wasn't here after all. I leaned against the wall, glancing at the second floor of the club. People were gathered by a banister that overlooked the main floor. As I watched, a familiar sandy-colored head came into view.

"Danny!" I yelled, but to no avail as he wouldn't have heard a bullhorn in this noise. With relief, I pushed my way to the stairs and sprinted up them toward Danny.

The broad smile of greeting I wore dropped from my face when I saw him more clearly. A blond girl was in front of him, her hands on his chest. She was grinning as he leaned down to kiss her. I stared, shocked, as Danny put his arms around the girl.

After a long minute, he broke the kiss—and finally noticed me. "Oh shit," he muttered.

I heard him. I shouldn't have with all the background noise, but my hearing wasn't normal. Neither was my eyesight, and I absorbed every emotion on his face as he looked from her to me.

"Catherine! Er... What are you doing here?" Danny stepped back from the pretty blonde, who gave me a belittling glance as she took in my jeans, sneakers, and T-shirt.

"Is this the girl you were telling me about, Danny? The one you just broke up with?"

"What?" It was a gasp of outrage, not a question. My hands balled into fists, and I took several deep breaths to calm down. *Control your anger. You can't let anyone know what you are.*

"Can you give me a second?" Danny asked the blonde.

She tossed one more snotty glance at me and then smiled. "Sure. I'll be at the bar."

Danny waited until she'd walked away before speaking again. "Catherine, I was going to call you, because I've been thinking. You're just sixteen; I'm almost twenty. You're too young… it wouldn't work out between us."

After everything he'd said to me the previous weekend, I couldn't believe what I was hearing. "You told me you cared about me, that you'd never felt this way before, that I meant so much to you…" Every item was ticked off in a low hiss. "That was five days ago, Danny! And now you've changed your mind?" My anger covered the hurt welling inside me. I desperately wanted him to take back what he'd just said.

Danny lowered his head, flicking his gaze around him to see if anyone else was paying attention to this scene. The dimple in his chin wrinkled when he pursed his lips, seeming to choose his words. "It's like this, Catherine," he began in a tone he'd never used with me before. "I thought we could have some fun, and you seemed into it as well. Right until it was time to actually have fun, and then you got all coy and hesitant. So I told you what you needed to hear. Get over it—it's not a big deal. It wasn't even that good. Now go on home. Isn't it past your bedtime?"

Danny turned around without another word. He went to the bar, slung an arm around the smirking blonde, and walked away. I watched them go, transfixed, while emotions slammed over me. I had been used, plain and simple. Used like the stupid hick farm girl I apparently was. All week long I'd been worried about Danny. Worried and happy and ignorant and disposable. Tears began to trickle down my cheeks. When I'd first begun dating Danny, I'd thought maybe there was a chance I could live a normal life despite what I was. Hopelessness felt so much harsher after I'd been allowed to hope. My hurt was soon followed by despair. It must be my bloodline. Maybe I was being punished for the evil inside me, no matter that it wasn't my fault it was there.

"He isn't worth it."

I didn't know who the voice behind me belonged to, but without turning around, I nodded. "I guess he isn't." My voice was a rasp. I barely recognized it.

"Have a drink with me."

"Okay."

Still I didn't turn around but kept my eyes on Danny and his blonde until they disappeared into the crowd. A cool hand touched my arm, making me flinch at the twinge of static electricity. I let the guy lead me to the nearby bar and sat on the stool as if in a daze. My unknown escort ordered two gin and tonics. When a cold glass was pressed into my hand, I finally glanced at my new companion.

My first thought was, *he looks familiar. I know him*, before realizing his face was entirely foreign to me. Black hair brushed his shoulders and his skin was almost the same pale shade as my own. But such skin. Smooth, opalescent... like cream poured over diamonds. Hazel eyes looked right into mine with a stare that seemed to pin me to my seat. The air around him held a faint crackle, as if somehow he'd managed to harness an electrical field as a coat.

Yeah, you could say I knew right away the man sitting next to me was a vampire.

"You're staring." He said it chidingly, but it didn't seem to bother him.

"Yes, I'm staring," I agreed, shock making me numb. Right next to me, sipping a drink, was a real live—sort of—vampire. I couldn't stop looking him up and down. After months of hearing about vampires, here was one in the flesh. My mother had said they looked just like normal people, but she was wrong. With the perfection of his skin and that tingling energy coming off him, I couldn't understand how anyone thought he was human.

A sudden fear gripped me. Could he tell what I was? Was that why he'd stopped me? My stomach gave a frightened lurch. I grabbed the gin and tonic, downing it in one swallow.

The vampire gave me a surprised glance before ordering another one. "Thirsty, aren't you?" he remarked.

"Aren't you?" I blurted out, then nearly choked. *Smart one, Catherine.*

"Of course." He brought his glass to his mouth and took a sip, then smiled. "That's better."

I suppressed a scoff, my mother's words ringing in my head. *They're demons, Catherine. Monsters. All they want to do is trick people so they can get them alone and kill them.* We'd see about that.

"What's your name?" My tone was steady, but nerves made me gulp my second drink as quickly as I had the first one. It was finished before he answered me.

"Anthony."

"Anthony what?" I stared right into his eyes now, challenging him. A strange peace had descended over me. It was a savage serenity, but with purpose. Danny had dumped me, I had no friends, and my life was a constant source of shame for my mother. What did I have to lose? This vampire was out for blood, but maybe I could turn the tables on him.

"Anthony Dansen. What's yours, beautiful girl?"

I knew he'd probably given me a fake name, and after Danny, I never wanted to hear another man call me Catherine.

"My name is… Cat." *And you are my mouse, or I am yours. May the best beast win.*

He smiled, confident and predatory. "Cat what?"

I looked at his hair. It was so dark it could have belonged on a bird's wing. "Raven."

"Isn't that unusual? One half on the opposite spectrum from the other."

With an answering, cold smile, I finished my drink, signaling the waiter for another one. "You have no idea."

After nine more drinks, I allowed Anthony to convince me that I was in no shape to drive. I was kind of surprised that I wasn't drunk from all the booze, but so far so good. Anthony was very considerate, helping me as I pretended to stagger toward the exit. He'd even been a great listener as I told him how I'd been dumped by Danny. Why not? One of us was going to be dead by sunup, so no need to worry about him repeating my humiliating confession. Anthony had oozed sympathy too. It was a good act. If I hadn't known what he was, gullible me might have bought it.

We stopped by my truck so I could get my purse, since I insisted I couldn't leave without it. What he didn't know was that I had a surprise inside that bag, something my mom had given me. I'd soon find out if it was as effective as she'd hoped. I gave Anthony directions in the exact opposite of where I lived. If I died, I didn't want him to look up my family. My driver's license was the fake one, so the address on it was bogus. In short, I was as ready as I was ever going to be.

When I climbed into his car, a lovely dark blue Passat, I put my purse between my body and the interior door. Then I pretended to snooze as we got underway, but in reality, I was reaching into my bag to wrap my fingers around a large silver cross.

I wasn't praying; the cross had a hidden silver dagger inside of it. Some kids got new cars on their sixteenth birthday. My mom had given me a big cross that had a secret switchblade in it. Soon enough I'd find out if silver actually killed vampires, or if crosses repelled them. I would have liked to have had a piece of sharp wood too, just in case, but I hadn't figured on running into a vampire.

Anthony drove in silence for about twenty minutes before he turned off the highway and onto a side road. I knew this because even though my eyes were closed, I could feel the ground change from concrete to bumpy dirt and gravel. Still, I continued my sleeping act. After about fifteen minutes, Anthony stopped. My hand tightened around the cross until it ached. Since my heart was pounding now, which even I could hear, I quit faking sleep and opened my eyes.

Rows of trees were in front of me. Through them, I could see the silvery outline of water. If you wanted to suck someone's blood and dump their body in a secluded place, this spot was postcard-perfect for it.

"Where are we?" I didn't have to fake the tremor in my voice. I was completely alone with a monster who would most likely kill me.

"I wanted to pull off and spend some time with you. You don't like the sound of that?" Anthony made his voice sound vulnerable and sexy. Quite an act, but then practice probably made perfect.

"I want to go home. I'm tired, a little drunk, and I think we should leave."

There. I'd said it firmly. If I was crazy and he was just a regular guy looking for a good time, he'd put the keys back in the ignition and drive off. No harm, no foul.

To my complete lack of surprise, he smiled instead and touched my cheek. "You're beautiful, Cat." He moved closer, leaning in until his mouth was inches from mine. "Kiss me."

His voice dropped to a lower, deeper octave. Smooth as the air outside. He didn't wait for my response but kissed me, his mouth slanting over mine. Anthony's lips were cooler than mine, but I'd been braced for him feeling cold and gross, and I was surprised when he didn't. The thought flashed through my mind that he was a much better kisser than Danny had been too. That was completely absurd, however, because we were here to kill each other.

"Anthony, don't." I pressed against his chest. It didn't move him an inch. My right hand tightened on the concealed cross. "I want to go home."

He stopped kissing me and lifted his head. I screamed, unable to help it. His eyes, which had been hazel at the bar, now glowed a clear bright green. A cruel smile wreathed his face, and yes, poking out from between his lips were pointy, murderous-looking teeth.

"I'm sorry, Cat, but you won't be going anywhere tonight."

His voice had lost that seductive tone. My heart hammered, seeming to be stuck somewhere in my throat. For a few moments that seemed to stretch longer, I watched Anthony bend toward my neck.

"Your eyes are glowing," I whispered. "Guess what? Mine can, too."

"What?"

Anthony glanced up at me right as I struck. My hand flew out, and with all my strength, I plunged that cross dagger into his back, aiming where I guessed his heart would be.

He howled so loud it shook the windows. Then he reared back, trying to reach the weapon in his body. I held on, knowing if I let go, it would be all over. With a savageness I didn't know lay in me, I twisted the blade, wrenching it from side to side. Anthony backhanded me so hard the window cracked when my head hit it. In the split second I let go, he grabbed for the knife.

I kicked at him, my body braced against the door. Since both his hands were clawing at his back, Anthony's face was unprotected. My feet landed with a solid *thunk*, snapping his head back. When his fist arced at me again, I threw myself forward, ducking to avoid his blow and groping for the knife. Fangs sank into my shoulder. I screamed as Anthony tried to chew his way up to my neck. His fists beat on my back until every one of my ribs felt broken. The pain was so great—I knew at any moment I'd pass out and never wake up. But even if I was going to die, maybe, just maybe, I could take him with me. I focused all my remaining effort on the dagger, missing it twice before finally grabbing it again. It was slick with blood, and I curled my fingers around the arms of the cross to anchor my grip. Then I scissored it madly left and right, my vision blackening as Anthony continued to tear at my shoulder and crush me with his fists. With the last bit of strength in me, I gave the dagger one final slanted thrust.

All at once, Anthony's mouth went slack, his arms dropped, and he fell onto me as if unconscious. Even through the haze of overwhelming pain, I smiled.

My last thought before the darkness claimed me was *This one's for you, Mom.*

Feelings returned slowly to me. My back ached. Something heavy was on me. My leg was twisted. My shoulder hurt. I tasted blood in my mouth. *I was still alive.*

That made me snap my eyes open. The first thing I saw was Anthony's face. His mouth hung open, his tongue lolled out, and his features had somehow sunken and withered. He was on top of me, and I was contorted at an odd angle so that I was halfway under the glove box. The blood I'd tasted in my mouth was apparently his since it had run in a disgusting red trail from the hamburger of his back down to my face.

I spat it out, terrified, because I'd clearly swallowed some of it. I pushed at Anthony's body but couldn't get enough traction to get out from under him. Fumbling, I reached behind me and groped around for the door handle. Ah, there it was. One tug later and the door spilled open. I wiggled backward, twisting, until I got enough space between us to kick Anthony back and fall out of the car. From my vantage point in the dirt, the car looked like a pig slaughter. Blood was splattered on the windshield, dashboard, and seats. Add that to a ripped-up man in the front, and there was no way I could drive this into town to get my truck. Somehow I didn't think the police would believe me if I told them the thing I'd killed in it was a vampire. "But honestly, Officer, he tried to suck my blood!" No, better not try to go public with this.

So, then. Unless I wanted to go to jail, I had to get rid of the car and the body. But how?

I gave Anthony's corpse an assessing look. Could I burn him? It would be hard trying to torch him with just the cigarette lighter. To be honest, I was a little surprised that he hadn't spontaneously combusted. They always did in the movies. Maybe he wasn't really dead after all. The thought chilled me.

All right, first things first. I needed to make sure the thing in the car really was a corpse before I worried about disposing of one. I got up, leaning cautiously over the open door.

The dagger still stuck out of Anthony's back like some macabre trophy. With a grimace, I rolled him over so he was faceup.

My stomach gave a sickening lurch. Anthony looked even worse than he had before. His skin was like cracked leather, his lips were pulled away from his teeth, his hands clawlike, and his chest seemed to shrink within itself. If he wasn't dead, he was doing an Oscar-winning performance. Still, I wanted to be sure, so I looked around the backseat for another weapon. Some part of me was afraid if I removed the dagger, Anthony would leap up and attack me.

The backseat was useless. There was nothing, not even a toothpick. The glove box was empty of everything but registration papers, which were not to Anthony Dansen but to a Felicity Summers. I said a quick, silent prayer for Felicity, although I knew it was probably too late. Then as a last resort, I got out and opened the trunk.

"Good God."

I spoke aloud, shocked into doing so. The trunk looked like a Hannibal Lecter starter kit. There was an ax, oversized garbage bags, duct tape, a shovel, extra clothes, and baby wipes. Baby wipes? Mentally I shuddered at the thought of why they were there. As horrifying as the objects in the trunk were, they were tailor-made to suit my purposes. Already I was thinking like a murderer.

Another tremor passed over me as I realized, belatedly, these things were here for me. It made my blood run cold to know these items would have been used in my body's disposal, if Anthony had had his way.

A feeling of vengeful satisfaction coursed through me. Never again would anyone be bled and killed by this vampire. Now, to be sure he was really, truly dead. After a moment of contemplation, I picked up the ax. Two hours later, I was finished. Sweat stuck to me, and I felt like if I showered a thousand times, I would still never be clean. But it was done. Anthony's head was buried about a quarter mile into the woods. His body was hidden half a mile away in the opposite direction. If that didn't ensure he stayed dead, I was all out of ideas.

After debating with myself about what to do with the car, I settled on cleaning it as best as I could with the baby wipes. Then I opened all the windows and pushed it down to the edge of the lake. With luck it would sink to the bottom and never be seen again. As though I were dreaming, I watched the car founder in the water for a few moments before it disappeared. Then I looked down at myself. My jeans and T-shirt were ruined. I stripped to don the extra clothes my would-be murderer had provided—and then stopped short, gaping at my shoulder.

There was no wound. Sure, it was still red from blood, mine and the vampire's, but where there should have been messy punctures from Anthony's teeth, there was nothing but smooth skin. Seized with memory, I gripped my ribs. They should have hurt. In fact, I shouldn't have been able to do any of the things I'd done in the past few hours, what with the beating Anthony had given me. But I felt... fine.

Panic surged in me. How had I healed that fast? Sure, I healed faster than anyone else when I scraped my knees or got a cut, but nothing like this had happened before. Oh no. What if...?

In desperation, I pressed my fingers to my throat. Relief coursed through me when I felt my pulse's strong, steady beat. Then I held my breath for as long as possible before gasping and gulping in air. Okay, I still needed to breathe and my heart was still working, so no, I hadn't turned into a vampire.

My head spun with possibilities. Could his bite have affected me this much? What about his blood? How much of it had I swallowed when it dripped into my mouth? It was all too disturbing to contemplate. Later I would think about it. Right now I had a murder to cover up. I pulled on the spare shirt. It was too long, but style was the least of my concerns. Next came the pants, which I rolled at the legs and the waistband. My bloody, ruined clothes I stuffed into one of the garbage bags. When I was farther away, I'd bury them, but not too close to the body—either piece of it.

With the last of the baby wipes, I scrubbed the blood from my hands, face and shoulders. No wonder Anthony had the wipes, they really did the trick. Lastly, I stuck the crucifix in my pants. There. I'd done the best cover-up and body disposal I could. Hopefully no one would ever find the remains of the vampire or the car. It was time to leave. I had a very long walk ahead of me.

When I finally pulled into the driveway of my house, streaks of sunlight crept over the horizon. It had taken me over two hours to find my way back to the club, then another hour and a half to drive home. Never in my memory had I felt so exhausted. The sound of the truck must have woken my family, because one by one, they came out of the house. My grandparents were in their nightclothes, but my mother wore the same dress she'd had on yesterday. Obviously she'd never been to bed. The look of relief on her face when she saw me turned immediately to anger, and she was at the truck window before I even had time to open to door.

"Where have you been? Do you have any idea what time it is? I've been worried sick! So have your grandparents. They called the police! What...?"

She stopped when she caught sight of my strange clothes as I got out of the car and stumbled toward the house. Her speechlessness lasted only a moment, however.

"Whose clothes are those, Catherine? Answer me!"

I opened my mouth to explain when my grandfather walked up and grabbed me by the shoulders, shaking me hard.

"You think you can run all over, doing God knows what? You will not bring more shame to me! It's been hard enough after what your mother's done. I won't stand by and let you be the same, you—"

He cut off his tirade when I grasped his hands and pulled them off me. For a few silent moments, we glared at each other, me with angry weariness, and he with shock at the strength in my grip. Then I turned my back on him and went to my mother, reaching in my pants. I'd kept one souvenir, just for her.

"Hold out your hand." My voice was harsh, but my eyes weren't.

She stared at me before stretching out her hand. Into it, I placed a small, hard object.

"This is where I was and what I was doing. I'm strong enough, and I know what it takes, so it's what I'll be doing from now on, I promise you."

She stared at the single curved fang in her hand for a long moment, tears overflowing her eyes. Then she reached out and touched my cheek with more tenderness than she'd ever shown me. Finally she wrapped me in her arms.

Tears came to my eyes as well. At last I'd made her proud of me.

My grandfather stomped over. "What in the Sam Hill is going on? Justina, I'm not finished with that girl yet."

"Oh yes you are." My mother's tone was so vehement that my grandfather gazed at her as if she'd grown a second head. She patted my shoulders before speaking again. "Leave her alone, she was doing a good thing. I am her mother, I am responsible for her, and I say it's okay."

With her arm still around me, my mother led me into the house. My grandparents gaped after us but didn't move to stop us. My mother had never spoken up to them before or overruled their wishes, so they were even more shocked than I was. I knew I'd always remember her standing up for me, but I didn't have the energy to dwell on that. As soon as I got to my room, I fell on the bed and passed out.

Later that night, I got up and ate dinner as though nothing had happened, and my grandparents never mentioned it again.

Like my mother before me, I acquired a scholarship to Ohio State University and used money from working the orchards to buy my books. Unlike her, the remainder of the money I used to put a deposit on my ramshackle off-campus apartment came from vampires. Dead vampires, that was. From sheer cold practicality, I'd taken to pocketing their cash after killing them, getting the idea when one of them robbed me before attempting to bite me. Waste not want not was their motto, and it was fast becoming my own. In the three years since my first one, I'd killed four more. I had gotten better at it.

For starters, I realized my weapon had to be bigger. The first vampire nearly killed me because it took too long to destroy his heart with the thin silver cross dagger. The question became, how did I increase my weapon size without giving away that I carried one? My answer came from making caramel apples.

The closest neighbors to my grandparents had an apple orchard. We regularly traded fruits with them. While I was making the apples, sliding the fruit onto its wooden stick for easy handling, the idea hit me. *Hide the silver.* That's what I needed to do. Conceal it in something a vampire wasn't afraid of. Thus the idea for my wood-covered silver stake was born.

It was a custom job, naturally. I took all my savings and bought a wide silver blade, five inches long and pointed. It was heavy but deadly sharp. Next came the disguise. Carefully I glued wooden strips over it, keeping them hard and smooth, contoured to the shape of the silver. When I was finished, I had a very ordinary-looking wooden stake with a surprise inside. Since plain old wood didn't kill vampires (I found that out the hard way with my second one, ending up with a dislocated shoulder, bloody lip, deep puncture wound and a fractured wrist), they weren't afraid of it. Indeed, the one I stabbed through the heart with only wood looked at his chest in amusement before yanking out the stake and ramming it into my thigh. If not for my silver cross with the handy dagger attachment, there would have been nothing left of me but a bad aftertaste in his mouth. Fortunately for me, the vamp thought that since I'd attacked him with wood, I didn't know what really worked. He never saw the silver coming.

My third one was almost downright simple. There was a pattern to it now. I went to any of the clubs within a three-hour drive and perused the patrons for the undead. They were easy to spot for me, their skin being so perfect compared to everyone else's, and their energy crackled the air around them. My false wide-eyed infatuation worked every time, especially when combined with my consuming enough alcohol to fell a horse. The drinks had little effect on me, only making me calmer instead of inebriated. They appeared to have no effect on my vampire companions as well, so I surmised it was an immunity in the tainted blood we shared.

However, it was becoming too risky to keep dumping cars into the lake; I was bound to get caught. It was much simpler to stake them, throw them in their trunk, and drive back to the where I'd parked my truck in a conveniently sheltered area. Once there, I transferred the body to the truck, concealed it with cherry bags, and took it home to bury in the far side of the orchard. Their cars I wiped down and abandoned.

Fingerprints were no longer of great concern to me; I took to wearing long black leather gloves. The vamps actually found it sexy, much to my quiet amusement. There was the added bonus that nobody reported the vampires missing. I figured they didn't stay too long in one place and so went unnoticed when they were gone.

With my fifth vampire, I ran into a snag. Everything had gone smoothly, as far as killing the undead went, anyway. He was a chestnut-haired Irishman who kept telling me funny stories in a lilting accent until he'd charmed the socks off me. I almost figured I had him pegged wrong until we got to his car and he backhanded me so hard I actually lost consciousness. He deposited me in the backseat, thinking I would have a nice long snooze, and drove to an empty parking lot. Fortunately for me, I'd stopped carrying my stake in my purse and had it tucked inside the pocket of the carpenter jeans I wore. When he flung himself on me in the backseat, he came crashing down on my new toy. He was dead before his fangs were fully extended.

After backtracking to my truck, I dumped him into the bed and covered him with bags of freshly picked cherries. When I was only about five miles from home, I stiffened at the red and blue lights flashing behind me. There was no way I could explain what was in the back of my truck.

Chapter Two
The Hair Salon Incident

Author's note: This scene originally took place in chapter 5, right after Bones tells Cat that she's reached the point in their training where he's going to turn her into a seductress. I had fun writing it, but it was eventually taken out in an attempt to keep the pacing more brisk. Plus by this point, I assumed readers were ready to get to the romance aspect of the novel, and this scene prolonged that, although it did show Cat starting to consider Bones as more of a man than a monster.

Hot Hair Spa was a full-service salon. Facials, body wraps, manicures, pedicures, every hair treatment possible, and waxings. Bones greeted the receptionist by name, smiling charmingly and asking after her family. She nearly tripped over herself to usher us back, casting openly admiring looks at him as she guided us through the modern beauty maze. I was incredulous at her behavior. My God, couldn't she tell he wasn't human? Apparently not, and she made it very clear she would offer him services above and beyond what the spa advertised.

"How do you know these people?" I hissed when we rounded yet another seafoam-colored corner.

He looked at me as though I were slow. "My hair, of course. You didn't think it was natural, did you?"

"No, I didn't think it was natural. I thought you just dumped a bottle of peroxide on your head every night!" My nervousness made me snippy. Well, snippier than usual.

"Darling, how good to see you." A perfectly coiffed older woman squealed as she threw her arms around Bones.

"Marlena, my sweet, always lovely to see you," he replied.

She patted his chest in a mock-reproving way. "What can I do for you, darling? You said it was an emergency."

I shot him an evil glare upon hearing that, but Bones ignored me.

"I call upon your genius to work a miracle. My cousin here—" He gestured in my direction and her head swiveled toward me. "My cousin desperately needs your help. She has countless split ends, her fingernails are a disgrace, her eyebrows need waxing, and I don't even want to tell you about her toenails."

Marlena stared at me as if I had just crawled out of the deepest, darkest swamp and had the algae coating to prove it. My face flamed, and once again I fantasized about me, Bones, and a long, pointed silver stake.

"Ah, my darling, I see what you mean. But what pretty skin she has. I'm sure we can salvage her."

Salvage? Why that arrogant, uppity—

"If anyone can do it," he said, interrupting my mental train of insults, "you can. Spare no expense. I want her dazzling when she leaves."

Marlena cast a dubious look first at me and then back to him. "Come back in five hours. We'll see what we can do."

When Marlena-the-evil-hell-mistress was done with me, I had an exact understanding of what it was like to go through the washer and dryer. I was washed, waxed, plucked, snipped, blow-dried, manicured, pedicured, painted, sloughed, exfoliated, curled, primped, and finally covered in different shades of makeup. My head pounded murderously by the time she was finished, but Marlena clapped her hands with the delight of a child.

"Look at you! You are *ravishing*."

She swiveled my chair toward the mirror and I finally looked at the image I'd avoided all day.

"I look... fake," I managed, staring in the mirror at my perfect hair, makeup, brows, and matching fingernails and toenails.

"Nonsense," she said, brushing the hair off me since her scissors had cut layers into my long tresses. "You look beautiful. Now, you must remember everything Charleen told you about how to apply the correct contouring on your cheeks and eyes. Bones was very specific—he wanted to make sure you'd know how to do this when we were finished. Oh, I can't wait until he sees you. He'll be so pleased."

"I *am* pleased."

His voice made me jump nearly out of my chair as he appeared in the mirror behind me. Yes, vampires cast a reflection. He stared at me in the most unusual way, running his tongue along the inside of his lip like did when he contemplated something dangerous. I met his eyes and then looked away, not wanting to see what was in them.

"Marlena, you are a goddess." He praised her, kissing her hands and then each cheek. She beamed when he was finished, her face flushed.

"Underneath all those country trappings was a beautiful girl waiting to be revealed. We didn't even have to bleach her teeth."

For the first time in my life, I fervently wished I had a pair of vampire chompers. I would have bitten the smug look right off her face.

"I already settled with Lisa at the desk. You're too miserly with your fees. For the work you did on her, you should have charged me double."

Pig! I thought. Marlena was either oblivious or didn't care about my obvious discomfort at being discussed as though I were a Buick that had just had some repairs done.

"You know I gave you a special price. After all, if it weren't for you, we'd still be in the red from that rash of robberies."

"Nothing to it, sweet," he assured her. "Just kids thinking they're tough. I gave them a good talking-to, and they saw the error in their ways."

I wondered if Marlena had any idea of what his version of a "good talking-to" was. Those kids had probably died horrible, screaming deaths.

"And don't forget your bag, Bones. We can't have this lovely girl leave without all her new friends, can we?" She handed him a large, department-store-sized bag stuffed full of God knows what.

He thanked her again, dark eyes crackling with flirtatious energy. It nearly had her quivering on her feet. I felt sorry for her.

"Come back soon. We miss you."

With those parting words, Marlena escorted us through the doors of her salon. It was dusk already, and I felt his otherworldly vibe increase degree by degree. He'd been right about the night increasing a vampire's power. During the day, he almost felt normal when I was near him.

"Happy with your new look?" he inquired when we got back to my truck, eschewing his motorcycle for obvious reasons.

It occurred to me that the last time we were in my truck at night, we'd been trying to kill one another. A sudden memory of him unzipping his pants and the flash of that tight, pale belly flittered through my mind before I could squash it.

"Penny for your thoughts?" He had a crafty curl to his lips that let me know he could pretty well guess what I had been thinking. Well, some of it.

I put the truck in gear and spoke without looking at him, concentrating on the roads. "Just remembering the last time we were in this truck after dark. You nearly punched a hole through my head. You might not want to do that this time. It would ruin my hair, and you just paid a lot for it."

He gave a low chuckle. "Still sore about that? Blimey, you should have seen how you looked that night to me. As rattled as a snake in a box filled with mongooses, you were. Thought you'd jump out of your skin when I pulled my trousers down. No wonder I had you pegged for an innocent. I've met nuns who were more promiscuous."

My knuckles whitened on the steering wheel while I sternly told myself that it wasn't wise to slam on my brakes in the middle of traffic. Seeing my reaction, he laughed again.

"The only thing I ever want to do with a vampire is kill them, Bones. I might be forced to kiss them and let them get a feel, but all I'm thinking about is the moment I'm going to bury my stake in them."

"Funny you should say that. I'm sure they're thinking right along those lines as well."

I will not blush, I will not blush, I hate him so much, I will not blush. "Yeah, well, may the best one blaze a trail, right?"

His eyes sparkled when I glanced over to see the effect of my words, and he clucked his tongue. "Well, well, luv. We might make a fallen woman out of you yet. You're going to have to get used to a lot of dirty talk and be able to respond back to it. A simple 'Want to fuck?' isn't going to cut it, quaint though the phrase may be."

"I can handle it." To hide my discomfort at him throwing my former words in my face, I concentrated on merging onto the freeway.

"Glad to hear it. For the next six days, we're going to dress you the way a vampire expects an easy shag to dress. And we're going to work on your flirting skills. Lastly, you'll learn how to talk with the most depraved, lust-crazed, undead blokes out there. I'll make you say things you've never even thought of. Opening night is next Friday, and you will be ready."

CHAPTER THREE
BONES'S POINT OF VIEW AFTER
THEIR "FIRST TIME"

Author's note: Readers have often asked me if I will ever rewrite Halfway to the Grave *through Bones's point of view. The answer is probably not. For starters, when you're in a character's head, that character loses a lot of mystery for the reader because readers know what he or she is thinking or feeling. Second, I've also found that being inside a character's head paints them in a much harsher light for the reader. Not only do readers experience the character through action and dialog, they hear everything the character doesn't say, and unfiltered thoughts can be ugly at times. So if I rewrote* Halfway to the Grave *through Bones's point of view, I fear that Bones would lose some of his mystique and sensual edge. After all, Cat might have thought that Bones was sexy and irresistible, but Bones would never think such a thing of himself. What character would? Oh, okay, Ian would, but that's another topic *wink*.*

However, years ago I did take a stab at writing a scene from Halfway to the Grave *from Bones's POV, and I'm including it below. It takes place immediately after the first time Cat and Bones slept together, and I was surprised by how introspective Bones turned out to be.*

Bones fell back against the bed with her in his arms, loath to part with her flesh, but letting himself slide out until his cock rested just below her warmth instead of inside it. Her heart still beat with a frantic pace, and she breathed in sharp gasps even as her eyes fluttered closed.

He held her and took in a long breath. Her sweat clung to him, masking his scent with her own, just as she now smelled more of him than herself. This created a new, mingled scent that was neither hers nor his, but *theirs*, and he breathed it in again so he could absorb it inside him.

I've waited so long.

He was surprised at the thought, because eight weeks to get her into his bed wasn't *that* long. Still, he couldn't dismiss his feeling of profound relief. Like something long denied to him was finally here. It wasn't just the usual relaxation he felt right after a supremely satisfying shag—and she was as passionate as he'd dreamed—but it was something else.

He was happy.

That sounded like such a trivial thing, but Bones couldn't remember the last time he'd been truly happy. Oh, he'd been satisfied, contented, pleased, charmed, exhilarated, impressed, and even emotional with the many women in his life, but this feeling of happiness was so foreign to him he wondered if he'd ever felt it before.

His past flashed through his memory, feminine faces blurring. When he finally remembered the last time he'd felt anything close to this, a lump formed in his throat.

There's my beautiful lad. Sleep now, Crispin, I'm here...

His mum. As a child, he'd stay up until she came to bed, always afraid if he fell asleep, something bad might happen to her. He used to hate the night, because darkness meant he'd be kept downstairs in the kitchen or sent out of the house to wait until very late, when one of the other ladies would sneak him upstairs. Then he had to wait longer, his eyes heavy but heart pounding, wondering if his mum would have bruises again or if she'd come to bed at all.

When she did, when she wasn't hurt or sick or suffering from the illness that finally claimed her, she'd hold him until he fell asleep. She'd smooth back his hair, hum to him, and whisper that he was the most beautiful lad in all of London, and one day he'd be a prince. He'd been happy then, knowing his mum was safe and hearing the lovely lies that youth had allowed him to believe. *Yes, Mum, I'll be a prince, and you'll live in my castle and never see any of those awful blokes again.*

But there was no castle. Just a bordello that was his home even after his mum died of syphilis. Then he'd been the whore, using the same beauty his mother spoke of as a bargaining tool for any woman with money to spare and an itch to scratch. He'd had no choice about selling himself, just as she had had no choice. Becoming a vampire changed all that. Afterward, he could pick who he pleasured, and there had been no shortage of women. But they hadn't made him happy. Nothing had... until this.

She sighed. Her breathing had evened out. So had her heart rate, which no longer beat against his chest like a small bird trying to break free. Her eyes were still closed, and a hint of a shiver went through her. Without their passion to warm her, the chill in the cave was gaining ground.

Bones pulled up the blankets, covering both of them. She burrowed closer to him with an unintelligible murmur. Her arms hung loosely around his neck, leaving her breath to tickle his chest with soft puffs. He inhaled once again, thinking he might breathe all night just to keep drawing her scent deeper into him.

I love you, Kitten.

He smiled at the words he didn't dare say out loud, yet. It didn't matter that she was too young, too stubborn, too narrow-minded, too temperamental... He loved her. If he were being practical, he'd have chosen someone far more compatible. But love wasn't something you chose. It chose you, proving that being practical had bugger-all to do with it. All those centuries of believing he was missing whatever ingredient allowed people the insanity of love, and here it had found him when he least suspected it. It was enough to make him believe fate might exist after all, even if Cat was far too good for him despite her flaws.

Her bravery left him awed, her streak of loyalty went straight to the bone, her wit made him laugh, and the vulnerability she tried so hard to hide made him want to tell her over and over how extraordinary she was. She didn't see it, of course. She only measured her worth by the number of vampire corpses she delivered to her mum, as if a mother's love was something that needed to be purchased with blood. One day she'd realize that either her mum loved her or she didn't, and if she didn't, no amount of vengeance could tip those scales.

She shifted, whispered his name, and then started to snore. The loud sounds made him grin. Millions of women in the world, and he'd fallen in love with a half-breed who snored. The Almighty had turned out to have a grand sense of humor. If he didn't think it would scare her straight out of bed, he'd wake her up and tell her how he felt. But she wasn't ready to hear it. *One step at a time*, he reminded himself. She'd already made tremendous strides from believing that all vampires were murdering scum to falling asleep in his arms after hours of making love.

But tomorrow things might be different.

The thought sent a cold shiver through him that had nothing to do with the cave's temperature. She'd had no

when her night began that it would end this way.
, she hadn't even been speaking to him for days.
at if tomorrow she told him this had been a mistake and
t could never happen again?

Bones pushed the thought away. He hadn't lived this long to give up on something he wanted, and he had never wanted anything more than her. If she woke up and regretted what had happened between them, well then, he'd just have to change her mind.

Because you're not getting away from me, he thought, smoothing her hair back from her face. *I promise you that, Kitten... and I promise myself.*

CHAPTER FOUR
AFTER THE MORNING AFTER

Author's note: This next section contains a different version of what happened after Cat finally succumbed to Bones's charms. In the published version, Bones and Cat go to Charlotte to look for a lead in the human trafficking ring they're trying to shut down. In the original version, the trafficking plotline didn't come into play until much later. Instead, the first half of the story was more focused on Cat's emotional battle as she deals with falling for a vampire when she still believes that vampires are evil. However, I ended up taking a lot of that out and adding the trafficking arc in place of these scenes because it revealed the story's overall external plot and its main villain, Hennessey, much sooner.

Finally, this also contains an additional sex scene. I ended up deleting it because I felt that the book already had enough sex scenes in it. For those of you who like more of the sexy stuff, however, now you get to see what didn't make it into the published version.

I had never been to an airport before, let alone on a plane. It was exciting, but I fought not to show it, carefully making my expression glum and angry. That wasn't all an act; I was furious at Bones for forcing me to go. Now that we were boarded and awaiting takeoff, my grim countenance began to slip.

He'd booked first-class tickets. The seats were leather and roomy. They reclined as well, but were upright now as the plane taxied down the runway. Glancing to my right, I saw Bones close his eyes when the aircraft picked up speed. With an incredible surge of power, it left the ground, sounds of engines groaning with the effort, and my face felt pulled back into my skull. It was amazing, and without realizing it, I grinned.

I had the window seat, and my eyes were glued to the grainy image of the ground disappearing from sight. The lights of the evening winked up at us, and after several minutes the plane eased into a horizontal position and the Fasten Seat Belts light flickered off. Flight attendants unclipped their belts and scurried to the beverage carts.

"Enjoying yourself, pet?" Bones had been staring at me while I was fascinated with the outside view.

Remembering myself, I dropped the smile from my face and scowled. "No."

He snorted in derision. "Yeah, you look right wretched."

Ignoring that, I accepted the offer of a drink from the flight attendant. When she passed our seat, I lowered my voice so only he would hear me. "Why did you come to my house before I was supposed to meet you at the cave? How did you know I had no intention of showing?"

Those dark brown eyes looked levelly into mine. "I saw your face when you left this morning. You looked as though someone had just walked over your grave. Give me some credit for knowing women after more than two hundred years."

"Keep your voice down." I looked around to see if someone had overheard him, but everyone appeared to be minding their own business. "You know it can never happen again, Bones. I made a terrible mistake last night, but now I've learned from it. You have to respect that."

"Nice speech," he commented. "Been working on it long?"

I poked him hard in the arm. "I'm serious! God was I thinking?" The last part was meant to be only in my head, but the words flew out.

Bones jumped all over them. "I'll tell you what you were thinking. You were thinking you were a woman, though admittedly a young one, and I was a man, and for once in your bloody life you weren't consumed with anguish about your heritage. You took a short trip off your high horse and found out you loved walking on the ground."

"Whatever!" I snapped.

He reached out and lightly fingered my neck where the hickeys showed. Silly me forgot to wear a high-collared shirt. "The marks you left on my skin have healed. I wish they hadn't. I would keep the proof of your response to me for- ever if I could."

"Then thank God for enhanced recuperative powers." Muttered because of the stab of remembrance that shot through me. The marks he'd left on me would eventually heal too, but I would never forget what had happened when they were made.

He gave a grunt of dismissal. "Tell yourself what makes you the happiest, pet. You could have walked away from me last night, but you didn't. I know it, and now you know it too. The rest is posturing."

He closed his eyes again and reclined the chair, leav- ing me to flip miserably though the pages of the flight magazines.

It was less than an hour and a half before we landed. Amazing how fast one could cross states while in the air. We collected our bags and went to the car-rental area. Bones had reserved an SUV, and after filling out the necessary paperwork we were off. He drove, of course, since I had no idea where we were staying or how to get there. The name signed on the registration forms was Phillip Arthur. So I wasn't the only one who had false identification.

We arrived at the Charlotte Towers around eleven thirty. When Bones signed the check-in forms, I saw he had only booked one room.

"You have a package waiting for me?" he immediately queried.

The man behind the desk handed him a FedEx box and Bones tucked it under his arm.

"There are two beds in that room, right?" I asked the concierge.

The man gave a flustered look at his paperwork while Bones arched a dark brow at me. "Um, let's see... No, the reservation requested a king size, not two queens. Ah, is that going to be satisfactory?"

"No, it's not," I began, but Bones gave a warning squeeze to my hand.

"Causing a scene, luv? Why don't you run an ad in the newspaper while you're at it? Let everyone know we're in town. Me, I love a good fight, but you tend to like the ones that are safer. Still, if you insist..."

Defeated, I yanked my hand out of his and looked directly at the mortified concierge. "We are *not* having sex." There. Had to tell someone.

He nodded briskly and passed over the room keys. "Enjoy your stay."

"Thanks ever so," Bones replied, eyes flashing dangerously at me.

With my head erect, I followed him to the elevator. The hotel was beautiful. It was the nicest one I had ever seen, albeit the only one I'd ever stayed in. The lounge was opulently furnished, and the room was on the top floor with lovely views of the city from the tall windows. If only I weren't here with Bones, I'd have cried out with joy. Of course, if I weren't here with him, I could have never afforded such luxury. You pay for your pleasure with pain, my mother had always said. A grim and often truthful motto.

Bones, ever practical, began to unpack. I busied myself with discovering the delights of the minibar and the snacks therein.

"Food! And liquor!" In my eagerness, I broke my stiff silence and heard a bark of laughter in reply.

"Is that the way to your heart? I'd have installed a mini-bar in the cave long ago if I knew you were so easy to please."

"For your information, I haven't eaten all day."

He finished with the bags and sauntered over. "Make it quick, pet. We can feed you when we're finished. You have to get dressed."

"We're doing it now?" Dismay filled me; I'd hoped for a quiet evening on the couch stuffing my face.

He gave a suggestive wiggle of his brows. "Well, we really should be going straightaway, but I know you could persuade me…"

"Not that, the job. But it's…" I checked the clock. "Midnight."

"Yeah, midnight, and time to kill some vampires. Come on, luv. Brought your stakes and knives in that package I picked up at the desk. Get dressed in your tight little clothes and make them drool. When you're staking them, you can always pretend it's me."

I dropped my snacks immediately. "That works."

Uptown Charlotte was a busier city than Columbus or Newark. There were streets lined with clubs and shops, all open until two a.m. or later. When we arrived at Club Flame, Bones had a more ambitious plan than we'd previously implemented. I was no longer going to lure the intended victim to take me for a drive but was going to lead them outside and go for them there. There was a neat little catch to that as well. There were two of them. One for me, one for Bones. Both needed to be quickly and cleanly dispatched and thrown in the SUV before anyone noticed that a murder had occurred. Personally, I thought we were both going to jail.

I wore the purple dress, cut high on the thighs and with crisscrossed straps covering my back. It was the smuttiest of all the dresses, in my opinion, but since I was acting as though two men at once was my bag... Well, there you have it. Bones went with me as well, saying that the marks didn't know him and therefore wouldn't recognize him. We would play the swinging couple. How romantic.

Bones looked sleazy as well, wearing a black leather vest that made his pale arms and chest almost glow next to the fabric. He actually wore pants that weren't black. They were deep purple to go with my dress. We looked like a pair of freaks, in my estimation. Once I would have said that I wouldn't be caught dead dressing like this, but now that was tempting fate to utter such provocative words. You just never knew what you'd be caught dead in.

Once inside we separated, not wanting to look overly cozy together. That suited me just fine. The less time with Bones, the better. At the bar, I ordered a gin and tonic and watched with paranoid concern that no one but the bartender went near the glass. Even when I looked around, my hand covered the rim at all times. Fool me once, shame on you and all that.

Bones had filled me in on the details of the two vamps while we were driving. The tall skinny blond would be Eric, and his short brown-haired friend was Ed. Eric was supposed to be distinguishable by a nose-to-jawline scar on his face, and Ed by extensive tattooing. Be still, my beating heart. When I asked what they'd done to piss off the person who hired him, he'd responded that they made a snuff film starring his employer's fourteen-year-old son, who was human and had been snatched off the street by pure bad luck. The bankroller was human as well and had gotten Bones's name by an elaborate hit man referral network. The vamps were supposedly no more than fifty years old each, so that was the reason for his lack of concern as to their fighting skills. Hopefully he was right.

With his height, Eric was the first one that I spotted. When Bones said tall and skinny, he wasn't kidding. Eric was probably six foot seven inches and weighed no more than one seventy-five. If that wasn't enough, there was the jagged scar on his face. Contestant number one. Sidled along next to him must be Ed. He was about five foot flat. As described, tattoos decorated his arms like clothing. They were on the dance floor, apparently boogying with themselves. Anxious to wrap things up before it got any later, I headed over.

Working my way through the people, I started dancing close to them. Truth be told, I'd discovered I liked to dance. It was an outlet my body responded to that didn't involve waking up with a vampire. I caught their gaze and smiled, dancing closer until I wedged myself nearly between them. To my surprise, they didn't seem interested. After a few minutes, Eric cast Ed a look and they moved closer to a guy about my age, making him their monkey in the middle. One look at the heat in their stare when they glanced at the other man made it perfectly clear.

Giving up, I made my way to the bar where Bones sat. He sipped a whiskey neat. It amazed me how vampires were able to eat and drink as they pleased even though their bodies didn't work like a human's. Plunking down next to him, I grabbed his glass and finished it in one swallow without asking.

"Looks like I could've kept my panties on," I remarked conversationally.

A dark brow rose questioningly at me. "Did I miss something?"

"You sure did. Looks like you're the bait tonight. They don't swing my way."

Bones ordered another drink and digested the information. Finally he gave a slight shrug. "Intelligence on these individuals only went so far this round. At least the location and time were correct. So be it, then. Keep a lookout. When I go out that back door, I want you behind me in three, got it?"

The wicked grin that slid across my face was unchecked. Good to see someone else be the meat instead of me. "I'll be behind you in three, or they will?"

He gave me a look. "Just be there."

"Oh, *honey,*" I called out merrily after he walked away. He stopped, arching a brow. "Don't forget to take your panties off!"

Laughing, I ignored the strange looks that were cast my way from people within earshot and instead relished the dark one he threw me.

To give him credit, he worked fast. After a few dances with the boys and some drinks, they were out the poorly lit back door within twenty minutes. As soon as the door closed behind them, I set my watch and waited, moving to be in striking vicinity when the timer went off. Counting down to the last ten seconds, I pulled my stakes out of my boots and gripped them in both hands as soon as the timer hit zero.

The alley behind the club wasn't lit. At nearly two a.m., it was deserted and pitch-dark. With my enhanced vision, however, I could make out three figures by the Dumpster, which was shaded by the long branches of a tree. One of them had just let out a scream that was abruptly choked off.

Charging forward, I launched myself onto the back of the nearest vamp, who turned out to be Eric. He spun around just before I hit him, sensing my attack. In that split second, the stake that had been aimed at his heart struck deep into his shoulder instead. He let out a howl, which I quieted by flinging one of the throwing knives dead center into his throat. Now the noise he made was more of a loud gurgle. Eric leapt for me but I sidestepped him, and he was unprepared for my speed. As he pulled himself up short, I struck out with a fierce kick, knocking him backward. When he was on the ground, I flung myself on him with a pile-driving elbow drop that smashed his ribs. Immediately I crashed my knee with brutal force into his groin. When he instinctively doubled up, the stake in my left hand found its mark and slammed home through his heart. Three wrenching twists and he went limp permanently. Springing to my feet, I looked around to see how Bones fared.

He stood a dozen feet away, watching me. From the head lying unattached at his feet, he'd been quicker than me in dispatching his target. My adrenaline pumped, blood rushing through my veins at the savageness of the brawl and the quickness of the ending. The stark reality was this: the fight was over and I wanted more. It was my first true taste of bloodlust.

"Stay here while I get the car," he barked.

In less than two minutes the SUV pulled up as far as it could in the narrow alley, headlights off. Bones jumped out and opened the back. He twisted Eric's head off and

then threw the remainder of both their bodies into a
Dumpster. Then he tossed the two heads into the hatch-
back and covered them with the plastic already laid out.
There was a thick blanket on top of the plastic. To the
casual observer, whoever that might be, it was just junk
thrown in the back. As soon as the back slammed shut,
Bones pulled me to him and kissed me with all the residual aggression left in him.

To say I responded was to put it mildly. Left with an over-
abundance of energy, I sought an outlet for release, and he
was better than violence. I ripped off his vest. Buttons flew,
and I dug my hands into his chest and opened my mouth to
rake my tongue with his. His mouth sealed over mine, and
my free hand clawed along his waist to pull him closer.

After a minute, he pulled back. "Too dangerous out
here. No telling who might come along."

"What about their corpses being discovered in the
Dumpster?" I asked, my voice still unsteady from the deluge
of passion and leftover adrenaline.

He grinned at me. "We're leaving this state tomorrow,
so it doesn't matter. As for their heads, that's why I brought
the box of dry ice. They'll ship out tomorrow to the client."

I wondered what the father would do with his grisly tro-
phies. The man couldn't really put them in the china cabi-
net next to the crystal.

"But what about the police?" I persisted when we sped
away from the Dumpster, the new home for the headless
bodies.

"Coppers? That's the funny part, luv. When a vamp
dies, their body decomposes to their true age. That's why
they look like bloomin' mummies sometimes afterward.
Just let them try to figure out how two stiffs dead over fifty
years ended up in modern clothes stuffed into the garbage.

Makes me laugh just to picture them scratching their chins about it."

"Really?" The more I learned, the more I realized how little I knew.

"Yeah, really."

We stopped at a red light. He leaned over and kissed me, lacing his fingers in my hair. I loved the way he kissed me, as though he were drinking in the taste of me and still coming back thirsty.

A horn blared at us, telling us the light was green again. He ignored it, even when it sounded several more times, until he was finished exploring my mouth and my lips were slightly swollen. Rolling down the window, he gave a one-fingered salute to the car behind us and sped through the light just as it turned red again. I leaned back into the seat, eyes half-closed, and watched his profile as he floored it through the sparse traffic. We made very good time back to the hotel.

As soon as he parked, he pulled me to him again. God, but he could make me ache with need, no matter that I knew being with him was a horrible mistake. I pushed at his shoulders when his hands began to creep under the short hem of my dress.

"Not here," I panted, which was as close to "stop" as I could force myself to say.

He wrenched away and then yanked open his door. I got out too, grabbing the coat I'd worn earlier to conceal the blood smears on my dress. After all, it wouldn't do for me to look like the murderess I was in front of the nice hotel employees. Bones pulled his denim jacket over his bare chest and kept his arm around me as we hurried inside the lobby. The same concierge who'd checked us in was alone at the desk. Poor man, he apparently worked the graveyard shift.

When we reached the elevators, Bones shot me a wicked glance before he called out to the concierge, "For the record, we *are* having sex tonight."

Mortified, I slapped him. He laughed and grabbed me, kissing me so soundly I didn't even notice when he propelled me into the elevator. The doors closed on the stupefied face of the concierge still staring after us.

We barely made it inside the room. As soon as the door opened, we fell through it onto the floor, knocking over a nearby table and sending the lamp crashing to the ground. Bones kicked the door closed while ripping off his pants, tearing them in his impatience. I slid along the floor under him. The carpet scraped against my skin as he pushed my dress around my waist and buried his head between my legs. My hands stretched out behind me, fingers mindlessly grasping for anything at his erotic assault on my sensitive flesh. Something solid brushed by my hand, the lamp from the table. His tongue stabbed into me and I gripped the base of the light. After a moment it shattered and cut my palm. I didn't even feel the pain. Only the sensation of his mouth registered, and it burned me as if he breathed fire.

"Now. *Now...*" The words were raggedly spoken in pure desire. Everything ached to have him inside me again.

"No," he growled, voice muffled against my skin and tongue ruthlessly tormenting me with pleasure.

"Yes. Now." My fingernails ripped the carpet in frustration, spine arching with every wet stroke.

"Tell me you want me. Say the words." He paused long enough to lift his head so he could see my face. His eyes drilled into mine, unrelenting, and his tongue flicked out to tease my quivering flesh.

Sparks nearly flew off me. "Yes, oh God, yes. I want you. *Now.*" If I had national secrets to spill, I would have. Anything to make him comply.

He dragged his mouth up my stomach, pausing to rend my dress from me and draw on each nipple before his body covered mine. I opened my legs and gave a shuddering moan as he slid inside me. He rocked his hips slowly, and my arms wrapped around him so that nothing separated us. My hand bled where the glass had sliced into my palm. He held my wrist and sucked on the cut while continuing to move within me. I pulled it out of his mouth and kissed him, tasting my blood and other things when his tongue caressed mine.

"I can't get enough of you," he murmured into my mouth.

Good, I thought. *Then you won't stop.*

Bones locked his arms around my waist and flipped us over, leaving me on top. This hadn't happened before and I hesitated, unsure.

His stomach muscles flexed as he sat up. His hands caressed my back, dark eyes bright green with lust. One sensuous arch under me as he rubbed his loins into mine took my shyness away.

"Bones," I moaned. "You feel so good it drives me crazy."

He smiled and bent his head to my breasts. "That's the intention. Now it's your turn. As hard or gentle as you want, you decide. You're in control."

I repeated the motion he'd just used. The hard slide of his flesh was punctuated by his pelvis hitting my most sensitive spot, sending heat flaring through me. Being in control had never felt so good.

"Let's see if I can make *you* crazy," I said throatily and began to move with single-minded purpose.

❧ ❧ ❧

"Shit!"

The word burst from my mouth when I woke up to sunlight peeking through the heavy drapes and Bones curled next to me in bed. What was wrong with me? When the sun went down, it seemed to take my common sense with it.

"Not this again…," Bones muttered, then tightened his grip on me when I would have bolted out of bed.

I squirmed, very aware we were both naked and repeated chafing was not a good idea. "Let me go."

He appeared to ponder it for a moment and then pulled me closer. "No."

"Come on, Bones! We have to stop this, can't you see? This is no good, not for either of us."

"You're the only one who doesn't respect yourself in the morning," he countered.

"All right, I admit it: I am clearly attracted to you. Why wouldn't I be? You're gorgeous and smart and funny, and you're also the only person in my life who hasn't made me feel like a freak. Oh, and you're unbelievable in bed. There, are you happy? You've gotten what you want, why can't you just leave like he did!" It came out of me before I even knew what I was saying.

Something flashed across his expression, and then his voice was low and resonating. "I am not him. You'd do well to try to remember that."

"But you're a *vampire*, Bones, and nothing can change that. There is no future for us. We have to stop this now." *Before I get hurt again. Before I care for you more than I already do.*

"'Fraid I can't do that, luv," he finally answered.

My fingernails dug into my palms. "Why? You don't need me, you can do the tracking on your own." Despair gripped me, because I was very afraid I didn't possess the willpower to end this on my own.

He touched my face, and the gentleness in that gesture pierced me to the quick. "Because, Kitten, I am in love with you."

My mouth hung open, and my mind briefly cleared of thought. Then I said, "No you're not," because denial was always my first response to something I feared.

He let out a snort. "That is one truly annoying habit you have, telling me what I do and do not feel. After living for over two hundred and thirty years, I think I know my own mind."

"I can't believe you'd stoop this low." If he hadn't been holding me, I would have jumped up in outrage. "You're not like Danny? He also lied about his feelings to get some action."

"And why do you think I haven't said anything before now?" he shot back. "I never wanted you to wonder if I was merely cajoling you into bed with meaningless prattle. However, I've already gotten you on your back, and it wasn't by declaring my devotion to you. I simply don't care to hide my feelings any longer."

"But you've only known me two months." Now I tried arguing the point, because denial apparently didn't work.

A slight smile curled his lips. "Kitten, I began to fall in love with you when you challenged me to that stupid fight in the cave. There you were, wearing almost nothing, blood in your hair from where I'd struck you, chained hand and foot, questioning *my* courage. Why do you think I made that arrangement with you? Oh, don't get me wrong, you ended up doing splendidly. Much better than I thought you would, but as you said, I can do this alone. So could you now, for that matter. You're strong enough, fast enough, smart enough. Truth is, luv, I struck that bargain with you so you'd be forced to spend time with me. I knew you'd never agree any other way. After all, you had such hang-ups about vampires. Still do, it appears."

"Bones..." My eyes were wide with his revelation and with the growing knowledge that he was serious. "We'd never work out together. We have to stop this now, before it goes any further."

"I know what makes you say that. Fear. You're terrified because of how that other wanker treated you, and you're even more afraid of what your dear mum would say, not to mention you still think all vampires are evil. But we are who we are, as men and as vampires. Just as you choose how to live your life with the power you have, so do we. You certainly never thought you'd shag a vampire, yet here you are in bed with me again. So although now you may think it could never work between us... Well. I don't give up so easily."

While he spoke, my death grip on the sheets loosened and the rigidity of my limbs relaxed. Not one to let an opportunity pass him by, he closed the distance between us and kissed me when my guard was down. His hands wound through the sheets until he pulled them away from my body. The sudden feel of his incredible skin pressing along the length of me caused me to gasp. Those hands began to move over me, seeking the places he knew were my weaknesses with unerring accuracy.

"You see, I told you," he whispered as I trembled under him, "I don't give up so easily."

We ordered breakfast later from room service. Well, by the time we ordered it, it was actually more like lunch, although I still chose the pancakes and eggs with bacon. Bones watched in amusement as I scarfed the food down eagerly, scraping my plate when it was empty.

"You know, Kitten, you can always send for more. You don't have to chew the dishes."

"Wouldn't matter if I did. I think you already lost your security deposit," I replied, casting a meaningful look at the shattered lamp, broken table, bloodstained carpet, overturned couch and various other items that were in a condition other than how we found them. It looked like a brawl had taken place. One sort of had. A sensual one, anyway.

He let out a contented noise and settled back with his arms flung carelessly over his head. "Don't fret. It was worth every farthing."

"What's that?" There was a marking underneath his inner left arm, and I traced it with a finger. "I never noticed this before. Crossbones. How appropriate." The tattoo was etched with just the outline, and his pale flesh emphasized the black ink. "When did you get it?"

He reached down and held my hand. "Over sixty years ago. Rather like a name tag. A mate gave it to me. He's dead now; he was a Marine in World War II."

Talk about a generation gap. That tattoo was over three times my age.

He had his laptop set up in the bedroom, and Bones went to it and logged online while I visited the bathroom. When I came out, he stared in satisfaction at the screen.

"Bank wire transfer completed. We'll be shipping the heads tomorrow before we board, and that a neat hundred g's for the lot. That'll be $20K for you, Kitten, and you didn't even have to kiss either of them. Not bad for a few minutes work, is it?"

"I don't want the money." The reply was immediate. I didn't even have to think about it. No matter that the shallow, greedy part of my brain screeched in protest.

He raised a dark brow at me. "Whyever not? You earned it. I told you that was always part of the plan, even though I didn't let you in on it right off. What's the problem?"

Sighing as I sat heavily on the edge of the bed, I tried to articulate the whirling of emotions and thoughts that consisted of my conscience. "Because it isn't right. It was one thing to take it when we weren't sleeping together, but I don't want to feel like a kept woman. I don't know why I can't say no to you and make it stick right now, but I won't be your girlfriend and your employee at the same time. Really, the choice is yours. Pay me, and I stop sleeping with you. Keep the money and we continue on in bed until I get my head fixed to where I can resist you."

He laughed outright, coming over to where I sat and putting his head on my lap while dissolving in hilarity. His arms grasped me around the waist, and when he finally pulled back, his eyes were pink from tears. "And you wonder why I love you. When you boil it all down, you're *paying* me to shag you, for as soon as I stop, I owe you twenty percent of every contract I take. Blimey, Kitten, you've turned me back into a whore."

"That's... that's not... Dammit, you know what I meant!"

Clearly I hadn't thought of it in those terms. I tried to wrest away, but his arms hardened like steel. Although still sparking with humor, there was a definite glint of something else in his eyes. Dark brown orbs started to color with green.

"You're not going anywhere, luv. I have twenty thousand dollars to earn, and I'm going to start working on it right now..."

"Wake up, Kitten. We have to be at the airport within the hour."

I didn't remember drifting off. Then again, my brain hadn't been functioning at all after the third shattering climax, or was it the fourth?

"Where are we going?" I asked, sitting up. We seemed to be always on the move, and all I wanted to do right then was sleep.

"Back home."

"Oh no, I never even called my mother."

Bones cast a sidelong grin at me. "Going to tell her how much you enjoyed Bible study? I seem to remember you calling out the Lord's name several times this afternoon."

"You're a pig."

He was too. An arrogant, dirty, insatiable pig, and God help me, I reveled in it when we were alone. "I'm going to tell her the truth." His eyebrow rose in amazement before I quickly amended, "Er, some of the truth. I'll tell her I went with a friend to do a job. Thanks to the marks on my neck, she knows I'm sleeping with someone. You'll be tickled to hear the day you came to pick me up, she was out buying me condoms."

"Really?" he said with a laugh. "Quite thoughtful of her. Are you going to bring them over so she'll think you're practicing safe sex?"

Something between desire and despair shot through me. "Any sex with you isn't safe, no matter how many condoms were involved."

He leaned closer until his mouth nearly brushed my ear. "Since when do you like to do anything safe?" His teeth caught my earlobe for a moment, and then he sat back again. The mere brush of him against me caused me to quiver, and no, there was nothing safe about it.

"What will you do, Bones, when one day I finally say no and mean it?" Even I recognized the grimness in my tone.

He looked at me sharply for a moment and then shrugged. "Write you a check, apparently. And then work on changing your mind."

The plane landed at five thirty, right on schedule. We picked up our bags and waited for a cab. Bones was very handy when it came to that; he would just glare at the drivers with his green gaze and compel them to stop. They did, even if they already had passengers. That happened twice, to my embarrassment. Finally we flagged one without occupants and started back to my house. He had been oddly quiet since our little chat. When we were within five minutes of my place, he suddenly told the driver to stop.

"What?" Turning to look at him, I saw his eyes were green again. Great, now what?

"Sit there and face forward. All you see is the road. All you hear is music."

He used that resonating voice again, the one that caused hairs to sit straight up on my neck, but he wasn't talking to me. The driver nodded, fixing his eyes forward with a dull stare.

"I am so not having sex with you in this backseat, Bones. Do you know how unsanitary that would be?"

He chuckled and put his arms around me. "That wasn't the idea. Not that you couldn't convince me of it, of course. Actually, I was thinking of your family. I take it you don't want me to walk you to the door and give you a kiss good-bye in front of them? As I said, I could convince your grandparents it was a girl they saw, but that leaves your mum. Somehow I don't wager you'd want me to hold her down and drink her blood so she'd believe whatever I told her."

"Absolutely not." The mere thought of him meeting my mother sent chills of horror down my spine.

The look he gave me told me he didn't appreciate my vehement response. "As I said, your grandparents think you've been to a Bible study with another girl, so that's what they would have told your mum. Yet you have fresh bruises around your neck. Unless this is a lesbian Bible study the likes of which crowd control would become necessary, those two things don't mesh."

"Maybe you shouldn't keep leaving bruises on me. Then we wouldn't be having these problems." The prissy tone of my voice sounded comical even to me. Who was I kidding?

A knowing smile curved his lips. "Kitten, if I didn't heal so fast, my back would be a river of scars from your nails and there would be bite marks all over me."

My face flushed and I cast a panicked look at the driver, who still hummed to himself. "Since when are you complaining about that?" I hissed.

"I'm not," came his instant response. "The point was that you don't like your family seeing such marks on you. One simple way around that: take some blood from me, and away go the nasty reminders you've shagged the undead. Really, pet, I'm being considerate. Doesn't bother me a bit that you look like you're wearing a bruise necklace. In fact, I rather enjoy—"

"You've made your point!" Exasperated, I poked him. He just eyed the spot and grinned.

"Subliminal message? Looking for a poke? All you had to do was say so. You might not fancy the backseat, but we could go right into those trees and—"

In frustration I kissed him, because at least *that* usually worked to shut him up. Bones responded without hesitation, pulling me next to him while his mouth moved over mine in a centuries-perfected way that left my head spinning. My arms crept up around him before I knew what I was doing. Then, tearing my mouth away, I attempted to slow my jagged breathing.

"How?"

He drew me against him again and leaned back so we almost reclined. "Kiss me again, Kitten."

His voice was husky and his eyes were emerald, telling me that he felt the same passion I did. Slowly, I lowered my mouth to his, and right before our lips met, I saw a flash of fang. When his tongue slid into my mouth, I tasted blood. It should have repelled me, but there was something disturbingly sensual about sucking his blood off his tongue as we kissed.

Bones ran his hands down my back, sliding over my hips. His tongue quit bleeding, but I hadn't stopped kissing him. His fangs were fully extended now, as were other things on his body, and either I had to stop or let him lead me out of the car to finish this in the nearby bushes.

"Bones, no." Chastity won out this round, and I pushed away from him.

"I want to see you tonight." The heat in his eyes told me it wouldn't be for training. Well, not battle training.

"No. I just got back, I'm barely ever home anymore. This weekend I move into my new apartment. These next few days with my family will be all I'll have for a while. Something tells me my grandparents won't be visiting often."

"Where is the apartment?"

Oh, I'd forgotten to mention it before. Silly me forgetting that soon I'd have my own place where no one could track his visitations.

"Near the campus, about six miles away."

A light sparkled in his eyes. "You'll be only twenty minutes from the cave then." *How convenient.* Bones didn't speak the last part. He didn't have to. "I could come to you tonight. No one would see me."

"No. I'll call you with the address on Friday. You can come over late after my mother leaves. Not before. I mean it, Bones. Give me a little time. It's already Monday."

He took my hand and kissed it, cradling it in his while that green light still glowed in his eyes. "Friday then. I'll hold you to it. No more running."

"Running?" Why? I certainly didn't feel in the mood for jogging.

Then his meaning penetrated. When I got home and looked into my mother's eyes, I would second-guess a relationship with him all to hell, I knew. He must have known that too. But right now the only face in front of me was his.

"No, I'm too tired to run, and you're too fast. You'd only catch me."

"That's right, luv." Soft, but with unyielding resonance. "If you run, I'll chase you. And I'll find you."

It was a busy week. There was final registration for classes, books to pick up, and the deposit and rental agreement signed with my new landlord. When Friday dawned, my mother actually cried, hugging me to her in bed and sniffling that tonight she'd be sleeping alone for the first time in over nineteen years. I wished I could have said the same.

There were precious few things to pack up. I'd bought a box spring and mattress and a dresser for my clothes. Add a few lamps and an old desk for studying, and that was the whole enchilada. I hoarded as much of the money as possible, knowing I would still have to get a part-time job to make ends meet. When Bones found out about that, he'd freak.

He had been underneath my thoughts all week. To my horror, one morning my mother asked me if I'd had a nightmare the previous evening. Apparently I'd been saying the word "bones" in my sleep. Yeah, it was a nightmare all right, just not what she thought. Mumbling something about graveyards, I brushed her off, but the reality remained. Friday came too fast, much too fast.

My grandparents let me keep the truck, which was nice of them. They had been less than pleased with me lately, but I received a stiff hug from each of them when it was time for me to leave. I was waiting until the last possible moment to call Bones with the address, because the thought of seeing him again made my knees weak. How was I ever going to break this off?

"Be sure and learn good, child," Grandpa Joe gruffly muttered to me when I started to pull away. My eyes pricked with tears, because I was leaving the only home I'd ever known.

"I love you both." I sniffed, blinking back the moisture which threatened to leak out of my eyes.

"Don't forget to keep going to Bible study with that nice young gal," my grandmother instructed me sternly. If she only knew what she was saying.

"Oh, I'm sure I'll be seeing her soon." Real soon.

I sat on the floor of my new apartment, staring at the phone before I finally picked it up and dialed.

The knock came less than twenty minutes later. Not knowing what to do with myself in the meantime, I'd taken a shower and put on new clothes. With the time apart this week, I'd rebuilt my determination to cease all activities with Bones that didn't involve a stake. Being with my mother had certainly helped that process. She couldn't stop talking about how vampires were demons from hell and deserved to die, between admonitions for me to study. My hair was still wet from washing it when I heard him rap on the door. My, but he was prompt.

I opened the door... and all my strong, self-righteous intentions crumpled when I saw him. Bones stepped through the entrance, locking it behind him while pulling me into his arms. God, but he was beautiful with those chiseled cheekbones and pale skin, his body hard and seeking. His mouth covered mine before I could get a breath in, and then I didn't need to breathe because I was too busy kissing him. My hands trembled when they reached up to grasp his shoulders and then clenched when he reached under my waistband to feel inside.

"I can't breathe." I gasped and wrenched my head away.

His mouth went to my throat, moving over the sensitive skin as he bent my spine until only his arms held me upright.

"I missed you, Kitten," he growled, pulling off my clothes.

All of my carefully rehearsed words on how we could no longer continue this flew straight out of my head. Instead, I ran my hands to the front of his shirt and pulled it out of his pants.

He swept me up in his arms and asked a single question. "Where?"

I jerked my head in the vicinity of my bedroom, too busy feasting on his skin to answer. He carried me into the small room and nearly flung me on the bed.

"Well, luv, I wanted to see your place before I bought you a housewarming gift. Little did I know that you'd need a whole bloody apartment."

Bones was sprawled out naked on the bed, looking for all the world like a fallen angel. He stared at the shabby bedroom with a look of mild disdain. "I should slaughter your landlord for charging you money for this hovel," he went on.

I wasn't entirely sure if he was kidding, but at the moment, I was feeling too languorous to be offended. "This from the man who lives in a cave. Hardly a Hilton there, is it?"

He grinned. "Hate to break it to you, but my cave is nicer than this. Anytime you want to go back on that silly refusal to take your cut of the money, just tell me. Never fear; I won't stop shagging you no matter how many checks I have to write."

"You actually have a bank account?" That was so... normal.

"Several. Why, want to try to coerce me out of my money? Steal my account numbers and rob me blind?"

"No, but if you have money tucked away, why do you live in a cave? Granted, it does have more amenities than this, but it is what it is." I had never thought about his finances, but now that the subject was open, I was curious.

He stretched. "Safety, for one. I can hear you coming a mile away when you approach. Good warning enough if some other beastie wants to take a stab at revenge for one of the jobs I've done. Or one of the things I've done for free, for that matter. Besides, it was only supposed to be temporary. Didn't plan on staying here this long."

"What changed that?" As soon as the words left my mouth, I regretted them.

"You know why," Bones answered softly.

He grasped my shoulders and forced me to face him. I stared at his collarbone, unwilling to look in his eyes. He traced my face with his fingers delicately, as though I might shatter. How true that was.

"Don't hide yourself, Kitten, look at me."

Although I would have given worlds to refuse, my pride wouldn't let me be so cowardly. Always pride before a fall.

His eyes were brown, and something about their lack of vampire green affected me more than if he'd tried to cloud my mind with his power. Maybe he already had. Maybe that was why I couldn't resist him.

"I meant what I said before. I love you."

It was unbelievable how three little words could smash through me with the weight of a wrecking ball, and how unfair that they could never change what he was.

"I wish you wouldn't say that." My voice was barely a whisper.

"I wish you would," he replied at once.

I dropped my head against his shoulder in defeat. "Isn't it enough that I can't say no to you? That I've gone back on everything I believe in by being here with you? God, you have no idea how every time I'm away from you, I build myself up to be so strong, and then it all comes crashing down as soon as I see you. Do you have any idea how hard it is to look my mother in the eye, knowing I'm sleeping with the same kind of creature that raped her?"

"Don't you dare compare me to him," he snapped. I blinked, because he looked as furious as I'd ever seen him, and here I was within biting distance. *Smart, real smart.* "Do I hold you responsible for the evil that humans do? No, because that would be ludicrous. At the same time, although you try so hard to forget, you are half-vampire.

Are you not responsible for half the misery the bad ones cause, then? No, because you are only accountable for what *you* do. When you finally get that through your head, you'll be a much happier person, if you live long enough."

Bones jumped up from the bed. Dumbfounded, I watched as he yanked on his pants and then pulled his shirt over his head.

"You're leaving?" This was a first. Usually it was me who stomped off in a huff.

"Yeah." Crisply. "Now you can sleep snug and not fret about waking up with any creatures beside you."

My mouth was still open in disbelief when he slammed the door behind him.

At once remorse filled me, followed quickly by rationalization. Okay, so perhaps I was out of line calling him a creature, but really, I'd called him much worse before.

Not after he told you he loved you, my conscience whispered.

Right, then, bad timing. But when was a *good* time to call someone a creature? Before or after breaking in the new mattress? Besides, how was I supposed to refer to his species? As the *formerly alive?*

Anything except creature, monster, or all the other names your mother has called them, that inner voice continued until it felt like I had a proverbial angel on one shoulder and a devil on the other.

Don't feel bad. Bones is a vampire *who beat your head in the night you met—*

Because I'd been trying to kill him.

He forced you to endure unmerciful training—

That will probably save my life in the future.

So what! He seduced you, took advantage of you—

Yeah, I was really fighting him off.

You can't trust him—

But he hasn't let me down yet.

He's using you, you fool, just like Danny did!

Then why does he act NOTHING like him?

Miserable, I burrowed into the covers, an ache growing in my chest from how big, lonely, and empty the bed now seemed. The truth was this: regardless of the fact that Bones was a full-blown vampire, I had treated him much worse than he'd ever treated me. Once again, I had been wrong, so wrong. But was it better to leave things the way they were? I'd started today with the goal of ending things between Bones and myself, and now it looked like I'd done a bang-up job of that.

But the thought of never seeing him again made that ache in my chest swell until I felt like I couldn't breathe. *Even if he's had enough and his walking away is for the best, he deserves an apology from me,* I decided, that ache easing a little at the thought of calling him. It was the least I could do, I told myself as I got up and grabbed my robe. Yeah. That's why I had to call him right away.

But when I got into the kitchen and stared at my phone, I paused. I should probably spend some time actually *thinking* about what I was going to say before I spoke. If I'd done that before, I wouldn't be in this situation now. I stood there for several minutes, holding the phone in a tight grip as I went down a mental list of possible apologies. If only there was a lovely, eloquent way of saying, *Hey, know what? I was a total ass and you had every right to leave.* But I couldn't find a way to pretty up those cold, harsh facts, and I was concentrating so hard trying to find one that I didn't notice the knock on the door until the second one.

I glanced at the clock on my phone. Almost midnight and I didn't know any of my neighbors. Who else could it be?

I opened the door and let Bones in. With an almost abashed look on his face, he thrust a bouquet of flowers into my hand. I gaped at them, speechless.

"I'm sorry I stormed off like that, Kitten. You're really blasted young, and sometimes I forget that everything seems only black-and-white at your age."

The selfish part of me was relieved and wanted to leave it at that. Yippee, he was sorry so I didn't have to be! But that damned little voice of conscience wouldn't shut up.

"No, Bones. I was wrong. Very, very wrong, and you didn't deserve that, so I'm the one who's sorry."

With a smile, he laid a gentle hand on my forehead. "You don't feel feverish, but you must be impaired to have willingly admitted such a thing. Or did you just down an entire bottle of gin and this is drunk-speak?"

That mischievous glint was back in his eyes, and I thrilled to see it even as I pretended to be flippant. "There isn't any alcohol in the place, thank you very much. And what did you just do? Knock over a florist?"

As I spoke, I looked around for something to put the flowers in. The gesture touched me so much; I was afraid I'd embarrass myself completely and start to cry in front of him. These were the first flowers I'd ever received.

Bones came up behind me. When I felt his arms fold around me, I leaned back into them like steel to a magnet.

"There's an all-night grocer down the road," he said softly. "I was in the midst of driving home when I spotted it and decided to pop in. It was either buy the flowers or smash the place, but I had to do something."

"I like the flowers," I murmured, turning around and reveling in the feel of him holding me tighter. "But most of all, I'm glad you came back."

Danny hadn't, even when I'd done nothing to deserve him walking out. Bones had, and I'd given him more than enough reason to keep going. I wrapped my arms around him, that ache in my chest returning as I inhaled, taking in his scent and closing my eyes as his lips brushed my neck. Right then it didn't matter that I was the only one of us who was technically alive. He didn't need to breathe because I breathed for him, and my heartbeat surely pushed the blood through his veins as well as through my own.

Right then, in my arms, he was as human as he needed to be.

Chapter Five
Death and Taxes

Author's note: This deleted scene took place during chapter 15 in Halfway to the Grave, *right after Bones meets Timmie and right before Cat has her encounter with Spade in the cave. It was cut because my editor didn't feel it revealed anything new to the story and thus slowed the pacing. To give a brief setup, Cat and Bones are investigating to see if a girl from a withdrawn missing person's report was another of Hennessey's victims.*

Bones sat next to me. He wore a suit and tie. A briefcase was at his feet, right next to his shiny business shoes. In his professional ensemble, complete with thin, rimless glasses, he appeared the very picture of mundane respectability. Talk about a disguise.

"So you see, Mrs. Phillips, why we would feel this was important enough to interrupt you at your place of employment," Bones was saying. "We at the Internal Revenue Service take tax evasion very seriously."

"Of course you would," the brunette sitting at her desk opposite us agreed. She kept twisting her fake pearls around her neck. Madeline Phillips was a real estate agent in Hocking County. Her office was tidy, with several pictures of her and a smiling Amanda Phillips in the room.

"Now, if I understand you correctly…" Bones consulted the paperwork in his hands, which had nothing to do with tax laws. "You filed last year that your daughter Amanda was living at home, still a dependent, and attending Hocking Community College. Is that your position for this current year as well?"

A firm nod. "Yes."

My head banged louder. The pantyhose I wore felt like a lower-body straitjacket. I'd never worn any before, and I wasn't going to make it a habit. They went well with my long wool skirt and matching jacket, however.

Bones leaned forward. "Mrs. Phillips. You called the police last July to report that your daughter hadn't come home. Then you never followed up with that. Are you telling me Amanda lives with you, even as of today?"

Her fingers drummed on the desk. "Yes. Granted, she had me worried that night, but she apologized and hasn't done it since. You're too young to have a twenty-year-old child, but let me tell you, they're a handful. She's always on the run."

Madeleine Phillips was wrong on both counts. Bones could be a great-great-*great* grandfather if vampires reproduced, and Amanda hadn't been on the run at all lately. She was dead. And if that weren't bad enough, according to Winston, she'd been dead for over a month.

I got up and closed the verticals without being asked. Our charade of being IRS agents in order to get a private meeting with Mrs. Phillips was over. It was time to go green and find out if this woman was the coldest bitch on the planet... or the most deceived.

When I turned around, locking the door as a last precaution, Bones already had his brights on. He leaned over the desk toward Madeline, his unnecessary glasses off.

"Look deeper, that's right... Now tell me, when did you really last see Amanda?"

Her eyes were crystal blue and transfixed on his. "I-I don't know… I don't know!"

"Kitten, you might want to turn your back."

"Why?" God, he wasn't going to start beating the shit out of her, was he?

"She's been bitten—I can feel it," he replied flatly. "I'll have to drink from her to push her past it. Otherwise she can't answer me with the truth."

Oh. I cleared my throat. No, I didn't care to see Bones feed, he was right about that. But it seemed cowardly in the extreme to turn around.

"Go ahead. Do what you have to do."

Bones met my eyes briefly, then circled around the desk to where Madeline sat. Her hair was already up in a bun, so he didn't have to bother with that. He undid a button on her shirt, pulling her collar open farther, and bent to her neck.

I only saw the back of his head and her face. Heard her slight intake of breath, saw her mouth open to make the sound, and then watched her eyelids slowly close. When they were all the way shut, he pulled back, rebuttoning her blouse and kneeling in front of her.

"No marks," I said, feeling very strange and remembering how there hadn't been any on the other girl I'd stumbled on him feeding from weeks ago. "How, ah… How do you close the holes?"

"You already know that."

My fingers clenched, which was ridiculous. Yeah, I had a good idea, but hearing it confirmed didn't make me any happier. He'd cut his tongue on a fang and held it over the spot until it healed. Since we'd been sleeping together, my method of swallowing his blood had gone from licking it off his fingers to sucking it from his tongue after he did that while we kissed. It was no surprise to discover he had more than one use for it and learn where he'd gotten the idea from.

"It's not the same," he said quietly, studying my face.

"We have more important things going on. Ask her about her daughter, for God's sake." My voice was harsher than I'd meant it to be, because I wasn't really mad at him. I was sick over this whole thing. So many girls missing or dead, and we still didn't know how many people were involved. Before we came here, we'd looked into the other names Winston had given me. Aside from Violet Perkins, whose human boyfriend had strangled her in a mescaline-induced rage, none of the others had even been reported missing. They were dead, and no one, not even their families, knew anything about it.

He stared at me for another second before returning his gaze to Madeline. "Now tell me, and nothing is hidden any longer, when did you last see Amanda? You don't have to be afraid. No one will hurt you."

She started to shake. Tears flowed, and her face transformed into an expression of agony. "I don't know where my little girl is! She went out after her birthday in July, months ago, and she never came home!" Her voice rose. "*She never came home!*"

Bones held a finger to her lips. "Easy now, Madeline. Shhh. I'm going to help you, so don't fret. Who made you believe Amanda was home? When did it happen?"

In a steadier tone, she relayed how the day after her daughter hadn't come home, someone else had. Madeline couldn't tell us what he looked like. She'd been hit with his eyes too fast, but she knew it was a man, for what little information that was worth. He'd instilled in her that Amanda was fine, she'd just seen her, and to go about her usual routine and do nothing further with the police. It had helped that her ex-husband was a loser neither of them had seen in years. Madeline's parents were deceased, and she had no other children. To any of Amanda's friends who called, Madeline had been programmed to say she'd moved. Just like the Spencers, though their daughter had told them that herself, and the jury was still out on whether Natalie was a victim or a villain.

So Madeline continued to pay for an education which wasn't utilized, kept Amanda's insurance current on a vehicle that wasn't there, and was oblivious to the fact that she'd never seen her daughter again.

"All right, Madeline," Bones said when she was finished. "I want you to look at the clock. It's three minutes to five. When its five o'clock, you won't remember anything you've just said. Or anything I've asked you. We're just two IRS agents who inquired about your returns, and now you're no longer going to lie on your taxes. We didn't talk about anything else, and nothing has changed with your daughter."

"What?" I gasped.

"She walks out of this room saying anything else, and what do you think will happen?" he asked me without looking away. "They know who she is. She'll be lucky if they just kill her, but in all likelihood, they'll have a waste-not, want-not attitude. You want to sentence her to that? I'd say she's had enough cruelty done to her."

"But... But it's..." There weren't enough words to describe how wrong that felt, leaving her in her state of instilled illusions.

"Not until they're dead, Kitten. That's the only way she'll be safe."

There was no other point I could argue. He was right. It was still wrong, but in this case, wrong was the best we could do for her.

Seconds ticked past. Bones moved away and was seated again when the clock struck five. Madeline blinked—and then her features settled back into polite wariness without a hint of their former pain.

"Thank you for your time, Mrs. Phillips," he said, rising. "We'll be leaving now."

She stood as well, unaware that tears were still drying on her face. "I'll have my accountant go over those figures more carefully next time."

He nodded. "We won't need to return if you do, I'm sure."

I left without speaking. What could I say? Have a nice day?

Bones placed a hand on my back as we left the building. His touch was light, barely discernable, yet it kept my legs straight as we walked. I wanted to cry. I wanted to kill someone. I didn't want to *ever* know things like this could actually happen.

"They kept her alive for two months," was what I said as we got into the rental car.

Bones didn't start it. He just looked at me. "You've already done a great deal to help these girls. More than can be expected. There's no shame in letting me take it the rest of the way. You won't be abandoning them."

I considered dropping out for a selfish, weak second. Then I shook my head. "I'm in it until the end. However long that takes."

He put the key in the ignition and didn't say anything else. I leaned back in the seat and closed my eyes.

After several minutes, something unrelated nagged at me. "Why did you tell Madeline to stop fudging numbers on her taxes? How did you know she was doing that?"

"Come now, Kitten," Bones said with a knowing grunt. "Who doesn't?"

CHAPTER SIX
THE MISSING GIRL WHO
CALLED HOME

Author's Note: *This scene formerly took place in the middle of chapter 15 in the published version of* Halfway to the Grave. *In it, Cat and Bones are trying to narrow down who the other girl was with Emily (the girl they rescued from Charlotte) when Emily was taken to the mysterious masked man's house. It was taken out in final revisions because my editor felt that Cat and Bones had already chased down enough leads to be plot-pertinent. When I deleted it, I had to go back and change the earlier scene at Tara's in chapter 14, where I'd originally written that Emily had said there was another girl with her when she was taken to the masked man's house. I also then had to go forward and change the climactic scene at the end where Cat confronts the governor at his home. In my original version, Cat finds the missing girl from this scene alive and chained up in the governor's basement. So as you can see, deleting even one smaller scene can cause a ripple effect of changes throughout several parts of a book.*

"Is this the place?"

Bones had slowed the motorcycle enough for speech to be productive. Even though I was facing his back, I could feel him scoping out the area with his gaze.

"Second house on the left."

It was almost twelve hours after my morning coffee with Timmie. Bones had arrived at my apartment right at dusk. He'd taken one whiff inside my place and then asked me with questionable politeness how I liked my new neighbor. That nose of his would put a bloodhound's to shame, but then again, Bones was a true bloodhound in every sense of the word.

"Remember, luv, don't use your real name."

Well, that was easy. I barely knew it myself anymore.

Bones pulled into the driveway of the modest one-story house, and I was the one who got off. He stayed where he was, casually resting the bike upright. A young girl would look a lot less ominous to the Spencers than he would after nine at night. Natalie's parents, if that's who they were, lived several counties away. If I had been driving instead of Bones with his damned speedy, unsafe bike, we wouldn't have arrived until after midnight.

My knock was greeted with slight grumbles, but then a man in his early fifties answered the door. "Hello?"

I smiled brightly. "Mr. Spencer, it's Suzy. Sorry to come by so late, and you probably don't even recognize me with this new hair color—gosh, it's been years, huh?—but when I got back into town I just *had* to come by and see if Natalie was home. The house looks great, by the way. Love the new paint color."

Bones was nothing if not thorough. When he said he'd researched the Spencers, he'd researched them. I bit back the urge to say, *Glad that prostate issue of yours cleared up!* The Spencers had lived in Bethel for twenty years, and though they weren't rich or influential, there was a break in the typical pattern with Natalie. She hadn't been a loner, on drugs, or prone to any problems. That's why we were proceeding with caution, because there was no need to green-eye or alarm these people if this was a wrong number.

George Spencer rubbed his eyes and blinked. "Um... Suzy. How, ah, how nice to see you again."

If there was one thing my young years had already taught me, it was that men hated to admit they didn't know someone who claimed to know them. If Mrs. Spencer had answered the door, I would have used a different ploy to get inside.

"I want you to meet my boyfriend, Cris." I said, waving Bones over when he pretended to be hesitant. I lowered my voice as if sharing a secret. "Can you believe I snagged such a cute guy? Don't tell him what a dork I used to be, okay?"

George Spencer appeared mildly dazed. I saw him glance up the stairs and knew if I had telepathy, I'd hear him screaming, *Honey! Get down here and rescue me from this chatterbox!*

"Natalie's not here," he said with an eye on Bones as he approached. His hand tightened on the doorway. "She moved to Los Angeles two weeks ago. Said some agent's gonna make her the next Nicole Kidman. Maybe you can talk some sense into her. She doesn't listen to reason if it's coming from her parents."

"Who is it, George?" a woman's voice called from upstairs. Must be Liz Spencer.

"Natalie's friend Suzy!" he yelled back, sounding impatient and weary.

"Suzy?" The voice was closer, and then a graying blonde came down the stairs with her brows furrowed in puzzlement. "Natalie doesn't have any friends named Suzy."

Bones hit the two of them with his gaze right then, pushing past George Spencer as I closed the door behind us.

"Don't scream," he commanded them in that hair-raising voice of his. Two sets of eyes were instantly transfixed on his glowing ones. "When was the last time you saw Natalie?"

"Two weeks ago," both of them answered in unison.

"And did she tell you then she was going to Los Angeles? Just you answer me, mum."

"No," Liz said.

"When did you first hear that?"

"The next night after I saw her. She called and said she wasn't coming home."

So far, just like Emily.

"And that's the last you heard of her?" Bones asked, tapping his chin.

"No."

That reply surprised both of us. He stopped tapping and his brows rose. "Indeed?"

"She called yesterday," was the unexpected response. "She didn't want us to worry and she said she was getting a phone in her apartment soon, so we'd have her number. She'd been calling from a pay phone."

Now that didn't make sense. Maybe this was way off. From what it sounded like, Natalie Spencer *had* just gone off to Los Angeles to pursue an acting dream. I didn't see any of Hennessey's people letting her call her parents from forced confinement just to chat.

"Get me a recent photo of her," Bones instructed.

Liz went to a picture on the mantel and handed it over without a word. Bones took it from the frame and tucked the photo in his jacket.

"Listen close, both of you," he said, laying a hand on each of them. His gaze brightened even further. "We were never here. You've been in your rooms just as you were before, and no one came to your door. If you ever see me or her again"—a jerk of his head indicated me—"you won't remember us. Once we leave, we never arrived."

They both nodded, and I shifted uneasily on my feet. Yeah, this was convenient, but it was still scary that people's minds could be manipulated so effortlessly.

"Kitten." Bones turned to me. "Let's go."

"We're taking my truck next time," was the first thing I said as we walked outside.

Bones let out a snort. "Not likely. First, it could very well break down on the way to wherever we're headed. Second, it's as maneuverable as a bus if we run into a spot of trouble, and third, it's registered in your name. I don't want someone on Hennessey's side to simply copy down a license number to find out who you are."

All three were valid points. Damn him for using logic when he argued.

"What do you make of Natalie's phone calls?" I said next, defeated in my attempt to avoid ever getting back on his bike.

"Not sure. That's why I took the photo. I want to show it to Emily and make certain that this is the girl she saw when she was taken to the man with the mask."

We climbed onto his bike, signaling the end of our conversation. Even with Bones's speeding, I wouldn't have time to shower before I had to be at class. I'd be lucky to make it on time if I only dashed in my apartment and changed my clothes.

"I have to drop something off at Ted's," he told me once we were back at my apartment complex and I gratefully got off his motorcycle. "Should be back later tonight."

"I'll be asleep," I muttered. "Do we have to—"

"Hi, Cathy!" Timmie opened his apartment door with a wide smile. He must have seen me through his window.

Bones gave Timmie a look that froze the smile on the younger man's face.

"I'm sorry, I didn't know you had company." Timmie apologized, almost tripping to hurry back in his apartment.

I shot Bones an equally hostile glare for rattling my already skittish neighbor. "It's okay," I said, smiling at Timmie. "He's not really 'company' anyway."

"Oh." Timmie gave Bones a shy peek. "Are you Cathy's brother?"

"Whatever would give you the idea that I'm her damn brother?" Bones snapped.

Timmie backed up so fast he hit the back of his head against his doorframe. "Sorry!" he gasped, and banged into the door again before managing to scramble back inside.

I marched over to Bones and stuck my finger in his chest. He regarded me with what I would have called sullen-ness—if he hadn't been over two hundred.

"You have a choice," I said, biting off each word. "Either you make a very *sincere* apology to Timmie, or you leave and slither back to your cave like the festering ball sack you just acted like. I don't know what's gotten into you, but he's a nice guy, and you probably just made him pee his pants. Your decision, Bones. One or the other."

A dark brow arched at me.

I tapped my foot. "One... two..."

He muttered something foul and then climbed the stairs, rapping twice on Timmie's door.

"Right then, mate, terribly sorry for my unspeakable rudeness and I do beg your pardon," he said with admirable humbleness when Timmie cracked it open. Only I could pick up the slight edge to his tone as he went on. "I can only say it was caused by my natural affront to the notion of her as my sister. Since I'll be shagging her tonight, you can imagine how I'd be distressed at the thought of rogering my sibling."

"You schmuck!" The words burst out of me as Timmie's jaw dropped. "The only thing you'll be 'shagging' tonight is yourself!"

"You wanted sincerity," he countered. "Well, luv, I was sincere."

"You can get right back on your bike, and I'll see you later. If you're not being such an ass!"

Timmie's head swiveled back and forth between the two of us, his jaw still swinging open. Bones gave him a smile that was more just a baring of teeth.

"Nice to meet you, mate, and here's some advice: don't even think about it. You try anything with her, and I'll neuter you with my bare hands."

"*Leave!*" I stamped my foot for emphasis.

He swept past me and then swiveled, kissing me hard on the mouth before jumping back to avoid my right hook.

"I'll see you later, Kitten."

Timmie waited until Bones had driven out of sight before he dared to speak. "That's your boyfriend?"

I let out a grunt that I suppose was an affirmative.

"He really doesn't like me," he said, almost a whisper.

I gave one last look in the direction Bones disappeared in before shaking my head at his bewildering behavior.

"No, Timmie. I guess he doesn't."

CHAPTER SEVEN
SOUND MEDICINE

Author's note: This training scene originally took place at the end of chapter 16 in Halfway to the Grave. *It ended up being cut because the book was already running long and my editor said we had to be ruthless about only keeping scenes that were directly related to the main plot. This scene might not have added new or crucial information, but I really liked it because it showed Cat starting to relax in her new relationship with Bones and also showed Bones continuing to work with Cat to hone her skills. Cat's training wasn't mentioned much after the first twenty percent of the novel, but it did continue as Bones gave Cat the skills she would later use to survive without him. And as this scene shows, with Cat and Bones's new relationship, both of them enjoyed it much more than Cat's early training sessions.*

"Is that all you've got?" Bones taunted me.

I glared up at him while crouching on the rocky floor of the cave. My lip was split and my ribs ached as if they were being beaten with invisible hammers. You would think that since we were now sleeping together, Bones would be a little gentler on the merchandise. Not hardly.

We still trained together regularly, and if anything, he pushed me harder now when we sparred. I'd insisted on joining his fight against Hennessey, and Bones was downright paranoid about something happening to me. Thus he intended to make sure I was up to whatever Hennessey and his men might dish out if I got the chance to tangle with them again.

Still, that didn't excuse what he'd just done. "You jerk, you sucker punched me when I thought I'd hurt you."

He'd gotten in that painful rib blow when I leaned over to see if the stake I'd thrust into his chest had injured him too badly. Even though it was only wood, I had barely missed his heart.

"How many times have I told you, when someone is down, you *kick* them, you don't ask if they're bloody all right," he shot back. "They're not supposed to be all right, are they? No, that's why it's called a fight and not a chat. You'll get yourself killed one day checking to see if someone's really hurt. When will you learn that someone isn't really hurt unless they're *dead?*"

He circled around me, cracking his knuckles and rolling his head around his shoulders. My eyes narrowed. Take advantage of my concern for him, would he? We'd see about that.

As if reckless from anger at his words, I charged forward, pummeling him with my fists and feet. I took a sound thumping in return. But when he went for his traditional head punch that left me seeing stars, I braced for it, following the motion like I hadn't seen it coming.

His fist connected and I dropped to the ground, sparing myself nothing in the fall. My face banged against the rocks hard enough to bruise, but I lay sprawled where I was, motionless.

"Down again. Well, I was knackered anyway," he muttered as he knelt next to me.

When I heard him take out his knife to pierce his palm and give me blood, I struck, snatching the weapon away from him while he was distracted. I shoved it into his abdomen before he could react, then, ignoring his groan of pain, I drove the wooden stake in my other hand straight into his heart. If it had been silver, he would have been dead.

At last I'd won a round between us.

"Good on you, you nasty wench," Bones said, his words more ragged than usual. "Now pull that out, it hurts like blazes."

Blood flowed briefly from his chest when I yanked the stake out. No use being delicate with a vampire.

"I think you broke my rib, maybe two," I replied conversationally when he took the switchblade out himself. That wound also released a flow of blood before closing as if with an invisible zipper. Some things you just never got used to seeing, and instant healing was one of them.

Bones gave me a crooked smile. "Never forget to follow your own advice, hmm? Bloody hell, I'm right proud of you. I'd be staring at my body from a block away now if this was real."

"Glad you approve," I said and lay down next to him on the hard cave floor.

He shifted until he put his arm under my head, and I moved even closer to him. What a strange, strange relationship this was. Beating the hell out of each other and then cuddling afterward. I wouldn't know normal if it shot me in the ass.

We were going out again tonight. Not the traditional dinner-and-a-movie thing, but something far less romantic. Bones had run what he knew about Switch through his contacts, but they'd come up empty. It was the same story with pinpointing Hennessey's location. No one knew where Hennessey was, or if they did, they weren't telling. Well, there was more than one way to skin a cat, and this Cat was in it to win it.

We knew from Charlie that Hennessey and the mysterious Switch needed to restock their human supply, and there had been a string of disappearances around Northeast Ohio. Bones had found that out after hacking into the police's computer mainframe. The cops weren't even investigating most of the cases. If no one badgered them to look for the girls, more often than not, they didn't. The unusual number of missing persons in the same fairly narrow geographic area smacked of Hennessey's involvement. After getting as much information as we could from the girls' acquaintances, we managed to get names of the places the women frequented. When we found ones that crossed over, presto. We had a possible location for a feeding ground.

Bones had argued until he needed to breathe just to get oxygen to argue more, but I hadn't budged from my insistence on going with him. The bottom line was, when you were looking to catch something that didn't want to be caught, you needed bait. *Someone* had to place themselves out temptingly for the unknown Switch or Hennessey to attempt to snatch up. Hennessey, of course, would go straight for me on sight. After all, I was the one who got away, though he only knew about that single instance and not how I'd nearly been nabbed by Stephanie the very next weekend. He wouldn't expect me to put up a fight either, since all I'd been able to do before was dazzle him with my vomiting skills.

If it was Switch I ended up stumbling across, well, that was just as good. Then Bones would find out his real identity, get the names of who else was in their illicit crime ring, and find out where Hennessey was hiding. Both possibilities were well worth me putting on my sleazy clothes and trolling around bars and clubs angling for a fang bang, regardless if

Bones thought it was too unsafe. He'd be close by, and those guys had a lot of paybacks coming to them.

"Let's go somewhere softer, pet," he said, urging me up. "You need patching up and I need you."

Even with me poking three different holes in him, he was still in the mood. In a sick way, it was admirable.

"Can't you just fake impotence and take a nap? You really bashed my ribs earlier. I hope your chest still hurts. You deserved it."

He grinned. "Here, this is what I was trying to do when you tricked me with that fake faint. Looked brilliant, by the way. Never saw it coming."

With the same knife that had recently resided in his stomach, he slit a neat gouge in his palm and placed it against my lips. Although I still found it repugnant, I swallowed his blood without complaint. I'd need my strength tonight. And my rib cage.

Almost immediately I felt better. I never ceased to be amazed at the incredible healing power of vampire blood. Bones had told me matter-of-factly that the older and stronger a vamp was, the more potent their blood. Apparently it was similar to wine in that regard, and Bones was a vintage brew. I still preferred gin and tonic for taste.

He picked me up and carried me, still protesting but with little force behind my words, into his bedroom. Bones was a firm believer in kissing something to make it feel better. And better and better. Who was I to argue with sound medicine?

CHAPTER EIGHT
THE OTHER RENFIELD

Author's note: This is an alternate version of the first half of chapter 24, where the police "Renfield" was someone other than Lieutenant Isaac. Lieutenant Isaac kind of showed up out of nowhere in the published version, but in my original draft, it was Detective Mansfield's sidekick, Detective Black. This version ended up being changed because of pacing concerns since the climax of the novel was already very long and my editor wanted to get Cat to the governor's house faster. I've included a little bit of the published version for context, and some of the dialog in parts is the same, but the person Cat is speaking to has changed. Oh, and the part where the nurse tries to kill Cat by injecting poison into her IV was totally inspired by the scene in Kill Bill. *I loved that movie, and Daryl Hannah's character merrily whistling as she dons a nurse outfit and attempts to kill Uma Thurman's character was so chillingly comical I wrote it into this version as an homage.*

They handcuffed me to the stretcher and drove me straight to the hospital in an ambulance. In no time the area was turned into a law enforcement and crime scene circus. None of it mattered to me because I'd seen two things which filled me with inexpressible gratitude. One was my mother, IV bag attached, being hoisted into another waiting ambulance. The other had been Bones, running unharmed after Switch. The bullet wounds would heal and he would catch him. Everything inside me believed it. What was a little multiple murder count compared to that?

A white-faced officer read me my rights and then burst into tears. Guess the sight of the living dead absorbing bullets like bubbles and still tearing throats out unnerved him. Not to mention the other vamps turning into shriveled mummies before his eyes. In my quick assessment, two had gotten away in addition to Switch, but I didn't worry about them. We'd get them later. It shouldn't be too hard since Bones now knew who they were. Switch was our first priority, and Bones wouldn't let him get away. After all, he had promised me vengeance, and I knew he'd deliver.

The rescue workers treating me were also perplexed by my condition. I was covered in multiple slashes, stab wounds, bite marks, bruises, bashed ribs, scrapes, and oh yeah, a bullet hole. Yet when the young attendant took my vital signs, he blanched in confusion.

"Heart rate... normal. Blood pressure... normal. Pulse... normal. That can't be right."

"Sorry, buddy," I murmured, enjoying the painkillers they'd injected into my IV. While the medication didn't affect me as profoundly as it should have, it still took the edge off the sting.

"Look at your arm. The bullet is extruding toward the point of entry. Holy shit, Tom, come see this!" Forgetting his professionalism, the tech pointed excitedly at my shoulder.

Another face peered at the wound. "Not possible," Tom stated flatly.

A strangled laugh escaped me. "That's what I've been saying my whole life, fellas."

"*I can see the goddamn bullet crowning!* Give me some Steri-Pads..."

Even in the midst of their awe, they still worked. Admirable quality. The bullet was pulled free from my flesh. When they unloaded me at the hospital under guard, I could hear them still mumbling to themselves dazedly.

"Did you see that? The tissue's already coapted at the edges. *The goddamn tissue's coapted at the edges, Tom!*"

Daylight lightened the sky with mauve and amber streaks. Sunrise. In the brief moments before the emergency room's automatic doors excluded it from my view, I looked over at the horizon and smiled. We had lived through the night after all, all of us. It was the most beautiful sunrise I'd ever seen.

I now knew how a celebrity felt when they had something wrong with them which required hospitalization. There were multiple guards posted at my room, and doctors came in droves to gape and gasp over me. Aside from being hand-cuffed to the bed, it would have been flattering.

The dawn brought weariness, with reinforcements. I slept through most of the poking, prodding, and futile attempts at stitches that were promptly removed when my skin closed over the sutures at my accelerated healing rates. None of this concerned me. Bones would come for me. Let them gawk at me and scratch their heads while they had the chance.

As it turned out, by noon I had my first visitor, and it wasn't my undead lover.

Detective Black entered the room with a nurse at his side. He smiled when he saw me. "Hello again, Catherine."

Both of his wrists were bandaged from where my knives had punched through them. Frankly, I was surprised to see him at all, let alone in a good mood.

"Well, hiya," I said, cursorily noticing the nurse fill a syringe from a tiny bottle on her tray. "Didn't know you could speak, Detective Black. You didn't say a word yesterday. Sorry about your wrists, but I didn't feel like getting shot. Happened anyway though, as you can see. How's my mother?"

He came near my bed. The nurse gave him a look as she tapped the syringe in a professional manner to get any bubbles out.

"No hard feelings, Catherine," he said genially, holding up his thickly bandaged wrists. His eyes were peat colored and not nearly as friendly as his tone. "I'm getting promoted because of you. My career's on the fast track, but Mansfield already mentioned that. Damn, is that old man annoying or what? I couldn't wait for him to retire, and thanks to you, he finally has."

"My mother?" I prodded, unnerved all of a sudden by how he smelled. There was something familiar about it. I wasn't used to diagnosing things by scent, however, so I couldn't quite place it.

"She's our next stop," was his reply.

The nurse motioned him out of the way of my IV. Irritably I wondered what they were injecting me with now. I'd even been given a tetanus shot.

He stared at me. "She and the other five girls they pulled out of that house are on the floor below you since none of them have been arrested like you have. Tragic, isn't it? How a young girl like you ran a human trafficking ring and even killed your grandparents to cover it up."

That pissed me off. "You shouldn't even be given the title detective since obviously you're a moron. My grandparents were killed right about the time you and Mansfield were chatting me up, as the medical examiner will soon confirm, and..."

His fingers were tapping impatiently on his leg as the nurse carefully stuck the needle into my catheter port. I watched his fingers, my gaze narrowing, and suddenly it all clicked into place. There was no way he could have such dexterity less than a day after being impaled through the tendons, and I knew what that smell was now. *Vampire.*

I ripped the IV out of my arm even as that bright pink liquid was snaking toward my vein. With all of my new speed, I catapulted out of bed, landing behind the two of them and throttling Black with one hand while I jammed the half-empty syringe into the nurse with the other.

The force of that action emptied it into her. I watched with harsh satisfaction as she dropped. Her heart had stopped before she even hit the floor.

"Well now, Detective." My grip tightened to prevent him from screaming. After all, a guard was stationed outside my room. "Looks like you brought me a female Dr. Kevorkian. My, my, that stuff must have been potent. She's as dead as Hennessey, or didn't you know that? Vampires all do look the same when they're shriveled."

"…ddnnt knww att alking outtt…"

It came in garbles. I relaxed my hold only a trifle.

"You speak above a whisper and you're getting the rest of what's in that bottle," I hissed, kicking the fallen glass container for emphasis. "Nice disguise with those bandages on your wrists. I bet you don't even have a scratch under them. Somebody pumped you full of vampire blood—you stink of it. Who sent you?"

"Fuck you."

At least he said it softly. I smiled. "Fuck me? Are you in the mood? Let's find out."

And I reached down and squeezed his nuts like they were stress-relieving orbs. Knowing how he'd react, I clapped a hand over his mouth at the same time. All that came out through my fingers was a frantic, tormented wheeze. The cop outside didn't even budge.

"Ooohh, squishy," I said pitilessly. "Now, I'm going to ask you again, and *don't* disappoint me. Who sent you?"

"Oliver," came the pained reply. "It was *Oliver!*"

That wasn't the mayor's name. In fact, it wasn't anyone on our list of human or vampire suspects.

"You'd better make me a believer. Oliver who?"

I hadn't let go of his parts. That's probably why his voice was about three octaves higher when he answered me.

"*Ethan* Oliver!"

I froze, stunned.

Black let out a gasping snicker. "You didn't know? Hennessey was sure Francesca told Bones. He wondered why he hadn't moved on him yet. We didn't know what he was planning, and we were scrambling for any edge we could get. When I found Danny's police report, I knew a vampire did it. And when Danny described him *and* his ex-girlfriend, we knew we had Bones at last."

"Ethan Oliver," I whispered. "*Governor* Ethan Oliver? My God, I voted for him! He's Hennessey's shadow partner? Why?"

"Let go of my balls!" Black rasped.

I got a firmer grip on them instead. "I'll let go when you make sense, and the clock's ticking. Every minute that goes by, I squeeze harder. You won't have any left inside of five."

"He wants to run for president, and he's using Ohio as his podium," Black rushed out in one breath. "He stumbled across Hennessey a few years ago. Think it was when he was buying pussy on the side. Hennessey came up with this idea to harvest people for feedings, like he did in Mexico, and Oliver loved it. Problem is, it's only the pretty young girls who sell the most, but things get messy when a bunch of them go missing. So they made a deal. Hennessey cleans the streets of the homeless, drug dealers, prostitutes, and degenerates as his end of the bargain, and Oliver makes sure the paperwork disappears on any of the high-end tail that Hennessey needs to keep his clients happy. But that got to be a lot of work, so Hennessey began getting the girls' addresses and stopping the reports before they started. Made *my* job easier. Crime rate goes down, economy goes up, voters are happy, Oliver looks like Ohio's savior... and Hennessey makes a bundle."

I was shaking my head in disbelief at the sheer callousness of it all. Frankly I didn't know who was worse— Hennessey for doing it, or Oliver for making himself out as a hero on the bones of hundreds of victims.

"And this afternoon? Oliver sent you to kill me, obviously. What about my mother and the other girls? *What were you going to do with them,* and I dare you to lie to me."

My new clench got a squeak out of him, but it also made my point. What he told me next was no candy-coated fabrication.

"I was planting a bomb on the second floor," he croaked. "In the back wing where they all are. Then Oliver was going to pin it on Muslim extremists. Leave a hate note, et cetera. He saw how Bush's numbers spiked right after 9-11. He thought it would push him over the top as the next presidential candidate."

"You *fucker*," I growled. "Where's the bomb?"

"In the morgue. Shelly hid it there. We were getting it later, after someone found you. No one goes in there. No one who talks, anyway."

I thought rapidly. Oliver would be expecting a kaboom within the next couple of hours, and when it didn't come, he'd send someone else to finish the job. A man like that didn't leave loose ends.

"Black," I said in a perfectly pleasant tone, "you're coming with me. I'm revoking my vote."

His eyes slid to mine and then to the door. "You'll never make it."

I laughed nastily. "You're right. Not that way we won't. Pick up your girl, what's her name? Shelly?" I pointed at the nurse.

His mouth curled in distaste. "Ew. She's dead."

That made me laugh even more viciously. "Want to join her? If I have to tell you again, you will."

He bent down in slow, wounded movements since I still had his balls. When he had her hefted in his arms, I changed my grip to hug him from behind.

"Ever been bungee jumping?"

His head turned. "What?"

"Me neither," I went on. "Who needs the bungee cord, anyway? I say it's for pussies." And I shoved him toward the vertical window, picking up speed as he started to scream. The door opened behind us right as Shelly, Black, and I crashed through the window, free-falling three stories to the grass below.

We landed on Shelly. Or at least Black did. I landed on him, to be specific, rolling us immediately to limit the impact. Glass was all around us, and more than a few bystanders began to scream louder than Black was.

"You crazy bitch! You *lunatic*—"

It came out in noisy wheezes. His ribs were probably broken. I couldn't seem to care.

"You die as soon as you lose your usefulness, so I suggest you get us to your car right now."

"Around... around the fountain! Ohh, my leg. My *leg!*"

In the interest of time, I swung him over my shoulder, leaving Shelly where she was. My hospital gown gave the shocked onlookers something else to see as I dashed off in the direction of the fountain, Black bobbing with every step. We made it to his car in less than a minute, and it was his good luck that his left leg was broken instead of his right, because I made him drive.

CHAPTER NINE
THE SHORT STORY THAT
NEVER WAS

Author's note: This is the original short story I'd started writing for the Weddings from Hell *anthology, but when I was about twenty-five percent into it, I realized it was all wrong for the theme of the anthology. So I wrote* Happily Never After, *the story with Chance and Isa instead. The timeline for this story takes place after* Halfway to the Grave *and before* One Foot in the Grave. *Since it was originally supposed to be a new anthology story, there will be some backstory with world building and explaining prior events from* Halfway to the Grave. *You'll also get to see the first time that Cat met Denise, as well as what happened to Juan when he made the mistake of calling Cat "Kitten."*

The vampire sat next to me at the bar. I was drinking a gin and tonic, light on the tonic. It was my fourth since Mr. Right walked in twenty minutes ago. I'd lost count of how many I'd had in the previous two hours waiting for him.

"Buy you another drink?" he asked, his eyes sweeping over my short, tight dress.

I could say yes. Make small talk with him, ask him to dance, or flirt for a while before getting him alone. But why waste time?

"I have a better idea." My voice was low and seductive. "How about I pour what's in this glass on your skin and lick it off. You pick which part."

He tossed some money on the counter for my tab without even counting it. "Let's go."

Vampires. If horniness was a crime, they'd all be under arrest.

Of course, I wasn't going to arrest him, and horniness wasn't his crime. Neither was being a vampire, in my opinion. But according to the data my boss, Don, gathered, the man now leading me out to the parking lot had killed five people in the past month.

That I wasn't going to stand for. Vampires didn't need to kill to eat, so this schmuck was doing it just for fun. Well, I had my own definition of fun, and it involved the silver knives concealed in my thigh-high boots.

"From the moment I saw you, I knew I had to have you," he said, taking me in his arms.

We were at the far end of the parking lot. The darkest part. Two of the bodies had been found in the Dumpster not fifty feet from here.

I smiled. "My thoughts exactly."

Then I slid to my knees, giving him a knowing look as I set my drink down and reached for the front of his pants. He groaned and closed his eyes, but not before I saw the flash of green in them. If his mouth hadn't been closed, I knew I'd also see fangs where before there had been square, normal teeth. Lust or feeding caused vampires to shed their human disguise. I was one of the few people with a heartbeat who could spot them without that. Their creamy crystal skin was a dead giveaway to me, pun intended, plus I could feel their power in the air.

Being half-dead had its advantages.

The vampire was getting impatient. His hands curled in my hair, bringing my head closer. I stifled an annoyed grunt and pretended to fumble with his zipper while my other hand slid into my boot. I had a treat for him all right, but it wasn't what he was expecting. Still, this was an effective ruse to distract him. I'd yet to meet a vampire who'd turn down a potential blow job, even if he did intend to murder me afterward. It was probably his motto that one good suck deserved another.

I was just about to clear my dagger from my boot when a loud voice shattered the quiet.

"Freeze!"

"What the hell?" the vampire and I asked in unison.

About twenty feet away, a man stepped out from behind one of the cars. He looked to be in his midforties with a respectable gut and gray hair hugging his temples. What held my main attention, however, was the gun he pointed at us. Or rather, pointed above my head at the vampire behind me.

"Police officer, don't move!" he said, raising his voice.

My fingers tightened on my concealed knife. There went my plans for a private game of stake and shake.

The vampire recovered from his surprise enough to laugh. "Ah, Detective Morrows. Have you been staking out this bar again? Maybe I'll let you watch me this time, not that you'll remember afterward."

This could still be handled quietly, I thought. If I could get fang-boy to mesmerize the cop into placid immobility, I'd plug his heart with silver and cart away his body before the cop even snapped out of his trance. Nice, quick, and clean.

It wasn't to be. A dozen men dressed in black and wearing thickly visored helmets fanned out around the parking lot, automatic weapons pointed at the three of us.

"Drop the gun, cop," one of them said, a Spanish accent marking his words.

"Jesus, Mary, and Joseph," I spat, coming to my feet. "Are you kidding me?"

The vampire looked around with an expression of amazement but no fear. "You brought a SWAT team, Morrows?" he asked the cop.

Morrows gaped as he shook his head. "I don't know who these guys are."

"Oh." The vampire shrugged, then a burst of green spilled out of his eyes. "Well, don't just stand there. Shoot them!"

Morrows, instantly mesmerized by the power in that glowing emerald gaze, took aim at the men. They abandoned formation and jumped behind various cars as Morrows squeezed off shots with robotic obedience.

I'd had enough. My dagger cleared my boot and I whirled, ramming it into the vampire's chest. He grabbed me, fangs snapping near my throat, but the strength in his grip—and the light in his eyes—faded as I twisted the blade several times. Silver in the heart was a vampire's kryptonite.

He dropped at my feet just as the doors to the bar flung open. Onlookers goggled at the cop still shooting at the dark figures who took cover behind the cars. I gave the cop an irritated glance and pulled more knives from my boots, far smaller than the eight-inch dagger I'd skewered fang-boy with. These were smooth, curved silver blades, no handles, perfectly balanced. I flung them at Morrows, burying them in the brachial nerve in his arm. The gun clattered from his hand as he screamed. Before he had a chance to pick the gun up with his other hand, I sprang at him and punched him in the side of his head. He went limp.

Then I marched up to the man who'd come out from behind a nearby car. He took his helmet off, revealing shoulder-length black hair tied back in a ponytail.

"What have I told you about keeping the perimeter clear, Juan?" I asked through gritted teeth.

He swallowed. "But... you looked like you were in danger, *querida*."

My fists clenched. It wasn't because of the endearment; Juan was forever calling me one of those, but he usually did it while following orders. Not while taking matters into his own hands in an idiotic, misguided chivalrous way that almost got people killed.

"Cat." Another of the black-clad men came forward, also taking off his helmet. "Your eyes."

Right. I took a breath, forcing down the surge of adrenalin that had kicked in my nonhuman traits. By the time I blinked, I knew the green glow had left my gaze and my eyes were their normal gray color again. Years of practice made perfect when it came to controlling the vampire parts of me.

Most people were happily unaware that vampires existed. It was my job to keep it that way while protecting them from the more unruly members of undead society. I hadn't asked for this job—it was forced on me because of the heritage I also hadn't asked for. Thanks, Dad, I thought with bitterness. One day I'll find you. And then I'll kill you for raping my mother.

You could say I had family issues.

"Let's get those people back inside and contain this area," my second-in-command, Tate, ordered. More helmets came off as the rest of the team obeyed. The helmets had specially-designed infrared filters that blocked ninety percent of a vampire's hypnotic glowing gaze. The rest of the helmet's purpose? Well, it had saved more than a few skulls from getting cracked after some impromptu flight time. Vampires were strong enough to hurl cars if they wanted to. Humans? They could be thrown so much farther.

While Tate made sure the bystanders were hustled back inside, other members of the team went about carting the vampire's body away. I returned my attention to Juan.

"This was your first time commanding a tactical operation, and what did you do? You allowed a police officer into the containment area where the vampire and I were. Then you brought the team out of hiding to confront said cop. And then you didn't attempt to neutralize the cop when he started shooting up the place. My God, Juan, the only thing you left out was setting off flares while calling the media!"

"You were right behind the cop, *querida.* I didn't want to risk shooting you," Juan said, defending himself. His Spanish accent was thicker than normal, a sure sign he knew he was in for it.

"Really?" I scoffed. "You've been with the team three months now, and you still think I couldn't move in time?"

"*Por favor.* You're fast, but you're not that fast."

"Juan." I didn't shake him, but I was tempted. "I didn't get to be leader of this team because I sweet-talked the right secret government official. I got it because of my high undead body count. Now, don't ever disobey orders again, or I'll throw your ass off this team. Clear?"

He smiled. "Crystal clear, Kitten…"

At that one word, all the emotions I'd buried over the past fifteen months came roaring to the surface. In a surge of grief, I shoved Juan backward. Too hard; I'd forgotten to check up my strength. He dented the car he landed on. Then his head smacked the concrete when he hit the ground.

Tate swung around to give me an incredulous look. So did the other team members who were still outside.

I cringed in guilt, resisting the urge to run over to Juan and check on him. He'd be okay—I'd give him some of the vampire's blood later to ensure that. But as for now... better the guys think I was a heartless witch than show weakness and spur their concerns that I wasn't tough enough to lead them.

"I hate that nickname," was all I said. "Now maybe Juan will remember that."

I walked through the graveyard, not needing the bright moonlight to lessen the darkness for me. There were crumbling headstones with fading inscriptions etched on them around me. A large evergreen towered in the middle of the cemetery. Several yards away, a scarred tree extended over a cliff like a wraith leaning over the edge of eternity.

I looked around with deliberate casualness, sensing I was no longer alone. A waft of charged air seemed to caress my back, announcing the approach of a vampire. *Come closer,* I thought, tightening my grip on the knife in my pocket.

The vampire came up behind me as silent as a shadow. I waited until I could almost feel the brush of his hand on my skin before I whirled, my knife raised to strike. Then I saw his face... and my weapon fell to the ground.

"*Bones.*"

His hair seemed almost white under the glow of the moonlight, and those deep brown eyes locked with mine.

"You left me," he whispered, but the accusation in his voice might as well have been a scream.

I dropped my gaze. "I... I had to."

He laughed, low and bitter. "Did you?"

I reached out to him, a stab of pain going through me when he pulled away. "The law was chasing me, other vampires were chasing both of us, and then the FBI's version of the Spook Squad found out I wasn't totally human. You would have been in too much danger trying to hide me and my mother. I couldn't let you die, Bones."

"You didn't give me a choice," he shot back, his eyes flashing green. "You left me with only a bloody note. How could you do that? You said you loved me."

"I do," I said brokenly.

Bones grabbed my shoulders, pulling me close. "I told you I'd find you if you ran from me, Kitten. I have, and you will never run away from me again, do you understand? Say it."

I stared at him, heartbroken. "I can't."

He started to fade. I snatched at him, but it was as if he'd turned to smoke in my hands. Desperately I tried to hold on to him, but the more I clutched at him, the more he dematerialized.

"Bones," I screamed, suddenly willing to say anything, do anything, to keep him with me. "I won't leave again, I promise. I love you, please come back…!"

The ground reared up to hit me—and I woke up on my bedroom floor. There was no graveyard, no moonlight, no Bones. Just me, tormenting myself with another dream about him.

"Goddamn it," I whispered, my heart pounding. I must have fallen out of bed during my dream, chasing someone I could never have. After being gone over a year, I should have a better grip on my emotions, but I didn't. No, I still missed Bones with the same gut-wrenching ache I'd had the day I left him.

One thing could be counted on to help. I showered, then got dressed and drove to work. The military compound Don recently renovated was about thirty minutes from my house. By the time I got on the road, I usually hit the lunchtime rush. It was my vampire blood that made mornings not my thing, plus you could safely say most of my job activities took place at night.

After my obligatory stop at the three—count 'em, three—security checkpoints leading up to the compound, I made it in the building. Most of the levels were underground, completing the image of "nothing strange goin' on here, folks!" that Don wanted to project.

He was waiting in his office for me. It was my routine to stop there first, go over reports from the previous evening's activity, and then get back to training my team. Unless there was another string of suspicious murders to discuss, of course. Then it would be flying to the scene of whatever gruesome event to figure out if we were dealing with the wrath of humanity against humanity... or something else.

Don's gray head was bent over his laptop when I entered. He didn't bother to look up as I sat down in the chair opposite him.

"Juan's still in medical, Cat," he said by way of greeting. "The doctors say he'll be unconscious for another day."

Guilt poked me again for my unwarranted reaction to the name I'd only let one person call me.

"He'd be back in the training room today if you'd bend your stupid rules. Between my blood and the blood from the vampire corpse the other night, Juan could be good as new," I replied.

Don's eyes were almost the same gray shade as his hair. "I won't have the men getting careless because they think vampire blood makes them invincible. And I won't have them becoming addicted to the other effects it would have on them."

Don thought vampires were evil, plain and simple. If not for my usefulness to his operation, I was pretty sure Don would be happy to see me dead. One less blight on society and all that, considering my mixed lineage.

I shrugged. "Your call, boss, but then don't blame me because you're afraid to use the resources available to you."

"How is your mother?" Don asked, changing the subject.

I glowered at him. Boy, did he go for the low blows. "Fine, thanks. She says she missed you at her last Undead Pride party."

A faint smile touched his lips. Don knew my mother was even more prejudiced against vampires than he was.

"We have a possible case I want you to review," Don said, bringing the subject back to business. "Here are several hard-copy files, newspaper microfilm, and floppy disks to go through." He pushed a thick manila envelope across his desk to me. "I'll want your report tomorrow on whether you think there's anything supernatural involved."

"What's the rush? If you're having me sort through old newspaper films and floppy disks instead of fresh bodies, why don't I have more time to do a proper evaluation?"

Don gave me a thin smile. "Just have the report ready when you come in tomorrow."

I stood up. Too bad for him he didn't specify what time tomorrow, because I was feeling a late start coming on. "Whatever you say, boss."

After a bruising day of running my team through staged drills and hand-to-hand combat, I left the compound at ten. It occurred to me that I hadn't eaten anything, so instead of heading straight home, I stopped by a fast-food place. It was chilly out, but despite that, I decided to eat my hamburger and fries sitting on a bench near a park instead of in my car. It was so rare to be out at night unless I was hunting something. Even more rare to be out without someone from my team spying on me.

Don didn't know I could hear the teams he put on me and the faint clicking in my phone that revealed the extra wiring. He knew a lot about my inhuman abilities, but I'd held back a few things. Like how far my hearing range really extended. I wasn't planning anything devious despite Don's suspicions, but some things were best left undisclosed. Don had relaxed somewhat in the past couple of months, to give him credit. Now I was only tailed a few times a week instead of every day.

I chewed the salty goodness of my fries and wondered for the millionth time what Bones was doing right then. Whatever it was, I hoped he was okay. He might be undead, but that didn't make him impossible to kill, and with his line of work, a lot of people wanted him shriveled. *Please, God, keep him safe,* I thought. *Let him understand why I did what I did and not hate me for it. Or, let him hate me if that'll make him happier. Just let him be okay.*

A choked-off scream snapped my head up. I fixed my gaze in its direction, moving toward the sound. *There.* Behind the thick clump of trees about a hundred yards into the park. I pulled out one of the silver knives I always kept in my jacket, concealing it in my sleeve.

"Is someone hurt?" I called out. Maybe that sound was the muffled scream of passion during a clandestine tryst. Or something else human in nature. I crept closer.

There was no response to my question except a slurping noise. I knew that sound.

When I burst through the trees, the vampire didn't even pick his head up from the girl's neck. Two things registered with me in an instant. *He's not feeding to get a harmless snack— his teeth are sank in too deep. And he hasn't even bothered to put her under.*

The girl's wide eyes met mine, silently pleading. This was no consensual exchange of blood. If it had been, I would have turned around and walked away, same as I'd done many times before. This was different, however. It was attempted murder.

"Hey, buddy," I said. "I taste better. Come see."

The vampire laughed, the sound muffled against the girl's neck. He wasn't alarmed—why would he be? I had a heartbeat, I breathed, and I was all alone. No undead person in their right mind would find such a combination a threat... which was why it was such a perfect disguise.

His emerald gaze drilled into mine as he lifted his head. Good. Fangs no longer in her artery where they could rip it open.

"I'll have to do that."

I flung myself at him with blurring speed. Fang Face didn't even have time to look surprised before my silver blade sank into his heart. One, two, three twists, and all the strength left him for good.

I knew it made me a homicidal witch, but oh God, did I enjoy that! There were few things that made me happy these days, but evening the score against murdering bastards like him made me still believe there was a reason to live. I couldn't be with Bones, but I could save a few people. I did have that to keep me going.

The girl was staring at me in disbelief, swaying on her feet. A flow of red leaked from the two holes in her neck with steady, rhythmic pumps. I gave that flow a swift, calculating glance before leaning down and hacking off the vampire's hand with one hard slice.

Her eyes bugged. Before she could do anything stupid, like run while her artery was punctured, I grabbed her. Then I held the severed end of the vamp's hand to the holes in her neck, clapping my other hand over her mouth so she couldn't scream.

Her heartbeat was a loud staccato in my ears as she struggled. I gave the unattached hand a few good squeezes to get the remaining blood out of it since it was already starting to shrivel. After a moment, I pulled the stump off her neck to examine her wound.

Her bleeding had stopped and those two fang holes were gone. Satisfied, I dropped the dead vamp's severed hand.

"Works like a charm," I muttered. Stupid Don and his prejudices. Nothing but *nothing* healed like vampire blood.

Then I took my hand off her mouth and let her go, about to give her my rehearsed speech on how trauma can make people see things that aren't really there.

"He was a vampire, wasn't he?" She asked it in a very matter-of-fact way.

I regarded her warily, wondering if this was a prelude to full-blown hysterics. "Miss, you're confused. Sometimes, when people go through a traumatic experience, their mind can play tricks on them—"

"You sure killed the shit out of *him*," she interrupted me. "I mean, wow. I owe you a beer at least."

I stared at her with the same disbelief she'd bestowed on me earlier. Most people, after having their necks chewed on and then seeing their fanged attacker stabbed to death, were pretty overwrought. Not poking the dead vampire with their foot and mumbling about how he hadn't even bought her a drink before getting one of his own.

I shifted on my feet, torn. Protocol demanded that I keep her here, call in the team, and let Don arrange a little memory-altering session between her and his staff of highly skilled, always-on-call hypnotists. After all, we couldn't have people running around screaming, "Nosferatu!" and rallying the villagers, could we?

"I have to call this in," I said. "Remove the body, gather up any evidence…" What was wrong with me? Why was I admitting that?

She nodded like it made sense and then sat down. Her pulse was steady now, though a little weaker than it should have been. Still, some iron pills and rest and she'd be good as new.

"Is this your job or something?"

Why wasn't she acting like every other victim I'd come across, male or female? She'd almost been eaten by a vampire! She should be screaming, crying, or demanding to talk to her lawyer. The usual stuff.

"Have you been around vampires before?" I asked suspiciously. That would explain it.

She shook her head. "No, this was definitely a first for me."

"Then why are you so calm?" I couldn't help but blurt.

She gave me a jaded look. "I just moved here from New York and my old boyfriend was a cabbie there. Does that answer your question?"

Caught off guard, I laughed. Yes, now her relative nonchalance about discovering the existence of the undead did make sense.

"I'm Denise," she said. "What's your name?"

I answered her with the fake name I went under. "Cristine."

She smiled. Though it was a trifle shaky, it was genuine. "Cristine, I'm *very* glad to meet you."

The vanilla-colored envelope landed in front of Don. I took my seat and propped my foot up on the edge of his desk. Few things pissed Don off as much as that, which of course was why I did it. It's not like I was worried about getting fired. Jeez, that was a dream of mine.

"Do you mind?" Don asked acidly.

I smiled. "I'm comfier this way, so why would I?"

He gave me a scathing look but picked up the folder and didn't comment further on the location of my foot. "Since it's almost six p.m., I assume you've conducted an extensive evaluation of the materials here?"

I nodded, rocking back in my chair just to see how deep his scowl could get.

"You've got yourself a creature on the loose, all right. Seven prominent husbands go missing right after their weddings, never to be seen again... unless you count the random parts. Coincidentally, their wives all look like the same woman, barring the changing hairstyles and clothes, but hey, you can't expect fashion to stand still for a hundred years, can you?"

Don leaned back with a satisfied expression on his lined face. "Just as I thought. She's a vampire, preying on these men after she marries them."

"Not so fast," I said. "She's not a vampire. She's a ghoul."

Don pulled on his eyebrow. He hardly had any hair left on the end of it. "Are you certain?"

"Certain as death," I replied. "Most of those photos are older—she obviously smartened up as picture quality got better and avoided the camera more—but the newer ones show more detail. She looks exactly human. No telltale crystal clarity to her flesh, so unless this chick uses the fountain of youth for her daily bath, she's got to be a ghoul."

Don digested this. Ghouls weren't our operation's forte, mainly because they weren't my forte. Bones had taught me everything there was to know about vampires, but ghouls? Bones had only covered the most essential basics there, i.e., how to kill them. Decapitation. And they didn't part easily with their heads.

"How much of a problem will this represent?" Don finally asked.

I shrugged. "On the plus side, ghouls don't have any power in their gaze, so we wouldn't need to worry about her mesmerizing anyone. But the rest is all on the negative side. For one, this chick goes after men. You've put me in a bunch of disguises, but unless you've got someone *seriously* talented in wardrobe, I won't be able to fake that. Two, she's not just trolling bars looking for an easy meal. She goes after rich men who don't have a lot of public visibility and even fewer family members. Three, she doesn't just eat them and run, she marries them first. I'm assuming that's to get her hands on their inheritance, but it throws a real curveball into our plans. We can't just check all the published engagement announcements to catch her before she eats her next husband."

Don pulled harder on his eyebrow. I resisted the urge to point him to the scissors so he could take care of it once and for all.

"Are you saying it can't be done?"

I'd been asking myself that same question since I realized what we were dealing with. On one hand, as Bones would say, we had to fight the battles we could win. It was impossible to bring every murderer to justice no matter how much he or she might deserve it, so sometimes we had to walk away. Live to fight another day and all that. On the other hand…

"It would involve a long-term operation the likes of which our team isn't properly prepared for," I said after a pause. "But yes. It can be done."

Don nodded, satisfied. "Then let's get started."

The forty-two members of my team stared at me with varying degrees of shock. Not that I blamed them. It wasn't every day I asked who wanted to volunteer to be a ghoul's boy toy turned chew toy.

Don stood behind me, a rarity. Normally he let me give the mission details to my team alone—unless you counted those secret sessions where he picked whose turn it was to spy on me. But in this case, his presence was a show of support for my dangerous, highly improbable plan.

"I'll do it," Tate said. His dark blue gaze swept over the men. "I'm second-in-command, so it's my risk to take."

My opinion of Tate had come a long way over the past fifteen months. When we first met, I thought Tate was a tight-ass who hadn't had an ounce of inspiration since he was a baby deciding on one tit or two. Now I knew Tate was someone who would walk through fire to save one of his men if they needed it. Hell, the only reason Juan led the last mission was because Tate still had some internal bleeding from the one before it, after trying to save a new recruit. Tate had almost worn his guts on his back after one hard undead punch. The recruit died anyway. Once someone's throat is gone, there's no saving them. But the point is, Tate had tried.

Yeah, Tate was fearless and tough. Which was why he couldn't be the volunteer.

"No," I said shortly. "You're right, Tate, you're second-in-command, so the risk *does* fall to you. But it's the risk to lead these men if I go down for the count. Not to be ghoul-bait on this mission."

"Juan would be perfect for this... once he wakes up." A recruit named Dave chuckled.

There was more laughter even as I cringed in guilt over Juan's condition. Yes, Juan was a real ladies' man, to put it nicely. Calling him a tramp would be more accurate.

Come to think of it, being knocked out for a couple of days might do Juan a world of good. *But if he doesn't wake up by tomorrow*, I promised myself, *I'm giving him a pint of my blood, Don's rules be damned.*

Three more of the men volunteered. I waited, but there were no more takers. Then I gave the three guys a cool, evaluating stare. *No, not Peter. He's too prejudiced against the undead; he'd puke in the ghoul's mouth the first time she tried to kiss him. Jeff, hmmm. He's a good soldier. Open-minded enough for the job too, but... Oh, forget it. He's as sexy as a vegetable sandwich!*

That left Edward. He was a newer recruit, which made me hesitant, but he'd performed well in the field, didn't have a pathological hatred of the undead, and he was easy enough on the eyes.

"You, Edward," was all I said.

He gulped and nodded. "Yes, ma'am."

Now to turn Edward into irresistible man-meat that no inheritance-hunting ghoul could refuse...

Chapter Ten
Original Beginning of
One Foot in the Grave

Author's Note: I mentioned before that I tend to overwrite my beginnings, and thus a lot gets cut later from them. One Foot in the Grave *was no exception. If anything, I had to cut far more from this than I did from the original beginning of* Halfway to the Grave. *In these original chapters, you see a lot more of Cat interacting with her team. Tate, Juan, Dave, and Don had become a sort of surrogate family to her, and in addition to that, she used saving people as a way of self-medicating the pain she still felt from leaving Bones. However, as much as Cat did grow up during the years that she and Bones were apart (and savvy readers will note the difference in those years from this version to the one that was published) she still hadn't outgrown her innate tendency toward recklessness.*

"Gentlemen." Tate's voice boomed through the thick walls I waited behind. He really got into his speeches. "All of you represent the top of your field in weapons, combat, espionage, or infiltration. You come from different branches of the military, the Bureau, the CIA, and even the criminal justice system. Gentlemen, you are the toughest there is." Tate paused for dramatic effect. I rolled my eyes. "And you are all going to fail."

Even through the solid concrete and metal, I heard a slight shuffle from the men at this proclamation. I shouldn't be able to hear anything, but my hearing was far from normal. Hell, *I* was far from normal, as these men were about to find out. If Tate would hurry it up already.

"Out of the twenty of you who enter this room, we only expect a few to make the cut. Do not remove any of your protective gear. Once these doors close behind you, they will not open again until this exercise is over. Remember, participation is voluntary. Any of you who choose to decline, step forward. This is your last chance."

More shifting, but no one chickened out. Usually no one did, not if they'd gotten this far.

"Men," Tate concluded, and the glee in his voice almost made me smile. This was his favorite part. "You have only one objective in this exercise. Defeat the enemy!"

The doors slid open to reveal a large square room lined with padding from top to bottom. Such insulation allowed for longer training sessions, but somehow I didn't think it was completely appreciated.

There was a shocked silence. Tate was grinning now. My other two captains, Juan and Dave, wore similar smiles.

One of the potential recruits looked to them in confusion. "Sir…? There's, um, nothing in here but a woman, sir."

Well, score one to him for stating the obvious.

"Lesson one, soldier," Tate said firmly. "Don't believe for a moment that because something looks harmless it is harmless. What's the matter with you men? She is the enemy. Defeat the enemy!"

"Come and get me, boys," I taunted, anxious to get started.

A collective bellow erupted from the group as they charged me. When the first few got close enough, I simply started flinging them into the air. There were muted sounds of bodies thwacking against the padded walls followed by surprised yelps. One after another I threw them, until all twenty had experienced the dubious joy of flight.

The men rolling around on the ground stared at me with disbelief. Guess they hadn't figured a five-eight chick with a medium build could toss them clear across the room.

"Cat," Dave called out. "Teach these slops what lesson number two is."

To demonstrate, I grabbed the nearest soldier and promptly broke his nose. It happened so fast he was bleeding before he even knew I'd moved.

"Lesson two is take every cheap shot."

Someone muttered, "Did you see that?" as if needing confirmation. Time for the third instruction.

"And lesson three is take every low blow."

A hard kick to the groin of one of the men caused him to bellow in agony. Sympathetic winces appeared on every male face. The one whose balls got blasted rolled on the ground, curled around his parts.

"But the most fun is lesson four. Always, always kick someone when they're down."

To punctuate the point, I drew back my foot and nailed the same poor recruit, feeling three of his ribs break with the contact.

"Let's get the bitch!" someone yelled.

If only I had a dime for every time I heard that.

The fighting began in earnest and lasted ten minutes. After all, cameras were rolling. I had been criticized before for being too quick and not leaving enough footage. My boss, Don Williams, always complained about something.

When it was over, all the potential recruits were either unconscious or flailing on the floor. My three captains—Tate,

Dave, Juan—and I picked through them to choose our new members.

"No, not that one. He wet himself. Thank God these mats are washable."

I nudged the next one in the face with my toe and got a bloodshot glare in return as the man slapped at my foot.

"That one," Juan nodded, pointing to the soldier at my feet.

A nod from me sent special personnel to retrieve him.

"What about him?" Dave inquired when we came to one who didn't even twitch. He'd been thrown through the air seven times before going night-night.

"Good pick," I said. "He just kept coming back." Another jerk of my head and he too was carted away.

"Fucking freak," a low voice hissed.

I walked toward its direction. The others hadn't heard him, but they followed me.

"You sure you want to be saying that?" I asked as I ground my heel into his bashed rib cage, forcing a wheeze of air from him. Brown eyes stared up with fury from a face that looked mulatto.

"Fuck you," the man spat.

I turned to Tate. "Oh, I like him," I said. "He'll do."

Tate chuckled his agreement and away Foul Mouth went, cursing me the entire time.

"Anyone else?" They looked around while I cracked my back to relieve a kink. "Right, then. Three. Well, that'll off-set the loss at least."

We hadn't had a banner month. One in our unit had died a gruesome death. Two more dropped out right after, unable to handle the horror of witnessing it.

"Hopefully they'll last," Dave added.

I shrugged. "We'll see. We play the hand we're dealt." Oh, if they only knew who had taught me most of the advice I now dispensed. "I'm off to the showers. Got blood in my hair."

The blood was only a few shades darker than my hair itself, which was a pure crimson red. Along with my pale skin and gray eyes, I looked exactly like my father, or so my mother had said. She hadn't meant it as a compliment.

Juan and Dave said good-bye, but Tate walked with me. He had a far-off smile on his face.

"What are you thinking about?"

"I was just remembering the day we met. Every time I see the recruit's faces when those doors open, it reminds me. When Don told me you were more than human, I didn't believe him. Not until you broke my arm and threatened to blow my brains out with my own gun."

A stab of grief went through me that I carefully concealed. I had vivid memories of that day as well, but not of him. No, not of him.

"If you reminisce further you'll recall that you were about to shoot me," I pointed out. "I was only defending myself. Now as for Don, well, okay. I broke his kneecaps out of spite."

"I can't believe it's been six years," Tate marveled. "Don thought you'd turn on us and I'd have to kill you inside six months."

"I'll bear that in mind when I buy his next Christmas present." My voice was dry but this wasn't news to me.

"Well, you have a while to hold that grudge. You'd be better off shafting him on his birthday in April."

We reached my locker room. Due to my gender, mine was separate. I was the only female in our unit. Don had once said he didn't want any internal "conflicts of interest," but I thought he was just being a sexist pig.

"If it makes you feel any better, I thought very little of you also when we first met. Who knew you'd be the one I counted on the most?"

Tate smiled. "Who knew you'd be the bravest, meanest bitch I'd ever served with? I'm glad you didn't shoot me. I would have missed out."

I smiled back. "I'm glad I didn't shoot you too, because I'd probably be dead if I had."

He laughed at that. "No, you wouldn't. I'm only good enough to take on the ones that are too easy for you. You do all the hard work."

I shook my head but didn't respond as I went inside. He didn't understand. If it weren't for him, Dave, and Juan, I would have given up years ago.

It wasn't easy being a genetic fluke. To all those who say there aren't things that go bump in the night, I say look closer. My mother didn't believe in vampires, either, until a blind date took a horrible, toothy turn. That vampire didn't just bite her, he also raped her, and then several months later there was me. To say I had a weird childhood was to put it mildly. I hadn't even known why I was different until I turned sixteen and my mother told me the real truth about my father. About the only thing I hadn't inherited from dead old dad were pointy teeth and the need for a liquid diet

Don found me at twenty-two when I got into a little trouble with the law. You know, the usual youthful stuff. Killed the governor of Ohio and several of his staff, but hey, they had it coming. After I was arrested, my funky pathology reports tattled on me for not being totally human. Don snapped me up to lead his branch of "Homeland Security" by giving me the quintessential offer I couldn't refuse. Or death threat, to be more accurate. I'd taken the job. What choice did I have?

CHAPTER ELEVEN
WHEN CAT MET BELINDA,
AKA SUNSHINE

Author's note: Some readers might remember that Belinda was one of the vampires Don had kept captive at the compound so that his scientists would have a steady supply of vampire blood in order to make Brams. Readers might also remember that Bones had a history with Belinda, and Cat was not happy when she found out about that. The scene where Cat first caught Belinda was in the original version of One Foot in the Grave, *but it ended up being cut because I thought readers would rather have Bones appear on the page sooner than see Cat on another hunt with her team. However, I loved Cat's interactions with Tate, Juan, Dave, and the rest of her team, so I'm glad that I saved this in a file instead of deleting it entirely.*

Don was in his office and I went directly there. He was my first stop every day. The routine was that I was briefed on any intelligence and then I shared it with my team leaders Tate, Dave and Juan.

Don glanced up from his computer when I walked in. "Cat. Good afternoon."

I looked at the clock. Yes, it was after twelve already.

"Don." Without invitation I sat down and stretched out my legs. He eyed me when I put my feet on the seat opposite me, but said nothing. We'd had the conversation about feet on the furniture many times before, and he'd finally given up.

"News arrived last night of some related deaths in Phoenix. Women with strange injuries to the throat, blood loss but no blood at the scene. Police think they were killed somewhere else and the bodies dumped. Needless to say, I disagree."

"Whatcha think? One or more vamps?" Blood loss only meant no ghouls or flesh eaters. They left very distinct corpses behind when they were too full to eat everything.

Don frowned. "More than one. The area is fairly narrow, but there are too many for just one vampire to be feeding. My guess is that you'll uncover a nest. Let's put it out of business."

I yawned and didn't cover my mouth. Sometimes I did things like that just to aggravate him. Like the feet. Even though I'd gotten over my resentment of him, a little devil in me enjoyed annoying him. Seeing his face darken made it all worthwhile.

"Am I keeping you awake, Cat?" There was a definite edge to his tone.

I blithely ignored the question. "Are the three recruits from yesterday patched up? Ready for more training today?"

That made Don lean forward with more enthusiasm. It was the one thing that would always put him in a good mood. "They were given the transfusions immediately after their removal from the Wreck Room." Ah, the cute nickname given to the place where the potentials first met me. Someone here had a sense of humor. "That last strain you brought in was of decent stock. With any luck, tonight you can procure more. We're running below the levels I'm comfortable with."

"Without me you wouldn't even know what levels you *were* comfortable with, Don." In that I'd proven my worth in gold. Before me, they never even knew that vampire blood healed.

Six years and a team of brilliant scientists later, they'd filtered through the components in undead blood and come up with ways to preserve it. Now the team and any wounded recruits were patched up in a day or so, courtesy of the vampires I brought back alive to be temporary donors. The tricky part was that only the younger ones were easy to damage sufficiently and transport without killing them. There was a drawback. The younger the vamp was, the weaker the power in their blood. The older they were, the more potent they got. Especially if they were a Master vampire. Those were extremely difficult to bring in alive. Hell, it was enough of a job to kill them. Don salivated at the thought of an old, strong vamp in his custody. He could concentrate the serum in the blood and stretch it ten times further.

"You've held up your end of our agreement admirably."

That caused me to look twice at him. It was the highest form of praise he'd ever bestowed on me.

"You feeling all right, Don? You're not drunk, are you?"

Another thin smile appeared on his face, which was lined with years.

"No, just remembering the day we brought you in. In my greatest imaginings I didn't think it would turn out this well."

I snorted rudely. "Yeah, Tate mentioned that yesterday. Nostalgia must be in the air around here. He said you were sure he'd have to shoot me within a year."

Don shrugged. We might have been discussing lunch. "I didn't trust you. You were filled with wild, unchecked power. I thought you'd try to run away on your first mission and warn the vampires about us. Tate knew what to do if that happened."

Now I pushed my feet off the chair and stood. This was too many trips down memory lane for me. "I keep my promises. If you didn't know that then, you should have realized it by now. I'm off to the exercise unit to meet up with the boys. Anything else I should know about tonight?"

"Only that you leave in five hours. With the time change there it will give us two extra hours to prepare. Oh, and one more thing. The person last seen alive with five of the victims was a woman. Looked very cozy with them too. You can review the rest of the data on the plane. Try to bring at least one in alive."

"Sir, yes, sir!" My hand rose in mocking salute and he glowered again.

Three dirty looks in thirty minutes. Maybe today would be a good day.

The exercise room was more than a gym. It was an extravaganza of an obstacle course, complete with ropes to swing from, falling debris, ground that shifted under your feet, and lots of room to run. Bones had trained me in a cave and in the woods. This was a more modern version, but the same principals held. Drive a recruit until they passed out, then wake them up and push them further. Boot camp was a pleasure cruise compared to this, or so I'd been told in profane and explicit language numerous times. When I stepped inside, I saw Tate and Juan berating an exhausted soldier from yesterday. Oh yes, the one with the potty mouth. Even though I was the length of a football field away and there was enormous noise from the activity, I heard each word clearly.

"You're not stopping, Cooper! Back at the ropes! If you think we're being rough on you, just wait until Cat comes over. She'll make you wish you had your bottle and your blankie."

Tate's voice sliced through the commotion and Cooper, obviously his name, panted hard.

"I don't believe this shit. I don't believe it. Yesterday twenty of my bones are broken, and today I'm running a fucking marathon. Vampires, who in the world would guess?"

"No one, pal, and that's the way it stays. You think you're shocked now? See how you feel when one of them comes for your throat. You'll be glad for your efforts here. They'll save your life later."

Tate spoke from experience. He'd been on at least a hundred missions with me and been comatose over a dozen times to show for it. He was one tough human. Without the recuperative benefits of the blood I harvested, he would have been dead years ago. At least some good had come out of my heartache.

"And they tell me that bitch is half one of them? How can you follow a fucking—"

The sentence abruptly ended with Juan's fist in his face. Cooper fell to his knees. Juan was a pretty mean cookie as well.

"No one talks about Cat that way in front of me." The Spanish accent seemed to emphasize the statement.

Cooper gaped at him. "Why? She's in charge, but you must have to watch your backs. One day she could snap."

Juan shook his head in wry amusement. "Yeah, we watch our backs if we're *conscious*. She's dragged my half-dead ass out of so many horror houses, I can't even count them all. When she goes back inside a place filled with vamps to haul your ignorant carcass out, you'll stop someone from insulting her too."

"That will never happen. No matter what you say, she's a freak."

"Hey, dumb fuck, she can hear you." Tate gestured in my direction and I waved.

"Bullshit. No one could hear us from that far in this racket," Cooper said with absolute conviction.

Boy, did he have a lot to learn.

Juan grinned at him. "Go on, whisper something to me, and when she walks up, she'll repeat it to you. She can hear you from a mile away. Hell, if you fart, she'll hear it before anyone smells it."

Oh, charming. Juan did have a way with words.

"Okay, I'll play." Cooper leaned in and whispered to Juan, who nodded and looked at me expectantly. They loved to show off my abilities.

I walked over to them, and Cooper looked at me in challenge.

"You aren't circumcised," I announced. Funny what people thought to say.

Tate and Juan laughed at the shocked expression on Cooper's face.

"No fucking way," Cooper breathed.

My brow arched at him. "Oh, *very* fucking way. Have respect for the freaks around you. The minute you don't, one will break you in pieces. Believe me, I've seen it." Hell, I'd done it, but that was more information than he needed just now.

"Tate, Juan, get Dave and meet me outside. We're on for tonight."

"Showtime," Tate murmured.

Juan groaned in mock disappointment. "I'll miss my show again!"

"DVR it like a normal person," I threw over my shoulder as I left.

When I was far enough away for even Tate to think I couldn't hear him, he addressed Cooper again. "One more thing. Critical safety advice. Whatever you do, *never* call her Kitten."

"Why not?" Cooper sounded intrigued.

"I'll take that one." Juan chimed in, with grimness under the humor in his tone. "Because if you do, when you wake up three days later… everything will *still* hurt."

Later, when I explained tonight's mission to them, Juan's face resembled a child's on Christmas morning when confronted with a pile of presents. "You're telling me we're going after a *lesbian* vampire? Cat, if you let me watch, she can suck all my blood as a diversion. I'd die a happy man."

"This is serious," I snapped. Juan and his perpetual hard-on. If he wasn't such a good fighter, I'd have killed him myself by now. "Over a dozen women are dead, remember?"

"Are you the bait or the hook tonight, Cat?" Dave asked.

What a relief to change the subject from Juan's fantasies.

"Hopefully both. If she's already picked out her treat for the evening, I'll see if I can tag along. If not, we follow her. We need to find the nest. There's probably a few vampires, judging from the body count."

"A threesome." Juan sighed in rapture.

"Juan, I swear. If you screw this up tonight, I will shove your gun up your ass and fire. You got me?"

"Loud and clear, *querida*." He grinned, unrepentant as usual. I pitied the poor fool who ever married him.

"Okay then. Tate, pick ten more men; we'll need a solid crew. Don wants another refill on his vampire blood supply."

"I hate bagging and tagging them," Dave muttered.

I did too. That's how we lost the last member of our team. One of them was careless for an instant. Before anything could be done, his throat was missing. Even I couldn't fix that.

"We have the new capsule, Dave," I reminded him, proud of my contribution to its invention. "That mistake won't happen again."

"Let's hope not," Tate muttered.

Just before I left to board the plane, I stopped by Don's office. He looked startled to see me. Usually one visit a day was enough for both of us unless something major happened.

"Don, I need you to do me a favor."

His forehead wrinkled. Those were words he never heard from me. "What is it?"

"Um, if I don't make it back tonight, I adopted a kitty. Would you make sure it goes to a good home?" I hated to sound so pathetic, but my mother hated cats and Denise was allergic.

His expression eased into a smile. Clearly he'd expected something far more involved. "Of course. But I won't need to. You'll be magnificent, as always."

"Yeah, well, the day will come eventually when I'm up against someone more magnificent."

"Not you," he said confidently. "You're unique. I knew it from the moment I saw you."

And took me away from Bones. Deep in my heart, I would never forgive him for that. Yet I'd made a bargain and I would hold to it.

"See you later, Don, if my ass still points to the ground."

"Beg your pardon?"

I smiled. "Australian expression. Means if I'm still standing. Really, brush up on your lingo."

Our team traveled in two planes. They never had my three leaders and me on the same flight, out of paranoia if the plane went down. Someone would still have to head the units and train replacements. At my request, Juan was with the other backup men on the second plane. He was still far too happy about tonight for my patience. At least he could be counted on to rally the men. Juan was an excellent leader.

"Cat, how about on Monday we grab some chow and play cards?" Dave suggested. "I still have to win back that fifty you stole from me last week."

I turned around to smile at Dave. My house was a favorite hangout place after work. Like me, everyone on our team was sworn to secrecy about our work. Not being able to relax around normal people because of your occupation made things very lonely. Hence, poker was a favorite pastime at my place, though why the guys kept coming back for more was beyond me. I beat them ninety percent of the time. They all loved the stocked minibar in the family room though. Amazing what an endless supply of liquor could accomplish.

"Can't Monday. I have… Er, I can't."

I tripped over my reply, almost admitting I had a date. The fact that I never dated didn't escape anyone's notice. Juan called me a spinster. Dave might not be gifted with my extra perception powers, but when I looked away in embarrassment, he pounced.

"You go, Cat!"

"Huh?" Tate was slower on the draw.

"Cat has a date."

Tate looked stunned. "No way. You're going out with someone? Really?"

"Oh, stop. It's not like that. He's a vet, new in town, and he helped me out last night with this cat I accidentally hit. So as a favor I'm going to... I don't know, have dinner. See a movie."

"Folks round here call that a date, missy," Dave drawled in a fake Southern accent.

Tate still looked shell-shocked. "Has Don run a check on this guy? It could be a trap."

That raised my hackles. No way was I going to ask permission to go on a simple date like I was fourteen. By God, now I'd go on two just out of spite.

"Tate, do you check with Don each time before you get laid? Does Dave? Does *Juan?* Of course not, or Don would have to hire a separate staff just to handle Juan's love life. I think I'm old enough to handle this on my own, so rack off!"

Occasionally Bones's expressions would leak out in my speech. He'd been English by birth and Australian by vampiric rebirth after he was one of the unfortunate prisoners sent to the New South Wales penal colony. Of course, that was back in 1789. Okay, so he'd been a little older than me.

"Now you're going to have sex with the guy? I thought you said it was just a date!"

"Easy, man," Dave warned Tate, seeing my features darken. "This guy could pick his nose at dinner and then leave her with the check. Don't load the shotgun yet."

This visual seemed to calm Tate, because he shut up and turned his attention to the paperwork in front of him. There were photos of the crime scenes, autopsy reports, and eyewitness statements. You know, the usual light reading material. Most of the victims were either lesbian or bisexual and were last seen leaving with an Asian woman with long black hair. Three of the victims had left from the same bar, Ophelia's, so that's where we were headed.

"What do you think?" Tate finally asked after mulling over the reports for half an hour.

I tapped a finger at one of the photos. "Two men inside, posing as a couple. Two around the back as lookouts. The other six split in two groups with separate vehicles. No wires inside, only in the van. If I leave with the target, switch out the tail so she doesn't get suspicious. Once at her home base, wait for my signal, then come in blazing. Have someone waiting at the van to pull up the capsule immediately for transport. Should be quick and clean."

"Oh, it might be quick, but it's never clean," Dave commented.

I shrugged. It was true that we usually looked like something out of the horror movie *Carrie* after one of our missions. This was not a job for the squeamish.

"Tate, you can pick the pair for inside. But absolutely not Juan. He'd be too busy beating his meat to be any good as backup."

Dave laughed, easing some of the tension that still lingered from earlier. "Cat, are you sure you were never in the Navy? You have the dirtiest mouth of any chick I've ever met. Who taught you to speak that way?"

A twinge shot through me, and I shoved it back down with all the other memories of Bones that I couldn't bear to dwell on. "It just comes naturally, I guess."

Ophelia's was pretty upscale. Velvet couches, high-end tables, and excellent drinks. They boasted a smaller dance floor that was mostly packed with couples of the same sex. I wore a tight, strapless crimson dress that hugged my breasts in order to stay upright. I carried a small purse that held only my fake ID and cosmetics because all my weapons were tucked away in my specially made knee-high leather boots.

As soon as Juan saw me in my low-cut, tight dress, he began to protest his assignment outside the club. "Cat, you never let me have any fun. I'll tongue-kiss whoever you set me up with if you let me inside. *Madre de Dios*, you look like strawberries and cream, my favorite—"

I slapped him. He rocked back on his heels, but the grin never left his face. Maybe why I tolerated him, aside from his effectiveness as a fighter, was because he reminded me of another pervert. Change the Spanish accent to an English one, and it would be like listening to Bones.

"That's exactly why you're not coming inside, so shut up and get serious."

We left Juan to sulk in the van while I went inside, hoping to get lucky with a murderous female vampire who might or might not show. If she didn't come around tonight, there was always tomorrow. If at first you don't succeed and all that.

Tate and Peter followed me inside, pretending to be a loving couple. Once in the club, we didn't make contact with each other. We didn't have to. Every so often, one of them would whisper, "All clear," and I heard them. Wires weren't necessary when I could detect their slightest breath. Being half-monster did have its advantages.

A few times different women asked me to dance. I accepted, wanting to blend in. My current partner looked to be in her early thirties with curly brown hair and big brown eyes. Bones had taught me how to dance, one of the countless things he'd shown me, so there was nothing chaste about the way I moved. My partners seemed to like it. When this one tried to kiss me, however, I pulled back. No point in her getting possessive if the vampire showed up.

"Not so fast, honey," I said. "I'm keeping my options open tonight."

"Your loss," she replied, walking away.

I stifled a snort. Had to love a girl with confidence.

"You've never looked better," I heard Tate say to Peter, and I went on alert. That was the signal that they'd spotted someone who might be our target.

"Let's dance," I announced to the girl on my left, who'd been eyeing me for the past half hour. She accepted with alacrity and I turned things up a notch, gyrating aggressively against her. Then I grasped her hips and turned her around, nibbling on the back of her neck. She gasped and arched against me, molding her rear to my crotch.

"Juan would be spewing in his pants by now," I heard Peter say.

Tate kept his talk to business. "Target approaching your left."

Out of the corner of my eye, I saw a swish of waist-length black hair, poker straight and thick. Then almond-colored eyes met mine for an instant before I looked away.

That must have been enough for her because I felt her as she approached. Judging from the vibe she gave off, she had been undead for probably around fifty or sixty years. Older vampires gave off a stronger current, like supercharged static electricity. Master vampires were even rarer. They positively vibrated the air around them. Bones had been one of those. He'd crackled with energy like a walking lightning bolt. No wonder he was the person vampires called when they wanted to kill one of their own. Bones had been a bounty hunter, to put it nicely. Hit man would be a more appropriate term since most of the creatures he delivered were missing their bodies from the neck down. I should know; for a time, I'd been his assistant.

Almond Eyes was still watching me, I could feel it. For effect, I raised my arms and let my head fall back as though absorbed in the rhythm of the music, displaying my neck to maximum advantage. My crimson dress would be a startling contrast against my pale skin, which had a faint, almost imperceptible incandescence. My skin had garnered me the highest praise from my former victims. Bones had once likened it to a homing beacon for vampires.

Apparently it still worked, because she headed right for me, and her aura parted the air before her. When a cool hand touched my shoulder, I glanced up as if in surprise.

"I like you," she purred in smooth, unaccented tones.

My dancing partner glowered at her. "Hey, wait just a minute."

The vampire pushed her aside as casually as if she were swatting back like a pesky fly. Vampires were as tactful as rampaging bulls when it came to something they wanted.

"Sorry, sweetie," I said to the sputtering girl and then put my arms around the vampire. She was my height and our faces were level as we began to dance. She pulled my hips firmly against hers and then twisted them for maximum friction.

"What's your name, lovely?" she murmured, licking red lips.

I smiled back and licked mine too, but more leisurely. "Cat."

"Ahhh…" She drew the sound out as the music continued to another song. "Curiosity killed the cat, or so they say."

A dark sense of humor. My favorite. "And satisfaction brought it back," I replied at once.

She gave a throaty laugh. "I haven't heard that before. Do you believe it?"

"Oh, yes," I said and kissed her.

It was the first time I'd ever kissed a woman. When comparing apples to oranges, it wasn't any different. Lips, tongue, mouths, all the same. Granted, I wasn't used to tasting lipstick, but then what can you expect? None of the men I'd kissed had ever worn any.

She reached down and squeezed my ass. Getting pawed was an unfortunate necessity when playing the part of bait, but I only let this sort of activity go so far. If it went beyond my tolerance, I simply pulled out the silver. The sight of a long, lethal blade was enough to douse any vampire's lust, particularly when that blade soon skewered them in the heart.

Then someone roughly pulled us apart. I looked up to see a man, roughly forty, with a medium build and wearing a poorly fitting jacket.

"Excuse me, miss," he said to the vampire. "I'm Detective Avery, and I'd like to ask you a few questions."

So my people weren't the only ones staking out Ophelia's looking for an Asian murder suspect. Kudos to the local law enforcement for doing their homework and taking the initiative. Not that it would do them any good. You couldn't exactly read a vampire their rights.

"Detective?" Her voice was all innocence. "Of course. One moment." Then she turned back to me and her sultry expression returned. "Go get a drink, lovely. I'll be right back."

Shit. I hoped she didn't take him outside and break him in half. Walter was out there, but if he intervened, that would give us away. Fortunately, she looked like she had decided that discretion was the better part of valor. She led the detective to a corner in the bar, facing him so that her back was to the majority of the people.

With my enhanced vision, I saw a flash of green and heard her speak with inhuman resonation, telling him he'd seen nothing and to go home. Nosferatu mind tricks. They worked on humans like a charm. The detective headed for the door without a backward glance.

She took her place next to me moments later.

"What was that about?" I asked, just like a normal person would.

She trailed her hand across my bare shoulders. "Rash of car thefts. He wanted to know if I'd seen anything suspicious." The lie slipped from her lips without pause. "You have the most beautiful gray eyes I've ever seen, Cat. Like darkened silver, and your skin... You are stunning. I want to be alone with you."

My, but she was quick. We hadn't even shared a drink yet. "You haven't told me your name," I pointed out, as if piqued.

She kept touching me as she answered. "Jade."

"Jade." I covered her hand with mine. "I would love to be alone with you."

The valet went to get her car. Jade made good use of the time by kissing me deeply. From a block away, I could hear Juan moan. This was his dream come true. Thankfully, she paid the noise no heed, and the valet didn't take long to bring her shiny silver Corvette around.

"I hope you live close by," I said when I climbed into the passenger seat.

She smirked at me. "Not far, lovely."

After about ten minutes, Jade pulled up to a three-story house in an upscale neighborhood. Her house was surrounded by a high iron fence that opened electronically with a clicker in her car. It was well past midnight, but there were lights on inside her home.

"Your house is so large," I commented as I counted the number of heartbeats I heard coming from the structure. Three humans at least, and they could be prey... or pets. Over the years, I'd come to realize what Bones had repeatedly tried to tell me. Having a pulse didn't make someone automatically better; it only made them automatically warmer. I'd witnessed firsthand how cruel humans could be, and they matched the undead any day in viciousness.

"A few friends of mine stay with me," Jade replied as we entered the front door.

"I can't wait to meet them," I said, which was the absolute truth.

We walked through a lovely foyer and entered a large living room. I counted seven more vampires, four female and three males. A human woman sat on the lap of one of the males, and aside from the dazzling amount of jewelry she wore, she had nothing else on. I measured the otherworldly energy in the air and did a quick estimation that none of the vamps were over a hundred years old. Maybe I wouldn't need the team as backup after all.

"What do you think you're smiling at?" a pretty, petite blond vampire demanded as she rose from her chair.

Then Jade grabbed me from behind. I made no effort to struggle. Instead, I let out a laugh.

"What's so funny, lovely?" Jade murmured as her lips grazed my ear.

"You are," I retorted. "Thought you were bringing home takeout, didn't you?"

"What?" In her arrogance, she let me go and faced me. She'd shed her human disguise, and her eyes glowed with pure emerald light while her fangs extended like daggers.

"You have entered the realm of death," Jade declared. "Now look into my eyes."

That made me laugh harder. She was downright cliché. "No, but how about you look into mine?" And I unleashed the emerald light in my own gaze. She gasped in disbelief.

"*You!*"

Oh, so she'd heard about me. It was nice to have fans.

In the split second that she froze with shock, I pounced, twisting her head off before she could flinch. Then I torpedoed it at first vampire who lunged at me. That bought me another second, and I yanked my knives from my boots. Several blades sank home, and two more vamps went down for good. Another one leapt at me, and instead of moving out the way, I caught her. She was unprepared for my strength, and with a brutal snap, I broke her back over my knee. Her spine shattered and she collapsed. Before she had time to heal, I drove a blade into her heart and twisted. She began to shrivel at once.

Instead of attacking, the other four tried to run. This is where my team would come in handy. I gave chase, grabbing the nearest vamp and plugging his heart with a silver knife before flinging him out the window.

That was the signal they'd been waiting for. Moments later, the van crashed through the metal gates, and I heard the guys yelling as they approached the house.

"Get the human!" I barked to whoever was close enough to hear me as I spied the naked girl trying to escape out the side door. To ensure that she didn't get far, I flung one of my knives and skewered her in the hamstring. She went down with a scream, but she was lucky that she hadn't been trying to go for a gun or I would have aimed to kill. My human body count had gone up along with my vampire one.

The remaining three vampires raced up the stairs. I followed in hot pursuit, my adrenaline flowing. It was a sad reality that the only time I felt truly alive was when I was in a fight to the death.

Noise behind the door to my right made me drop low and kick it open. I rolled through the entrance, avoiding the arms that struck empty air instead of me since I was near the ground. Then I buried my dagger into the nearest body part, which turned out to be my attacker's groin. Hair-raising shrieks filled the room, and I yanked the knife out and thrust it through the vampire's heart next, jerking it brutally.

Two more to go.

On the third floor, I heard sobbing and movement. I ascended the stairs as quickly as I could and kicked through the only door at the top of the landing. One look revealed that it was a prison. My two vampires were in there, but so were two naked, weeping girls, and the vampires had them by the throats. Bite marks and bruises covered the humans' bodies, confirming that they'd been the vampires' version of an in-house snack. Even though I'd seen this sort of thing before, it still filled me with a blistering rage.

"You want to see them die?" the pretty blond-haired vampire hissed at me. She didn't look afraid, but the other vampire, a brown-haired man, stared at me with frightened fascination. "Come closer, and they will," she went on. "Leave, and they'll live."

"I have another proposition." As I spoke, I could hear one of my guys come up the stairs, so I kept talking to mask the sound of his footsteps. "The first one of you that lets a human go lives. The one that doesn't dies. Well? Who feels like living to bite another day?"

"I've heard of you," the male vampire said with a moan. "You're the Red Reaper. We told Jade not to bring home any redheads, but she thought you were a myth."

"Shut up, Taylor!" the blonde snarled.

"I'm not a myth, Taylor," I said. More footsteps started on the staircase. I talked louder, faster. "You know how many of your kind I've killed? *Hundreds.*" Now that was a gross exaggeration, but it had the desired effect. Taylor visibly quailed.

The blonde turned to him in fury, and I took advantage. Three of my blades shot across the room and pinned her hand to the wall, away from the helpless girl's neck. Tate burst into the room at the same time and fired, striking Taylor several times. Tate was a crack shot and his gun was filled with silver bullets, so Taylor slumped to the floor. By the time the blonde yanked her hand free, I already had her gripped in my arms, and my final knife was in her chest.

"Don't even think of moving, Sunshine, or this silver will shred your heart," I warned.

Cornflower-blue eyes glared into mine. "What *are* you?"

"Homeland Security," I replied and left it at that.

Juan and Peter entered the room while sirens started to wail in the distance. The gunshots had no doubt disturbed the peace of this opulent neighborhood, not that I was worried. The other members of the team would hold the regular police at bay until the scene was contained.

"We've got a chopper coming to take these girls to a hospital," Peter informed me as he broke the chains around their wrists. Not surprisingly, both women were hysterical. He looked around the room for something to cover them with, but there was nothing.

"Bedsheets, lower floor," I said.

Juan went to fetch them. Then Arnold and John popped into the room. "Capsule's ready."

"Okay, Tate, cover me. I'll bring her downstairs, and you shoot if she even *looks* like she's thinking of making a break for it."

The blond vampire continued to glare her hatred at me, but she didn't try anything as we slowly made our way down the stairs and then out the front door. A tractor-trailer had been backed up as close as it could get to the house, and when my men saw me, they slid up the door.

The capsule was open, and the interior resembled an escape pod from hell. Four long, strategically placed silver pikes protruded from the capsule door, facing inward. Five sets of reinforced titanium clamps were awaiting the vampire's waist, wrists, legs, ankles, and neck. The capsule was soundproof, airtight, and blastproof, so once she was inside, she'd be truly helpless. She must have realized that because when she got a good look at it, the vampire began to scream.

Then she tried mind control, which didn't work on me, and my men had been trained never to look a vampire in the eye. Still, as a precaution, they snapped the opaque visors down from their helmets so their eyes were covered. Now they couldn't see, but we had run through this drill so many times they didn't need to. They knew this part by heart.

I shoved the blond vampire inside the capsule and began fastening the clamps. In less than a minute, I slammed the door shut, cutting off her wail when the silver spikes thrust into her torso. Too much struggling on her part, and they'd rip through her heart. That's how we made sure the vampire we brought back didn't wreck our transport on our way to the compound.

Once the capsule was safely loaded into the tractor trailer, Tate took off his helmet. "Don will be doing cartwheels about having a female vampire. We've only brought home males before."

"I don't think there'll be any difference in her blood," I muttered.

Juan gave me a wicked grin as he pulled his gloves off and flexed his fingers. "Cat, tonight was the best job we've ever pulled. Seeing you play tonsil-hockey with that gorgeous bloodsucker made my year. I'm going to burn new calluses into my hand just remembering it. Hey, do you think you could loan me that dress—?"

A punch to the jaw stopped him from saying anything else, and he rubbed his face. Dave coughed to cover his laughter, but I heard it anyway. Even Tate, usually more circumspect, had a curl to his lips, but then he sobered.

"That vamp said they weren't supposed to take home any redheads because of your reputation. Do you think it's going to become a problem?"

My forehead wrinkled for a moment, then I shrugged. "I think it means I'm going to the salon."

Chapter Twelve
Cat and Noah:
Her Greatest Mistake?

Author's Note: *When combined with grief from the loss of a friend and the additional years apart from Bones, Cat's inherent reckless-ness caused her to make a colossal mistake. This never made it into* One Foot in the Grave *because my editor flatly told me that I could not write such a plotline into a romance novel. At the time, I didn't understand why. I had been a long-time reader of romance, but I didn't realize the genre had certain rules. After my first book came out, it didn't take me long to learn those rules, and in hind-sight, I am endlessly glad that I edited out Cat's "greatest mistake." You'll get to see a watered-down version of it in these deleted scenes, however, and I am bracing for the hate mail.*

This alternate version also contains a small chunk of what did make it into One Foot in the Grave *because the context is essen-tial for understanding Cat's mindset at the time.*

My mother sat at the table, and she vibrated with excite-ment. I was less enthused. Noah and I had been dat-ing for two months now, and the poor schmuck said he wanted to meet her. She'd been over the moon to find out I had a boyfriend who was both alive and not in the military. Her brown hair was swept up and she even wore an outfit that wasn't dowdy. For her to take care with her appearance spoke volumes to me. Though she was only forty-four, she often dressed like she was eighty-four. It was a waste because she was an attractive woman. To my knowledge, she had never been on a date since the night she was raped. Too bad she had as tough of a time letting go of the past as I did.

"Catherine, I'm so happy for you!" she said for the fifth time.

"Cristine," I corrected her. She was forever reverting back to my original name, probably because she gave it to me.

She waved a hand in apology. "Oh, right. Gosh, I hope I don't slip in front of Noah. He might think something strange was going on."

That made my lip curl. No, mustn't let Noah be confused by the fact that there were *always* strange things going on.

He'd made it amazingly difficult for me to come up with an excuse to stop seeing him in the past couple of months. Whenever my pager went off and I had to rush out in the middle of dinner, he would simply have the waiter bag my food to go and tell me not to forget to eat. If I had to cancel at the last minute, he didn't complain about being stood up. When Tate and the guys waited at my house one night after my cell died and a vampire was spotted three counties away, Noah shook their hands and told them how glad he was to meet my coworkers. The fact that I'd climbed into a van filled with five athletic, muscular men didn't seem to faze him. If the shoe were on the other foot, I'd have demanded to see their identification.

No, Noah was the perfect gentleman. Even Don, who ran a full background check on him without my knowledge, was happy with him. To give him credit, Noah did take the edge off my loneliness. He was a great guy and I liked him tremendously.

But... I still cried at night when I thought of Bones. All the warm, friendly feelings in the world couldn't hold a candle to fact that my heart still belonged only to him. Perhaps I would continue feeling like I'd had a hole blown through the center of me for the rest of my life. At least I could say I tried.

A car pulled up in the drive and my mother shot out of her chair. "He's here!"

"Calm down. Here, check the roast. I'll get the door." I wiped my hands on a towel and opened the door to let Noah in.

He gave me a quick kiss before extending his hand to my mother. "Mrs. Russell, what a pleasure to meet you. Cristine has told me so much about you, I feel as if I already know you."

I'd told him lies, of course. There wasn't a shred of truth I could share with Noah. He thought my father had died when I was a baby and that my parents' marriage hadn't been a happy one. In my pretend life, I wasn't illegitimate. Then again, I wasn't half-vampire, either. He also thought that I was Irish. Hell, for all I knew, I could be. With all the resources of the United States government at my disposal, I still hadn't been able to find out my real father's identity.

"Call me Jussie," my mother said.

She'd taken less liberty with her name than I had and simply abbreviated it. She also had no idea that Russell was Bones's surname. If she had, my mother would have flatly refused to use it for her alias.

"Jussie, then. Can I help you with anything?"

"Not at all, Noah," she assured him. "Ca— Er, Cristine and I have it under control. Have a seat and tell me about yourself."

My cat picked that moment to jump onto the counter and leisurely eye the mashed potatoes. I handed Noah and my mother a drink while I swatted him away. He sat on the floor, watching everything with bright green eyes that were almost identical to my own when my other nature flared. My mother frowned at the kitty. She rarely visited me at home anymore because of him, which could be why I'd grown to love the cat so much.

"Cristine, can't you lock that... critter in your room?" she said with a sniff in my cat's direction. "It's unseemly."

I gave a short laugh. "Mom, Noah's a vet, so the only person my cat is offending is you. Get over it. He stays."

She huffed at that but gave up. She must still be trying to make a good impression on Noah, or she would have fought me for at least another few minutes.

"Why haven't you put his collar on him, Cristine?" Noah asked me, petting my cat. He purred before leaving with a flick of the tail. The feline was fickle in his affections.

"I keep forgetting," I lied. "He never goes outside, so it's not like he'll get lost."

In truth, I couldn't because Noah still thought that my cat's name was Bones. I didn't have the heart to tell him that he'd totally misunderstood why he'd overheard me saying that name to myself, and I hadn't come up with a different name for the kitty yet.

"What collar?" my mother asked.

I flashed her a look that said to drop it. She ignored me, as usual.

"I gave Cristine a collar for her cat on our first date, but she never remembers to put it on," Noah said with a forgiving smile at me. He was impossible to piss off.

My mother wasn't. "Cristine, that is so rude! When someone gives you a gift, you don't let it languish. What a thoughtful gesture, Noah. Where is the collar? I'll put it on the mangy feline myself."

Oh, *now* she was going to get it. "Right-hand drawer, next to the oven."

I watched with dark satisfaction as she fetched the collar and approached my cat. He watched her balefully, his tail swishing back and forth.

"Let's see now," she mused to herself. "Here is the buckle and here is the strap. Oh look, it's got his name on it. Cristine, I didn't know you named him. What—?"

The name finally registered, and my mother pitched forward in mid-crouch. My cat scored her hand with his claws before leaping away with a hiss. Noah blinked at the foul word she shouted as she sprawled on the floor. I shook my head without sympathy. She'd asked for it.

"Let me help you up, Jussie!" Noah said, recovering from his surprise. "Are you all right?"

My mother let him help her to her feet and then gave me a withering look. "What a perfect name for that *animal*, Cristine. It fits the horrid beast."

"Huh?" Noah didn't get it.

I did, and steam nearly poured from my ears. "See, something bad always happens when you mess with Bones. Did that scratch hurt? I hope it doesn't leave a mark like the one I got the last time I petted Bones. He practically kept me up all that night licking it."

Noah glanced back and forth between us, feeling the tension but not knowing the reason. My mother's face flamed in furious embarrassment, but I didn't care. One low remark deserved another.

Noah coughed, trying to defuse the situation. "Let me check on the oven. Something sure smells good in there."

The rest of the dinner passed without further incident. Occasionally I would look up and see my mother give me a scathing glance, but she dropped the entire matter of the cat's namesake. Noah was charming, as usual. You were just weird if you didn't like him. Soon he had her warmed up to where she was laughing again. By dessert, she quit with the underhanded dirty looks and instead was obviously pleased with my choice of a boyfriend. So pleased, in fact, that she faked several yawns even though it was only eight o'clock and was out the door in record time. I usually had to force her to leave when she visited.

"I don't know why you hesitated about having me meet her, Cristine," he remarked. "Your mom is terrific. She really doesn't like the cat, but then no one is perfect."

I gave him a level look. "She was behaving, Noah. Believe me, she can be a real bitch, but she loved you. I'm shocked she didn't grab your ass on the way out."

He laughed. "That would've been different, but then things are always unpredictable around you. It's what I like most."

He put his arms around me and kissed me. I responded, but it was surface level only. We hadn't slept together, but it was definitely to the stage where it was inevitable unless I broke it off. Kissing Noah was enjoyable, but it hardly inflamed me with passion.

He was worked up about it, judging from his accelerated breathing and the hardening of his body. I continued to kiss him while a cold list of pros and cons ran through my mind. I liked Noah, but I wasn't turned on by him. The truth was, I hadn't been turned on by any man in over six years. Finally, my choice boiled down to a single question: did I want to go to bed tonight with my loneliness or with Noah? He wasn't the man I loved. Not even close, but there was someone pressed against me instead of no one, and at the moment, it was better than being alone.

I pulled back to whisper against his lips, "You don't have to go home tonight, Noah."

He stared down at me while his hands tightened on my back. "You're sure?"

I kissed him and reached down, pulling his shirt out of his pants. He gasped when my palms traced his bare stomach and then moved lower.

"I'm sure."

The next morning, I woke up to hear him whistling as he clanged around making breakfast. He would make someone a wonderful spouse one day with how domestic he was. For a few minutes, I stayed in bed and wrestled with the unavoidable comparisons.

In the plus column, he was miles better than Danny had been, that worthless jerk. On the other hand, I had gained about as much satisfaction out of the two times last night as I did from a good gin and tonic. Still, I'd woken up in the middle of the night with a warm form next to me that wasn't just the cat. Orgasms weren't everything. After all, I could have those alone.

"Breakfast is ready, Cristine," he called out. "Come down before it gets cold."

The clock showed nine a.m. I never woke up this early if I could help it. What a closet sadist he must be. I headed straight to the bathroom and was occupied when the phone rang. No one called me at this hour unless there was trouble. What now?

"Noah, get that for me!" I yelled.

He answered and I heard him tell the caller to wait. Once I left the bathroom, I grabbed the phone next to the bed. "Noah, hang up. I've got it."

My tone was brisk and he complied without comment. There was a second of silence on the other line, then Tate's voice. "Is he off?"

"Yes. What's wrong?"

"What's he doing there this early, Cat?" An edge was in his words.

"Did you call me for a reason? Or did my mother resign and you took over?" Tate was the only person who didn't seem happy with Noah, even though he'd only met him twice.

"Yes, I called for a reason. You need to come in right now. Don's calling in Juan and Dave as well. I'm already on my way to your house; I'll be there in five minutes."

Tate lived close by, and my house was on his way to the compound, but still it annoyed me. Noah lingered in the doorway and his face fell when he saw my expression. It was one he recognized well by now, the one that said I was leaving.

"Right." I hung up without saying good-bye and started to pull on some clothes.

"You're going." It was a statement, and I shot him a look.

"Noah, this is the part where I remind you I don't live a regular life. If you can't handle that, let me again tell you that you should reconsider dating me. Trust me, I'd understand."

He came forward as I dropped to the floor to put on my boots. "How can you think I would just walk out on you after last night? I don't want to pressure you or move too fast, but I think I'm in love with you."

Oh no, no, no. "Noah, please... I told you I don't do normal." My boots were on and so were my clothes. I splashed water on my face and began to brush my teeth.

"I know what you told me. Yes, I am reminded of that whenever I'm with you. But I don't care. Cristine, what do you feel for me? Is this just... casual to you?"

He looked so vulnerable with his black hair tousled and gray-blue eyes pleading. I felt like a heel for using him to relieve my forlorn existence. An abrupt knock at the door saved me from replying. I brushed past Noah, running down the stairs to answer it.

"We'll talk later," I threw over my shoulder. "You can stay here as long as you want. Just lock the bottom knob when you leave and set the alarm. I have to go."

Tate positively glowered at me when I opened the door. His indigo gaze took in Noah's shirt lying on the carpet, his pants resting on the banister, and finally Noah himself, clad in only his boxer shorts.

"Sorry to interrupt," he said sarcastically.

I gave him a dangerous peep of emerald light in my eyes as a warning. "I'll call you later, Noah," I said, and left without looking back.

Tate started in on me as soon as the car door shut. "I thought you said you weren't serious about him?"

"Drop it, Tate. Do you know what's going on? Why didn't Don call me first?" That miffed me, because I was the leader of this band of freak fighters, and I'd earned my place in the pecking order.

He snorted. "He wanted to ask my opinion of what the situation was before speaking to you. There were some murders last night in Ohio. Pretty graphic ones, no attempt made to hide the bodies. In fact, you might say that they were displayed."

"What's so unusual about that?" We didn't jet around to every nasty crime scene in the nation or we would never be able to cover them all.

"I'll let Don fill you in on the rest. My job was to pick you up. Guess I'm glad I called first. If I would've just used my key, I might have walked in on you two."

He only had a key in case of my untimely death, but still. "Since when would you have barged in without knocking? God, Tate, if I didn't know better, I'd say you sounded jealous."

The guards waved us through the gates at the compound. Tate and I were such a common sight we didn't even have to show identification anymore. We both knew practically all the guards by name, rank and serial numbers.

"Maybe you don't know as much as you think," he responded.

[Author's additional note: To save you from reading a big chunk of the published version, I cut out the chapters where Cat and her team find out that it isn't Bones who's lured her back to Ohio but a vampire hit man named Lazarus. During a fight, Lazarus murders Dave, and Cat blames herself for not killing Lazarus when she had the chance. She returns from the trip grief-stricken and guilt-ridden, and Don forces her to take time off to recuperate. This is where the next deleted scene starts.]

Noah called me every day. I didn't call him back. The only two people I spoke to outside of work were Denise and my mother. Denise had met Dave on a few occasions, and I had once even entertained the notion of setting them up. She declined, stating she couldn't handle the stress of being with someone who risked his life every time he went to work. Since he was dead now, I was glad they hadn't been involved. At least I hadn't contributed to her misery as well. When I told her he died, sparing any other details, she hung up the phone and drove straight over. She brought a bottle of top-shelf gin and held my hand while I finished it. Denise was a true friend who didn't need to press for more than what I was willing to tell her. In the end I hadn't divulged anything more than his death. Better for her not to know particulars. Particulars could only endanger her, and she knew too much already.

The fourth night after Dave's death, there was a knock at the door. It was after ten p.m., and my only company was the cat and a pint of Häagen-Dazs. Denise was out on a date and my mother was more harm than help. She never wanted to hear about the rigors of my job, content to know I came back alive and the vampires didn't. In that regard she was easy to please.

There were only three people who would come by without calling: Tate, Juan, or Noah. Noah was my unplanned visitor and stood outside on the front porch under the light at the doorway. I hadn't seen him in nearly a week and hadn't missed him. In fact, I'd barely spared him a thought. Depression turned me into a selfish monster. I would have sold my soul for one night of mindless bliss inside the pale, chiseled arms that had been my only source of comfort.

The condemnation I felt over Dave's death ran even with the staggering knowledge that Bones was truly lost to me. Somehow I'd pictured him still in that cave, waiting there should I ever decide to return. Illogical, irrational, and incorrect, as it turned out. He was long gone. The scent of him to my improved nose was so faint as to be almost nonexistent. Bones hadn't been there for years. Yet the tiny whiff that lingered in the bedroom with the decimated mattress had been enough to level me emotionally. Maybe I could have run fast enough to save Dave from Lazarus had I concentrated more. Either way, it was my fault. No matter what Don said.

"Can I come in?" He shifted on his feet and looked searchingly at me.

There was no reason why I shouldn't want him to. He was kind, gentle, sincere, considerate, and handsome. That meant, of course, that I felt nothing for him beyond the benign affection I gave Tate and Juan. Less than that, actually. With them there was the deeper bond of facing death together regularly and the accompanying sense of responsibility. Noah had none of those ties with me. At the moment, however, he offered me one thing they couldn't.

Escape. There was no reality with him. No death, no vampires, no ghouls, no buried bodies of close friends who had trusted me to protect them. I could be Cristine, the research and field analyst who was utterly human and just worked odd hours.

"Come in."

Drowning hands grasp at anything, and Noah was my final gasp of oxygen before taking that lethal plunge. I shut the door behind him and didn't object when he folded me in his arms.

"I've reconsidered what I told you before, Cristine. I don't think I love you. I *know* I do. I don't care if this is moving too fast, I've been crazy all week without you. You can throw me out afterward if you want, but I'm going to say this anyway. I want to spend the rest of my life with you, no matter how many times your job interrupts us. Marry me, Cristine. You don't have to say anything now, but give me a chance to prove that I can make you happy."

My head whirled with thoughts too fleeting to cling to. Above them all was a warning: Don't do it. *Dave's blood splashing my hands as I tried to stem the flow...* Don't do it. ... *Bones's last words to me. "Don't fret, luv, I'll be back before you know it."* ... Don't do it. ... *My old house littered with new body parts...* Don't do it. ... *My mother's face when she called me a whore for sleeping with a vampire...* Don't do it. ... *Don's smile when he forced me to come work for him...* Don't do it. ... *The headstone I'd glimpsed before leaving Ohio, engraved with the name Catherine Crawfield and dated six years ago...*

"Yes, Noah. I *will* marry you."

"You *what?*"

Don's voice was almost comical in its incredulity. He was my second call after my mother. She'd cried with happiness.

I repeated the sentence slowly and clearly. "I got engaged to Noah and took off to Niagara Falls to celebrate that."

Nothing but silence as he digested the news. I could just imagine him tugging madly at his eyebrow. "I see," he replied at last. "Congratulations, I suppose, although you took my advice to start living a bit literally, didn't you?"

Asshole. "You always tell me to pay attention, Don."

Another pause. "Are you sure about this?"

"I'll tell Noah you offered your congratulations," I cut him off, then hung up. For once, it had been nicer talking to my mother. That was scary.

"Was that your boss?" Noah inquired in a careful tone.

I leaned back. "Yeah, it was."

"Will I ever meet him?" Again, he sounded like he was choosing his words.

"Not if you're lucky," I murmured and flipped over to kiss him.

Sex with Noah still didn't excite me, but he didn't know that. I told myself that one day I might feel Noah inside me and not wish it was someone else. How easily the lies came.

I'd developed a neat self-defense mechanism since Dave had been murdered. *Think about nothing. React blindly. Fuck the consequences.* We'd see how it worked. Noah certainly wasn't complaining. He was too busy moaning and arching his back.

I looked down at him and knew I didn't have to worry about my eyes changing color. My vampire nature hadn't flared up once. See, there were some advantages to not being satisfied by my new fiancé. I just had to look at the bright side.

The hotel-room phone rang thirty minutes later. I answered it, which was a good thing since Tate's first words were, "Are you out of your fucking mind?"

"Didn't take long for Don to trace the call, huh?" No surprise that he'd scrambled to find what hotel I was in.

"You *don't* love him," Tate went on as if I hadn't spoken. "You don't even know him! I doubt you even know his middle fucking name. And he sure as hell doesn't know *you*. He'd shit his pants if he knew the real you. Look, we're all upset about Dave, but do you think Dave would want you to go and do something as stupid as get engaged to some chump who wouldn't know the dangerous end of a gun if it were shoved up his—"

I hung up. Okay, so maybe this *had* been hasty, but I was going to see it through. After all, it couldn't be the worst mistake I'd ever made. My life was a glorious account of one bad decision after another, and usually those decisions ended with someone dead, like my grandparents. Or Dave. What was a quickie engagement compared to that?

Next to me, Noah began to stir. Sex was like a sedative to him. I didn't know whether to be flattered or offended. Since I was trying to think positive, I picked flattered.

"Who was that? Did the phone ring?" he asked me drowsily.

"Just Tate, wishing us all the best." How easily the lies came.

Noah kissed me and got out of bed, heading for the bathroom. Moments later, the shower turned on and I heard him whistling as he stepped inside. I grabbed a pillow and hugged it to me. *Please,* I prayed, *please let me have done the right thing by agreeing to marry him.*

"I love you, future Mrs. Rose," Noah called out.

"I love you too, Mr. Rose," I replied immediately.

How easily the lies came.

CHAPTER THIRTEEN
ALTERNATE VERSION OF CAT
AND BONES'S REUNION

Author's Note: *Cat's "greatest mistake" had a ripple effect in other places in the book, such as the scene where she and Bones finally see each other again at Denise's wedding. The original version below differs from the published one because in this, Cat is engaged to Noah instead of merely dating him. And Bones is not happy about that, as you can imagine. As I've had to do before in some places, I included some parts of the published version with this alternate version. Otherwise this section would consist of a lot of new sentences without any context.*

Felicity was delighted at having Bones as her wedding partner for the pictures. She managed to squeeze herself indecently close to him in every shot. My jaw ached from how hard I had to grit my teeth to keep from backhanding her. To make matters worse, he was being charming, and she ate it up.

When I could stand it no longer, I turned my head away to face a wall and spoke under my breath so only he could hear me. "Keep it up and she'll need a new pair of panties."

"Jealous, luv?" he said, covering the words with a fake cough.

Hell yes. Even though my fiancé waited for me, my feelings had no sense of fairness. So I took the offensive, as I usually did when upset.

"Not at all. Why don't you take her around back and fuck her real quick? Then maybe she'll simmer down and stop acting like such a whore."

"Ah, Kitten," he said while he refit the rose in his lapel so no one would see his lips move. "You know how I like to take my time…"

"Just the wedding party," the photographer said and ushered us to stand together.

I stomped over gracelessly.

"Move in closer, that's right, a little closer. Now smile and think about the one you love."

Just as the flash went off, I glanced up and saw Bones staring at me. He wasn't smiling, and neither was I. But we looked at each other and no one else.

I made a beeline for the bar right after the last click of the camera. There was only one thing that could help me tonight, and that was gin. Lots of gin. I downed the first glass without budging from in front of the bartender.

"Another one."

The bartender made an inquiring face but poured another gin and tonic.

I eyed the level he selected and gave him a dirty look. "More alcohol," I said succinctly.

"Whiskey neat when you're done with the lady," a familiar voice behind me directed. "Drowning your sorrows, Kitten?"

"Follow me," I replied, fed up. One way or another I had to find out what he wanted. I passed by my mother's table to whisper to her. "Keep Noah busy. I'm going to have a chat."

"Don't do it, Catherine," she pleaded, calling me by the wrong name again.

I walked off to the patio before she could say more.

The country club was surrounded by trees with low-hanging branches. Light turned into shadows as the sun set. I heard Bones approach but kept looking at the dying rays of the sun.

"Tell me straight out, why are you here? Is it because you… you still have feelings for me?"

He let out a harsh grunt. "I think *you* should answer that first. After all, you're the one who let me come back to an empty house and a bloody Dear John note."

I couldn't look at him, because I hated myself for what I'd done. "It was the only way," I murmured.

"Bollocks," he snapped back.

"They knew what I was, Bones." Now I faced him and tried to my keep composure. "The men who came to the hospital that day, they knew everything from my pathology reports. And they knew about vampires. The one in charge—"

"Don?" he supplied.

Oh, so he'd done his homework. "Yes, Don. He said he'd looked his whole life for someone who was strong enough to fight vampires but who wasn't one of them. And my darling mother informed them I'd been sleeping with one, so they knew about you too. Don offered me a deal. He would relocate us, and I would lead his team. In return, he promised to leave you alone. Then you caught us on our way to the airport and demolished ten square miles of highway. You put five agents in a coma, Bones! If I hadn't taken the deal, we would have been hunted like animals, and you know my mother would rather die than be sheltered by you. She'd also rather see me killed than changed into a vampire, and let's face it, that's what you would have eventually wanted me to do!"

Bones ran a hand through his hair in exasperation. "Is that what this whole bleedin' thing was about? Your mum telling you I'd turn you into a vampire? Bloody hell, Kitten, when did I *ever* force you to do anything you didn't want to do? You should have trusted me. I trusted *you.* I never saw it coming when you ran away without a word."

I had to look away at that.

He began to pace in short, angry strides. "Did you truly believe I couldn't handle whatever it was your government tried to do?" he went on. "Blokes like that have chased me most of my undead life, yet I'm still here while they're not. But no, you had to be a hero and take the fall. Do I still love you? You don't deserve to know, but I will tell you this." Suddenly he was so close that the breath from his words fell onto my lips. "I still want you, Kitten. When I look at you… all I want to do is rip your clothes off and hear you scream while I'm inside you."

"I'm engaged," I blurted out to cover my skyrocketing pulse. I couldn't stop looking at the chiseled planes of his cheekbones or how close his mouth was to mine. That mouth twisted at my reply.

"Yeah, I know. Threw me good one, it did. Is that why you didn't come to Chicago back in April? Because of that pet vet?"

The derisive way he spoke about Noah stiffened my spine. "You mean when you kidnapped and murdered Danny Milton? You swore to me that you would never touch Danny, but I don't suppose he's off in Mexico sipping margaritas, is he?"

Bones straightened. "You made me swear not to kill, cripple, maim, dismember, blind, torture, bleed, or otherwise inflict any injury on Danny Milton. *Or* stand by while someone else did. You should save your sorrow for someone worthy. Danny gave you up like a bad habit straightaway. You know that brainwashing rot doesn't hold up under a Master vampire's eyes. At least the bugger was finally useful. He told me where you lived. Virginia. I had you narrowed down to three states, and he saved me some time. That's why I told Rodney to kill him fast and painless—and I didn't stay to watch."

"You bastard," I managed.

He shrugged. "Takes one to know one, luv."

I lowered my head and rubbed it, thinking of Dave. How needlessly he had died. How absolutely it was my fault, first by my rescuing Danny instead of killing Lazarus, then by my shouting at them not to fire. I might as well have ripped Dave's throat open myself.

Bones stared at me. "You're actually grieving over that wanker? That sod would have gotten you killed one day, make no mistake about it. I couldn't let him live. Your boss might have done a bang-up job hiding *you* away, but I found him in three days."

"It's not grief over him." My voice was thick with self-recrimination. "I lost a friend that day. And for the record, I didn't know about Chicago until a month ago. Don had given me some time off to deal with my guilt, so he sent someone else to Chicago when Danny went missing. He only told me about it when Ian got away." I gave a dry, humorless laugh and looked at him. "When I heard, I demanded to see all the evidence from the hospital. I found the watch and knew it was from you. I'll say this; I didn't worry about Danny after that."

Bones held my gaze, and I shivered even though the outside air was warm. There was a sense of unreality to standing here and talking to him. Some part of me thought I'd wake up and this would all be a dream.

"Would you have come?" he asked softly.

That was a dangerous question, but he deserved a little honesty, even if I couldn't tell him most of what I was feeling.

"The state of mind I was in, chewed up with grief and looking for any source of comfort, yes. I would have come to you. It would have been a mistake, of course, because nothing about our situation has changed and everything would have gone to shit, but yes. After I got engaged to Noah, no. I made a commitment, Bones. That means something, despite..."

"Despite the fact that you don't love him?" he finished brutally.

"That's not true! Anyhow, it doesn't matter. You and I are over." The words tasted vile, but I said them. The next ones positively choked me, but they had to be uttered too. "I..." I looked away. "I don't love you anymore."

"There you are!" Noah called from across the patio. "Darling, people were wondering where you were. What are you doing out here?"

The lies came quickly. "My ankle was bothering me from my slip down the aisle. I was just stretching it out, didn't want to make a fuss."

"We haven't met," Bones said, and held out a hand to Noah. I glared at him, remembering how he'd crippled Danny's hand this same way. "My name is Cris. Cris Pin."

Cris. Pin. Why hadn't I clearly looked at the invitations when I helped mail them?

"Noah Rose," my fiancé replied, shaking Bones's hand. I breathed a sigh of relief when he let go and no bones were broken. "This is my wife-to-be, Cristine, in case you haven't met."

"We've met before," Bones said with a knowing look my way. "In fact, she was just telling me the history behind her last name."

I groaned inwardly. Noah frowned. "Russell? I didn't know there was a history behind your last name, Cristine. What is it?"

Well, what did I expect? I had practically named myself after Bones when I switched identities. Did I think he wouldn't mention it?

"Um, er… Cris's mother's maiden name was also Russell, that's all. You said people were looking for me? Let's get back to the party. My ankle feels better."

I walked away so fast that Noah had to trot to keep up. Even still, Bones's voice chased after me, too low for Noah to hear.

"Kitten, when you said you didn't love me anymore… you were lying."

Dinner was a living hell. Felicity kept up a stream of suggestive chatter with Bones that had me digging my nails into my palms until I drew blood. Worse, her hand kept finding its way onto his thigh whenever she leaned in to whisper to him. And he did nothing to stop her.

Unable to watch anymore, I turned and speared my dinner roll viciously. From the corner of my eye, I saw Bones glance at me and chuckle.

"I have to go powder my nose. I'll be right back," Felicity cooed, brushing her breast against his shoulder when she bent to retrieve her handbag.

He winked at her when she walked away, the bastard. I twisted my knife into my helpless dinner roll and imagined it was his heart.

"Trying to warn me about something?" he asked with a knowing glance at my roll.

"Just wishful thinking," I shot back evilly.

Bones took his own dinner roll and split the center, buttering it. Then, lowering his head, he ran his tongue along the center until he'd licked away every drop of moisture. The air left my lungs in a rush as I watched.

"Wishful thinking," he murmured, giving me a heated look.

I stood so hastily my chair upended, and my face burned with a full crimson blush that had nothing to do with causing a distraction among the wedding guests again.

"Um, a toast to the bride and groom," I improvised. "Denise, Randy, may you always remember the commitment you made to each other today. Marriage is the pledge you make that come hell or high water, you will stand together and not be knocked over by what life throws at you. Today and always, I wish you the strength, courage, and tenacity to overcome any obstacles that threaten your relationship. Once again, congratulations."

A smattering of applause sounded, with more than a few sideways glances. Okay, so maybe I sounded like a drill sergeant, but I was trying to keep my head above water here.

Randy came over to give me a kiss, as did Denise, and I sat back down feeling slightly better. Then Randy stood and raised his glass.

"I'd like to thank Cristine for strongly reminding everyone of the seriousness of marriage. Since she's usually armed, I'm not going to disagree with her."

His statement garnered genuine laughter and applause. Most of the guests knew that I worked for the government in some capacity, and they knew it wasn't secretarial duties. Poor schmucks, if they had any real idea.

"But let me deviate a bit," Randy went on. "Denise and I have known each other for just six weeks, a very short period of time, many would say, and they would be correct. We have different backgrounds, different upbringings, and different religious beliefs. None of that matters. The first night I met her, I knew she was the one for me. The night before I asked her to marry me, I had a talk with my friend, Cris."

Randy gestured to my right and I tensed, afraid to listen further.

"Most of you don't know Cris, but we met six months ago, and I asked him if he thought I was rushing things by proposing to a woman I'd only dated for two weeks. I want to share with all of you what Cris said, because I think it bears repeating."

Randy moved to stand behind Bones, and my knuckles whitened on the edge of the table. Something told me I didn't want to hear what was coming.

"He said, 'Randy, mate, don't bother about how long you've known this girl if you love her. Time has no dominion over love. Love is the one thing that transcends time.'"

There were sentimental *oohs* and *ahhs* from the guests. I didn't dare look to my right, because tears coursed a slow steady trail down my cheeks. How right Bones was. Love *did* transcend time, because my heart was breaking as much now as it had the day I left him.

"I would like to thank new friends and old, family and extended family, for sharing the happiest day of my life with the woman I love," Randy finished.

Heartfelt applause broke out when Randy and Denise kissed.

When they broke apart, her eyes widened when she saw me over Randy's shoulder. "Cristine! You're crying. I've never seen you cry before."

I smiled and lied through a throat almost closed off from emotion. "I'm just so happy for you, that's all."

Grimly I vowed to make it through the entire reception. But I sat closer to Randy than Denise did in my vain attempt to put as much distance between Bones and myself as possible.

Felicity, bitch that she was, took one look at the gin I kept guzzling and faked a shocked gasp. "Cristine, can't you keep a lid on your drinking?" she hissed behind Bones's back. "This is my cousin's wedding, for heaven's sake."

Her prim tone made me squeeze my drink so hard that it shattered. Gin spilled on the front of my dress, and my palm started to bleed.

"Motherfucker!" I shouted.

Every head turned. Bones smothered a laugh by faking a sudden cough.

"Are you okay?" Randy looked worriedly at me and wrapped his napkin around my hand. He glanced at Bones, who gave him an innocent shrug.

"I'm all right, Randy," I yelped, mortified.

Denise poked her head around her new husband. "Do you want us to switch the seats?" she murmured quietly.

They thought I was rattled because Bones was a vampire. That was the least of my concerns. His nearness was shredding my control, and the reception wasn't over yet.

"Darling!" Noah came to the table and took the napkin off my hand. "Is it bad?"

"I'm fine," I snapped harshly. His hurt face made me cringe with guilt. "Just embarrassed," I covered. "First I trip, now I break glasses and scream obscenities. I'll be okay. Go back to your seat. Let's not make it worse."

Noah looked mollified and he went back to his table. I gathered the shards of glass and began to pile them on the bloody napkin. "I'm going to the ladies' room to wash this off and throw away the glass," I told Denise.

"I'll go with you," she offered.

"No." I gave a glance to my right at Bones and then back to her again. Her eyes widened, and she got the picture. Part of it, anyway.

"Cris," she addressed him. "Would you mind going with Cristine and seeing if they have any bandages? Randy says..." She paused and then continued wickedly. "Randy says you have a great deal of experience with bleeding wounds."

"Are you a doctor?" Felicity cooed.

Bones stood and gave Denise an appreciative grin at her choice of words. "Back in England I was many things," he answered Felicity evasively.

"Keep Noah busy," I whispered to Denise, and she nodded. God knew she would do a better job than my mother had.

I made a stop at the bar first. The bartender gave a wide-eyed look at my red-stained napkin.

"Gin. No glass, just the bottle," I said bluntly.

"Um, miss, maybe you should..."

"Give the lady the bottle, mate," Bones interjected, his eyes flashing green.

Without delay, an unopened gin was thrust in my still-bleeding hand. I twisted the top off, threw away my broken glass and the bloody napkin, and took a long swallow. Then I led Bones into the far corner of the parking lot where there were the fewest cars. He waited patiently while I drank again. I was smearing blood all over the outside of the bottle, but I didn't care.

"Better?" he asked when I came up for air. His lips twitched with suppressed amusement.

"Not hardly," I countered. "Look, I don't know how long my mother will keep quiet, but in case you hadn't noticed, she hates you. She'll call in the troops and try to have you skewered over an open flame with a silver stick. You have to leave."

"No."

"Dammit, Bones!" My temper exploded. Why did he have to be so gorgeous, why did he have to stand so close, and *why* did I love him so much still? "I work for the government killing vampires, ghouls, and even humans when necessary. They own my ass for another thirteen years if I don't die first, and that's a big if. *You cannot be here.* I told you I don't love you anymore. I might have some—some residual feelings of attraction for you, but it's only because I have eyes and you're breathtaking. Now please, before this turns ugly, will you just leave?"

He tilted his head. A slight breeze ruffled the curls in his hair, and in his tuxedo, he was more than breathtaking. He was devastating. "You don't love me? Then why didn't you kill Ian? You had a knife in his heart. All you had to do was twist. You said it yourself, your job is to kill vampires, yet you let him go. You might as well have sent me a bloomin' valentine."

"Sentimentality." I grasped at straws. "For old times' sake."

"Right." Bones let that go. "Well, luv, you *should* have killed him, because now he's looking for you. You made quite an impression. While I would never force you to do anything against your will, Ian wants to find you to do just that."

"What are you talking about?"

Bones smiled, but it wasn't pleasant. "He's enamored, of course. Ian's a collector of rare things, and there's no one rarer than you, my beautiful half-breed. You're in danger. He doesn't know I found you, but he'll find you himself soon enough."

I mulled over that while I took another drink. "Doesn't matter. I beat Ian before and I can do it again."

"Not the way he'll play it." There was something in his voice that made me look sharply at him. "Ian won't just come at you one night and try to take you on in a fair fight. He'll grab everyone you love first and strike a deal, his terms. Believe me, you won't like them. Now, your one advantage is me. Because of your clever little description of our relationship, Ian believes you hate me and vice versa. Nice touch, that. Especially the money part. Still want a check?"

"I'll write *you* one if you leave," I muttered.

Bones ignored that and moved closer, holding out his hand. "Mind if I have a drop from your bottle?"

I handed over the gin, careful not to let my fingers graze his. Instead of drinking from it, he stared into my eyes as he licked my blood off the smooth glass surface. His tongue curved around every contour of the bottle, and heat flared through me as I watched, mesmerized. When there was not a red drop left on it, he passed it back into my suddenly shaking hand.

"Residual attraction?" His voice deepened. "Oh, Kitten, you're only deceiving yourself."

Think about Noah! my brain screamed. *Think about anything but what that tongue felt like on your skin!*

"I appreciate the warning about Ian." I tried to sound firm, but my voice came out breathy. "But I will handle this myself. If need be, I'll relocate with Noah and my mother. Noah loves me. He'll go where I go."

He gave a harsh, brief laugh and his eyes glowed green. Anger or passion, I wasn't sure. "You hold Noah up like a shield, but he's your weakest link. Let's talk about your fiancé, since you're so quick to mention him every time you feel your willpower weakening. Tell me, how did he take the news that you're half-vampire? Supportive, was he? Or what about how you risk your life to slaughter the undead? Does he give you a kiss and tell you to stake one for him? Your mum has bigger balls than Noah does."

"His balls are fine!" God, did I just say that?

He moved in for the kill. "Let's talk about that as well. Little wonder you're hot as a firecracker around me. The best shag you've had all these years has undoubtedly been yourself." Then he leaned forward until his mouth was mere inches from my ear. "You know, luv, I've been wondering something ever since I found out you were engaged. Which is more frustrating for you? Having to hide your eyes every time Noah's inside you so he doesn't see their glow… or not needing to shut them at all?"

Bastard. I swung the bottle at his head, and he caught it in a blur of speed. As soon as I felt his fingers near mine, I dropped it, and it shattered at our feet.

Bones smiled with cruel satisfaction and stepped back. "That's what I thought."

"Bite me!" I snarled venomously and oh, how stupidly.

His eyes gleamed. "I've been dreaming of that for years. I'll hold you to your offer."

"Figure of speech, Bones," I said as I backed away toward the safety of the clubhouse, although nowhere would be safe now. His expression told me that.

"Not to a vampire, yet out of respect for Randy, I'll let this go for now. You and I will finish this later."

"No, we won't. Do me a favor. Go fuck Felicity and leave me alone."

"You reckon that wouldn't faze you?" he called out as I reached the clubhouse door. "We'll see."

I ran inside and didn't reply.

CHAPTER FOURTEEN
BONES DISCOVERS CAT'S
CROSSBONES TATTOO

Author's note: I cut out the rest of the wedding scene and the scene where Bones followed Cat to the club because there wasn't much new material. This next section is a revised version of what happens after Cat kills the vampire at the club and includes a deleted section where Bones first sees the crossbones tattoo on Cat's hip. I honestly can't remember why this part didn't make it into the published version. It might have been a simple case of my thinking that it was there but accidentally deleting it during one of my many revisions. And yes, there were a lot of revisions, as you can now see.

"You forgot one."

I was just about to fling more knives when his voice stopped me. Bones came in and cast a thorough look around the carnage. Most of the vampires I'd dispatched with my blades, but the ones who'd killed the kids I'd torn apart with my bare hands. It was the least I could do.

"Really? Who?"

His smile was pleasant. "The little bitch who was sneaking around for a gun, but she's not doing that any longer."

Must have been Brandy with the pink toenails. His benign expression didn't fool me. Knowing him, she'd be wearing that shade in hell.

"Two of these girls are still alive. Give them blood. Yours will work faster than what I have to offer."

All I had was my own, but with my humanity, it was weak when it came to healing. And I didn't have any Brams on me since this wasn't supposed to be a worknight.

Bones took the knife I handed him and sliced his palm, going to each girl and making them swallow his blood.

"Will she be okay?" the ghost asked, hovering over his girlfriend.

Gradually I heard her pulse return to a slow but steady rhythm as Bones's blood went to work in her. After a moment, I smiled. "Yeah. She will be now."

He smiled back, showing that in life, he'd had dimples. God, he was so young! Then he started to fade at the edges, growing fainter until there was nothing left of him anymore.

I stared in silence. Then, "Is he... gone?"

Bones knew what I meant. "I expect so. He accomplished what he wanted to and so he's moved on. Sometimes a few stubborn people hang on long enough to do one last thing. He must have truly loved her."

True love. That snapped me back into my foul mood. "Why are you here? Finished with Felicity so soon? That's hardly up to your usual performance."

A brow rose. "I had no intention of shagging Felicity. I only kissed her to prove that you care far more than you're admitting to."

I was so glad nothing more had happened with her that I almost smiled. Then I caught myself. "I *don't* care."

Bones snorted and gave another look around at the blood-smeared walls. "Right. Cool as a cucumber, you are."

He'd left his tuxedo jacket somewhere else but still wore the shirt and pants from the wedding. His tie was also missing, and his shirt was casually opened at the neck. Over that, he had on a black leather coat that trailed down to his calves…

"Holy shit, is that what I think it is?" I blurted.

Bones did a circle. "You like how it looks on me? After all, you kept your Christmas present. Only seemed fair to retrieve mine, especially since you took my other jacket."

The leather coat I'd bought him for Christmas over six years ago fit him perfectly. When I told him where it was the day before I left him, it never occurred to me that he'd go back for it. Then again, it never occurred to me that he'd search for me this long.

I shook my head to clear the images. I had to get away from Bones. When I was near him, I couldn't think straight. *Work, concentrate on work.*

"I have to call this in, you got a phone on you?" All I had on me was my underwear, blood, and some knives.

Bones pulled one from his pocket and passed over.

"Tate, it's Cat. I need a cleanup crew at the GiGi bar. Got a bunch of dead vamps and some victims who need medical attention and new memories. Couple of human bodies also, unfortunately."

"Why aren't you at the wedding? The GiGi bar was supposed to be with us, tomorrow."

From his tone, Tate was pissed, but I was in no mood to argue with another man.

"Are you going to berate me or get the crew?"

"What number are you calling from? This isn't your cell."

"I stole someone's phone," I lied. "I'm giving it back now. Hurry up, this place is crawling with people."

I hung up without saying good-bye. "You have to leave," I said for what must have been the tenth time. "The guys will be here soon."

"I'm in no hurry," he replied, his voice husky.

Belatedly, it occurred to me that I stood six feet away from Bones clad only my bra and underwear. Granted, I was covered in blood, but that never turned off a vampire. It was their equivalent of whipped cream.

He hadn't missed a thing, and his eyes slid over me with the intimacy of a touch. "You're exquisite, Kitten."

He came toward me, but I leapt back. Something flashed across his face and his eyes narrowed as he stared at my bared hip. Uh-oh. I'd forgotten about that.

"You really did duplicate my tattoo. Ian told me you did, but I didn't quite believe him. Yet there it is, etched on your flesh." There was faint wonder in his voice.

"Don't touch me. Don't." My voice quavered because I knew if he did, it would be all over.

"You want me to. I see it in your eyes, and your scent betrays you." Bones's flat, hungry tone frightened me. His next words did even more. "Yet I told you long ago, I don't come in unless invited. You'll be the first to lay hands on me, and I'm not going anywhere. You want to get rid of me? Then you'll have to kill me."

Oh, *shit*. He knew I couldn't do that. Hell, I hadn't known if I could kill him when I thought that he'd slaughtered an entire family.

"Then I'll leave," I said. "Don hid me once, he can do it again."

"I dare you to try," he replied menacingly. "We have unfinished business, and we *will* settle it, ready or not. After nearly seven bloody years, you've had enough time as it is. Set an hour, luv, finish up here if you like, but I'm not waiting another day. If I have to follow you home and have it out in front of Noah, I will. Won't bother me a bit to pull the wool off his eyes as to who he hopes to marry. What will it be? Private or public, take your pick."

He wasn't bluffing, he never bluffed, and there was no way I was letting him near Noah if I could help it. The fact he hadn't murdered him already amazed me.

"All right, you want me to pick a time? Dawn."

His lips curled at the spitefulness of my choice. A vampire was weakest at dawn. So was I, but in this one instance, my humanity would help me instead of hinder me. Take every cheap shot, every low blow. He had taught me that.

"Where?"

I thought for a minute. "There's an unfinished park outside Richmond called AdventureLand. Construction's been halted due to permits, so it's empty. Meet me by the bridge connecting the golf course to the far green. Don't be late—I won't wait for you."

He smiled and gave a last, long look down the length of my body. "I won't be late, Kitten. You can count on it."

CHAPTER FIFTEEN
BONES AND CAT, REVISED
REKINDLED PASSION

Author's note: *In the published version of* One Foot in the Grave, *Bones and Cat go on several dates before giving in to their passion. At one point shortly after Bones returns, Cat even tells him something like "I'm not just going to fall back with my legs open while declaring my undying love to you." *grin* That line was me being a smart-ass to my editor, because in the original version below, that's pretty much what happens. Cat had never stopped loving Bones, and she'd made herself a miserable, self-destructive mess without him, so I couldn't imagine her putting Bones off for any length of time once he was back in her life. I also couldn't imagine Bones wanting to take things slow now that he'd finally found her. He's a patient man, but not THAT patient.*

However, I did end up rewriting what happened when Bones returned because my editor reminded me that new readers who started with One Foot *had never "met" Bones before, and thus had no background for their romance. Having Cat and Bones jump right back into bed would therefore diminish the sexual tension that could otherwise be used to introduce them to Cat and Bones's relationship. Since I'd written this well before I had any readers, that thought had never occurred to me, but I could see her point, so I revised. I did use some of the original sex scene below in the published version, but I changed the setting as well as what inspired Bones to bite her. So in this version, you'll get to see both an amended version of their first sex scene as well as some of Bones's temper with regards to Noah.*

Dawn had just broken when I pulled up to the bridge. I hadn't slept a minute all night.

Bones was already by the bridge, waiting for me. Some idiotic part of me had hoped he would oversleep, but no. In fact, to my bleary gaze, he looked as rested as could be. He wore a navy sweater and blue jeans, and my heart began that damned accelerated beating when he met my gaze. I'd picked a place out in the open deliberately. Although it was deserted, it was hardly private.

He laughed outright when I got out of my car. Okay, so maybe I'd gone a bit overboard in an attempt to look dowdy. I'd even debated whether or not to shower or brush my teeth, but hygiene had won out. I had on loose-fitting overalls, a high-necked top with long sleeves, and three pairs of panties underneath the overalls. My hair hung in wild strands after I'd roughly towel-dried it following my shower. I hadn't even bothered to comb it.

"Where's your chastity belt?" he said in greeting, still chuckling. "You must be very concerned about your will-power. I'm flattered."

"Save it," I said shortly. "I'm here. Let's settle this."

"All right." He walked under the bridge. I didn't move. "Going to rain soon, I can smell it. Stay there if you like, I'm going to keep dry."

The air did feel moist, and gray thunderclouds were holding the sunlight at bay, but I held my ground and remained where I was. "I'll risk it."

That signaled the beginning of the showdown. "What you're willing to risk makes my hair stand on end," Bones snapped. "Taking off and hunting vampires with only humans as support. I can't believe you're still alive. How many times have you put yourself in danger to bail out your team? Must have been hundreds. Last night I could have picked them off one by one. Without you, they're just food."

"I'm glad we agree," I interjected. "My team needs me. Noah needs me. Don needs me. My mother needs me. You have to respect that and go. Let me handle my own problems."

"I don't give a rot about them." Brown eyes glared into mine. "I need you. That's all I bother about."

Last night lying in bed, I'd rehearsed dozens of arguments. Here went the first one. "I am not the same teenager you plucked out of a bar. I'm a grown woman. If Ian comes for me or mine, I will fight him. Frankly, I'm more concerned about you hurting Noah than about Ian coming after him to get to me."

He snorted rudely. "If I meant to kill him, I'd have done it already. I followed the sod to his office the morning after I found you, then picked him up by neck and told him my name. Of course, he had no idea who I was. Only took another minute to confirm he also had no bleedin' clue who you were, either. That's why your human teddy bear is safe from me. He's too soft, naïve, idealistic, and weak. You got engaged to a man you knew you could never truly love, and God knows he wouldn't love you if he had a clue about who and what you really are. That bloke from your team has more to fear from me than Noah."

"Who?" I had no rebuttal for what he'd said about Noah. Maybe I was just happy that he had promised, in a round-about way, not to hurt him.

Bones gave me a scathing rake of his eyes. "Tate. He's so in love with you I could smell it from a mile away. Interesting you didn't choose him as your playmate since he accepts you and has a bit of strength. No, you went right for Noah's Furry Ark."

I stomped closer to shout in his face. "First of all, Tate doesn't love me. He just wants to get laid. You and he have that in common."

"Too right he wants to shag you, but he'd walk through flames for you. After over two hundred years of watching men and women, I know real love when I see it."

"I don't love him."

"Of course not. Be too dangerous for you, wouldn't it? After all, you might have to trust someone then. Tell them the truth when you feel threatened instead of disappearing." Bones stalked over.

We were now toe-to-toe.

Then his voice softened a trifle. "Kept the car though, didn't you? Do you know how many people in America own a Volvo similar to yours? I do. That's how I had you narrowed down to three states. Don changed the year and make as well as the registration, yet even the government keeps service records of their vehicles. And fuel records for their aircrafts. Knew you weren't flying commercial with all your weapons, so after every scene you went to, I tracked the flight paths of nearby military planes. Do you know how many times I arrived only hours after you'd left? I could still smell your scent in the air, almost as clearly as I can now."

Bones had told me last night that he had searched for me, but I hadn't realized how extensively. My heart constricted.

"Bones, I'm sorry for leaving the way I did. It was cowardly, but I... I wasn't strong enough back then to look at you and tell you good-bye, even though I knew it was the right decision. It still is. If it makes you feel any better, I've cried every night about what I did to you. Literally every night." Bitterness crept into my tone, because it was true.

"No, it doesn't make me feel better, Kitten." Frustration and tenderness mixed on his features. "If anyone else hurt you like that, I'd kill them, yet you did it to yourself. What am I to do about that?"

"Please just leave." I forced the request out with will-power alone. "Please. I'm telling you this to your face, like I couldn't do before." I met those dark brown orbs I'd dreamed about incessantly and didn't falter. "Good-bye, Bones."

He gazed at me for several moments. I put all my deter-mination, strength and will forward for him to see, not the quaking emotions underneath. Finally he blinked, and the stalemate was over.

"All right, Kitten. If you're sure that is what you wish, I'll go. I told you long ago that I'd never force myself where I wasn't wanted. Give me a hug, pet. Let us part as friends."

Part as friends, that was better than before, wasn't it? In fact, it would be downright insulting to refuse such a mag-nanimous offer. All these excuses sped through my mind and overruled the inner warning that told me not to do it. When did I ever listen to those warnings?

I stepped forward and put my arms around him, but as soon as I did it, I knew it was a mistake. A colossal one. Bones folded his arms around me, and it was like a match igniting across my every nerve ending. His body seemed to pulse with voltage begging to be let free, and his embrace was the only thing that had felt right in the past six and a half years. I should never, ever have touched him. He had always been my kryptonite.

"I'm sorry," I whispered, but it wasn't to Bones. It was to my mother, Noah, Don, and everyone else, because nothing short of my own death would stop me from what I did next. Impatient to feel his flesh under my palms, I grabbed a handful of his lovely blue sweater and tore it open.

I would have gasped when my fingers touched his bare skin except in that instant, his lips covered mine. He ravaged my mouth with blind need, tongue ruthlessly raking the interior. His grip on me turned unyielding, crushing, and he lifted me off my feet as I wrapped my legs around his waist. Only the pressure from our bodies kept his sweater on; I'd rent his sweater into strips in my greediness to touch his bare skin.

"Don't... *ever*... say that... to me... again," he growled while kissing me into mindless oblivion. My conscience slept, comatose from the flash beating it had just received by my lust. I couldn't get enough of kissing him, tasting him after so long, and I sucked on his tongue as if meaning to swallow it.

I moved my hand between our tightly molded bodies with the single-minded intention of destroying his pants. Then all thought fled as his fingers slid under my overalls and pushed into me. I arched back hard enough to hit my head on the wall behind us, harsh cries of need spilling from me. My loins twisted in pleasure from each new rub, the intensity inside me building—until his hand was gone, leaving me wet and aching.

"I can't wait," he muttered fiercely and dropped to the ground with me underneath him.

If speaking was still in my control, I would have immediately agreed. But all my vocal abilities were used in gasping at the unbelievable sensations his fingers caused. Bones shifted, I heard another rip, and then my overalls, shirt, and three pairs of panties split down the middle.

I cried out when he entered me in one hard stroke, my flesh ecstatically stretching to clutch his. He didn't pause to savor the sensation of our joined bodies but thrust forcefully into me while still tearing off my clothes. It only took the third thrust for me to shudder in frenzied climax, unable to handle the bombardment of my senses.

A growl escaped him that might have been a laugh. "Oh, Kitten, you did miss me, didn't you?"

My mind was seized with a single, jumbled rant: harder-faster-more-yes! It was all I could think as I clawed at his back. His muscles rippled with his movements, and his skin positively crackled with inhuman energy.

I was still in the throes of orgasm, nerve endings shredded with pleasure, and only the concern for oxygen gave me the ability to talk. "Can't... breathe..."

Between his ceaseless kissing and his iron grip, my lungs were deprived. He loosened his hold and tore his mouth from mine, leaving a hot trail down to my breast. A strangled moan tore out of me when he sucked hard on my nipple. I took in rapid breaths and then bit my lip at the intensity of his motions. He was rough enough for it to have been rape, except I strained toward him and reveled in the ravishment. No pain had ever felt this good. Strangled sounds escaped me and I punctured his back with my nails.

"Forgive me," Bones moaned into my ear. "I can't be gentle. It's been too long."

"Don't stop." I raked my nails down his back for emphasis, sparing him nothing in the gesture. The storm broke around us, rain pelting down in sheets. I felt more wild than it was, what with the passion that had my nerve endings contracting and twisting in a frenzy.

"I can't stop," he muttered as a twist of his hips shot rapturous torment into my loins. The muscles inside me clenched and unclenched in furious competition. I unleashed all control over myself, tearing into him with the same force he inflicted on me, and the thunder and downpour absorbed our cries. There was nothing tender in the way we took each other. We were both too desperate for that.

When Bones finally convulsed, tremors shaking him, I'd almost fainted. My heart pounded and my ears rang with the blood thrumming in them. He gathered me closer and let his mouth rest over my pulse, and I could feel its rampant beating against his lips.

"That took some of the edge off," he breathed into my neck.

I managed a wheeze of a laugh. "If that only took *some* of the edge off, you'll kill me before you dull the blade." It was true. I'd be black and blue by nightfall, and my walking abilities were in serious jeopardy.

I felt him smile against my skin, and I opened my eyes. His glowing emerald gaze held mine and the reality of him being with me, me actually inside his arms, struck me belatedly. The anguish I'd carried for so long eased bit by bit, reluctant to break its stranglehold. Tears came to my eyes, and I couldn't hold back the truth any longer.

"Everything I said to you before was shit. I still love you. I couldn't stop, no matter how hard I tried! Oh God, Bones, I've been so lost without you..." I couldn't speak anymore. I tried to fight the tears, but they came anyway, and a sob choked off my words.

"It's all right, Kitten," Bones said softly. "You're not lost any longer. I found you, and I love all of you. I love the narrow-minded teenager who tried to kill me when we first met because she thought the world had two categories: human and evil. I love the budding fighter who made a deal with a vampire to protect her family, and I love the sensual young woman who hid underneath. I love the lying bitch who left me because she thought she was protecting me. I love the hardened warrior you've become. I can even love you for getting engaged to that fluffy scrap of humanity you thought would change you into something you'll *never be*. I love you whether you're Cristine, Cat, Cathy, Kitten or even Catherine, and I will love whoever you become in the future too."

That did it; I burst into full, wracking sobs that shattered the walls within me. More than anything else, I'd longed to hear that he still loved me, and more incredibly, as he'd pointed out, he loved the real me, in all my flaws and forms. It was an inexpressible relief to break down, drop my shields, and be emotionally defenseless without fear of rejection. Bones held me the entire time that I cried, and when the storm of my tears finally passed, I kissed him with such fervor that I tore my lips on his fangs.

Bones made a guttural noise as he swallowed my blood. Then one hand tangled in my hair and his mouth sealed over my throat. I had a split second where I guessed what he intended, and tensed in instinctive defense.

"Don't be afraid," he whispered, then his fangs sank into me.

Just like that one time years before when he'd bitten me, what logic told me should hurt only felt good instead. Really, really good, and increasing with each pull from his mouth. I tried to talk and couldn't. There seemed to be an invisible highway connecting my artery to my loins, and I felt him there as if he were inside me again. The last time he'd bitten me hadn't been like this. It had been fast and explosive. This was slow and sizzling, both alarming and erotic. He wasn't draining me by inches; he was doing it by millimeters.

Another pull from his mouth curled my fingers and toes in delirious reflex. A hoarse sound left me when his tongue laved the punctures before sucking again. Heat raced through my veins with searing alacrity. My head fell back, and my fingernails dug into him while I trembled.

"How does it feel?" His voice was a growl.

I couldn't keep up with the deluge of new sensations. I was faint and exhilarated all at once. Goose bumps rippled over me, gray spots danced in my eyes, and I clung to him as my world tilted.

"Hot. F-feels hot. I think... I'm dying." Strangely, the thought of my demise had never bothered me less.

"You're not dying." He drew on my neck again and I shuddered, wondering how I could be so feverish when Bones was warmer than I'd ever felt him. "Give in to it," he urged me and bent my spine back, his fangs still locked on my throat. "Let yourself go."

My heartbeat seemed to rage inside my chest. Nothing felt separate anymore, and with every continued suction from his mouth, my pulse flamed with heat until my body felt incinerated. I cried out in a voice I didn't recognize as my own as he sucked harder, deeper. There was a burst of color behind my eyelids, an even stronger suction, and those incredible sensations built until it felt like I emptied into Bones along with my blood. When the climax crested through me, I stepped off the edge of consciousness into the blissful, waiting darkness.

Chapter Sixteen
After the Vampire Wedding Ceremony

Author's note: Over the years, many readers have asked what Cat wrote to Bones in the note she left him at the end of Halfway to the Grave. In this deleted section, you will find out, as well discover a few other tidbits. This deleted scene would have taken place before chapter 39 in the published version, for reference. It ended up being deleted so that readers would get to the graveyard scene where Dave is raised faster.

We hitched a ride with Spade, who drove us back to the airstrip where the same helicopter that brought me here would now take all of us back.

Ian had fumed, but a stern remark from Mencheres sent him off. Noah was summarily released from his cage and sat as far away from me as the SUV would allow. Who could blame him? I didn't. Perhaps my greatest shock was when the other vampires began to disperse without trying to kill me. Bones informed me that since I was his wife, if they attacked me they attacked him. No one wanted to try their luck with all his people milling about.

We changed helicopters twice to throw off any tail before landing at the base five hours later. Sunrise broke the horizon, and I was tired. Bones was also, but there was one more favor I was going to ask him to do, and it couldn't wait until later.

I whispered what it was in his ear. He stared at me for a moment before nodding shortly. "If that's what you want, Kitten."

"Yes. I'm sure."

Bones and I made our way to the back of the helicopter where Noah huddled. We had landed, but no one disembarked yet. Nosy bastards.

Noah took in the sight of me in my barely there dress with Bones following close behind and turned his face away. "I don't know who you are or what you are, Cristine. How am I supposed to live the rest of my life when the only person I've ever loved turns out to be... a monster," he finished at last.

"You don't have to live the rest of your life like that, Noah." I tried to smile but couldn't, and he was too terrified by me for it to be comforting, anyway.

Bones pushed me gently aside and knelt in front of him.

Noah sighed. "You're going to kill me now, aren't you?"

"No, mate, I'm not," Bones said steadily. "Now don't look away, look right in my eyes..." Once Noah was lost under their hypnotic power, Bones began to repeat what I'd asked him to say. "Your fiancée left you, but that's all right, because you've come to realize that you don't love her. In fact, you're glad she's gone, and you're not bitter or afraid to trust someone again because tonight, you were involved in a car accident. You survived, so you feel like you've gotten a second chance at life. Tomorrow, you'll wake up without any guilt or pain over your broken engagement, and you'll be happy one day when you meet a nice girl who wants a family. Sleep now; you're very tired. Sleep..."

Noah's eyes fluttered closed, and a hint of a smile creased his mouth. It was the only thing I could do for him, and I prayed that it held for the rest of his life.

I half staggered through the door to the house, exhausted. The silver heels on my shoes were stained with blood, and I kicked them off. When I reached up to unfasten the halter of my dress, anxious to shower so I could wash the rest of the blood off me, cool hands stopped me.

"Ah, Kitten, that's my job, remember?"

I smiled, but it slipped when I remembered the other thing I'd sworn to do tonight, if I lived through it. "Wait a minute."

I pushed him back and went to grab the folder I'd picked up at work.

"Is this how it is?" he teased me. "The shagging stops as soon as the wedding's over?"

"That's not it, but I have something for you." I reappeared and sat on the bed. "Something I want you to see."

Bones watched me curiously as I set the trash can in front of me and flicked his lighter until the desired flame appeared. With the other hand, I pulled out the wadded piece of paper that had shattered both our lives.

He recognized it and closed his hand over the page. I watched him reread the words and didn't need to see the page to know what they said. They had branded me with pain when I wrote them nearly seven years ago.

Don't come after me because I'm already gone. I've taken Hennessey's body and told them it's yours, so they think you're dead. We could never be safe together, and I won't kill you or my mother trying. Every word I ever told you about how much I loved you was the absolute truth. You are my life, Bones, and now consider me dead because I am. I will always love you, right down to my final breath. Your name will be my last word, I promise you.

"Rodney saved it. He gave it to me yesterday. I cried the whole time I wrote that, Bones, and now I want to destroy it along with every doubt I ever had about you. I love you, and no matter what, I'm never leaving you again."

Bones traced his finger over the page and then over the healed slash on my palm. "Let's get rid of this, Kitten."

He smiled at me and held the paper over the trash can as I set fire to the edge. When the flames brushed his fingers, he dropped it and we watched it burn.

CHAPTER SEVENTEEN
ORIGINAL ENDING TO
ONE FOOT IN THE GRAVE

Author's note: In the published version of One Foot, *Bones allows Justina to have Cat's team capture him because he wants to infiltrate Don's compound. Justina had thought she was setting Bones up to be killed, but in reality, she was playing right into Cat and Bones's hands.* One Foot *ends without readers seeing how Justina took the news that she had been outfoxed, but in the unpublished version, I had written all that out. So here is the original ending to* One Foot in the Grave, *which includes an additional chapter to show Bones giving Justina a little of the comeuppance that she so richly deserved.*

"**M**om, there's good news and bad news, and you don't get to pick the order." I opened the door of the single barrack where she'd stayed the past couple of days.

She looked up from the book she'd been reading. Her expression was guarded, understandably, and faint smudges of bruises still darkened her eyes.

"Catherine, I—" she began.

"Save it." Shortly. "I already know more than you do about what happened, and here's the good news. I'm not angry at you for calling Tate or bringing the boys over. Not a

187

bit. Wouldn't have expected any less from you, in fact. Now for the bad news…"

Bones stepped out from the doorway where he'd been concealed, a jaunty grin on his face.

She screamed as soon as she saw him. "They told me you were dead! *Shriveled.* Why won't you just die and leave her alone? Guards? Guards! There's a vampire here! Somebody come quick!"

Tate appeared and shook his head at her. "Sorry, but he's allowed here. Much as I hate to say it, he works here now. In a way. For Cat."

I had never seen someone look so close to a stroke without actually having one. Her face went five shades of red and purple before settling on dead white.

"He's corrupted you too, I see. Is there no end to his evil? Isn't there somebody here who can't be influenced by his tricks?!"

Don was the next batter up. "I'm not influenced, Justina, and Tate is correct. I'm the only other person who's hated vampires as much as you have, but necessity makes for strange bedfellows. Until Cat sends him away, he stays. No matter if we like it or not."

A rash of profanity next spewed from her lips, enough to make Don wince and Bones laugh as he rubbed my shoulders. "I told you, Kitten, you're just like your mum. No matter who you resemble physically. Old chap, do you mind…?"

A set of handcuffs exchanged hands, and my mother was shackled before she realized he had even moved. Next came the gag, stemming the obscenities that grew even more shrill.

"Should have done this to you from day bloody one." He grinned at her and hoisted her effortlessly over his shoulder.

I helpfully manacled her madly scissoring legs.

Don coughed. "Are you two going to be all right with her?"

I looked back at him as we headed out the floor and to the exit.

"We'll be fine. Just need a little family time, that's all."

"You'll be in tomorrow?" From Tate.

"Afternoon at the earliest. This might take a while."

We borrowed a car since his motorcycle wouldn't suffice. Bones drove and my mother rested comfortably in the back-seat, bound and gagged. God help us if we were pulled over for a traffic violation. Then again, those glaring green eyes of his would settle it.

The house he drove to was unfamiliar to me, set back off the road and larger than his previous one in Richmond. *At least this one might come with all the kitchen chairs intact,* I thought to myself. Maybe it also had a bar. A gin would do me wonders about now.

"Wait here for a second, luv, I just have to settle Bertrand. This is where he's staying for the week; he just drove in."

"Settle him? You owe him money?" I was confused.

Bones chuckled and climbed out of the car. "No, that's not it. You'll see."

With those intriguing words, I sat and watched as Bones rapped on the door. A dark figure opened it. They exchanged a hug, and Bones rested his hands on the other man's shoulders as he spoke.

"Now, mate, you don't have to fret because we've got her tied up, right? We won't untie her, promise, and you'll be safe because I'm here. Don't let Cat frighten you because of her heartbeat. She's half-vampire and won't hurt you. Come on, mate, I'll introduce you. That's it."

Huh? Bones waved me over and the form cringed as I drew near. From appearance he was a man in his forties, albeit a vampire. He had dark curling hair and pale blue eyes, high patrician cheekbones, and was the same height as Bones. What made him stand out startlingly was the way he cowered away from me and turned his face in fear.

"Show him your eyes, Kitten, lights on," Bones urged me.

In compliance I flashed their glow at him. There was visible lessening of anxiety when the emerald brightness fell on his face.

"Bertrand, this is my wife. Her name is Cat. See, she's not all human. Don't be afraid."

Icy blue eyes met mine in quavering nervousness even as he forced a smile. "Honored to meet you."

I held out a hand. As soon as he touched me, he jerked back in terror. "Her skin is warm! Oh, Bones, I don't know if I can do this!"

"Have I ever led you astray? You'll be all right. Kitten, wait here with him whilst I fetch your mum. Won't be a moment."

Bertrand led me inside the house while giving me a wide berth. When Bones entered with the squirming body of my mother under his arm, Bertrand actually tripped over his own feet to back away.

Now that was a first. Vampires were notoriously graceful in their movements, yet here this one was petrified to an outstanding degree of a human. Granted, my mother could be a real piece of work, but still. Bertrand could snap her in two, cowardly lion or no.

Bones deposited my mother in the first available room. Then he accepted the length of cords Bertrand extended to him and tied her to a velvet chair. When he was done, he squatted in front of her.

"Justina, you and I have a dilemma to sort out. You despise me, and quite frankly, I don't care for you. What we do have in common is our love for your daughter. That is why I'm willing to overlook your continued plots to kill me. However, I don't fancy spending the rest of my life with my wife sad that her mum won't visit on the holidays."

Her eyes bugged at the word *wife*, and unintelligible, furious grunts snuck out from behind her gag. Bones ignored that.

"You and I are going to have to agree to dislike each other and get past it. Now, I know you think vampires are the scum of the earth and you're downright livid that your daughter is with one, but look at her." A wave of his hand indicated me. "You have done nothing in your life you should be more proud of than raising her. Remarkable things usually come at a high price, and she is more than remarkable, isn't she?"

He leaned forward. "When I was forcibly changed into a vampire, I thought God had abandoned me. For several years, I brooded over my fate, then I decided that since I couldn't change it, I'd try to have a grand time being dead. It didn't work. Truth be told, I thought my heart had died the day my humanity did. And then I met your daughter. You'd be proud to know she hated me on sight and kept that opinion for weeks. I forced her into spending time with me because something had happened that I couldn't believe. I'd fallen in love, and nothing would do but that she love me too."

Dismissive shrug. "You know the rest, but this you don't know. Every night we were apart, that same Almighty who hadn't heard from me in over two hundred years suddenly had me ringing his phone off the bloody hook with prayers begging for her to be alive. When I saw her again, I knew that God had a plan for even a wretched bugger like me.

I'm telling you this so you'll understand that you *will never be rid of me*. If a hardened sod like me can be changed by love, I'm convinced that you can be too. Perhaps one day you'll realize that she is worth all the pain you've been through. Maybe one day you'll even tell her that."

My tear ducts had been overworked these past few weeks. This was no exception, and steady streaks of liquid coursed down my cheeks. I went to Bones and wrapped my arms around him, kissing his finely sculpted cheek before facing my mother.

"Mom, you can hate me, forget me, disown me, whatever, but I am never leaving Bones again. You will always by my mother, and I hope you'll still be in my life, but if it's you or him... it's him."

Bones untied the gag around her mouth.

She swallowed several times and, after a long moment of silence, finally spoke. "Water?"

Well, at least it wasn't vulgarity. That was a start. Bertrand went to fetch some without being asked. He only handed it to me, however, and scurried back over to where he'd stood before.

I tilted the glass for her until she indicated she was finished.

She pursed her lips at Bones and her eyes narrowed. "You have an eloquent way of speaking, but there is nothing you could say that would convince me that you won't turn on her one day. Perhaps not today, but it's in your nature as a vampire, no matter how you might attempt to hide from it."

I sighed in defeat, but Bones gestured to Bertrand. "Tell this woman who made you a vampire."

"The priests," was Bertrand's instant reply.

I blinked.

"Go on, tell her why," Bones prodded.

Bertrand looked almost shyly at my mother. "I was accused of heresy by a neighbor and sent before the priests for my trial. One of them held a vampire captive. When I refused to confess any wrongdoing, they made her change me over as punishment. Then *he* found me."

The ominous way he said the word caught my attention. Bones smiled reassuringly at Bertrand before turning his attention back to my mother.

"'He' was Tomas de Torquemada, the head priest of the Spanish Inquisition. Torquemada took Bertrand and had many gruesome years with him. His followers continued to torment Bertrand after Torquemada died. I came across him in 1797 after hearing rumors of a vampire held captive by priests. For over three hundred years, humans had inflicted more agony, torment, and despair on Bertrand than you or I could ever imagine."

Bones rose and I followed him to the door.

"I wager you'd agree that God is not to blame for the horrible actions of a few of His followers, Justina. Likewise, the entirety of my kind is not to blame for the horrible actions of a few. Free will is given to us all, undead or alive. But if you disagree, you can tell Bertrand all about how you feel that his race is worse than yours. I know that he has much to say on the evils of humanity as well."

Bones took my hand and we left. He led me up a nearby staircase and then into a bedroom. We were peeling off each other's clothes before he kicked the door closed.

"He won't hurt her if she pisses him off, will he?" I asked between searing kisses.

Bones snorted. "He wouldn't go near enough to her to injure her, Kitten. Don't fret." Then he smiled as his mouth slid down my neck. "He's the only person I've met who is as prejudiced against a race as your mum. They'll be at this all night."

I smiled as well and pulled him closer. "We'll be at it all night too. I promise."

CHAPTER EIGHTEEN
THE ORIGINAL BEGINNING OF
AT GRAVE'S END

Author's note: Once again, I had to chop the first couple of chapters of my novel in order to start with more "action." Therefore, the scenes below aren't heavy on life-and-death drama. Instead, they're heavy on character interactions. They show Cat attempting to stretch her abilities, how she handles some vampire prejudice from her team, and an additional sex scene between her and Bones. It's ironic: the most common complaints I hear from readers are that I have too many sex scenes or not enough of them. For those of you who fall into the former category, I actually don't publish a lot of the sex scenes I've written, so what's in the books IS the version with less sex. For those of you who fall into the latter category, well, happy reading *wink*.

Oh, and to keep from copying material that hadn't changed much from what had been published, I skipped some scenes in this section, such as the scene where Bones agrees to change Tate into a vampire.

Wind blew my hair in different directions as I peered at the ground fifteen stories below. "Don't jump, lady!" a man called from the street. A brunette stood next to him, and even from up here, I could see that her gaze was wide and anxious.

"You don't have to do this, you know," said the man only ten feet away from me. "You can just come off the ledge and go down the normal way."

"Since when did normal ever apply to me?" I asked and turned my attention back to the concrete below. Jeez, it really was a long way down.

"Are you going to jump, or do I have to toss you off there myself?" An English accent decorated the words from another male bystander below. "Bloody hell, luv, make up your mind. It's chilly out."

One deep breath later, I had gathered my courage. Here went nothing.

I sprang off the balcony as if it were a diving board, keeping my body erect even in the free fall toward the rapidly approaching street. My eyes stung from the rushing air, and that instant surge of adrenaline made my heart pound. Only five more floors to go. Four… Three…

With a burst of inner energy, I willed myself to slow down, picturing waves of thickening water between me and the inevitable impact. The floors I passed stopped blurring together and separated into distinct shapes as my velocity decreased. When I hit the ground, I landed heavily, but I managed to stay upright on both my booted feet.

"Holy shit, Cat, you did it!"

Denise, my best friend, launched herself at me. When she reached me, she threw her arms around me. "That was the coolest thing I've ever seen!"

I laughed and returned her hug. It still felt strange to hear her call me by my real, albeit abbreviated, name. For years she'd known me as Cristine. My mom would forever call me by my birth name, Catherine. As for the English vampire behind her, I would always be Kitten, the name he'd first called me just to be sarcastic.

"You don't want the side effects that come with being half-vampire, Denise. Although lately the perks have outweighed the perils."

Bones, my vampire husband, laughed. "Happy to tip the scales for you, Kitten."

I went from her warm arms to his cool ones, not minding the change in temperature a bit. "You didn't have to catch me this time."

"I told you that you could do it yourself. Just takes willpower and practice."

"I wouldn't have known it was possible if not for you."

That was certainly true. Before him, I hadn't known much about vampires at all, let alone what abilities I'd inherited from my very deadbeat father.

"Can't you keep your hands off her for even a minute?" an irate voice asked, signaling that Tate and the rest of my coworkers had finally made their way down from the roof to join us.

Bones didn't even look up. "No," he said, and kissed me.

Several long moments later, a familiar cough behind me made me push him back.

"Very impressive," said Don, my boss and uncle. "I must admit, Cat, your skills have broadened considerably since Bones has joined the team."

Bones let out a snort of laughter. "You have no idea, old chap."

I elbowed him, fighting the blush that came so easily now. Out of the corner of my eye, I caught Tate scowling at Bones.

"If you're done cuddling, we have actual business to discuss."

I ignored Tate's snippiness and so did Bones. "We'll be right in, but I promised Denise something. She's been waiting, and I'm sure she and Randy want to go home. Bones? Ready?"

He uncurled himself from me and gave a theatrical bow to Denise, his leather coat sweeping the ground. She giggled, letting go of her husband's hand to place her arms around Bones's neck.

"Hang on tight, madam. One amusement park ride, going up."

Bones propelled them straight into the air as though yanked by a string. Denise squealed, but not in fright.

Tate shook his head. "Show-off," he muttered.

Bones took her so high I was the only one who could still see them in the darkness. He flew in a circle around the entire military compound before zooming toward us and then coming down in a rush that had her legs flailing. Bones landed them both neatly on the ground and then handed Denise to her husband, who gaped at him. Randy had never seen him fly before.

Denise was laughing as she wiped away her wind-induced tears. "That was so much fun! If I were you, Cat, I'd make him do that every night! Come on, Randy, let's go. Cat, call me tomorrow after you get up."

They waved good-bye and I watched them leave with a smile. She knew that call wouldn't come until the afternoon. Being half-vampire meant that I wasn't a morning person.

"Can we get on with business now?" Tate said, pulling on my arm for emphasis.

Bones glanced at his hand on me and then smiled.

"Aw, shit," Juan, one of my other captains, mumbled.

In the next instant, Tate was tossed straight upward into the night like he'd been fired from a cannon.

My uncle cleared his throat. "Ahem?" he said pointedly.

"You'd better catch him," I told Bones, speaking louder to be heard over Tate's screams.

"I'll catch the wanker," Bones responded, snatching Tate in his grasp just before the other man splattered on the ground. Then Bones set him on his feet with none of the care he'd shown Denise.

"You keep your hands off her, or I'll forget where you're landing next time."

"Fucking… tomb trash." Tate panted, struggling to regain his breath. He hated heights, and Bones knew that.

Don gave Bones a reproachful look. "Was that really necessary?"

"You'd think the sod would have learned by now," was Bones's short reply.

I rolled my eyes. Don should have learned too. Bones couldn't care less that my uncle disapproved of him chucking Tate like a Frisbee. As far as vampires were concerned, that was a mild response to Tate's continued sulkiness.

"This has been great, but I can't wait to go home," I said.

"Actually, Kitten, we're not going home," Bones said, surprising me. Normally, he couldn't wait to get away from the compound that served as home base for our clandestine "Homeland Security" operation. "I have to leave for a few days. There's something I need to pick up in Australia."

Alone? "You don't want me to go with you?"

He drew me aside until no one from my team could overhear us. "Not this time."

I was instantly on guard. "Why? What's so important you have to go there yourself to get it?"

His face gave nothing away. Over two centuries of learning how to control his features also made Bones an unbeatable card player. "I'll tell you afterward. Will you trust me and not ask why?"

"Depends. Is it dangerous?"

"Not at all. I'll tell you everything when I get back, promise. As a precaution, I told Charles to look out for you while I'm gone. Don is aware not to have anyone on your team try to stake him."

He sounded amused at the thought. Charles, or Spade as I knew him, was one of Bones's oldest friends. He was also a Master vampire in his own right. My team would have a hell of a time trying to take Spade down.

"You are so paranoid."

"Yes." Shortly. Then with a softer tone, "Stay at the compound, Kitten, it's safer. Max might know roundabout where it is, but he never knows when you'll be here."

I grimaced. Max, my father, had hired an assassin to blow my head off when he found out about my existence. Even though my new vampire marriage to Bones meant that I was now under his protection, we both knew that one day my father would come after me. After all, I'd sworn to his face that I would kill him. It was logical to assume he'd try to beat me at my game.

"I'll stay here," I said, trying not to let my reluctance show. "Call me when you land."

He drew me into his arms. "One more thing. Don't go on any jobs. If something comes up, it can wait until I return."

"Fine. I don't like the secrecy of all this, but… I won't ask about it until you get back."

He smiled. "Thank you."

The next day Tate was waiting for me at the entrance to the administrative floor. "So, where did Mr. Wonderful go?"

"Did Spade get here?" I asked, ignoring his question.

"Yep. He's in your office, where he's made himself quite at home. You know, your lover really should give more notice before he orders all operations to come to a halt and takes off."

"Something came up." What, I didn't know, but damned if I'd admit that. "Maybe you can call Bones and tell him he doesn't have your permission? I'm sure he'll turn right back around."

Instead of snapping back a reply, Tate was silent. Then he said, "I'm such a dick sometimes, aren't I?" in such an abashed tone, I stopped in mid-stride.

"Well...," I hedged.

He laughed a trifle grimly. "Half the time he smacks me around, I know I deserve it. I hear some of the things I say, and I can't believe it's me talking. It's hard, Cat. You know I love you; hell, everyone knows it. The team jokes behind my back about it. And you're so happy with him. I never realized how depressed you were before he showed up. It also doesn't help that he's got one hand in your panties at every opportunity, but who can blame him?"

I didn't know how to respond. His directness was refreshing, and his attitude problem of late was now gone. I finally settled on saying, "I wish it wasn't this way, Tate. One day you'll feel differently about me, I know it." And since Bones wasn't there to throw him a hundred feet in the air, I patted his arm.

He grasped my hand and brought it to his lips, faster than I believed him capable of. I should have remembered that he'd been imbibing heavily of vampire blood in preparation for his upcoming change into becoming a vampire.

A slow whistle interrupted whatever Tate had been about to say. I turned around and saw Baron Charles DeMortimer, aka Spade, at the end of the hallway.

"Now I owe Crispin money," he drawled. "He said your fellow would have his hands on you in five minutes. I bet on fifteen. Appears I lose."

Spade always called Bones by his human name, Crispin. Vampires were downright confusing when it came to remembering how the hell to address them.

"Tate, back away," I said, flashing Spade a rueful grin. "Bones probably gave him orders to terminate."

Spade's chuckle didn't deny anything.

Tate let go of my hand and his attitude was back with full force. "I should be flattered. If Boneyard thinks she needs a chaperone around me, I'm further along than I realized."

"You can both cool it," I said tartly. "I've worked almost five years with you, Tate, so I think I can handle not falling back with my legs open in less than three days."

Spade came forward and kissed my cheek. "Crispin doesn't doubt your fidelity. He simply feels that your empathy toward this sod would give him false hope. When you're in love with the unattainable, any scrap of pity can be misinterpreted."

"You arrogant piece of—" Tate began.

"Have you met Don?" I interrupted. Bones might take Tate's incessant insults, but I didn't know how Spade would react. He might snap his neck.

"The gray-haired gentleman? I saw him, but we weren't introduced. This one forgot his manners. He led me straight to your office and then practically guarded the door."

I sighed. "Come with me, Spade, I'll show you around. Tate, don't even start. He and Bones have been friends for over two hundred years, so he has no intentions of infiltrating our operation. God, sometimes you're as suspicious as my mother."

I brought Spade to Don's office and introduced the two men. Don eyed the hand Spade extended to him for a long second before finally shaking it.

"Don't be offended by that," I said with a laugh. "Don's always wary to shake a vampire's hand after seeing what Bones did to someone else's with a handshake."

"Ah, of course," Spade said, his mouth curling down. "Crispin told me he should have just killed Danny Milton that day instead of years later."

Don was shocked. "Bones was the vampire who kidnapped Daniel Milton out of his hospital room when he was under Witness Protection? And killed him, you say?"

Had I forgot to mention that? "Yeah. He went to Ohio looking for me and found Danny instead. Bones green-eyed him into spilling what he knew about me, then killed him so he couldn't repeat it."

I still wasn't happy about Danny's murder, even though there had been no love lost between us. Bones had stated that Danny would have gotten me killed one day and that was that. Dinner for Rodney the ghoul.

Don lifted a shoulder in a half shrug. "One less potential leak to worry about, though so many vampires know about you now, it's hardly relevant anymore."

Spade watched the interaction between me and my uncle with interest. "You are nothing like your brother," he said to Don.

Don straightened. "You know Max? Exactly who are you to my brother?"

"No one except a friend to his sire. I met Max a few times while visiting Ian. Didn't think much of Max—he seemed shifty."

That was an understatement if I'd ever heard one. "Ian made Bones, but who made you?" I asked. "Bones told me the story of that day, but he didn't mention who the other two sires were. Unless it's rude to ask."

Vampire etiquette still escaped me sometimes. It had been so much easier when I just killed them.

Spade waved dismissively, his black, spiky hair moving with the gesture. "You may ask me anything, Cat. Mencheres changed me. You remember him, don't you?"

How could I forget? Unadulterated power aside, he'd settled the dispute over who got to keep me when Ian and Bones were arguing over me like a cut of beef. Ian had gotten the hots for me after I nearly killed him. People get turned on in strange ways, if you ask me.

"I remember Mencheres. He's old, isn't he? He felt... different," was all I said.

Spade smiled. "You look so human I forget you can feel us as another vampire can. Yes, he's very old, and one of the most powerful vampires in existence."

I changed the subject because something about Mencheres unsettled me in ways I couldn't explain. "Let's get you a room, Spade. If you're babysitting me, you may as well have a bed. I'm beat myself—I didn't sleep much last night."

Don turned away in a flash of disquiet. Spade's smile turned knowing. God, me and my big mouth. Why didn't I just draw them a picture?

Spade's grin widened. "Yes, I am rather knackered. I'll take whatever abode is near to yours, thank you. Don"—he faced my boss—"you can be assured I shall be no trouble to your men. My only purpose is to ensure Cat's safety."

Don looked mildly offended. "Bones doesn't think she'll be safe even inside these walls?"

Spade held open the door for me and gave my uncle a look. "He values her above all else. Why wouldn't he be overprotective of what he can't bear to lose?"

Don had no response to that. Neither did I. Instead, I left to show Spade to his room.

There were barracks for my team downstairs on the third sublevel. Simple, military-style accommodations. Two cots to a room. Few amenities. Not that Spade needed one, but they didn't even have private toilets. The shower and bathroom facilities were on either end of the hall. My shower was at the farthest side of the sublevel and it was private, so I offered it to Spade.

"No need for me to put on airs, Cat. You don't want your team thinking all vampires get preferential treatment, do you?"

"Just a thought. You might be shy."

He smiled. "Few vampires are. That's nearly the first thing to go after the heartbeat."

"You've heard that Bones is going to change over Tate, I suppose?" I sat on the cot, adding an extra blanket for myself by taking it from the second bed. There would only be one occupant in this room. Spade didn't need to watch me *that* closely.

"I did. Can't say I agree with the decision, but it's Crispin's choice. I for one wouldn't endow another man with this kind of power if he openly lusted for my wife. I'd kill him instead."

The casual way he made the statement didn't make me doubt its sincerity. Vampires weren't all bark and no bite.

"Maybe he just trusts me. Besides, if he killed Tate out of spite, I'd be furious."

Spade shrugged. "All a matter of respect. Tate shows contempt with his blatant affection for you. One day he may well go too far, and then your wrath will be wasted because the deed will be done."

I fluffed the flat pillow twice before giving up. "I disagree. After all, Bones didn't kill Noah, and I was *engaged* to him."

"Speaking of that, did you know many people in the undead world think Crispin only married you to provoke Ian? Ian also thinks it was a sort of payback, since Crispin knew how much he wanted you. The fact your former fiancé still lives only increases the weight of this rumor. They figure if Crispin truly cared for you, he would have slaughtered your human paramour first thing."

That stopped me in mid-snuggle. "From what Ian and Mencheres both said, you vampires take your blood-vow marriage real seriously. Why would Bones make that kind of commitment if he only wanted to piss off Ian? Seems a bit extreme to take a grudge that far."

"You forget the exception. Death releases a vampire from marriage. You are after all part human, and much more susceptible to demise than a vampire. In your line of work, who's to say you'll even live out the year? That's what people reckon, making Crispin's marriage to you potentially a short commitment."

I had never thought of that. "Do *you* believe that?"

He smiled. "No. Nor does anyone who knows Crispin. Ian would realize it himself if he weren't so fixated on his injured pride. I'm only telling you this so that when you hear it, and you will eventually, you won't let it trouble you."

I smiled back, mollified. "If that's why they think Bones married me, then why did I marry him? What do the busy-body undead gossipers say about that?"

Spade chuckled. "Oh, for his shagging, of course. There wasn't a dry feminine eye in the house the night he declared himself to you. You are as hated as you are envied."

Nice. Just what I liked to be reminded of. "Yeah, Annette was kind enough to fill me in on that. She told me all about his penchant for multiple women at once and how he out-shined the countless other poor schmucks she'd fucked. If there were women crying that night, she cried the hardest."

He shrugged. "What do you care about them? When you were missing, Crispin only thought of finding you."

"Do you know what he's doing now?" I impulsively asked.

Spade started to laugh. "He didn't tell you? That's priceless."

Okay, it must not be dangerous, or I didn't think Spade would be so amused. "Well?" I prodded.

"Wouldn't dream of spoiling the surprise, so don't ask. You'll know before long, I'm certain."

I chucked one of the small pillows at him in exaspera-tion, but he caught it and handed it back to me.

"Go to sleep. I'll speak to you later."

Hours later I reached over, grasping empty air when there should have been cool flesh. My eyes snapped open, and for a second, I thought I was in bed at my old house in Richmond before Bones found me. Alone, like I'd been for years.

The door flew open and Spade was there. "What's wrong?"

"Huh?" I looked around, fully conscious now and remembering why I was in bed alone. Spade relaxed when he saw my cubicle was empty.

"Bad dream?" he queried.

"How would you—" I began, then stopped. "My heart rate, right? My, you're being attentive. Have you been listen-ing while I sleep? I hope I wasn't talking as well."

His lips twitched. "You might have been. The snoring would have drowned that out."

I snorted in an unladylike fashion. "Did Bones tell you to say that? He always makes fun of my snoring, but personally I think it's a lie. My mother never told me I snored."

He laughed outright. "Then she was being gracious."

In mid-stretch, I stopped to give him a jaded look. "You *clearly* don't know her to assume that. Didn't Bones ever tell you about her?"

His laughter subdued, but the twitch was back. "Not in any terms I would repeat."

It didn't offend me. Whatever Bones had called her, she'd deserved it. Trying twice to murder him allowed him a few unsavory comments where she was concerned.

"I'm off to shower and then to the Wreck Room. That's what we call the training room. You're coming, I assume?"

He nodded. "Of course."

Thirty minutes later, I felt a refreshing surge as the sun set and darkness fell. Some things about me were more vampire than human, and my affinity for evening was one of them. Even as a child, I'd had a hard time going to sleep until it was close to dawn. I glanced at my watch as we entered the Wreck Room. Most of the team was inside training. They kept nocturnal hours also due to the nature of what we hunted.

"*Querida*." Juan greeted me, stopping what he was doing and coming over. "Tate tells me you'll be staying with us for a few days. *Qué bueno*, I've missed you since you're always gone with that pale, pulseless man. No offense, *amigo*."

Juan had mellowed considerably about vampires since he'd gotten chummy with Bones. Now he constantly pestered him for tips on how to seduce women. Bones spoke Spanish; I didn't. It scared me to think of all the ribald conversation taking place under my nose, but Bones had laughingly refuted my attempts to discourage him from mentoring Juan in *that* area.

"Kitten, if he's going to shag every woman that holds still long enough, at least he should be doing it properly. Heavens knows I'm helping them more than I am him," had been his reply to my outraged protest.

Jeez, I was in trouble if that memory was enough to make me miss him again.

Spade looked around the training area with interest. It was about the size of two football fields, complete with obstacle courses that had shifting ground, ropes for rappelling up the faux building sides, impromptu mock attacks, and sudden blackouts. Roughly half of the sixty troops that made up my team were here, panting away under the relentless eyes of my four captains.

"Who is that?" one of the newer recruits, Jeffrey, whispered to the sweating guy next to him. Both were on the other side of the huge room, and none of my older team members were nearby to warn them that I could hear them.

"Got to be another monster, look at his skin. It's like hers. Man, she sure likes her dick room temperature."

"Don't," I said, gripping Spade's arm when he would have done something about that. "They don't know I can hear them. Let's see how far they'll take it."

"This one's a brunette," Jeffrey went on, heedless. "Whatcha think? Dracula—or his college roommate?"

They both snickered. Dumb jerks hadn't even looked up to see who was around. They'd learn.

"Cat, I was just talking to Cooper, and... What're you glaring at?" Tate walked up, giving me a curious look.

My hand was still on Spade's arm, just in case. "Who's the kid with Jeffrey? Apparently neither one of them believed the lesson about advanced senses, since they're prattling away like two teenagers. Concentrate. Try to hear them."

Tate cocked his head. With the daily blood he'd been drinking, he should be able to hear them if he mentally turned up the volume in their direction and managed to filter the other noises out.

"You paying attention to this?" Dave asked, sidling up to me.

"Shh!" Impatiently from Tate.

"...at least now we can check out her ass without getting thrown through the air. Bones has radar when it comes to someone looking at his all-you-can-eat treat. She's a full-service menu for him—blood for dinner, pussy for dessert. I bet she—"

"Are you out of your minds?" Angus, one of my seasoned team members, interrupted him. "Sorry, Cat, they were taking a breather," he added to me. "They won't be doing that again soon."

Angus hadn't raised his voice when he switched between speaking to Jeffrey and me. The new recruits stared at him, bewildered.

"She's all the way over there, she can't hear us!"

Angus shook his head. "She heard every word you said. See her hand on that vampire? He's probably licking his lips, deciding which one of you he's going to drink first. Leftovers go to Dave."

"But—" the one named Toby began and got a smack to the back of his head.

"Move it, soldier."

Angus marched the two reluctant men over to us. Juan had been filled in on the dialogue by Dave as they approached, since he hadn't heard on his own.

"Well, hello boys," I drawled when Angus shoved them the last few steps. "Some recruits weren't paying attention to who was around when they spouted off at the mouth, hmmm? So, you two think I'm an all-you-can-eat treat, huh? That's funny, because to a vampire or a ghoul, *you're* food. Dumb food, but hey? Who refuses to eat a burger because the cow was stupid, right?"

They stared at the ground, carefully avoiding my eyes. Now for the fun part.

"Men, fall out!" I roared. The thirty-plus soldiers ceased their activities and came to stand in rows in front of me.

"All right, men, Jeff and Toby here have concerns. Now, who else has been mouthing off about my sleeping with a vampire? Come on, step forward!"

No one moved. There was some shuffling of feet and a few coughs, but no takers. I smiled.

"I'll get the names of the other bigmouths, believe me, and because whoever it was didn't step up, now they'll get both legs broken as well as a severe beating. Don't you know? Cowardice gets you hurt worse. And as for you two." Back to Tony and Jeff. "Like my ass, huh? You're about to get real familiar with it kicking yours!"

I punched both of them in the mouth to punctuate my point. This kind of crap had to stop before someone got hurt. Or worse. Death took anyone, even the imbeciles.

"All right, boys…" I gestured for them to form a circle, then cracked my knuckles and rolled my head around my shoulders. "Let's get started."

My cell phone rang seven hours later. I was still in the Wreck Room, and so were all of the team. Well, those that weren't in the medical lab being pumped full of Brams. I snatched my cell up and answered it breathlessly.

"I miss you so bloody much, Kitten," were Bones's first words. "Thought I was being unselfish to leave you where you are, but it's the last time I'm doing that."

The frustration in his tone made me smile. Bones hated to fly, and he'd been cooped up in a plane for over fourteen hours. At least I'd been able to relieve some of my aggression.

"If I knew that was why you wanted me to stay, I would've insisted on going. We could have renewed our membership to the Mile High Club. You would have enjoyed your flight more."

A snort of laughter squeezed my heart. "Infinitely more. I can't wait to see you again. Tell Don you'll be unreachable for two days, sod how much he'll bellow."

I wasn't about to argue. "I'll tell Don something came up."

His chuckle was instant. "Right you are. Now, let me speak to Charles."

I handed the phone over to Spade, who had wandered by.

"Crispin, I've just had the pleasure of watching her pummel her poor crew into a state of misery these last several hours. She's just spectacular to observe. Liking your solitude?"

The reply he got in return sent Spade into delighted snickers. "Oh, you do sound out of sorts. I owe you money, by the by. It was three minutes before your potential changeling had her hand to his lips. The rest of her men might long for your swift return, but he doesn't. Bloke even seems to like it when she beats him, probably because it's the only time she touches him, wretched sod."

"Tattletale," I barked.

Spade ignored that. "Don't bother yourself over her, Crispin, I won't let her out of my sight. See you soon, mate."

"He sounds entirely too happy for my liking," Bones commented when I was handed back the phone. "Don't make it so pleasant for him, luv. Neglect your toothbrush or something."

That made me laugh, and he made a soft sound when he heard it. "Blimey, I'm getting off before I hop the next flight without retrieving what I've come for. I'll ring you again before I get on the plane to come back. I love you, Kitten."

"I love you too."

The connection severed, but I didn't let go of the phone. Absurdly, I wanted to hold it, like it was a tie to him. Then with a shake of my head, I turned back to my troops.

"Rest time's over, buddies. Who's next?"

There were no takers. I was about to pick the most weary face among them when there was a polite tap on my arm.

"If I may?" Spade said, with a gleam in his eye. "You've owed me a rematch for years."

I laughed at his reference to what had happened the first time we met. "How rough do you want to play? Knives, swords, staffs, or hand to hand?"

"All of it," was his response.

My smile widened. That's the way I liked it too.

"Back off, boys. Watch and learn," I called without taking my eyes off my new opponent. Spade removed his shoes and shirt, leaving him only in his pants so his movements would be less restricted. Since I was in flexible spandex, I didn't have that concern.

"Well, sir." I tossed a staff at him and held mine at attention. "Shall we dance?"

A little over a day later, Spade and I were at the airport, waiting for Bones to come off the plane.

"You don't have to stand here with me," I commented. "Driving me over was enough, thanks, but you know we're taking a shuttle back to the hotel from here."

Spade had been practically glued to my side for the past thirty-eight hours while I'd taken out my frustrations on my men, even calling more in from off-duty. If anyone missed Bones more than I had the past couple of days, it was my team. They had been all smiles as I left for the airport with Spade.

"You're perfect for him, you know," he said, ignoring my advice. "Checking in to the nearest hotel on the airport grounds in advance so all you have to do is run straight there instead of driving the arduous forty minutes back to the compound."

I didn't allow myself to blush. "He'll be exhausted from the flight and the time change. I'm only being considerate," I said primly.

Spade didn't comment. After a moment, his eyes narrowed. "I can feel him, he's almost here. Don't bother with a shuttle, I'll drive you to the hotel myself. See you in front."

I stood as close to the arrivals entryway as security would allow, craning my neck to see around the throngs of people. True to Spade's prediction, I soon saw Bones striding though the passengers waiting to collect their luggage. He had only one bag slung over his shoulder, and he moved with long, predatory steps that easily outdistanced those in front of him. His eyes met mine, and the rush of joy I felt at seeing him made my heart skip a beat.

Bones pulled me to him, slanting his mouth over mine before I could even smile at him. I wrapped my arms around his neck as he lifted me off my feet, running his free hand down my back.

I could feel people staring at the blatant display, but I didn't care. Only the knowledge that the hotel room beckoned gave me the incentive to push him back.

"Let's get your stuff and leave. Spade's waiting with the car."

He lifted his head but kept his eyes closed for a moment. When he opened them, they were hazel but not glowing. Blazing emerald would have attracted too much attention.

"This is all I have, we can go. Best hurry. Charles might have to pull off the road and take a walk, because I want you right now."

The flat concentration in his voice made my belly clench in anticipation. We nearly ran to the exit, his hand gripping mine.

Spade had the passenger door open. Bones threw his single suitcase across the seat and then gathered me into his embrace, slamming the door behind him. The car took off without even a hello exchanged between the two men since Bones had already returned to kissing me.

"Wait," I gasped, coming up for air. "We're almost at the hotel I checked us in to."

"Brilliant you are, Kitten." He smiled. Then to Spade, "Drive faster."

"Absolutely, mate. I can see you need your sleep." Laughter vibrated under his words. "Ah, here we are. You can ring me later about how you fared."

I'd picked a room on the top floor near the elevators. Less people to disturb if we were closer to the low-flying planes. In the elevator, I dropped my plastic room key as Bones kissed my throat and rubbed his body sensually against mine. He picked it up, glaring at the shocked elderly couple who had the misfortune to be in there with us.

"Mind your own business," he snapped.

Thankfully they didn't get off on our floor.

The hall was empty when we stepped off the elevator. I jerked my head in the direction of our door, already unzipping his pants. We stumbled into the room where a Do Not Disturb sign already hung on the knob. When I checked in, I knew we'd need it.

"Don't even think of foreplay," I said, already burning with desire. I threw off my coat and backed toward the bedroom. Bones followed, mouth locked on mine as his hands slid underneath my skirt to bunch it at the waist. The mattress was high off the ground, hitting the back of my thighs as his upper body covered me while he remained standing. Fingers ripped off the thin material of my panties. He cast them away, and I wrapped my legs around him while he thrust inside me.

"Yes, oh God, yes." I groaned, thrashing under him.

He straightened for better leverage, gripping my waist with one hand. The other untied the sweater I wore, unclipped my front bra snap and unbuttoned his shirt. His pants had fallen to the floor already.

"You're so hot inside. Like wet fire. I love to feel you, Kitten."

Each pumping motion of his body felt sharper to me. My skin was oversensitized from PMS, my breasts fuller and more tender, loins heightened to exquisite sensation. Bones didn't have to increase pace or force to feel like he was slicing through me straight to the center. Moans became shouts and shouts became screams of ecstasy. Nerve endings stretched, winding faster and tighter together until they snapped with a rush of aching heat that vibrated from the inside out. Even my fingers tingled.

"A thousand tiny hands." Bones groaned in satisfaction. He slid up the bed to where he lay fully on top of me, still pulsating within.

"What?" I could barely speak.

Pale arms held me closer. He nuzzled my neck, pushing my hair back. "That's what it feels like inside you when you come. Like a thousand miniature hands pulling me in deeper, squeezing me, burning me. It's incredible. You strip my will from me each time. Do you know what I'm going to do to you now?"

No idea I would have responded, but all that came out was a cry. He rotated his hips in an erotic twist that arched my spine and made me rake my nails down his back.

"I'm going to bite you," he whispered.

I wound my fingers in his hair and pressed him to my throat.

A low chuckle rumbled in his chest. "Not there, luv. Here."

He ran his hand between our joined bodies to rub his thumb over my clitoris. I jumped from the contact. He moved down my body, his other arm holding my legs. His tongue delved into the top of my crease before flicking in a series of licks. Then a slow glide from top to bottom, seeking. I trembled under his mouth, helpless. Somehow my skeleton had been replaced with jelly. He moaned and then swirled his tongue over my clit.

"I love you," he murmured, then bit.

The white light descended, blotting out everything in a blizzard of rapture that transcended pain while matching agony for sheer pleasurable intensity. It took reason, will, and sanity on a merry ride through the wonderland of chaos. Time blinked by, minutes fusing into microseconds. When my eyes focused again, Bones had his hand clapped over my mouth to silence the shrieks that couldn't be stopped. He shuddered repeatedly on top of me, in the throes of his own release, before relaxing with a final groan.

Shivers still rocked me. His hand left my mouth since my screams had died down to ragged panting. My throat was sore from the muffled cries. The first time he had done that to me, I'd been insensible for thirty minutes and lost my voice. Since I figured I could still talk, this must have been shorter.

"Blimey, now I can think straight again. I felt like a rabid animal before. Knew I could only hold out another ten minutes, and how is that fair to you?"

Who in the hell is he talking to? I wondered in a daze of afterglow. Chiseled arms lifted me and carried me into the bathroom.

"Still out of it, hmm? Just as well. You'd faint if you saw the bed. Broken like a bunch of twigs. No one makes anything durable anymore."

Author's additional note: *If you're wondering why Bones went to Australia in this version, he went there to pick up the red-diamond engagement ring. He proposed to Cat right after this scene, and Cat's acceptance, as well as Bones calling her mother to give her the news, remained pretty much unchanged from the original version to the published one.*

Chapter Nineteen
The Dress Shop

*Author's note: This deleted section shows Cat, Denise, Annette, and Justina going dress shopping for Cat's upcoming wedding. Sound like a recipe for disaster? *grins* It was. It ended up being cut because my editor thought that it was funny, but she wanted to get to the main plot faster. As you can tell, a lot of scenes were cut in an attempt to keep the pacing as tight as it could be. I understand the reasoning, but I admit that I hated cutting scenes like this. I love showing the characters doing "normal" things—or at least, attempting to—and in hindsight, I think At Grave's End could have used a few more light scenes to balance out the darker ones.*

"I must be high," I mumbled as I waited at Denise's two weeks later.

She gave me a sympathetic pat on the arm. "You're right. You must be stoned, cracked, smacked, juiced, whatever. I just hope you're also armed, because you're going to need it."

Randy smiled at his wife. "Honey, I'm sure it won't be that bad. If Cat's mother agreed to go with her to pick out the material for her wedding dress, then she must have mellowed. As for the other lady, Annette, well, she'll be on her best behavior, no doubt."

"*You* must be high," I amended with a shake of my head. "First of all, my mother is only going so she can ruin

219

everything. Second, the last time that other 'lady' was on her best behavior, I came *this close* to killing her."

Annette might be a first-class slut, but she was still the chicest woman I'd ever met. Bones had been cautiously pleased by my offer to include Annette in today's excursion. One phone call later and here I was, waiting for her and my mother to arrive. Annette had come all the way from London. My mother was pissed about driving an hour to get to Denise's.

"What does your mother know about Annette?" Denise prodded me.

"Oh, nothing much. Just that she's an old friend of Bones's who also happens to be a vampire. That guaranteed my mother's hatred."

"This is going to be one wacky wedding," Denise said with a grin.

Probably. "Annette's here," I grumbled. Two minutes later, a car pulled up in the drive.

Annette DeWitt, formerly Lady Ormsby, stepped out of the shiny silver Mercedes as gracefully as if it were a throne. Her strawberry-blond hair was arranged in a purposefully messy chignon, and she wore a navy-blue tailored jacket over matching designer pants. She went to the door and rapped once.

"Jeez," Denise whispered as she peered through the window, then looked at me in consternation. "Do I have something in my teeth?"

"That's exactly how I felt when I first met her." I sighed and went to answer the door. "Hello, Annette."

Champagne-colored eyes considered me from a lightly lined face that was smolderingly attractive. Annette had been thirty-six when Bones changed her. Times were different back in the seventeen hundreds, so she looked around forty-five, but she made it look good. Real good, damn her.

"Cat, I'm going to say this straightaway so there's no misunderstanding." Her accent was pure upper-crust Brit, each syllable perfectly pronounced. "I know it's because of you that I'm here. Crispin would never have done this on his own; he's still too cross with me. I behaved quite dreadfully when I thought there was still a chance for him and me, but then he bound himself to you and that settled it. In truth, I'm astonished you showed so such maturity as to include me in your human celebrations."

"Thank you for clearing that up, and I'm glad I impressed you with my grown-up behavior. The fact of the matter is, Bones cares for you. I love him, I trust him, so here you are. As long as you can tolerate the new standards of behavior around him, I have no issue with you."

There. Didn't that sound better than *fuck off, you condescending bitch!*

"This is Denise, my best friend, and her husband Randy," I added. "Guys, this is Annette."

After proper greetings were exchanged, she took a seat in the living room on the sofa. We were waiting for my mother, who was late.

"Drink, Annette?" Randy offered.

Her lips curled. "Thank you, but I had one from a flight attendant on my way over."

I closed my eyes. If she said that kind of thing in front of my mother, the shit would hit the fan. I was sure the drink she referred to hadn't been on the beverage cart.

"Oh, by the way, Cat," she went on. "I have Crispin's birthday present in the trunk. Do remind me to give it to you to take home."

"It better not have a pussy." The words flew out before my mental filter could stop them.

Denise spewed her iced tea all over Randy in a fit of laughter.

Both of Annette's perfectly shaped eyebrows rose. "I seem to remember you informing me those items were off the gift list. If they're back on, I'll have to rethink your wedding present."

Poor Denise was going to choke. Randy pounded her on the back while hiding his own smile.

"I'm sorry." I hated to apologize, especially to her, but in this case, she deserved it. "To tell you the truth, the thought of spending the day with my mother is enough to give me a Tourette's seizure, and I also have to apologize to you in advance for all the terrible things she will no doubt say."

"She's aware of my former relationship with Crispin and disapproves?" Annette didn't sound like she cared. Why would she? She'd certainly been proud of it.

I gave a short bark of laughter. "No, all she knows is you're a vampire. What did Bones tell you about her?"

Annette shrugged. "Practically nothing."

I stared at her. "He didn't warn you? You're right. He *is* still pissed at you, and not just a little."

The sound of a car pulling up tightened my gut with trepidation. She was here.

My mother swept into the room with none of Annette's gliding grace. Instead, she had a stomping, angry gait that was punctuated by her slamming the front door behind her.

"So this is the latest bloodsucking murderer you've befriended, Catherine."

No "hello, how ya doing, nice to see you." Not her. Just straight to the throat and tear. She and vampires had a lot in common.

"Mom, are you going to say hi to Denise and Randy? You like them, remember? They both have pulses." Dryly.

"Barely, and thanks to *that* one"—a stiff finger pointed at Randy—"who had your evil ex-lover in his wedding party, you left a wonderful man who was devoted to you. Each day I cry when I think of Noah. Isn't there any chance you would reconsider...?"

"Don't go there, Mom." Now I was upset. Didn't she know it was tacky to discuss reconciling with one's ex-fiancé before shopping for a wedding dress to marry the new one? "Noah is so much better off without me, I can't even articulate. I thought I'd throw that in, since the fact that I never loved him seems unimportant to you."

Annette rose from the couch and extended her hand. "Hello. I am Annette De Witt, charmed to meet you. I'm afraid Cat never told me your name."

My mother stared at her hand with more revulsion than if it had been a snake. "My alias is Justina Russell, and if you think I'm dumb enough to *touch* one of your vile, iniquitous paws when you've probably killed more people than the plague, you're very mistaken."

Denise handed me the gin bottle without bothering to include a glass. I ripped the top off and took a long, deep pull and then another. And another.

Annette withdrew her hand and gave me a look of growing awareness.

"I see now what you mean, Cat. Crispin is clever in his omissions, is he not? Very well. She's not the first outraged mortal I've encountered. Justina." Back to my mother. "You say you bear the name Russell? How appropriate, since it's what your daughter's married name will be. I hear Crispin's marrying her under his birth name—how sentimental."

My mother gazed between us in momentary confusion. "Who the hell is Crispin, Catherine?"

"That's Bones," I supplied. She had this coming. "His real name is Crispin Russell. But he called himself Bones after he became a vampire. Something about being raised in an ancient graveyard."

She looked aghast. "You called yourself by his name when we left Ohio? And let me use it as well? God, Catherine, were you never free of that scum!"

I could tell Annette wanted to smack her for how she was talking about Bones. She knew, however, that any misstep with my mother wouldn't be overlooked, even if it was in his defense. Wisely, she pursed her lips and didn't comment.

"Mom, there isn't enough gin on the market for me to be able to handle you. I let you unleash some steam since you just can't help yourself, but that's enough. I am marrying that vampire whether you like it or loathe it. Don't bother; I know, I know, you loathe it. But if you call him even *one* more insulting name, I'm going to throw you out. That goes for in the car too. Or the dress shop. Or anywhere else we may be. You'll walk home, because I won't listen to your poison about him. Can you behave long enough to be my mother? Or am I saying good-bye to you now?"

There was silence as she considered this. Time enough for me to take another drink.

Finally she settled for a muttered curse on all things undead and straightened her shoulders. "I'm going with you. Someone has to make certain you look presentable when you go to the altar like a lamb to slaughter."

"Right," I said wearily. "Let's go."

We took my car since it was the only one with bulletproof glass. Behind us I saw Dave and Cooper following at a discreet distance. Bones had flatly refused to let me drive around without some kind of escort, and they'd chosen to remain unseen. Smart men. After all, they'd met my mother before.

We went to Magdalena's, a lovely dress shop that specialized in handmade wedding gowns. I would have just shopped at a regular store and gotten it adjusted, but Bones had looked at me as though I'd lost my mind when I suggested that. The miser in me protested at spending all the extra money just for personal fittings and fabric selection. Still, it made him happy, so I was here.

The owner's name was Elise, despite the shop name, and she greeted us warmly as we walked in.

"Come in, please, you must be Cat. How beautiful you are, what coloring!"

Oh shit, bad way to start out. My mother's lips twitched with a thousand stinging comments, but she managed not to do more than grunt. My looks came from my father, down to my luminescent skin that was just a shade too creamy to be human.

Elise went on, heedless. "Which one of you lovely ladies is the mother? From your pale skin and strawberry hair, I'd guess it was you!" she gaily said to Annette.

Denise laughed and then began to cough to cover it.

My mother bristled. "*I* am her mother," she snapped.

Elise attempted to cover the slip and instead made it worse.

"Oh, of course. Are you two ladies sisters, then?" She indicated Annette with an inclination of the head. Denise lost it again.

"Look, Mom, gloves!" I yanked my mother safely away from the shopkeeper and ground out a warning between clenched teeth. "Don't even. Long walk back, remember?"

It wasn't really Elise's fault for her gross misidentification. Come to think of it, I probably *did* resemble Annette more than my mother. Of course, Annette was four inches shorter and far more voluptuous, but still. Our skin and hair similarities were there. The sister remark hadn't been without reason, either. Annette and my mother looked about the same age, even though in human years Annette was younger. Since they were shopping with the bride, it had been an honest mistake.

"They're not related," Denise hastily murmured to Elise when she ceased giggling. "Um, this is a friend of the groom's. Cat's mother is a little disapproving of him, so ignore any obscenities."

"Ah." Knowing smile. Apparently she'd dealt with this kind of thing before, but on a much lower scale, I'd bet. "Well, ladies," she continued, coming over and taking my arm. "Let's look at the fabrics, shall we? Are you interested in white, ecru, cream, eggshell, mother-of-pearl, alabaster, or another color?"

"I have no idea." I sighed. "Let's see them all."

Who had any idea dresses came in such a multitude of materials? I'd grown up on a farm where denim was the staple of my wardrobe, and the clothes I wore on jobs were mainly of the sleazy variety. I felt lost in a sea of silk, satin, velvet, brocade, and lace. We hadn't even gotten to style yet, and it had been over an hour.

"What about this one?" Denise fingered a bolt of delicate-looking lace and held it up.

I obediently uncurled myself from underneath a pile of cloth and went to her.

"It's so soft, Cat. Feel it," she urged.

She was right, it was soft. Holding it felt like holding spiderwebs, and the stitching was as intricate as one.

Elise beamed. "Our most luxurious lace, straight from Italy. Against your skin it would look magnificent."

Annette reached for it just as my mother did, and dear old mom snatched her hand back to avoid their fingers grazing.

"How much is it?" my mother bluntly asked.

Elise carelessly rattled off a number that had me dropping the fabric like it had burned me.

"On to the next one," I said.

Annette took the lace swath and held it next to my arm, ignoring me.

"It's perfect." Her tone was brusque. "You'll look radiant. Crispin means too much to me for me to watch him marry someone that looks like a peasant. His closest friends will be there—don't you want to look your best on your wedding day?"

I smiled tightly and spoke so low no one but she could hear me. "It costs more than half the cars on the fucking road. Are you out of your mind?"

She didn't bother with the same subtlety. "Cat, you must be the most ignorant person alive."

My brows shot up.

"Do you have any idea how much bloody money Crispin has? What do you think he's been doing with it after all those jobs over the centuries?"

Elise backed away a foot. Denise pulled my mother out of harm's way, anticipating a bloodbath at any moment.

"You know, Annette." Acidly. "In the time I've spent with Bones, a total of just under a year combined, we never got around to discussing his portfolio. Maybe it's because I was too busy either fucking him or trying not to get killed, I don't know which!"

That put a perplexed look on Elise's face.

Annette advanced a step and pointed emphatically at my hand. "That stone on your finger is worth more than seven million dollars, you blithering ingrate. Do you know how many red diamonds there are in the world today of similar size and color? Only one, and it's smaller. The cost of your dress and this wedding won't even put a dent in Crispin's funds, so will you stop acting like a child and think about him for a moment? What *he* would want? You could at minimum concern yourself with his wishes."

"You are the biggest bitch I have ever met," I burst out. "God, if you hadn't saved his life two hundred years ago, I'd stake you and wear your blood for a week!"

Elise looked alarmed now. She backed away farther.

"Do it, Catherine!" My mother played the cheerleader. It was the first thing she'd agreed with me on in months.

"But," I continued in clenched tones, "you did save his life. More than that, according to him, you've stood by him loyally through the years. I think he more than thanked you by fucking you up one side down the other, but that's just me."

A horrified gasp came from my mother. She wasn't as enthused now.

"However, Bones has put up with so much shit from me, I can stand to deal with you. You're absolutely right, Annette, the lace is gorgeous. Elise, get back over here. We're taking this one. Now let's pick a frigging style and then get the hell out of here."

"Catherine!" My mother pulled on my arm, shocked. "This *creature* and that *animal* together, what is wrong with you? How can you tolerate that?"

I was in no mood. "Mom, probably every female who will be at my wedding except for you and Denise has at one point in time fucked the groom."

Annette gave a shrug in concurrence.

"I'm not *wild* about it, but there you are. What can I say? He was busy in his years, but as long as he keeps his cock away from anyone but me from now on, we're square."

That was the last straw for Elise. She turned and sprinted for the phone, presumably to call 911.

"Get her, Annette, and make her happier," I instructed needlessly.

She had already grabbed Elise and bared her fangs. This caused my mother to charge forward, but I held her back.

"You are not my daughter if you stand by and let her murder that woman!" she railed.

Even Denise gave me an inquiring blink.

"Watch, Mom."

Annette bit into Elise's neck. Her eyes were now emerald green. They'd changed the instant she touched the shop owner. My mother screamed. Thank God we'd chosen to be the last appointment of the day and the store was empty. I watched as Annette took a few pulls and then daintily scratched her thumb, pressing it to the punctures on Elise's neck. The wounds closed almost as fast as the cut in Annette's thumb. One vampire bite, erased from sight.

Annette stared into Elise's dazed face. "Your customers have decided on a fabric. Your last recollection since giving the price is that the bride accepted it. Now you're going to help them choose the style. That is all."

There wasn't a drop of blood on anything, even Annette's lips. After centuries, you could be neat if you wanted to. Denise was openly fascinated by the exchange. She'd never seen a vampire feed before, except the one who'd tried to kill her when we met and I saved her life. Elise nodded once and smiled, a contented expression on her face.

Annette's eyes bled back to their normal color. Once free of their entrapping glow, Elise shook her head and then brightly announced she would begin showing the styles.

"Perfect," I stated. "You all go on, we'll be just a second."

The three of them left us and went to the other side of the shop.

"Do you see now, Mom? That's how easily a vampire can control someone's mind. Hell, Master vampires can do it without even taking blood, and Bones is a Master vampire. He could have changed your attitude problem with him countless times before, but he hasn't. If he were a low-life scum like you say he is, why wouldn't he?"

"Is that why you can't leave him? God, Catherine, is this how he keeps you under this thrall?"

I sniffed in annoyance. "He doesn't have me in any thrall. That stuff doesn't work on me, Mom, because I'm half-vampire. Believe me, many of them have tried over the years. I wanted you to see this... so you'd know that what happened with you and my father could have been orchestrated. He could have tranced you into doing whatever he wanted, and you would have believed anything he told you..."

If I'd punched her, she would have looked less stunned. My father was an asshole, no doubt about that, but the two of them had different versions about the night I was conceived. My mother called it rape. Max said it was consensual and that she'd only cried foul after she saw his glowing eyes and realized he wasn't human. She had no idea I'd ever met him, let alone heard his side of that story, and I wasn't trying to say who was right. My motivation was to show that she would have been compelled to believe whatever he'd said. Especially his laughing assertion that all vampires were demons. I'd heard that since I was sixteen, and it had been a hard thing to bear, thinking half of me had roots in the pit of hell. Max said he told her that because he thought it was funny. Yeah, real funny. Made a laugh riot out of my childhood. Maybe this scene with Elise wouldn't make a dent in my mother's beliefs, but she deserved to know this much at least.

Elise was musing over selections with Denise and Annette, oblivious that she had just been a blood donor to the undead. It was how vampires managed to remain undetected by the rest of the world. As far as ghouls, well... Dead men told no tales, as the saying went, and there was no shortage of natural deaths for them to choose their meals from. My mother would faint if she knew most funeral homes were owned by ghouls. Both species had that in common: they didn't need to kill to eat, they only killed if they wanted to.

Then again, the same could be said for humans. I guess in that regard, *all* species were equal.

"Come on," I said softly. "Let's go see the styles."

She gave me a sharp look but pursed her lips and didn't say anything else.

Bones came out of the front door before we came to a complete stop in Denise's driveway. How he got there, I didn't know. Randy could have picked him up, or he could have flown from the compound, I suppose.

Annette straightened in her seat and smoothed a hand across her hair. My mother, who hadn't seen him in about two months, mumbled something about vultures.

Bones just gave her a merry smirk and tapped on her window. "Justina, don't you look fetching? If you weren't about to be my mother-in-law, I'd be tempted to steal a kiss."

"I just bet you would, you depraved whoreson!" she replied, incensed. With her car available, she wasn't concerned about walking home anymore. "And here I thought you only preyed on young girls, but clearly your debauchery runs the full gamut of feminine ages!"

Bones arched a brow as he opened my car door. "Didn't *you* ladies have an interesting chat? Annette, you haven't been entertaining your companions with tales of me again, have you?"

There was thinly veiled menace in his tone. Even though a shallow part of me enjoyed his displeasure with her, I spoke up in her defense.

"She didn't spill it, I did. Along with a few other points of interest regarding your past love life. I might have lowered my mother's opinion of you, I'm afraid."

"That wouldn't be possible," she growled and stomped off toward her car.

"Lovely to meet you," Annette called out after her.

A rude expletive was my mother's response as she drove off without even saying good-bye to me. Typical.

"Crispin, that was a particularly wretched thing for you to do," Annette said. "That woman called you more names than I have ever stood to hear without killing someone. She will destroy your wedding."

"Hallo, Annette, and you well deserved it. Don't fret about my wedding, she'll pull it together. She loves her daughter. She just doesn't know how to express it."

He's giving her more credit than she deserves, I thought darkly. Instead of throwing rice, my mother would probably fling silver knives.

Annette flicked a piece of lint off his dark shirt, her hand lingering a second longer than necessary. "You look well."

Bones pulled me closer. "I'm very happy," he said simply.

I almost pitied her. She loved him, and it must hurt like a motherfucker to see him with me. If I were honest, I'd admit I didn't blame her for her prior attempt to sabotage us. If she didn't care for him enough to fight dirty to try to keep him, I wouldn't respect her at all.

"Where are you staying, Annette?" I asked. Respect aside, I wasn't about to have her over for the next few weeks until the wedding.

She glanced at Bones and hesitated.

"She's staying with Tate, Kitten," he answered for her. "Helping him with learning our customs and such. Invaluable opportunity for him, really. He'll learn far more with her than he would with me."

My hand tightened on his. Tate had slept with her before, mostly to spite me since Bones and I had been in the same house at the time, and apparently Annette thought he'd been worthy of a repeat performance.

I raised a brow. "Oh, I'm sure he'll learn plenty of new tricks." Wait until I got ahold of Tate later, that hypocritical son of a bitch. He hadn't said a word to me.

Annette overlooked my pointed observation. "He'll make a strong vampire, Crispin, but one day he'll be trouble for you because of her."

Bones shrugged. "I have my reasons, aside from my promise to her uncle. I'm not concerned."

"Coming inside or leaving?" Denise asked us, heading to the door.

"Leaving, regrettably," Bones smiled. "Duty calls. Kitten's boss wants to meet Annette. I think he's fretting she'll take a bite out of his top soldier if she stays with him."

Denise giggled. "Didn't she already?" Okay, so I told her *every*thing.

"Love you, thanks for your help," I said.

Annette got in her car to follow us to the compound, and Denise was in the process of closing the front door, but then she flung it back open with a bang.

"Wait!" Denise started laughing so hard she could barely speak. "Don't forget Bones's birthday present in Annette's trunk. It might run out of oxygen!"

She dissolved in a seizure of giggles that bent her over. Bones looked at me in wonder. "How much gin did you drink?"

I slid into the car and fastened my seat belt. "The whole bottle. But that part I let slip before I touched it. Annette told me to remind her that your present was in the trunk, and I told her it better not have a pussy. Sorry, it just flew out."

He snorted with laughter. "I love you, Kitten."

I smiled back. "I love you too."

CHAPTER TWENTY
AFTER THE S&M CLUB

Author's Note: This scene originally took place at the end of chapter 12 in At Grave's End. *It was later cut because I thought the sex scene would be somewhat gratuitous and might drag down the pacing. So why did I write it to begin with? In this version, Bones intends to leave Cat at the compound for the next few days while he goes out of town to secretly check out a lead on Patra, so "going away" sex made sense. Since Bones didn't leave in the published version of the book, having them pause for uninhibited nookie felt like it took away some of the seriousness of what Bones and Cat were facing at the time, and I deleted the scene.*

We flew back to the compound, dropping the humans off first at a local military hospital for checkups. Actually, we didn't even have to give them new memories of the night. All three knew about vampires and ghouls and had gone willingly to the club with them as playthings. The only thing they hadn't figured on was the merriment turning so sour. *Not my business,* I reminded myself. My job was to save them, not lecture them on their lifestyle.

When we reached the third sublevel, Bones tugged me right past Don's office where my uncle waited up for the evening's report. He didn't reduce his stride as Tate called after us.

"Where do you think you're going?"

Both of us had coats on for propriety as well as practicality. Miami might not have needed the outerwear, being still seventy-plus degrees even in November, but Virginia was chilly. Mine was belted modestly over my skank wear; his flew open with a swirl and trailed behind him.

"Less than three hours before dawn," Bones replied. "I'm not wasting it on show-and-tell. Not with you sods, that is. He'll get our input come the morning."

I would have argued, but what Tate didn't know was that Bones had an early flight tomorrow. We'd have to be at the airport at nine thirty, and it was a half-hour drive. For vampires, that was practically the crack of dawn. He was right. Time was of the essence.

Bones led me to the only really private place I had at the compound—the shower. Since I was the sole female on the team, there were no concerns about anyone coming in and interrupting us. In recent months, Don had even enlarged the area, adding sufficient room for Bones to have closets, his penchant for showering with me instead of the men infamous. Don had also added a chair and ottoman to the corner of the room. I supposed a bed would have been too blatant. Besides, we'd never required one before.

Bones locked the door behind us, wrenching me into his arms as soon as it shut. "I have been waiting all bloody night to do this," he growled, kneeling in front of me. He took off my jacket, threw it aside, and then snapped the chains which held up my leather bra. His lips locked over my nipple, that spike in his tongue grating the sensitive peak in a way that made me gasp.

Yet in addition to the heat rising inside me, a stab of jealousy remained. "How do you stand it, Bones?" I wasn't talking about the discomfort it must have caused putting in those pieces of jewelry. "Dave had to slap me to prevent me from ripping that bitch's head off when she kissed you. How do you watch me, job after job, making out with other men to lure them into position?"

It was hard to form coherent words when he paid such thorough attention to the task in front of him. Both my nipples soon throbbed, and his hands hadn't been idle.

A muffled grunt sounded against my skin. "Helps that they're dead soon after touching you, Kitten. I'm old enough to have learned patience, but no, it's not easy. Let's not bother about that now though. You have a question to answer, remember?"

Bones picked me up and carried me to the chair without breaking contact with his lips. He spread my legs, making me tremble, and then nuzzled my leather panties before hooking his fangs into them and dragging them down. His incisors neatly split the fabric while his tongue snaked inside the rents. Multitasking at its finest.

I moaned and gripped his shoulders. God, I loved what his mouth could do to me and told him so in a voice made rasping with desire. He laughed into my flesh, licking and probing with knowing, wet strokes that felt even sharper by the chafing of the prong. By the time my orgasm hit, I was sweating and arching against him, digging my nails into the pale arms locked around my waist to hold me closer. The scream that tore from my throat at the rush of ecstasy would prove whether or not the new insulation Don had installed held. If it didn't, they could probably hear me all the way back in my uncle's office.

"You're so beautiful," Bones whispered, sliding up to cradle me. I kissed him greedily, not caring that his fangs nicked my lips before I drew his tongue into my mouth to suck on it. Metal clanged together as his chain-link pants fell to the floor before the hard length of his body pressed on top of mine.

My nails scratched down his back while I wrapped my legs around his hips. "Now. Now. I want you so much."

Another chuckle, but throatier. "Ah, pet, I love how anxious you get. Yes, now, and I have one more surprise for you…"

A hard thrust bent my spine, eliciting a strangled cry while I arched back so strongly that I almost fell off the chair. Bones gathered me into his arms before lowering me to the floor, grasping my hips as he plunged deeply into me once again.

"You didn't," I managed, shuddering at the feel of added friction to the hardness sliding in and out of me.

His lips curled slyly. "There were two more silver rings. Call me a method actor. Hate to waste a good prop."

"That is… going to hurt… like hell… taking them out," I said around the raggedness of my breathing. I squeezed my legs tighter around him, reveling in the feel of him moving inside me with increasing fervor. That ring seemed to add a sharper edge to the pleasure, making my nerve endings clench and contract in growing sensual demand. I played with the silver rings in his nipples, gently tugging and twisting them while I kissed him as if I were trying to drown.

"Faster. Harder. More." In any order.

Bones complied, thrusting with an intensity that had me shouting in delirious bliss before begging him to stop. Or not to stop. I couldn't keep it straight. Either way, he had his own agenda. When we struck our bargain with Don, Bones had agreed to follow my orders at work, lecherously asserting he'd rather have control in the bedroom. I hadn't objected, which turned out to be the smartest decision I'd ever made. He dominated me in bed or out, as in this case, we were on the floor, and I loved every moment of it. When it came to anything sexual, Bones was truly a master.

CHAPTER TWENTY-ONE
WHITE WEDDING

Author's note: *I can't count how many times readers have asked me if Cat and Bones would ever have a "real" wedding. In the published books, they only had the vampire binding ceremony because their plans for a traditional wedding were ruined by events in* At Grave's End, *but in the original version, they did have their white wedding. It ended up being cut because of—you guessed it—pacing concerns, and also because my editor felt that it signified a happy-ever-after even though the series was far from done. I'd intended to put this in a later book, but I could never find a place where it would fit. Eventually I decided not to put it in the final books because it seemed to trivialize their prior blood-binding ceremony. Bones always considered that as the only wedding that mattered. It took Cat a little longer to feel the same way, but she did. In the scene where Don dies in* This Side of the Grave, *she thinks about how that strange, very unconventional blood-binding ritual was so much more important than any fancy dress or extravagant party, but both did happen in these deleted scenes, and I'm glad to finally share them you.*

The end of this section also contains a never-before-published sex scene where I broke a worldbuilding rule, so if it reads like what Bones and Cat do isn't possible according to previously known vampire abilities, you're right. That's why I've never tried to duplicate this scene in any other books. And for those of you who might be thinking "another sex scene?" this shows that I probably ended up

deleting more of those than I published. When I write, I let the char-
acters lead and then edit out later what I think is too gratuitous.

"How in the hell did you breathe in these things when you were human? My ribs are broken in ten places!"

Annette ruthlessly tightened the corset strings. "Back in the day, these things were much more constrictive. Be grateful."

"I think you're enjoying this a bit too much, to tell the truth." I grunted. "A little looser, please. I *do* want to be alive through the ceremony, even if pulses are the minority here."

They were, no mistake about that. When we had discussed the wedding, Bones said he wanted a small, intimate gathering. You'd think after years of dealing with vampires, I would know better. "Small and intimate" to him meant well over two hundred people. After two centuries, he'd built up a much larger network of friends than I had in my twenty-five years. Thank God he hadn't wanted a large wedding; it would have swelled to over a thousand.

It was Christmas Day, my wedding day. I hadn't seen Bones since yesterday morning. I'd even refused to speak to him today, finding myself unexpectedly superstitious. Maybe Denise had rubbed off on me.

Denise grinned at me as she held my dress up for me to step into. My mother hadn't been much help. She was in the corner of the room, crying. Even the Valium I'd snuck into her tea hadn't calmed her, but at least it kept her cursing at a minimum.

"There," Annette said with one last tug.

At last she was satisfied, which meant I was in pain. Silly me thought to pay homage to my groom's eighteenth-century days and had a corset made to go under my dress. Barring a few modern additions, it looked like the real deal.

Just cut a little sexier and with convenient snap buttons at the crotch. I even had on silk stockings.

I gingerly put one foot and then the other in the dress, praying I didn't fall and rip the whole damned thing. My mother would have cried tears of joy. One ruined wedding, just what the doctor ordered. Denise had just started to zip me up when the parlor door opened without a knock.

Spade came inside right as Denise finished with my zipper. At least now my chest was covered instead of my breasts bulging over the top of the low-cut corset.

"Crispin sent me," Spade said. His lips twitched. "He wasn't this nervous when he was killed, and I should know because I was there."

That made me pause adjusting the cleavage on my gown. "Is he having second thoughts?" I asked stiffly.

My mother perked right up.

Spade chuckled. "No, he's fretting over *you.* Said something about you always making a dash for the exit right before the finish line or some such. I'm to check on you to make sure you have no intentions of backing out. Any signs of indecision, and I've been given strict instructions to throw you over my shoulder and carry you to him. Or hold you down and yell for him to come. Well? Are you quite determined in your course of action?"

Even though we were on opposite sides of the church and there was a multitude of noisy guests, I knew that Bones was tuned in to my answer. I raised my voice to be more helpful. "You tell my vampire husband he's about to become my human one." My mom went from hopeful back to depressed in a flash. "And you can give him this."

I handed Spade a piece of parchment with something hard inside. He took it and kissed my hand.

"I'll do that. Annette, Denise." He nodded at each of them and left. Now it was my turn to strain my ears as the two women helped me with the finishing touches to my dress.

"Crispin," Spade said, his words carrying back to me. "Poor girl can't be talked out of marrying you. Heaven knows I tried. This is for you, in case you didn't eavesdrop."

"She's eavesdropping as well, aren't you, Kitten?" His voice seemed like it touched me, even with the distance, but I didn't answer. After all, we weren't supposed to be talking. "Ah, aren't these lovely? Frightfully expensive; you must have cried when you purchased them."

His teasing made me laugh, giving away the fact that I'd been eavesdropping. He knew how penny-pinching I normally was. Still, the antique platinum-and-diamond cufflinks were beautiful. My bank account had taken a hit it hadn't previously seen before, yet I could hardly buy Bones a gift using *his* money.

"I heard you, luv, naughty little snoop. Now, what did you write here?"

The last letter I'd written him had been good-bye when I ran off with Don, but this one was markedly different. *I love you, and nothing will keep me from walking down that aisle and proving it. See you there.*

"You will," he answered me. "Soon."

Denise finally finished with my dress, then backed up to get a look at me and smiled. "You look amazing. Let's do this."

Annette judged my appearance as well, but with more objectivity. She looked very elegant in a charcoal dress with matching bolero jacket. "You're perfectly smashing," she finally settled on saying. A spark of something else lit in her eyes, but it vanished in an instant. "And you're the luckiest girl I've ever met."

Right now, about to marry the man I loved, I did feel lucky. Very lucky.

"Wait, I forgot to get you something blue!" Denise said with a gasp. "I'm a terrible maid of honor. Quick, help me find something!"

She began to rummage through the parlor with the desperation of the condemned. Annette helped, muttering an oath about useless human customs.

"Here."

The word didn't come from either of them. I stared in shock at my mother as she shoved herself off her chair and came to me, holding out a ring. It was a small sapphire-and-gold one I'd bought her for her birthday years ago. A lump made its way with lightning speed to my throat as I accepted it.

"Thank you," I said huskily.

She wiped her cheek with a dash of her hand. "I expect it back, hence the term 'borrowed.' And one last time, I will beg you not to do this, Catherine."

There went the tender mother-daughter moment. Oh well. At least I'd had a split second of bonding. Progress, not perfection, and all that.

"Don't worry, Mom. He won't hurt me."

"Doubtful." She turned away and went back to her chair.

Annette rolled her eyes heavenward. Denise fluffed my dress one last time.

"Are you ready? Or are you going to make your mother's universe and let her drive the getaway car?" Denise gave me a gleeful smirk.

I smiled back and mentally thanked God for the night a vampire tried to make her a snack as I walked nearby. Without her, I would have been heavily dependent on Prozac the past several years.

"I'm ready."

Annette made a noise that might have been a sigh. "Come on, Justina, we have to take our seats now. Bother it, woman, I wasn't going to touch you. You don't have to shrink back from me every time, do you?"

My mother strode past her without a word, only allowing herself the pleasure of a filthy look as she headed for the sanctuary. At least that's where I thought she was going. She could have been trotting straight to the parking lot.

"You should have just let Crispin bite her into better disposition," Annette said, clearly aggravated. "Would have done her a world of good."

"Thanks for the suggestion, but we'll keep my mother's senses the way they are. Even if it makes me crazy."

Annette paused in the hallway. A small, self-deprecating laugh came out of her. "Well, Cat. You've certainly shown good form today. I would have rubbed Crispin's rejection of you in your face until you cried, but you've been quite gracious. Now, do hurry up. Don't keep the man we love waiting."

Denise watched her go and then tilted her head. "She's hell on heels, Cat, and a bitch besides, but sometimes I like her."

"I know." A reluctant trace of admiration colored my words. "Sometimes I do too."

"Cat." Don approached us, wearing a black tuxedo.

It was the first I'd ever seen him so dressed up. His gray gaze took in my strapless lace dress that fishtailed into a minor train behind me. The long skirt wasn't made of a single piece of fabric, but several different swaths that swayed as I walked. Only the multitude of layers provided modesty, because there was no lining underneath. The veil was a thin billow of gauze attached to my hair with a comb, trailing cathedral style down to the floor. My neck and arms were bare. Only a pair of gothic platinum-and-white-diamond earrings adorned me.

"You're stunning," he said.

I smiled at the compliment and accepted the arm he held out to me.

Denise gave my shoulders a parting squeeze and offered one last piece of advice. "Don't trip!"

"I'll do my best. At least I expect him at the altar this time."

Don didn't get the joke since he hadn't been at Denise's wedding. "What?"

"Nothing." I tightened my grip on his arm. "Thank you for doing this."

The lines in his face creased as he smiled. "Thank you for asking. Shall we go?"

I straightened my shoulders. "Yes."

The sun had just set and there was snow on the ground, making it a white Christmas after all. The church was small in size but big in privacy, so we'd erected a tent complete with portable hardwood flooring for the reception. The caterers specialized in preparing traditional and, um, exotic foods. God help my mother if she got the wrong plate, because nothing short of suicide would relieve her revulsion.

Instead of a normal wedding singer with a piano or even a small band, Bones had hired a full orchestra. Most of them were shivering outside, waiting for heaters to warm their separate tented area, but a pianist and a violinist were in the church. Small and intimate wedding, my ass.

Orchids, lilies, gardenias, hyacinths, tulips, amaryllis, poinsettias and other flowers I couldn't name covered the interior of the church. A rain forest would be less fragrant. The flowers had been dusted with a sparkling powder that reflected in the candlelight, and there were candles everywhere, replacing all but the most essential artificial light. Don and I came into view of the guests and the groom with our next steps as we entered the sanctuary.

Even the steady pressure of Don's arm on mine faded into insignificance next to the smile that lit Bones's face. True to his word, he wore white too. His suit was a combination of twenty-first century and eighteenth, with lace spilling out of his collar and cuffs. A silver-braided waistcoat added antique style to the more modern pants the jacket draped around. He looked dazzling. I had to resist the urge to pinch myself, because this man couldn't be mine.

Don formally relinquished my hand and Bones took it.

"I have never seen anything more exquisite in all my life," he whispered before kissing me until I was breathless.

"You're not supposed to kiss me *now*," I managed when finally he let me up for air.

"I don't care," he answered with such feeling that laughter rippled through the spectators. "Sod the proper order of events."

Spade's lips twitched as he leaned forward. "Crispin, all of us came to see a *wedding*. Perhaps you can abstain from the consummation until later?"

That definitely brought more amusement from the guests. His side, anyway. Few of my guests were that cheerful.

"Later. Right you are, Charles."

Bones pressed my hand to his lips before turning to the minister. I had only met him once before when we filled out the necessary paperwork. He was on loan from his home parish in Wisconsin.

"Welcome, family," the minister began, eschewing the usual "Dearly Beloved." "Tonight you bear witness to the reaffirmation of one marriage and the beginning of another. While the dissolution of their vampire union is impossible, custom demands that I ask the following: If anyone here can show just cause as to why these two should not be joined together in human matrimony, speak now. Else forevermore hold your peace."

My mother shot out of her chair like a rocket on full launch. I had just begun to mutter something completely inappropriate for church when Bones flicked his hand and Rodney appeared behind her. The ghoul clapped his hand over my mom's mouth before she could voice her lengthy, strenuous objections.

"Thanks ever so, mate," Bones said, saluting him. "Some people seem to need assistance holding their peace. Oh, I wouldn't bite him, Justina, he's a ghoul. Might make him want to return the favor. He'll let go if you sit quietly. Otherwise, you'll get a mouth full of flesh-eater palm for the rest of the ceremony."

Who knew if she recognized Rodney from seven years ago? After all, she wasn't exactly facing him at the moment.

I glared at her in silent warning. Whether it was that or the unappetizing taste of Rodney's hand, she nodded and Rodney released her. A loud sniff was the only noise she made when she sat back down.

Bones turned back to the minister. "It appears our objector has changed their opinion."

By the gleam in the man's eyes and his sudden need to cough in a manner sounding suspiciously like chuckles, I guessed they knew each other fairly well.

"Um, so it would appear. Let us resume."

The rest of the words were somewhat standard, but they skipped by my attention. I was mesmerized by the lights glowing off Bones's hair, his sculpted features, and those deep brown eyes staring into mine. My vision dropped to his lips when he sounded out a two-worded reply to the minister's question.

"I do."

"And do you, Catherine, take this man to be your lawfully wedded husband? To have and to hold, for better or worse, for richer or poorer, in sickness and in health, forsaking all others as long as you both shall live?"

"I do."

Those lips opposite me curved into a smile.

"May we have the rings?"

Denise and Spade handed over the requested jewelry.

"Repeat after me, Crispin. With this ring, I thee wed."

He copied the words as the red diamond slid onto my finger, accompanied by its new companion of a thin platinum band. Tears sprang to my eyes. Thank God for waterproof mascara.

"Catherine, repeat after me. With this ring, I thee wed."

I breathed the words out and placed a matching platinum band on his finger. When I looked up, I saw his eyes were also tinged in pink.

"By the power vested in me, I now pronounce you man and wife. You may kiss your bride."

Bones wrapped his arms around me and slanted his mouth across mine. I pulled him closer, hearing the cheering applause from our guests. I was almost out of oxygen when he broke contact to smile down at me.

"I love you, Kitten. Or shall I call you Mrs. Russell?"

"Take your pick. I'll answer to both."

Bones kissed my hand, and then we proceeded back up the aisle together. Even the sound of my mother's heartbroken sobbing couldn't wipe the smile from my face.

We went straight to the entrance of the tent to greet our guests as they filed back from the church. Right away I knew that I'd never remember all the names and also, I'd need another coat of my guaranteed all-day lipstick. These vampires and ghouls were heavily into the custom of kissing the bride.

After the sixth consecutive polite "May I?" before another unknown pulseless man planted his lips on mine, Bones threw up his hands.

"For the sake of not standing here all night, you may *all* kiss the bride. Just be warned that if you see her at a club and she kisses you, it generally means she's about to kill you."

Laughter broke out at that, but Don must be having a fit. He would hate having his operations be the butt of the joke.

Ian was next in the receiving line. Bones had invited him out of respect for Ian being his sire. I had thought that Ian would refuse, but that showed how much I underestimated him. Ian had the same English accent Bones did, and his chestnut hair was offset by vivid turquoise eyes. He was pretty, all right. Pretty frigging dangerous.

"Crispin, so happy you included me on your memorable occasion. It's only fitting, isn't it, since I was at your binding. And Cat, how devastating you look. Am I excluded from kissing the lovely bride after our former misunderstanding?"

He considered kidnapping my ex-fiancé and three of my friends to blackmail me into becoming his new toy a misunderstanding? I'd show him. "Not at all, Ian, step right up."

When Ian leaned in, I grabbed him and pressed my mouth against his, even running my tongue inside and biting his lip. With the same abruptness, I pulled away, and my smile widened.

"Say hi to my father for me, Ian, and you can thank him again for trying to kill me instead of giving you my location like he was supposed to. Just think, if Max would've told you where I was, you would have found me before Bones did. Who knows how things might have turned out? Great to see you, you look swell."

He also now looked pissed. "Quite," Ian said testily as he walked away.

Bones gave me a sideways grin at my vindictiveness. "You might not want to show such enthusiasm with your kisses, pet. They'll all be lining up for seconds."

Don was next, but he settled for a kiss on the cheek. Then came the other two dozen members of my team, Tate being the last of them.

"Cat." There was raw emotion in his eyes. "I've never seen you look lovelier."

"Thank you." My voice was quiet.

Tate sniffed. "Guess you feel I already cashed in my kiss ticket with her, hmmm, Crypt Keeper? Don't worry, I wasn't going to take advantage."

Bones narrowed his eyes. "By all means. Since this will be your only opportunity, you shouldn't waste it."

There they went again. I leaned forward, and Tate's lips caressed mine lingeringly. I pulled away first, and his eyes stayed closed for a fraction longer. Then they snapped back open.

"You lucky bastard," he growled and walked away.

Bones watched him go with something akin to pity. "Poor sod just torments himself."

Mencheres was next. "May I also kiss the renowned Red Reaper without my life being in danger?"

Oh, so he had a sense of humor. How valuable. I leaned in, and his lips brushed across mine for only an instant, yet it left them vibrating. His power was so palpable—now I knew how it must feel to kiss a power line.

Annette was the last in line, and I turned to her almost in relief. "Thank God. My mouth is nearly numb. What's that in your hands?"

She held out two glasses, one with whiskey and the other gin. "Thought you'd both appreciate a drink."

I thanked her and finished my gin a single gulp.

"Better?" she queried. At my nod, she smiled silkily. "And now it is *my* turn to kiss the bride."

With that, Annette laid her mouth on mine. I was so taken aback she had time to trace her tongue past my lips before I straightened, breaking the contact.

"Apologies if I offended you, Cat," she said while not sounding sorry in the least. "You know my inclinations run in both directions, and you really do look lovely." She turned to Bones. "You break my heart with how fair you are, Crispin. I shall always remember how you look tonight. I wish you joy, dear friend, from the bottom of my soul."

Pink glazed her vision as she stared at him. He took her hand and gently kissed it, and I was reminded that they'd been together for over two hundred years. I couldn't even imagine that length of time, but I was hoping I'd get the chance to find out.

"Go on and kiss her, Bones. Hell, she just French-kissed me, you might as well."

He arched a brow. I nodded again firmly.

Annette blinked at this and then turned toward him as he cupped her face in his hands. He kissed her with all the tenderness of remembrance, and she had colored tears trailing down her cheeks when he stopped.

"My dear Annette, you have brightened many days for me. I can only assure you that I am truly happy now. I wish the same for you."

She swiped at her eyes, regaining her composure. "We are not all as fortunate as you, Crispin. Now do come on, both of you. Your guests are waiting."

"We'll be in straightaway."

Annette went inside and Bones took me in his arms, brushing the stray hairs away from my temple. I smiled up at him.

"Hi, Mr. Russell."

He smiled back. "Hallo yourself, Mrs. Russell."

We held each other wordlessly after that. I could have stood there forever.

After the cake, everyone cleared out of the church and the tents. It was almost midnight, the witching hour. The snow looked pristine settled on the ground in thick white blankets, cold air billowing out in the breaths of those who took them. Bones had me in front of him at the edge of the trees. He said there was one more surprise.

With a blast, fireworks shot into the night, exploding over the church in a dazzling display of colors and shapes. For several moments, I stared, then Bones picked me up and carried me rapidly into the woods, chuckling as I craned my neck to catch another glimpse of the artificially lit sky.

"We're making our escape, Kitten, while they're all distracted."

The helicopter waited a mile away. I climbed inside and fired the propellers. Flying was a skill I'd learned years ago with Don, and helicopters were my favorite to operate. We were airborne and away from the still-exploding spectacle in minutes.

"Don't fret, luv. I know what you're thinking. I left a check for twice the amount of what that church is worth. No one is getting ripped off. Couldn't leave such an obvious scent trail for anyone to pick up on, now could I? It'll burn to ashes. Less chance of people discovering exactly who was there."

I glanced sideways at him as I flew the Bell Jet Ranger expertly. "You really do plan ahead, don't you? That light show was magnificent. I almost wish I could have seen it all."

"Go faster, pet, and I'll show you what else I have planned."

We were forty minutes away by air, a deliberate calcu- lation. When we talked about where we wanted to go for the two weeks off for our honeymoon, I'd been adamant. I wanted to be alone, not in a hotel room or seeing sights which would occupy valuable time, but alone. He hadn't needed persuading. We were spending one week at our Blue Ridge home and then one week at the Jackson Hole one. Both of us loved the mountains. The Blue Ridge loca- tion won the first round due to location. It was much, much closer than the Wyoming house from the church. Patience wasn't one of my virtues now.

The chopper landed neatly on the helipad and was garaged out of sight. Bones picked me up and sprinted up the stairs of the sparsely furnished house that was my favorite of our homes. My cat was rudely locked out of the bedroom as Bones kicked the door closed behind him. The feline had a tendency to want attention at the most inopportune moments.

Bones set me down to light the candles that were conveniently arrayed. I had just begun to kick off my shoes when he stopped me.

"Don't." His voice was soft but resonating. He finished with the candles a moment later and returned, running his hands up my arms. Green flame spilled out of his eyes.

"Don't take anything off, not yet. I want you just like this, with everything you have on now. You've never looked more stunning, and I want to be inside you while you're wearing that beautiful dress. All night I've been wondering what you've got on under it. Let's see, shall we?"

He knelt at my feet, hands sliding up my legs underneath the skirt of the dress. An approving noise left his throat.

"Silk stockings, hmmm? Lovely. And garters as well. Ah, what's this? Is that a corset, pet? Blimey, I haven't felt one of those in almost a century. Authentic replica, except for these. How terribly thoughtful of you, Mrs. Russell. These snap buttons would have come in right handy back when these things were all the rage."

"Glad you like it." Breathlessly.

His fingers had been busy. I sucked in a sharp gasp when he flipped my skirt up enough to cover him as he explored inside. The aforementioned buttons came free with a decisive pop as he unsnapped them. I backed up toward the bed in two unsteady steps when his mouth glided up my thigh.

"Say my name. I want to hear it when I taste you," he entreated into the red curls between my legs.

"Bones," I sighed.

He gave an inhaled breath at the center of me underneath my skirt.

"The other one. Just this once, call me by my other name."

The mattress was behind me. I scooted onto it to support my trembling knees. In a gesture of blatant desire I hadn't shown before, I spread my legs and pressed his head between them while groaning out the name I never called him.

"*Crispin...*"

An oral assault from lips, tongue, and teeth began on my flesh. He didn't bite me in the way he had previously but used his fangs as instruments of pressure without breaking my delicate skin.

When I felt near the edge of release I rolled away suddenly, panting. "Not against your mouth. I want to come when you're inside me."

He rose up from his knees, emerald eyes burning into mine. I stilled his hands with a quavering smile when he went to shrug off his coat.

"You were right. Keep them on. And then call me by my real name when you come."

Bones crawled up the bed toward me, fully clothed. I shivered as I drew down his zipper to grasp the hard flesh it concealed. He leaned back against the pillows, lifting the skirt of the dress as I straddled him. His mouth smothered my cry as I impaled myself on him.

The fabric of his pants rubbed my flesh. He murmured a warning about the zipper and undid his trousers, easing them out from under me without taking them down past his thighs. I rested my hands on the lacey neck of his shirt, fingering the silver threads braided in his waistcoat. His back arched with each rocking motion of my hips.

"You're so bloody beautiful," I rasped as the intensity built.

He laughed into my neck. "That's my line, luv. Tell me if you like this, Kitten. I think you will…"

His thumb sought out and found the top of my cleft, pressing erotic circles into the jumping knot of flesh with each movement I made. My hands clenched in the material of his coat.

"Stop that, I can't— I can't…" Every flick of his thumb caused me to jerk back uncontrollably with ecstasy. "I can't *concentrate*," I finished.

He let out an amused noise. "You're not supposed to. Still thinking? Let's put a stop to that."

He increased the pressure, causing me to grind in frenzied rapture on top of him. The climax burst inside me in tremors that felt like they might tear a muscle. Bones rolled me over and buried his head in my cleavage as I shook.

"That's better," he groaned into my skin. His fingers began to undo the buttons of my dress.

"Didn't you…?" I asked raggedly.

He shifted up to kiss me, sucking on my tongue and thrusting strongly within me.

"Not yet. Told you, I have a plan. For each time you come, I'll remove a piece of your clothing. Once you're naked I'll let myself go. We still have the corset, stockings, shoes, garters and your veil to work through. A man should have goals, don't you agree?"

Oh, I agreed. "I will be… ah, yes, right there… happy… to assist you."

Bones didn't cheat by biting me into submission, he took the long way around my clothing. Two hours later I was finally naked and drenched in sweat. He surged on top of me, alternating between kissing my face and my breasts. I'd raked bloody scratches into his back that healed just in time to be re-inflicted.

"Kitten," he moaned. "I'm going to pour myself into you now."

"Yes," I urged, twisting under him.

A jagged chuckle. "Not just that, luv. Something new. I've been saving this for tonight. Put your hands on my shoulders, like that. Now. Look in my eyes, Kitten, don't close yours. That's right, look straight into them…"

God, they began to really glow. Not just gleam, but sparkle and spin with a thousand tiny lights. I watched, fascinated, and gradually became aware that his skin started to shimmer as well. It was as if a light had been switched on that leaked out of his pores and through his eyes. A humming energy built up inside him. This was similar to what happened when he levitated, but stronger. And I couldn't look away from his eyes; they started to suck me in…

I fell forward into the spinning wheels of emerald in his gaze, lost. Bones seemed to grow and expand all around me until I didn't feel the bed underneath me, or my arms, legs, or anything of me. There was nothing but him, and I felt everything he did.

My body was hard, masculine, pulseless. The skin covering me was cool and rippled with lean sinews, and I was sizzled by the hot flesh of the woman underneath me. Her heartbeat drummed in my ears frantically, loud cries searing my mind as I thrust harder inside her. The sweet, musky scent of her filled my nose and flavored my mouth, arousing me to move faster, each stroke causing her to clench internal muscles around me. Wet ridges of scorching flesh welcomed each penetration, crunching in anticipation and tension. I loved the viselike grip she held me in and wanted to drink her and feel her blood inside me.

The hunger curled in my throat. I licked her neck, rolling her pulse underneath my tongue. She clutched me closer, screaming now, yes, yes, yes, her muscles compressing me in a scalding rush of liquid which ripped my control from me. I sank my fangs into her throat, blood splashing into my mouth, so warm, luscious, empowering me. Revitalizing me, running to every nerve in my body in an instant. Another deep pull that was better than the first. Ah, so close now.

Her red hair clung in wet strands to her face, green eyes huge and glowing. I still felt the squeezing of her body around me, but with less force. Her heartbeat slowed a trifle as her hands flexed on my shoulders with aftershocks. Roughly I gathered her into my arms, holding her hips hard against mine and plunging repeatedly into her hot, narrow depths. Over and over, each cleaving motion inciting more, yes, oh Christ, so good, a little more...

My skin exploded, molten sensation poured over me and through me, wracking me with shudders that shattered me. I shouted out her real name hoarsely as I came, just like she'd asked me to.

"Catherine...!"

"What do you think, Kitten? Did you like that?"

What did I *think*? Every part of me was shaking. So many thoughts raced through my mind, I couldn't pick one fast enough before it was replaced. Add that to the aftereffects of a near-simultaneous orgasm with my*self*, and Play-Doh was more coherent than I was.

"Is it... like that... every time?" was all I came up with.

He lay spooned behind me, a sheet tangled around us. I'd started to get the chills as soon as I was mentally back in my body.

"Close enough, yes. You should take a trip inside me after I bite you between your legs. Whatever you are feeling then, trust me, I am feeling more. It's like shagging a volcano that just erupted. Perhaps now you won't wonder if I'm satisfied with you in bed. You have your answer."

"How? I mean, how did you do that?" I peered around my shoulder to look at him as he smiled at me.

"You know a vampire can steal the mind of a human with their eyes. Well, pet, that is what I did with you. Only I didn't steal, you see, because you're too strong for that. It doesn't work by force with you since you have nosferatu blood in your veins. But I could ask, and you could choose to surrender your will to me. That's what I did, Kitten. I asked. You accepted."

Bones nestled against me, kissing the spot on my neck he'd bitten, we'd bitten, whatever. Hell if I knew the proper way to describe it.

"It was incredible," I settled on saying softly. "I can't even begin to articulate how much. Although technically, I just had sex with another woman, even if it was me."

He gave a sinful chuckle and began to unwind the sheet. "And you said you'd never have a threesome."

"That's as close as it comes, Bones," I said without anger. My body was too languorous for that. I'd actually been inside his skin, closer than I ever thought to be. Astonishing. "How often can that, um, be done? Is there a burnout factor? You were leaking power like a ruptured oil tanker—it must have cost you something."

Bones successfully got rid of the cotton barrier separating us. He began to caress me as he answered. "Cost a bit, Kitten. Everything worthwhile does, right? I'd say at a guess without it affecting me unduly… twice a month?"

"Really?" I mulled the response, stretching under those probing hands. He closed the distance between us.

"You know," I murmured as his head lowered to my breast, "I heard some of those things as you thought them. You have a very dirty mind, Bones. Just depraved."

He smiled against my skin. "Absolutely. What do you think I've been trying to tell you? Now let me prove it once again, Kitten."

CHAPTER TWENTY-TWO
BELINDA GETS FIRED

Author's note: In At Grave's End, *Belinda gets killed after a calamitous sting operation at Chuck E. Cheese's. In the original version, the Chuck E. Cheese's scene never happened, and thus Belinda died very differently. In both versions, however, Belinda has brief contact with another vampire and tells him the exact date and time that Tate was going to be changed over, giving Max the information he needed to attack Cat when Bones and her team would be occupied. In the published version, Cat killed Belinda before they had to chance to discover that. In this version, Belinda deliberately goads Cat with some very explicit recollections, but the end result is the same.*

Two weeks later, we strolled back into the Virginia compound. If I weren't so afraid of the word *perfect*, it would be what I used to describe our honeymoon.

We had originally intended to spend a week at our home in the Blue Ridge and then go to Jackson Hole, but an extended snowstorm nixed our travel plans. I could honestly say I didn't care. We toasted marshmallows, made snowmen, had a freezing version of a strip snowball fight and spent hours in our outdoor hot tub. The house was stocked well with food, and we only ventured out a few times for Bones to feed. He didn't want to only take blood from me for practical reasons, and a couple of flashes from his eyes later and the gas station attendants were unaware of their contribution to his appetite.

The time passed too quickly. I hadn't even spoken to anyone from work. They'd been given strict instructions not to bother us unless there was a serious emergency. Since there had been no calls, I assumed all must have been well.

Don looked up from his computer as we came in his office. Instead of taking my usual seat in the chair opposite him, I sat on the couch with Bones. Obnoxious maybe, but I couldn't stop touching him yet. Maybe in another couple of weeks.

Don cleared his throat. "You're both looking well. It appears you had a nice honeymoon."

"Very much so, old chap. Too short, of course. Were it not for our vampire-in-training, you wouldn't have seen us for over a month."

The intimate tone he used, combined with the light brush of his lips on my temple, made my uncle shift in his chair. Open affection between me and a vampire never failed to unsettle Don. I put him out of his misery by changing the subject.

"Did anything noteworthy go on while we were gone?"

Don started tugging his eyebrow. Oh, so there *had* been activity. "We had some incidents locally," he began. "A disturbance at a restaurant that serves vampires. Apparently you knew about this place, Cat, and didn't bother to enlighten me."

I shrugged off the accusation in his tone. Before Bones, Don had had a pretty stringent policy when it came to vampires. See 'em, kill 'em, find out later if they were being naughty. I had my own way of handling things. If the vampires didn't hurt humans, I didn't hurt them, hence my relaxed attitude about the places they frequented where bodies didn't turn up.

"What restaurant?"

That earned me a dirty look. "How many of them are there? Aren't you concerned about a large number of vampires congregating in the city when your mother lives?"

"Bloody hell, mate, vampires and ghouls are everywhere," Bones interjected. "Roughly ten percent of the population is undead. Going to have her try to hack her way through all of them?"

Don blanched at the statistic but returned to the subject. "The place was Arturo's, an Italian restaurant where they served blood side by side with the red wine, it seems. Some humans who were there called 911, and since we monitor those calls for supernatural content, we sent a team."

"Who went?" I hated it when my team went anywhere without me. Although Dave was great at filling my shoes, being undead and all, protective instincts died hard. No pun intended.

"Dave, Tate, Angus, and Belinda. We brought her to give a low profile since she's a vampire. Cooper stayed nearby with more soldiers for backup, and only those four went inside. As it turned out, it was just a couple of vamps being very indiscreet by feeding off their playthings at a table, and the sight of that naturally freaked the other humans out. The owner of the restaurant apologized profusely and swore that nothing like that had happened before. He even mentioned you, Cat. Said you'd been there and you knew the place was okay. You can imagine how much I liked hearing that."

His reproachful tone made me squirm, and then I took the offensive. "They have great lasagna, so what? No one else knew who I was. The owner guessed because of my frigging hair and skin. I didn't go back, and that was a year ago! They didn't let their clientele get rowdy, so why should I have called in the troops?"

Don twisted his lips. "That's not all there is to the story. Belinda vanished for about ten minutes until Dave sniffed her out. She didn't try to run, which surprises me, but she did have, ah, *contact* with another vampire before she was discovered. We have her in lockdown now."

I didn't get it at first, but Bones did. He gave a short bark of laughter. "So you caught her shagging the first undead sod she came across, did you? Undisciplined chit. Doesn't say much for the rest of them, to let her wander so off her leash."

"That little slut," I muttered.

Don nodded. "As I said, she's been confined to her cell since then, blood allotment decreased by fifty percent. I was waiting further decision on her punishment until you returned, Cat. Nothing else out of the ordinary has happened. The restaurant remains open, but it's being monitored now."

"Was Belinda questioned when she was brought back? What about the vampire she was nailing, was he checked for any weapons?"

My uncle shook his head in frustration. "She was questioned, yes, and also searched, but nothing was found. The vampire she consorted with managed to run away, as the team was more concerned with securing Belinda. We've watched the restaurant, but he hasn't returned since. Belinda claims never to have seen him before. According to her, she wasn't being particular."

Bones stood. "We should talk to her, Kitten. Find out if there's more."

I stood as well. "What a good idea."

In place of a warm hello, Tate, Dave, and Angus all received stinging rebukes from me for letting Belinda out of their sight. Even though she'd done nothing more than screw around, the point was that she could have. Since she'd behaved while training the men and had gone on a few missions without incident, they'd dropped their guard. Forgotten how dangerous she was. I never forgot. After all, she had once tried to kill me.

The vampire cells were on the fourth sublevel, the most heavily guarded area of the compound. We'd once housed four of them; now there was only her. The others became unnecessary after Bones began to supply Don with blood for Brams. Belinda was a training toy, and we didn't need more than one of those.

Bones lounged in the doorway as the reinforced metal doors were opened. A silver blade dangled from in his hands. I smiled at her as I entered the small room.

"Did you miss me, Belinda? You must have. I heard you were so lonely you snuck away for comfort while on a mission. Now tell me, whatever did you and that other vamp talk about?"

Her cornflower-blue eyes glowered at me, and she tossed her fair hair over her shoulder. "We didn't talk, as I told your other goons. You've had me locked up here for over a year, Cat. I deserved a little fun. I didn't try to run away, I knew *he'd* just hunt me down and stake me."

The "he" in question stared at her. "Why, sweet, that's the first intelligent thing I've heard you say. You're quite right, and I would have been horribly displeased about your interrupting my honeymoon. It would have taken me weeks to finish killing you."

The flatness in his voice sent a shiver up my spine. This was a side of Bones I didn't see very often. From his expression, he'd meant exactly what said.

"Oh, so you're married now?" She flicked her gaze between the two of us. "Congratulations."

"Thanks, I know you really mean it," I growled. "Back to the question, and don't give me that wide-eyed little-girl look. Who was the unlucky schmuck, and what did you say?"

"What did we say? Word for word? Well, it went something like this: 'Hurry up and fuck me before these idiots notice I'm gone. Um, oh, yes, mmm, harder, ah...'"

Her mocking grunts continued until I slapped her.

"You asked," she snapped.

"You'd better cease the grunting, Belinda, and be more helpful," Bones warned her.

She blinked at him. "You liked hearing it before, remember? You know, your face looked so much better when I was sitting on it."

I threw her across the room with such force I heard multiple bones break. Belinda managed to give a strained chuckle even as she huddled in pain.

"Do you know how the four of us fucked him back then?" she grated. "One on his cock and one on his face, and then we just kept switching—"

A gurgle interrupted anything else she'd been about to say. Belinda had the strangest look on her face as she stared at the twin knives protruding from her chest. I hadn't seen Bones throw them, but they were buried so deeply in Belinda's sternum that their hilts were past her rib cage. Then Belinda's pretty features began to shrink, wrinkle, and shrivel. She tilted over, withering more with each passing second.

Bones came behind me and gripped my shoulders. "Bugger," he said softly. "I should have asked her more questions first. Lost my temper, Kitten, I apologize."

I was still transfixed by the sight of Belinda withering in front of me, not to mention the images she'd inserted into my mind with her words.

"I can smell your anger," Bones went on. "Is it at me for killing her, or at her for what she said?"

"At her," I breathed. "I don't care that you killed her. In fact, I'm pretty pleased about it. I doubt she told the other vampire anything useful. My location is random, my identity has been common knowledge since Ian's, and this compound is too big for Max or anyone else to try to wage an assault against it."

Finally I looked up and met Bones's gaze. "I'll get over the rest of it. While I didn't need her giving me a mental picture, it's in the past. I can't walk around all the time being pissed at things you did before meeting me, can I?"

He kissed my palm. "I'd take them all back, Kitten, if I could."

Juan picked that moment to walk by. He took in the sight of Bones and me standing over Belinda's mummifying corpse, and his eyes widened.

"What the hell happened here?" he asked in astonishment.

I brushed the hair from my face. "Belinda just got fired."

CHAPTER TWENTY-THREE
BONES REALIZES CAT ALMOST "JUMPED"

Author's note: This is more of a snippet than an actual scene, but I'm including it because many readers who previously saw it on my website said that they really liked what Bones said to Cat. Because of that, I deeply regret not including it in the published version of At Grave's End. *At the time, I thought I had too many emotional statements already, and I didn't want to venture into purple prose or cheesy territory, so I left it out. In hindsight, that was a mistake. Emotions should be on overload when you realize you almost lost the person you love most, and I've tried to remember that when I write the rest of my stories. For context, I've included a few sentences of the published version, which starts when Cat and Bones are finally alone after Bones returns from the "dead."*

"Your body aged almost to the point of truly dying. That's why your hair's white, isn't it?"

"Yes. I expect so."

It hit me then, staring at his unlined, beautiful face and that stark white hair framing it, that neither of us should be alive. He'd almost been killed by a knife in his heart, and add one more step on a rocky ledge for me, and Bones would have returned to my body being broken beyond revival.

His hands closed around my face, and his whole body stiffened. "What is this you're remembering?"

I let the memory come, restricting none of it, hearing once again Vlad's pitiless admonishments and the final question that saved my life. *What are you?*

Bones let out a cry and clutched me to him. Pink liquid streamed from his eyes, matching my own tears in volume if not in color.

"If I would have come back to that, Kitten, it would have killed me more certainly than any silver in my heart. Promise me, promise me, *promise* me you will never do such a thing. If I die, I will wait for you, do you understand? No matter how long. I will watch from beyond to make sure you live every year you have to its fullest, and then we'll have so much to talk about when I see you again... Promise me right now, Catherine!"

I held him back just as tightly even as I choked out a laugh. "Did you miss that part? My name isn't Catherine. It's Cat."

CHAPTER TWENTY-FOUR
ORIGINAL BEGINNING OF
DESTINED FOR AN EARLY GRAVE

Author's note: This is the original beginning of Destined for an
Early Grave, *cut to get to the main plot point of Cat's dreams sooner. It was also set about a month before Cat and Bones take their
boat trip and features Cat and Bones's first meeting with Geri, the
woman who ended up replacing Cat as "bait" on Don's team. This
was an enjoyable scene to write because I got to show Cat and Bones
having a little fun with the new recruit. As I've said before, a lot
of the "just for fun" scenes got cut in the name of pacing, but it
wasn't all blood, danger, jealousy, and despair at Cat's former job,
and this scene gets to showcase some of the lighter moments between
Cat, Bones, and her team. Even Denise came to help out, and as
you can see, Denise had a great time moonlighting as a temporary
team member.*

The blonde sat at the bar, her finger tapping against the
rim of her glass. She was drinking scotch and soda, easy
on the scotch. The soda was diet. Even the thought of its
taste made me grimace. I favored gin and tonics myself.

She kept glancing at the man across the bar. His hair was
dirty-blond with dark roots, and underneath the illumina-
tion of the strobes, the lighter tips gleamed. So did his skin
with its pale crystal texture. His eyes were in stark contrast to

his coloring, as were his brows. Both were a brown so deep they could be mistaken for black.

From my position overlooking the bar, I gave an inward smile. *Gorgeous, isn't he? Go on, keep checking out those high cheekbones and those nice broad shoulders. If you like all that, just wait until you see his ass.*

A beautiful woman with strawberry-blond hair came down the staircase and went straight over to the blond man.

"Tell me you're straight, horny, and want to dance," she said with an upper-crust English accent. "After that, conversation is optional."

I shouldn't have been able to hear her with all the people, blaring music, and distance. But her words were as clear to me as if they'd been spoken in my ear. Being half-vampire had its advantages.

The man's lips curled in amusement, making him even more attractive. "Yes to all the above, luv," he replied in a matching English accent.

The blonde at the bar watched them and her mouth thinned. She paid her tab, keeping her eye on the couple as they made their way into the throng of dancers. The man spun the woman around, moving with a prowling grace, all leashed energy and sexiness contained in a lean, rock-hard package. Next to him, everyone else looked clumsy by comparison.

The blonde from the bar marched over, maneuvering her way through the other dancers.

"Can I cut in?" she asked bluntly, giving the other woman an unfriendly look.

"Why?" the man asked in a casual, cool tone. "What can you offer me that this lovely woman can't?"

The blonde balked. "Um, well... I can, er—"

"I'm already bored," he said, cutting her off. "Run along."

His dancing partner laughed. "Carry on." She smirked.

The man turned his back and continued dancing, leaving the blonde to gaze at him in disbelief before she walked away with brisk, angry strides.

"Asshole," I heard her mutter.

After a few minutes, I watched the couple make their way from the dance floor to the back exit. The blond woman watched, too, and almost shoved people out of her way to follow. I followed as well, but more discreetly, taking the long way around.

The alley behind the club was a dark, narrow stretch. Perfect for a secluded, if not private, quickie.

Or a great place for a hungry vampire to snack off an unknowing donor.

The man took his dancing companion behind a metal fire escape that hung from the three-story club like a spiderweb. I crept closer with much more discretion than the charging blonde, watching as he enfolded the woman in his arms with his mouth going to her throat. The woman's head fell back while her eyes closed.

"Get away from her, asshole," the blonde barked as she flung open the side door. She had a gun trained on him.

The man lifted his head, fangs visible and pearls of red on his lips.

"Really want that dance, do you?" He laughed. "Give me a moment and I'll be right with you."

The blonde fired. So did the three men who appeared behind her in flanking formation. Then the four of them stared at the empty space where he'd been, seeing nothing now.

"Secure the perimeter!" the blonde shouted. "I want—"

Her voice was cut off by a piercing creak as the metal fire escape fell on the four of them. It landed with a twisting screech that drowned out their screams, barricading the side door to the club with the wreckage. From start to finish, it took less than five seconds.

From out of the shadows, a ghoul crept up to me. "Hicks looks pissed."

I smiled. "You should have seen how pissed I was the first time I came up against Bones. Woke up with a concussion and chained to a cave wall, with him laughing at me. I think I was more mad than afraid."

"You were most definitely furious," Bones replied as he leapt down from the rooftop, Annette in his grasp. "Called me a coward and told me to choke on your blood. Was it any wonder I fell in love?"

Dave, the ghoul, grunted. "People get turned on in strange ways, if you ask me."

"Fucking... bloodsucker." The pained insult came from underneath the debris.

Bones stalked over and pulled a piece of metal up to reveal the blonde's dirty, bleeding face. "You are as witless as your mates when it comes to handling the undead."

Bones kicked at a nearby pile of the fire escape. A low moan was the response. Then Bones gestured to Annette with a disgusted shake of his head.

"Instead of me, they shot *her*. Do you see your blouse?"

A man with thinning gray hair and a face lined with age walked down the alley. One tug of the eyebrow preceded his reply.

"Did you think Cat would be easy to replace?" my boss and uncle, Don Williams, asked wryly.

I snorted. "Don't try to guilt me, Don. I'm not staying just because of this fiasco."

"...can't... feel my... legs," the blonde gasped.

"Too right you can't, your back is broken," Bones noted. "Your arms as well, I suspect."

Sirens sounded in the distance. None of us paid any attention to them. With our credentials, the police wouldn't be allowed to sneak a peek past the soldiers on both sides of the alley and the rooftops. My uncle ran a special brand of "Homeland Security" that outranked the local cops, FBI, CIA, and even the military.

I stood next to the tangled metal, ignoring the groans of pain coming from under it.

"All right, pay attention. That vampire," I said with a nod at Bones, "could be ripping your throats out now and inviting friends for leftovers. When you have a vampire in your sights, you don't give him a warning. You open fire before he knows you're a threat. And maybe you need to be reacquainted with the term *innocent bystander*."

I waved at Annette, illuminated under the street-lights, unhurt by the bullet because she'd been dead for centuries.

"A bystander is someone you get out of the way. If you don't, they *stand by* and screw things up. You certainly don't shoot them because you're too rattled by the vampire to aim properly."

"Who... are you?"

The question came from Lieutenant Geri Hicks, the blonde from the bar who was supposed to fill my spot as bait for my team. I squatted in front of her, tossing aside the few pieces of iron pinning her down.

"I'm Cat."

Geri studied me as we piled into the waiting van. She cracked her back and flexed her fingers, astonishment still on her face.

"It doesn't even hurt," she marveled.

"Vampire blood is a powerful healing agent, but don't forget it's also dangerous," Don said.

"So." Geri quit wiggling her parts to stare at me. "You're the one."

The freak.

She didn't say it. Unlike Bones, I couldn't read minds, so maybe she hadn't even thought it. Still, after growing up stuck between two worlds, it was how I considered myself. I had the strength, speed, vision, hearing, and glowing eyes of the nosferatu, but parts of me were very human. My teeth, for one. No fangs.

"Yeah, I'm the half-breed."

Her lips pursed. "This was all a setup? There was no vampire prowling Bellissima's, no two girls were found in the alley?"

Bones whistled. "Catch on right swiftly, don't you?"

She opened her mouth to say something and then shut it.

He laughed. "That's the first intelligent thing you've done all night."

Geri glared at him. That knowing, arrogant curl to his mouth didn't falter. *She must be cursing you up one side and down the other*, I thought to Bones in amusement.

"Okay." Geri lifted her chin. "Tell me what I should have done differently."

Bones leaned forward. "First, you waited too bloody long at the bar. If a vampire's looking for blood, he or she is impatient. Don't wait for someone else to get their attention as Annette did."

"I was just about to—" she began.

He waved a hand. "Then you failed to arouse my interest when you attempted to cut in. You had an opportunity to get rid of the other girl and maneuver me into position, yet you squandered it. If a vampire asks you what you can offer them, have an answer! Make it memorable."

"Such as?" She scoffed.

"I'll take that," I replied with a grin. "With a vampire, memorable means dirty. 'I can suck the skin straight off your cock,' would have probably worked, as well as 'bend me over and you'll find out why I'm better.' If the above two fail, then trip the other woman and bust her ankle. Then your advantage is that you're not the one who's limping."

Dave chuckled. So did Bones. My uncle Don looked a little uncomfortable, but he didn't disagree. How could he? I had a nearly flawless record when it came to my targets.

"I don't think I should have to stoop accomplish my objectives," Geri said icily. "I'm a soldier, not a whore."

Uh-oh. Bad choice of words.

"Got something against whores?" Bones asked in a silky voice. "Careful, it's my former profession. Do you have any other prejudices we should be aware of?"

She looked between me and Don. I shrugged. My uncle tugged his eyebrow and looked away.

"Pride and prejudice are two luxuries you can't afford in this job," I said. "People's lives are on the line. That has to mean more than your comfort level."

"If it means that much to you," Geri asked, "why are you giving it up?"

My uncle sighed while pale fingers tightened on my arm.

"I'm too recognizable now, so my position has to be filled by someone else."

That was one of the reasons. There were more, but I wasn't getting into all of them with her.

Geri digested this information. She'd been handpicked out of thousands of soldiers, field agents, spooks, and policewomen. The criteria was tough. She had to have the mental strength to deal with the supernatural, and physically she had to be attractive as well as strong.

At last Geri smiled, but it wasn't at me. It was at Bones. "You were really a whore?"

He arched a challenging brow. "Yes."

"Men or women?"

I didn't know where this was going, but Bones didn't hesitate. "Women."

"Were you any good at it?"

I laughed. My uncle looked like he'd swallowed something pointy.

Bones wore a ghost of a smile. "I've been told that, yes."

Geri nodded. "Good. Maybe you could meet my boyfriend for drinks? Sweet guy—he's great at everything except sex. If you could casually drop some hints...?"

My sides hurt from holding the laughter in. Bones nodded with complete seriousness. "Tell him to expect my ring. Don't fret, I'll inform him in such a manner he won't know he's being instructed. It's not the first request I've had like this."

"I think she'll do just fine," I whispered to my uncle as Bones went on, getting the particulars on Geri's boyfriend.

Don regarded me with solemn features that in no way resembled my own. "It won't be the same without you."

We were almost at the compound. I sighed. "Everything ends eventually, Don."

CHAPTER TWENTY-FIVE
DELETED FLASHBACK TO WHEN CAT WAS SIXTEEN

Author's note: This was the original start of the flashback when Cat's memory of her time with Gregor was finally restored. It was cut because of—all together now!—pacing concerns. In it, you see a young, naïve Cat being manipulated by both Gregor and Cannelle. Gregor was the worst, of course, using both charm and implied threat to get what he wanted, but Cannelle didn't lack for cruelness. As in the book, this flashback takes place just before Cat met Danny and the course of her life changed, putting her on a direct path to her future identity as the Red Reaper and her meeting with Bones. Some things are just meant to be, aren't they?

Licking Falls, Ohio
Summertime

I shaded my eyes against the late afternoon sun glinting through the branches. Soon it would be dark. That relieved me as much as it bothered me. No one else could see in the dark like me, but I wasn't supposed to let anyone know that.

"Joseph," my grandmother called from the front porch. "Go get Catherine and have her come inside for supper!"

"She'll be along shortly," was my grandfather's reply. From the sound of it, he was still working on the old Chevy. "She can smell the food, I tell you."

Another conversation I'd unwittingly eavesdropped on, even a few acres away. At least this wasn't anything embarrassing. Hearing them discuss erectile issues or his bowel movements in what they thought was the privacy of their bedroom would scar me forever, I was sure.

I left the tree I'd been sitting in to run farther into the orchard, away from the house instead of toward it. I didn't have much time until I had to get back, but I loved the orchard. Especially at night. Natural sounds surrounded me instead of the chatter from my family, and it felt peaceful. Often I'd sneak out here when everyone at the house was asleep. It was one of the few times I could relax.

After about thirty minutes, however, I headed back toward the house, walking at a fast pace. It was getting chillier out. March could still produce snow on occasion. Maybe winter wasn't done with us after all.

I was almost to the house when I heard the man's voice, low and cultured, with a French accent. It nearly made me stumble on my way up the front lawn. No car was in the driveway and this was rural Ohio. If you were a Southerner, you were still considered foreign here. I also hadn't heard him arrive, but then again, I had gone to the edge of the twenty-acre property. Too far away for even my ears.

When I went inside the house, my grandparents were already seated at the dining table, which was set for five instead of four. My mother was in the kitchen, her hair out of its normal tight bun and hanging messily down her back. That, in addition to the tall man with his back to me, was unusual, but my grandparents seemed relaxed so they must know what was going on.

"Sorry I'm late," I began, moving to help my mother with the heavy cast-iron pot she was removing from the oven. "I lost track of time."

The stranger turned around and faced me. This time I did stumble over my own feet. His arm shot out to steady me, making me blink at how fast he'd moved. My grandparents sat serenely as if nothing was occurring, and my mom just brushed by me to place the stew on the table.

I stared at the hand on my elbow and the tall man connected to it with mild shock. Golden hair combined with darker strands gave it an ash-blond color, and his eyes were grayish green. A scar ran from his eyebrow to his temple and his skin was as pale as mine, but his hummed with a taut vibration that made me tingle where he touched me.

"Who are you?" I blurted, pulling free and rubbing my arm briskly. The pins-and-needles sensation left it as soon as his grip was released.

"I'm Gregor," he said, looking me over in the most unusual way. My chemistry teacher studied items in a petri dish in the same manner. "I'm an old friend of your mother's."

My eyes bugged at that. Mom didn't have old friends. She didn't have new ones either. She stayed as solitary as I did and only ventured into town when absolutely necessary. I did a quick estimation of his age. Slight lines around the eyes, that scar didn't appear new, and he appeared to be in his early thirties, like my mother.

Could this be my *father?*

"Mom?" I asked hesitantly. "You know him?"

"Of course, Catherine." Her reply was almost mechanical. "He's an old friend. We'll talk about it after dinner."

Oh my God! Was this the man I'd been denied the slightest knowledge about? The one whose mere mention caused her to fly into an ugly rage? The way he was examining me looked like someone appraising what was his, that's for sure. My chin lifted and I went to the sink to wash my hands thoroughly. Talk after dinner, would we? I knew what my first question would be—where the hell have you been all my life?

The meal passed awkwardly. My mother barely spoke, only answering direct questions in a monosyllable. Clearly she was uncomfortable about having Gregor here, but she didn't act angry or confrontational as was her norm when upset. My grandparents talked between themselves, seemingly oblivious to the tension, and Gregor kept his conversation directed at me. How old was I? When was my birthday? What grade was I in? Did I have any hobbies? Had I met many people? Have I ever been to a dance club?

The polite interrogation was starting to wear on me. It was all I could do not to snap, "They have paternity tests if you're not certain!" Something about him made me nervous. It wasn't just the very odd reaction I'd had to him touching me, although that sensation I chalked up to shock at meeting my potential father. He moved differently. His eyes followed everything, and the air around seemed to be charged. *You're just freaking out*, I told myself. *There's nothing weird about him. You're the only bizarre one at this table.*

When dinner was over I stood, practically snatching up everyone's plates and clearing the table. Like someone possessed, I rinsed them and had the dishwasher running before five minutes passed. Gregor watched me the entire time, as if he'd never seen anyone do dishes before. I was seized with anxiousness. My illegitimacy had been a painful stigma ever since I was a child. What would I say to this man who'd contributed to that?

"I'm taking a shower," I announced, finding a way to delay the inevitable. "I'll be back down later."

Even though I didn't want to, I couldn't help but sneak a glance behind me as I climbed the stairs. Yes, Gregor was still staring, and yes, he seemed to see right through the thin excuse.

"I'll be waiting, Catherine."

It was spoken so softly I almost thought I'd imagined it. But I hadn't. Now he was smiling, and it was pleased and... chilling.

My reprieve didn't last long. Right after my shower, my mother hustled me outside onto the front porch with Gregor. My grandparents were inside watching TV, as if they didn't know or care what was going on. Their apathy baffled me, because Grandpa Joe hated the scorn from my illegitimacy about as much as I did. A change had come over my mother that held my attention. She seemed relaxed and cheerful. Those were two words I'd never before used to describe her. And she was smiling.

"Catherine," she began with a glance at Gregor, "I'm going to tell you about your father...."

Ten minutes later I sat transfixed in disbelief, staring at her. Good God. Somewhere along the way, my mother had gone completely crazy. My father was a vampire she'd been dating who was killed when he was set upon by well-intentioned Marines? There was an entire undead subculture existing side by side with humans? And I wasn't completely human myself?

She'll need inpatient psychological therapy, was my first thought when she finished. *And medication. A lot of it.*

"Mom, sometimes our minds make things up to help deal with what we don't want to face," I started out hesitantly. "I'm learning about it in school—"

"She's not lost her wits," Gregor interrupted. Oh yeah. I'd almost forgotten about Mr. Strange since she told me he wasn't my long-lost father. "You're half-vampire, but you needn't worry. I'm going to take care of you."

Crap, he was nuts too.

"I've waited to tell you this until I thought you were old enough to understand." My mom tried to take my hand, but I pulled away. "I know I've been hard on you at times, but it was just so no one else would find out about you. Still, it's time you know...."

"Seeing is believing," Gregor interrupted her, standing also. "Look at me, Catherine."

I turned around—and screamed.

Gregor's eyes glowed a bright, shining emerald, as if lasers had flicked on in his gaze. His smiled revealed two curved fangs in his upper teeth, and he was elevating in midair. A faint breeze came off him, blowing his hair. Then suddenly I was grasped in his arms, my legs kicking at nothing while he laughed. It was a joyous, frightening, knowing sound that silenced my scream. This wasn't an act. This was real.

"Haven't you always known there was something special about you?" Gregor whispered fiercely. "All your life, that you possessed something no one else had? I'm going to take you away from here. You'll come with me, meet people you've only read about, experience things you can't imagine—"

"I can't go anywhere," I said breathlessly while my mind reeled. "I have school tomorrow."

Gregor laughed again. He dropped down from the dozen feet we were suspended and spoke low and intimately in my ear. "I'll teach you everything you need to know, *ma chéri*."

The way he caressed the words while almost nuzzling my ear made me shiver. I hadn't been in such close proximity with a man before. It made me nervous on top of shocked and confused.

"Mom?" I asked hesitantly.

"You have to go with him, Catherine," she answered. "He's a trusted friend, and he'll take care of you. There are things I can't protect you from if you stay here. Don't worry about school; I'll tell them you're staying out of state with a sick relative. You'll call me whenever you want to. You'll be all right."

This wasn't happening. This *couldn't* be happening. Yet the arms imprisoning me weren't my imagination. The very big, tall body next to mine wasn't a hallucination. I had to go with this… man, creature, *vampire*? Leave everything I knew behind? Sure, I'd wanted to get out of this town, but never in all my imaginings did I think it would be this way!

"You're—" I had to stop, lick my lips, and try again because my mouth was dry. "You're really a vampire?"

Gregor's face creased into a smile. "Yes."

"And I'm…" Deep breath. "I'm not completely human because my father was a vampire? That's why there's something wrong with me? Why I'm not normal?"

"*Oui*, that is so." Unperturbedly.

He hadn't let me go yet. I didn't know if I should ask, push away, or just stand there stupidly.

"You, ah, have your fangs near my throat," I said with a self-deprecating laugh, trying for humor instead of demands. "Should I play the swooning victim or the indignant maiden? I feel like an actor who doesn't know my lines."

He didn't smile again. The light glowed brighter in his eyes, and he leaned in to whisper against my shivering neck. "I'm not going to bite you, Catherine," he answered. His hands dropped and he let me take a quick step away. "Not yet."

"Passengers, please observe the Fasten Seat Belts sign and return your tray tables to their upright and locked position," the flight attendant intoned in her falsely cheerful voice. "We'll be landing in Paris in about twenty minutes. Thank you again for flying Air France."

I glanced to my left where Gregor sat. He'd been sleeping since just before dawn. Normally I'd have slept as well, but my mind was whirling.

After the incredible pronouncement of my parentage, I was marched upstairs to pack. Or at least, my mother told me to. Gregor followed, took one look inside my closet and then crisply announced that I wasn't taking anything with me. The disdain in his expression made me give an embarrassed look at my outfit, seeing it through his eyes. Compared to his upscale shirt, jacket, pants, and shoes, I suppose I did look like a grubby hick. Then I was shuttled out the door with barely a good-bye to my mother and grandparents, speeding away to the airport before you could even say white trash. First flight, nonstop from Cleveland to New York. Next stop after a two-hour layover, Paris.

Gregor barely spoke to me the entire time, talking instead in French on his cell phone. In the air, he'd texted nonstop until he decided to nap. It was just as well. I didn't know a single thing to say. Oh, I had questions. A thousand of them. I just didn't know if he'd answer me.

When we stepped off the plane in the afternoon sunlight and he didn't burst into flames, there was one mystery dispelled. At the gate he was greeted by two pale-skinned men with dark sunglasses and equally thick accents. They each gave me an appraising once-over that made me uncomfortable. Gregor didn't bother to introduce them. He simply grasped my shoulder and propelled me toward the exit. A car was waiting, and I turned to him in surprise when we climbed in the back and left the others standing there.

"Aren't those men coming with us?"

Gregor said something in French to the driver and then turned his attention on me. "They're collecting my bags and following afterward. Don't concern yourself. I have everything arranged."

In other words, *zip it.* I bit back a frustrated sigh and reminded myself that my mother said to trust him. Since she didn't trust anyone, Gregor had to be really something. I wondered why he was interested in me. Was there a Vampire curriculum I had to learn? Would I meet other half-breeds like me? A friend would be so nice to have. Maybe here I wouldn't be considered weird. Maybe here no one cared I was illegitimate. The thought cheered me.

Certainly it *looked* different. I'd never been in a big city, and Paris was magnificent. The architecture, countless people, buildings... I was dazzled. Soon I forgot to ponder my predicament and became engrossed in the sights as the car sped by.

"It is beautiful, *non?*" Gregor said. He wore a trace of a smile when I looked back at him. "We will see more of it tonight."

"How's that?"

But he only gave me a secretive grin and refused to elaborate.

Thirty minutes later we arrived at a tall, imposing building of dark gray stone. Gregor nodded at the structure and the driver hurried to open my door.

"This is where we will stay, Catherine."

What should I say? Looks cozy? It didn't. It appeared large and intimidating, much like the man next to me.

"H-how many people are staying here?"

He held my gaze. "Just us and a few of my staff."

Oh! Immediately I felt uncomfortable and sought to allay my rising fears. *This guy is how much older than you? Decades, at least. He's big, blond, handsome, and he's probably got ten girlfriends. You're fifteen, ugly, and backwoods. Hell, he might just be fulfilling some promise to your long-dead dad and can't wait to unload you.*

"It's nice." Thank God my voice didn't waver. "How long will we be here?" I didn't ask what I really wanted to know. *When can I go home?*

Something snapped shut in his face and he gestured to the open door. "As long as it takes. Now come inside."

Left with no other option, I took the hand offered to me and went into his home.

A woman with rich chestnut hair and full curves waited just inside. She smiled when she saw Gregor, clasping his hands and getting a kiss on both cheeks in return.

"Cannelle, all is prepared?" he murmured, drawing me back when I made to walk away.

"*Oui*," she replied, dissecting me with her gaze. "*Mon Dieu*, is this she? *Très es le enfant!*"

I didn't know what that meant, but it didn't seem like *Hi, how are you.* "I'm Catherine." I introduced myself, taking a dislike to the way she eyeballed me. "Nice to meet you."

She accepted my hand after only a second's hesitation. As soon as her warm fingers touched mine, I had my confirmation.

"She's human," I stated the obvious to Gregor. "Are you the only… um, other one here?"

It suddenly occurred to me that I should watch what I say. Who knew if his undead status was a secret?

"Are you so certain of what she is?" he said, watching me closely.

I considered the woman in front of me. After a pause, I nodded. "No sheerness to her skin, her vein's jumping in her neck, she's warm… and she also doesn't give off a vibe like you do. I'm a hundred percent sure."

Gregor let out a satisfied chuckle at the astonishment on Cannelle's face. "You see? She can feel my essence. You can't." Then he turned and suddenly grasped my bare upper arms. His eyes flashed with tiny lights. "Describe what you feel, Catherine."

The intensity in his voice scared me. So did the way he was looking at me. From the curling of his lips, he liked my reaction. That frightened me even more.

"It… It feels like you're shocking me," I replied, fighting to stay calm. "Your skin tingles and vibrates."

"Yes…" It was almost a hiss. "Yet I feel none of that from you, *chéri*. You feel utterly… human."

The way he said it could have been disparaging. I was glad when he let me go.

"Cannelle will show you to your room," he said. With that, he walked away, leaving me still trembling slightly from the encounter.

Once he was gone, Cannelle gave me a sharp frown. "Follow me." It was thrown over her shoulder. "*Mon Dieu*, but you need a bath."

My mouth dropped at the blunt slur. Anger replaced my confusion, and I resisted the urge to plant my foot up her butt. Instead, I reminded myself that this was where my mother wanted me and followed her up the winding stairs.

The bedroom she led me to was so beautiful I forgot to be mad. A canopy draped over the circular bed, all the furniture looked elegant, and the room was about as large as my grandparent's whole house.

"This is awesome," I breathed, reaching out to finger the tapestry on the wall. "Does this all belong to Gregor?"

"Who else?" came Cannelle's short reply from the bathroom. "Take off your clothes. I will clean you."

Huh? That snapped me back into reality. Europeans must have a funny way about showing hospitality.

"Er, thanks, but I've got it covered."

She came out with her hands her hips. "I have been a lady's maid for fifty years, and Gregor's instructed me to wait on you. Don't make me return to him and tell him I've failed in so simple a task. He won't understand."

The ominous way she finished that last sentence spoke volumes. Sure, I was embarrassed, but even if I didn't think we'd be friendly, I didn't want to get her in the kind of trouble she was implying.

"Can you, ah, let me use the bathroom? I'm sure he won't mind my doing that on my own."

Cannelle shrugged and left the room, closing the door behind her. The tub filled rapidly with water as I availed myself of the facilities. When I was finished, I undressed and sank in the tub, hugging my knees to my chest.

"Look, I'm all set here, so you don't need to—"

Cannelle swept inside and stopped short when she saw me. "*Sacre bleu!* You look even skinnier naked. You have barely any breasts at all!"

Now I was mortified and sank farther into the water. Jeez, why didn't she call me an ugly bastard next? Take away the French accent and it was like listening to my classmates.

"I'm a size five," I answered defensively. "That's not so skinny. And I'm just... petite in the chest area, but I could still grow."

She gave me a look that plainly stated she doubted it, but rolled up her sleeves and settled herself on her knees next to the tub.

"We will wash your hair," she announced. "Then put a mask on your face while you soak. And we must shave you at once. You are so hairy, Catherine; do you not shave your pussy at all?"

I felt my cheeks flame. Oh no, she did *not* just say that.

"Cannelle," I managed through gritted teeth, "this isn't going to work. Just sit in the other room and we'll tell Gregor that you scrubbed me like a stain on the Pope's robes. But you are not, I repeat, *not* laying one hand on my... my stuff!"

"If you send me away, he will know it," she said darkly. "Even now, he hears us. There is no deceiving Gregor."

At that, I whipped my head around before letting out a humiliated groan. Great. Gregor could hear everything? Then he'd caught Cannelle loudly trumpeting that I was a titless, scrawny wonder with a crotch resembling a female Sasquatch!

"Let's get this over with. I'll talk to him about it later," I muttered, handing her the shampoo and mentally cursing up a storm. "You can help me wash my hair, but you're not getting anywhere near my goods, got it? Some things aren't happening no matter what you think of my shaving habits."

"As you say," she replied disdainfully before attacking my head like it offended her. "I am, after all, to obey your commands."

❀ ❀ ❀

"...*oui*..."

The muted cry woke me. I'd fallen asleep with surprising swiftness, but then again, I hadn't slept the day before. A glance at the clock on the wall showed four a.m. Still dark out.

A moan sounded next, low and guttural. I sat up in bed. Somewhere on the first floor, a woman was sobbing. I was halfway to the door when the next series of noises stopped me and a blush seared across my face. *Oh.*

The metallic sound of a bed creaking made me cover my ears, but it wasn't enough. I could still make out the feminine panting and masculine moans of a couple in the downstairs bedroom. It didn't take me more than another moment to recognize the voices. Cannelle and Gregor.

I got back into bed, knowing I should stuff the pillows over my ears and try to sleep, but I didn't. At least they were speaking in French when they were using words, so I didn't know what they were saying. Gregor was probably telling Cannelle she was gorgeous. Sexy. Big-boobed and shaved like a baby's bottom.

I kept listening, watching the time tick by with growing awe. Jeez. Really putting in a full day's work, wasn't he?

Finally, two hours later, he let out a culminating groan and the bed went silent. Cannelle murmured something unintelligible, and then I heard a door open and shut.

Footsteps sounded on the stairs, padding down the hall on the same floor I was on. I stared at the doorknob with growing dread, willing my heartbeat to stay slow. Did Gregor know I'd been listening? *Please don't let him know.*

Thankfully those footsteps only paused by my door before moving on to the other end of the hall. There was another opening and closing of a door, and then silence throughout the house.

I stayed where I was, clutching my pillow until weariness made my eyelids heavy and I fell asleep still facing the door.

"Good morning, Catherine. Sleep well?"

My head jerked up guiltily, but there wasn't any sarcasm in Gregor's face.

He gestured to the full plate opposite him at the table. "Eat something. Cannelle's made blintzes and poached eggs."

"She's a talented one, huh?" It came out before I could curb it. Immediately I regretted it. *None of your business*, I reminded myself as I sat.

That scar near his eyebrow twitched with his frown. "You don't care for Cannelle? She has offended you?"

"No." Great, how to get myself out of this? "She's fine. I mean, she's nice. Sort of. I don't like her giving me a bath!" I finished with vehemence.

An amused curl formed at his mouth. "*Oui.* I gathered that yesterday."

It was all I could do not to defend my chest size, weight, and alleged hairiness. "And it's not appropriate anyway, since she's..."

I stopped, cursing myself again. *Can't shut up, can you?*

"Since she's what?" With unyielding resonance.

No use trying to weasel out of it. The way Gregor's eyes were nailing me to my seat, I couldn't just change the subject. "She shouldn't be waiting on me like a servant since she's your, um, girlfriend."

If I thought he'd be upset, I was wrong.

Gregor laughed as if I'd told a joke. "Whatever gave you that idea?"

A steadily squeaking bed frame. "Oh, um, it's just a feeling I have."

"You're lying," he stated flatly. "Don't lie to me; I can smell it. Answer me or Cannelle will."

The way he said it made me remember her odd behavior when she said Gregor wouldn't understand if she failed to do her "duty." She was sleeping with him; he wouldn't really be mean to her. Would he?

"I-I heard you this morning." I had to look away when I said it, embarrassed to the bone. "I didn't mean to. I hear things I'm not supposed to. Believe me, it's gotten me in trouble my whole life—"

"You heard us in bed?" he asked bluntly. "Three floors down on the other side of the house?"

My cheeks were warm. With my head still bowed, I nodded.

"I see…" He drew it out thoughtfully, then his voice changed. Became powerful, raising the hair on my neck and arms. "Look at me, Catherine."

Up came my head to meet his blazing emerald eyes. They seemed to hold mine in a grip.

"You heard nothing this morning. You were dreaming," he said, his voice vibrating with power.

I blinked, taken aback by his intensity. "Okay. It's none of my business anyway."

That made him cock his head, like I'd just said something unbelievable. Gregor stared at me, almost bewildered, and then suddenly he was in front of me.

His hands grasped my face and didn't let me turn away. "I said, 'You heard nothing this morning. You were dreaming.'" His voice practically echoed and if his eyes gleamed any brighter, they'd leave burns on my skin.

"All right, you've made your point! I'll forget I ever heard it. You don't have to get all glowy and loud."

He sat back on his haunches with a stunned expression, his eyes fading back to their normal gray-green. A sharp laugh escaped him. "Extraordinary," he murmured.

"What?" Was I in *really* bad trouble for overhearing?

Gregor shook his head and fixed me with a bemused look before returning to his chair. His fingers drummed on the white table cloth.

"'Twasn't meant for your ears," he said at last.

I controlled the rude urge to snort, *No shit.*

"I didn't realize your abilities were to such a degree, and so now I must explain."

"You don't have to." Me and my big mouth.

"But I do." Softly. "I don't want you under a misapprehension. Cannelle and I are, shall we say, no more. She is in stewardship to me and on occasion, I have permitted it to go further, but this morning was... good-bye. She will stay on here, but our relationship will not alter from employee and employer again. Do you understand?"

Yeah, I did. A strange relief spread over me, mixed with apprehension. I was very much intimidated by the vampire sitting across from me. He could switch from jovial to callous in an instant, and I was more than a little afraid of him. But still...

"Why are you telling me this?"

Gregor leaned forward, and there went that herd of butterflies in my stomach. "Why do you think?"

My mouth went dry. Without thinking, I licked my lips, almost bolting from my seat when he slowly licked his. It was like kissing without touching, and it was a lot to handle for me, going from being shunned by all the boys my age to having breakfast with a gorgeous vampire who looked at me as if I were dessert. This was too fast, and nothing had really even happened.

"Um, did you say these were blintzes?" I wanted to break the weighty silence and snatched at the plate like it was a life raft. "Great. I'm starving."

Gregor settled back into his chair. He had a slightly superior, pleased expression. "As am I."

Chapter Twenty-Six
Alternate "Middle" Version of *Destined for an Early Grave*

Author's note: *This is the last and longest of the chapters. It contains roughly thirty thousand words, or the length of a large novella. In this version of* Destined for an Early Grave, *when Bones left Cat after the infamous "piano scene" to go to New Orleans, Gregor found a way to erase Bones's memory of Cat, similar to how Mencheres had erased Cat's memory of Gregor when she was a teenager. As you can imagine, having Cat erased from his mind changed Bones's behavior dramatically, and thus the original middle of the novel was very different from the version that was later published. I decided to take that subplot out because so much had already happened to Cat and Bones in* DFAEG *that the memory loss seemed too burdensome. However, I'm sentimental, which is why I took the chunk out of the final manuscript but didn't delete it from my computer.*

So, if you want to see Cat and Bones interacting with each other while Bones has no memory of their previous life, read on. For context, this alternate "middle" version starts on page 207 of the published version of Destined for an Early Grave. *You'll see some scene overlap with only small changes at first, then the new content starts after Cat arrives at the military base. In case you're wondering, the entirety of the alternate "middle" ends right before Cat is turned into a vampire. After that, the story was pretty much the same as in the published version, which is why I call this a* deleted "middle" section of DFAEG. Also, among other notable differences, Spade and Denise are already a couple in this version. Their romance originally happened off page, which changed when I got the green light to write First Drop of Crimson.

Bones fangirl warning: *His memory of Cat has been stolen, as stated above, so it starts out with Bones acting like he used to before he met Cat *cough, slut, cough*. If you don't want to see Bones that way, don't read this.*

The knock at the door didn't wake me. Must have been too soft and tentative. Only when Vlad said, "Come in," in a less-than-pleased tone did I wake up. God, he was right. My reflexes were shit.

Shrapnel stuck his head inside. I mentally berated Vlad for not giving me a chance to disappear into the bathroom. How incriminating did this look?

"Forgive me, but the caller says it's urgent. May I give you the phone?" He held it close to his side, obviously nervous. Maybe Vlad was really grumpy when he woke up.

Vlad gestured in annoyance. "Very well, bring it."

Shrapnel moved like a jackrabbit and then hurried out, closing the door behind him.

"Who's this?" Vlad snapped into the phone.

Spade's voice blared out loud enough to cause me to bolt upright. "If you don't put Cat on the line this time, I'm going to roast you alive in your own sodding juices—"

I snatched the phone away from Vlad. "What is it? I'm here, what's wrong?"

There was a loaded moment of silence. Too late, I realized what I'd done. Vlad lifted a shoulder as if to say, *You're stuck now.*

"I was told he couldn't be disturbed because he was in bed." Each word was a blistering accusation. "That he was extremely indisposed. Lucifer's bloody balls, Cat, is this why you haven't returned my calls?"

"I-I-I didn't..." Good God, I was stammering.

"Indeed!"

"Look, don't even!" My anger came to the rescue. "If something's wrong, tell me, but if you're just going to play Pussy Police, you should start with your best friend. He's probably nose-deep in one right now."

"He's arse-deep in mortal danger, if you still care," was the icy reply.

That took the hostility right out of me. Spade wasn't one for hysterical exaggerations. I clutched the phone like it was slippery. "What happened?"

Maybe I sounded as fearful as I felt, because Spade's voice lost some of its anger.

"Fabian, your helpful ghost, has been in New Orleans trying to speak with him. From what he can deduce, which is little, Crispin's mind has been altered. And Gregor's lying in wait outside the city to kill him."

"What do you mean, his mind has been *altered*?" My voice couldn't get more shrill.

Vlad winced.

"Just as part of your memory was erased years ago by Mencheres, it appears Gregor's found a way to do the same thing to Crispin. He doesn't remember Fabian. He doesn't even know he's at war with Gregor."

I was so stunned I couldn't even gasp. How could Gregor have done that? How?

"Crispin went to New Orleans to have a meeting with Marie," Spade continued. "After it took place, from what I've gathered, he started acting strangely. Then Marie closed the Quarter to any more undead visitors, and Gregor's assembled a slew of forces beyond the city's outskirts."

That knocked me out of my temporary paralysis. I jumped up and began rummaging for clothes. Vlad scooted into my spot, unperturbed.

I asked, "Are you there? On your way?"

"We can't, that's the whole bloody problem! Because of you, Gregor has clear rights to take Crispin out under our laws. And now Crispin doesn't even know he's under a death sentence. He'd likely walk right up to Gregor with a 'fancy seeing you here' before that filthy git slaughtered him!"

"He doesn't remember why he's at war with Gregor?" The ramifications of that finally began slamming into me.

"Although Fabian's very careful in what he says since Crispin still doesn't know what to make of the ghost, Crispin has never mentioned you, either," Spade said brutally.

I sat on the floor, my knees weak. For a second, I couldn't even breathe. Then I pushed my feelings aside and began to plan.

"He'll need to be airlifted out of there. A helicopter would be best. We can arm it with silver bullets. We'll do a midair transport onto a plane. Did you say you've been leaving messages for me about this?" I gave Vlad a truly menacing glare.

"I've been leaving messages for you to call, but we only found out tonight about Crispin's condition and Gregor's ambush."

Vlad shrugged, unapologetic. "You said you didn't want to speak to them. This part is news to me. I would have told you had I known."

I didn't bitch at him. After all, it was my own fault for hiding, not Vlad's.

"There's a problem with your plan, Cat," Spade said tightly. "Else we would have already done something similar.

No one of any line is allowed in the city, and that means above it too. It would be sentencing them to death by Marie's decree, and she's too powerful to dismiss. I'd risk it myself, but if one vampire or ghoul crosses the line into the Quarter, Gregor and his people will follow. It has to be humans of no vampire affiliation, do you understand?"

Yeah, I did. Now I knew why he'd been in such a twist to get ahold of me.

"Give me your number. I'll call you right back."

"...testing three, two, one... You read me, Geri?"

Lieutenant Geri Hicks, my replacement with Don's team, coughed and muttered, "Affirmative."

She had a receiving line surgically planted under her skin, pumping my voice directly by her eardrum. If I shouted, she'd be in pain. Her microphone was less invasively located in her necklace.

"What's your location, Geri?"

"Crossing St. Ann Street and heading toward Bourbon. The bird still show he's there?"

I checked the satellite imagery of the French Quarter on my borrowed laptop. The plane's turbulence didn't help, but I could still spot Bones. And the woman next to him.

"Affirmative. There's a small time delay, but he should be there. You doing all right?"

Geri was nervous. I couldn't blame her. She had to bring Bones in without getting him or herself killed. Bones was lethally powerful, plus there was a good chance he wouldn't recognize her. Yeah, I'd have been wigged too.

"I'm good," Geri said.

"Roger that. Now go show him that he can't turn you down twice."

She made a noise that was almost a laugh. On her first mission, she hadn't known her mock target was also her trainer. "This is so weird."

No shit.

I was the only person Spade knew who had human connections without direct undead affiliations and who could amass airpower and support complete with cutting-edge weapons and technology. Sure, it could be argued that my old team had connections to Bones, but none of them were under his command anymore since I'd quit. I owed my uncle big for this.

We weren't sure how "altered" Bones's memory was. Only a few things were certain. Bones didn't know about the strife with Gregor. He didn't seem to be able to read human's thoughts anymore, either, or he wouldn't be with the double-crossing skank in the photo. Oh yeah, and he *definitely* had no idea he was married. What—if anything— he knew about me remained to be seen. Maybe I'd been reduced to old-girlfriend status in his mind.

Or maybe I'd been vanished completely.

Since she was human, Geri couldn't see Fabian. He was there though, trying to convince Bones he wasn't deranged while not getting noticed by any of Marie's people. That wasn't an easy task. When this was over, I'd owe him big too. How does one repay a ghost? That was an issue I'd ponder later.

"Approaching target, going silent," Geri whispered.

On-screen I saw her nearing Bones. He was at Pat O'Brien's in the outside area, drinking what I guessed was his usual whiskey. His arm was slung around a pretty brunette who was almost glued to him. Even now, her hand ran along his hip.

I clenched my fists. *Bitch, you and I are going to have a long, bloody chat after this.*

Cannelle couldn't hear my mental warning, but Vlad could. He lounged in the chair opposite me, the jet's turbulence not bothering him. We were on our way to the rendezvous point if all went well.

"You really don't like her."

I didn't answer out loud. That might confuse Geri since I was wearing a headset.

No. I really, really don't.

"I know this is forward," Geri purred through my earpiece as the satellite showed her reaching Bones and his companion, Cannelle, "but after seeing the two of you gorgeous creatures, I can't decide who I want to fuck first."

"Attagirl," I whispered. God, cheering someone to hit on the man I loved! Why couldn't I have a normal life?

With dark appreciation, I watched Bones set his drink down. Not any line would have worked. The man was a frigging chick magnet, and Geri wasn't his usual type. But with that opener? She'd gotten his attention, all right.

"Easy decision, luv." Her necklace picked up every nuance of his accent. "Ladies first. Isn't that right, Cinnamon?"

Cannelle's knowing laugh pierced me straight to the heart. The plane's armrest lost a chunk.

"She looks very fierce, *chéri.* I was hoping for softer company, *non?*"

Geri didn't let Cannelle's disparagement stumble her. She flicked her fingers in Bones's drink, then made a good show of licking the alcohol off them. "I'll be as gentle as a lamb, honey."

Geri really had come a long way since the person I'd trained months ago. Cannelle might still be wavering over her, but Bones wasn't. He caught her wrist, slowly ran his mouth along her palm, and then did something I couldn't see that made Geri gasp.

"Never let a drop of something precious go to waste."

His voice was deep with promise, an orgasm for the ears. Hearing it directed at someone else was another stab in the heart, but I masked it. I had a job to do. Everything else was secondary.

Geri sounded promising herself. "Maybe you'll show me what you mean?"

Bones handed her his glass. "Drink."

She took a sip. I tensed everywhere when Bones set it aside and then took Geri in his arms. Through Geri's microphone, I heard his body rubbing against her, her muted moan of enjoyment, and his masculine rumble as he pressed her closer.

A full two minutes later, he lifted his head. By then I almost *wanted* him dead.

Vlad watched me without pity. "Someone else could be doing this."

He was right. I'd insisted on being the relay. I didn't trust anyone else for something so important, no matter that it was brutal for me.

"That's what I mean," Bones told Geri softly.

"You, ah…" She sounded breathless and a little flustered. "You certainly get your point across."

"You're doing great," I said to Geri, very low. She couldn't be distracted by worrying about how I was taking this. "Get him moving."

"What was that?" Bones asked sharply.

We'd been worried about this. Vampires had great hearing, hence the receiver being under her skin. It was also why I'd insisted on being the relay. If Bones overheard us, I'd be the one talking him down. No one knew him better than me.

"What?" Geri tried playing innocent.

Bones began running his hands down the front of her, all business now. Cannelle's confusion showed even on the satellite image. Something had to be done. Now.

"Sorry about this," I said to Geri. Then louder, "Bones! Lean in and listen up, and for God's sake, can you *be* less conspicuous?"

That startled him. Apparently a hidden voice snapping at him wasn't what he expected.

"*Chéri?*" Cannelle inquired.

She shouldn't be able to hear me. She was still human, even after all these years.

"Calm the bitch," I barked. "She'll get you killed."

"Don't fret, sweet, it was nothing," he told her. Then rustling sounds preceded the image of Bones moving closer to Geri, holding her shoulders. "What a lovely neck you have. Let's see how it tastes."

If I were Geri, I'd be gulping at the blatant warning that translated into *Anything goes wrong, and your jugular is* mine. Fortunately, it allowed him to be right by the receiver.

"What's your name, darling?"

Although Geri answered him with a fake one, I knew Bones was really talking to me.

"Don't you recognize my voice?"

"No." To Geri, "You don't look an Alexander."

A sob almost choked me as my worst fears were realized. I was completely gone from his memory. After everything we'd been through, now I was just an unknown voice.

"That's the name of the ship that took you to Australia in 1789," I replied, controlling myself. "You can trust me. I'm a... friend of Spade's."

"You'll have to do better than that," he said as his hand wound in Geri's hair.

She began kissing his neck, making it look like he was giving her instructions. Cannelle seemed to be getting fidgety. I had to make him a believer.

"Your mother's name was Penelope. She died of syphilis when you were seventeen. Madame Lucille poured a bottle of her favorite perfume on Penelope before her body was burned. Every time you smell violets, it reminds you of your mother."

A highly personal thing to recount with someone else listening, but I had no choice. Loaded silence followed my words.

"Do I meet your standards?" Geri asked.

Bones still had her neck angled. I sucked in my breath.

"You'll do," he said at last.

I let out that breath in a sigh of relief. Bones might not know me anymore, but for now, he'd listen to me.

"First things first. Cannelle's a traitor, and the city is surrounded. You need to get to the top of St. Anthony's as quick as you can, but be subtle. You're being watched."

"You're so gorgeous, baby," Geri said, catching his shirt in her hands. "Do we have to get to know each other? I just want to fuck like you can't imagine."

Bones disentangled himself from Geri to take Cannelle's hand. "Hate to keep a lovely girl waiting. Come on, Cinnamon. This is who I want tonight."

"Don't I get to choose?"

I heard the pout in Cannelle's voice and it was all I could do not to scream.

"Not this time, luv."

"*Chéri—*"

"Everyone else has been your choice." He led them through the crowds. "Keep whinging, and I'll make you wait until I'm done before you have her."

"Little French whore," I spat, unable to help it. *Everyone else? Wasn't that just great!*

Bones stopped at a curb. "Careful, Alexander," he said pleasantly. "Or you'll trip over your narrow perspective."

I knew that was directed at me, so I answered it. "Don't go there, buddy, I *married* a whore."

Vlad gave me a look. I waved a hand at him as if to say, *I know, I know. I'm trying!*

"Keep heading toward the church," I said, back to business. Then I removed my headset and spoke into my cell phone. "Okay, Don. Deploy. They're on their way. Tell Cooper not to drop the ladder until he's fifty yards away."

"Got it, Cat."

I readjusted the headset. Geri had just been telling Bones that she wanted to have sex on the church's roof, but Cannelle was protesting.

"*Non,* there could be rats! Why can we not leave here for an evening? I told you I have very beautiful friends in Metairie I want you to meet."

"Tell you what, sweet. We'll go tomorrow. You've wanted me to meet these lasses for days; they must be terribly special."

"*Oui. Très magnifique.*"

"Bitchsticks has been trying to get you out of the city, huh?" I said with rising anger. Maybe Vlad's impalement thing wasn't such a bad idea. "Now you know why."

"Tomorrow we'll do what you fancy, and tonight shall be my evening," Bones went on. "I promise you'll see a new side of me."

And me too. I was *really* looking forward to seeing Cannelle in person again.

I couldn't see the three of them anymore. They'd been off my satellite since they started walking. "Look around, Bones. Are you being followed?"

"It's a beautiful night, isn't it, ladies?" Pause. "I love this city. It's so deliciously haunted."

"Don't worry about the ghost, if he's the same one who's been bugging you for days. He's a friend."

"I like haunted places," Geri replied, keeping the conversation going. "You don't think anyone will catch us climbing up on the roof, do you?"

Bones kissed her again. I couldn't see it, but I could hear it. "Not at all."

Okay. It was clear. God, I wanted this to be over soon. Safely, and soon.

"Here's the score, Bones. A chopper's going to do a pass over the church about two hundred yards up. He'll have a chain ladder dangling. When you see him coming, you blast up with both chicks and grab it. As soon as you're clear of the city, you'll leapfrog onto the back of another plane. Spade will be on it."

"Ah, here's the church," he said in reply. "Alexander, my lovely, look at me for a moment. You don't need to fret about my eyes or my teeth, right? You don't notice anything unusual about them. You're not afraid, because you know I won't hurt you. Say it."

"You won't hurt me," Geri repeated. "I'm not afraid."

So, that's how he got around the glowy gaze and pointy teeth when he fucked humans. I'd thought as much but had never wanted to ask. I knew more about his past than I already cared to. This scene was for Cannelle's benefit, I guessed, since Bones knew Geri was in on his secret. Just going through the usual motions.

I thought I'd puke.

"Cinnamon, shall we?"

"If we must, *chéri*."

"We must."

After a few moments of noisy rustling sounds, Bones spoke again. "The roof at last. No rats, petite, quit cringing."

Vlad, get the chopper's ETA, I thought.

He complied with the mental directive and took my cell, hitting redial.

"They're on the roof," he informed Don briefly. "How long? ... Yes." He set my cell back down. "Six minutes."

"You've got six minutes, Bones. Remember, you have to have both of them with you when you jump, and Cinnamon won't want to go."

"Come here, lovelies. That's better."

Bones's voice changed. Became that luxurious purr that used to melt me. Listening to it now only made me pissed. Worse, next there was the breathiness and the soft chafing noises of kissing.

Then Geri said, "Hey now, sugar. Ease up a bit."

"Why?" Cannelle's voice was belligerent. "I am ready for you to please me."

I glanced at the time. "Two more minutes. Stall but be cool, Geri."

"Cinnamon, don't be so greedy. I'll sweeten her up for you. You'll like it better for the wait. Why don't you find a better use for your mouth than complaining, petite? Ah, yes. Like that."

"Sonofa*bitch*," I spat. It didn't require a satellite to know where he'd directed her mouth.

"You, um, might not want to do that." Geri sounded rattled.

Cannelle made a reply that was garbled. Vlad got up and started rubbing my shoulders. I was crying now. Silent, furious, useless tears.

"Accomplish your objective," Vlad said, soft yet stern.

I beat my fists against my legs but didn't scream like I wanted to. Instead, I watched the seconds tick past and tried to listen with clinical detachment for signs of danger. Unfortunately, most of what I heard wasn't sounds of danger.

Ninety seconds... sixty... thirty... twenty...

"Ten seconds," I rasped. "Nine, eight, seven..."

"Know something, Cinnamon?" Bones lost the seductive timbre to his voice and it turned into cold steel. "You're not any bloody good at that."

"...one!" I yelled with all the bitterness in me.

Then there were only the sounds of the helicopter before I heard a clanging of metal, a thump, and the words I'd been waiting for from Geri.

"We're in!"

The chopper had special silent blades that reduced its normal noise. It made Cooper and the two copilots inaudible, however.

Geri wasn't, of course. "Zip up, Bones, and I hope you're rich."

He laughed. "Why?"

"Marriage counseling," she replied. "You're going to need the best that money can buy."

"Drop it," I told her very softly.

"I don't know who misinformed you, luv, but I'm not married."

"Is she still breathing?" Geri asked, wisely changing the subject. "You hit her pretty hard."

"She's alive."

There was a thumping noise, and then Geri said harshly, "Try to shove *my* head between your legs, huh? Who's happy now, bitch?"

"She can't feel you kicking her," Bones said, no criticism in his voice.

"Yeah, well, I can feel it, and I'm enjoying it!"

"Are you a friend of Charles's also?"

Charles was Spade's real name. Vampires never could just pick one. Great, now he was asking questions. That was my cue.

"She's a friend of mine, Bones. So are the guys flying. Spade will explain everything when you see him. It should only be a few minutes until you're clear of the city."

"Then it is you I owe thanks to." He sounded closer now. Must be right next to Geri. "How did you know my mother's favorite perfume? I don't recall ever telling Charles that."

"Long... long story." My throat closed off with suppressed tears. What was I going to say? *You don't remember me, but once we were madly in love?*

"You can tell me about it. I'll take you and your husband out for a grand evening. Former whore, was he? We have something in common."

Geri gave a bark of laughter. "Boy, you have *no* idea what you're saying."

I couldn't break down now, so close to the finish line. "Don't bother. We're, ah, we're separated."

"Oh?" Pause. "Then it shall just be you and me."

"I'm three hundred pounds, have bad scoliosis, and I just turned sixty," I snapped.

Bones didn't miss a beat. "Dinner theater then."

I laughed even as the tears started to flow again. I'd wanted confirmation that things were really over between us, and here it was. He didn't even know me. It couldn't get more over than that.

"I'm glad you're safe, Bones. Tell Fabian thank you— he's the ghost. He's been a good friend."

"And who shall I say is thanking him?"

"Cat." I waited a second, but he had no reaction. "Cat says thanks."

I waited until Bones had transferred to Spade's plane as planned before unhooking my headpiece. Geri was probably delighted not to have my voice pumping into her eardrum anymore. Only Bones was doing the aerial jump; she and Cannelle were staying in the helicopter. Spade's plane was supposed to rendezvous with me at one of Don's locations, but that wasn't necessary now.

I called my uncle. "Change Bones's flight plan," I said. "Don't tell me where to, but don't fly him where I'll be."

My uncle didn't ask unnecessary questions. "All right, Cat."

I hung up. Vlad had been watching me the entire time.

I managed to muster what had to be a terrible imitation of a smile. "That answers that."

"He doesn't even remember you, and it's not as if his prior habits were unfamiliar to you," Vlad replied, no false sympathy in his voice.

No, they weren't. But I hadn't expected to listen while Cannelle found the soft chewy center in Bones's Tootsie Roll Pop. He'd been on the other plane over two hours now. Spade had called my cell several times, but I didn't answer. I knew they were safe. Nothing else needed to be said.

We finally landed at a base, though I didn't know where. From the outside, most military installations looked the same anyway, not that I was looking. I had my eyes shut and my hand on Vlad's arm as I got off the plane.

"Hello, Commander," a male voice said.

I smiled with my eyes still closed. "Cooper, I'd say nice to see you, but give me a minute."

He grunted, which was his version of a belly laugh, and soon I was inside the facility.

"You can open your eyes now," Cooper said.

His familiar face was the first thing I saw, dark skinned and with hair even shorter than Tate's. I gave him a brief hug, which seemed to surprise him, but he was smiling when I let him go.

"Missed you, freak," he said.

I laughed even though it was hoarse. "You too, Coop. What's the news?"

"Geri's chopper arrived thirty minutes ago. The prisoner was secured and is awake. Ian is here. He's been questioning the prisoner."

That made me smile for real. I'd had Ian flown here because he was a cold-blooded bastard—and right now, I liked that about him.

"You can stay here or come with me, it's up to you," I said to Vlad.

"I'll come," he replied, giving Fabian, who'd just floated up, a cursory glance. The ghost hovered over the ground next to Cooper, who as a human couldn't see him.

"Fabian, you've been incredible," I said. "No matter what, I'll take care of you. You'll always have a place to stay."

"Thank you," he said, brushing his hand through mine in his form of affection. "I'm sorry, Cat."

He didn't need to say what for. That was obvious.

My smile turned brittle. "Whoever said ignorance was bliss was shortsighted, if you ask me. But what's done is done, and now I have an acquaintance to renew."

The ghost looked momentarily hopeful. "Bones?"

"No. The little bitch inside, and you might not want to follow me for this one. It's going to get ugly."

I didn't have to tell him twice. In a whirl, Fabian vanished. Neat trick. Sucked to have to be a phantom to do it.

Vlad gave me a slanted look. "You're not intending to see him at all, then?"

"No. We have no official ties anymore, and now he wouldn't even be able to pick me out of a lineup. Plus I'm a walking LoJack to the vampire who wants nothing more than to kill Bones. I'd say the best thing I could do is get away from Bones… and go back to Gregor."

Vlad looked at me like I'd suddenly sprouted a second head. "Don't be a fool. You can't trust Gregor."

I let out a noise that no one would misconstrue as a laugh. "I don't. But I trust that I can keep Gregor occupied enough to lay off Bones until he and Mencheres can figure out how fix Bones's mind."

"You can stay with me. Gregor won't dare to attack me to retrieve you; he has enough powerful enemies as it is."

I touched his hand with a sad smile. "I appreciate the offer, really. But then Gregor will only use Bones to draw me out, and no matter how mad I am at him, it'll work."

Vlad said nothing, merely staring at me with a look I couldn't decipher. I didn't want to hear more arguments, so I headed toward my uncle's office without waiting to see if Vlad followed.

Turned out, Don was waiting for me in the hallway. He looked… bad.

"Is something wrong?" I asked, instantly worried. Had Bones's plane been tailed, or attacked, or worse?

"No." He coughed. "I just have a cold."

"Oh." I gave him a hug hello. It surprised me when he squeezed back and held on. We weren't a cuddly family.

Vlad sniffed the air. "A cold?"

Don let me go and gave him an annoyed look. "That's right. Don't concern yourself. I'm not contagious to your kind."

He said it harshly. Jeez, maybe Don really did feel like shit. My uncle wasn't normally so surly, even though vampires weren't his favorite group of people.

Vlad looked him up and down and shrugged, taking out his cell phone to signify that Don didn't merit a response. His fingers flew over it, texting the fastest message ever.

Don went right to business. It was his defining characteristic. "Dave radioed to confirm that Bones's memory of you has been completely erased. He was astonished to hear he was married, and now he's insisting on seeing you. Dave's requesting permission to come here."

"No," I said at once. "You tell Dave to forget changing course. If Bones wants to satisfy his curiosity about me, someone can give him a picture. Gregor's going to be mad as hell as soon as he realizes Bones has flown the coop, and if I'm with him, it'll only make Bones easier for Gregor to track."

"Is that the only reason?" Don asked in a quiet tone.

I had to look away and blink to clear my suddenly fogged vision. "Whatever chance we might have had—which was slim anyway, considering Bones left me and said everything but good riddance—it's over now. I don't know how Gregor did it, but when he carved me out of Bones's mind, he killed any hope of a future for us. You can't regret losing someone you don't even remember, so... that's that."

My uncle didn't argue even though his expression said he was doubtful. "Ian's been asking the prisoner about how Gregor did it. She hasn't been very forthcoming."

Oh, hasn't she?

"Then it's time for me to see my old friend."

Cannelle didn't appear to have aged a day in the twelve years since I'd seen her. In fact, only her reddish-brown hair was different with its new, shorter length. I guessed it was where she got her name. Cannelle. French for cinnamon.

She sat on a steel bench which took up an entire wall in the square, boxlike space. Cannelle wasn't restrained since Ian and Geri were in the room with her. Even if by some miracle she got past them, there were still three more guards outside the door. Her eye was black, and blood dripped from her mouth and temple, but she wasn't cowed.

When I walked in, she blinked, then laughed.

"*Bonjour*, Catherine! It's been a long time. You finally look like a woman. I am very surprised."

I felt a nasty grin pull my lips. "*Bonjour* yourself, Cannelle. Yep, I grew tits and ass and a whole lot more. What a difference a dozen years makes, huh?"

She went right for the throat. "I must compliment you on your lover, Bones. *Qu'un animal, non?* In this instance, his reputation was... not gracious enough."

Bitch. I wanted to rip the smirk right off her face. "Too bad he didn't seem bowled over by your bedroom skills. I mean, the fact that you couldn't get him to leave the city for a *ménage a cinq* doesn't speak well, does it? And how *do* you even give a bad blowjob? Those words are usually an oxymoron."

Ian chuckled with malevolent humor. "Oh, you two ladies have a history, do you?" He looked at Cannelle. "You might want to start speaking now, poppet. I've been gentle with you, but Cat has a wicked temper. She'll likely kill you before I can reason with her."

"Her?" Cannelle flicked her finger contemptuously at me. "She's a child."

Boy, did she pick the wrong girl in the wrong mood.

"Hand me that knife, Ian."

He passed it over, his turquoise eyes sparkling. Geri looked a little nervous. Cannelle didn't even blink.

"You won't kill me, Catherine. You play the hard woman, but I still see a little girl before me."

Ian regarded Cannelle with amazement. "She's unhinged."

"No, she's just remembering who I used to be. Gregor made that mistake also, at first."

I smiled at Cannelle again while twirling the knife from one hand to the other. Her eyes followed the movement, and for the first time, she looked uncertain.

"Remember that big bad bitch Gregor didn't want me turning into? Well, it happened. Now, I'm in a hurry, so here's what I'm going to do. I'm going to circumcise you, and the only way you'll stop me is by talking, so please. *Please.* Don't talk."

She didn't believe me. When Ian held her and I cut her panties off, she was still giving me that I-dare-you glare. When I used my hips to open her legs, she still thought I was bluffing. Only when I severed the aforementioned tissue with a single upward swipe did she get the picture.

And couldn't stop screaming.

"Whoa, I bet that hurts," I said coldly. "Ian's licking his lips at all that blood. You have a choice, Cannelle. We can put this thing back on and a dab of vampire blood'll have you good as new. Or…"

"Put it back! *Put it back!*"

"You'll tell us what we want to know?"

"*Oui!*"

After listening to her go down on Bones, I was almost disappointed. "Ian?"

Cannelle was still screaming when he took her severed hunk of flesh, coated it with his blood, and slapped it between her legs like he was playing pin the tail on the donkey.

Then he sliced his palm and cupped it over her mouth. "Quit wailing and swallow."

She gulped at his hand. In seconds, her bleeding stopped and her flesh knit itself back together.

Geri couldn't tear her eyes away from Cannelle's mending clitoris. She shivered and rubbed her own crotch as if in reflex. I was more concerned with Cannelle's face and judging whether or not she'd go back on her word.

"Since we've established that I'm in a really foul mood, let's move on to the question-and-answer phase. Oh, and if you make me use this knife again… I'm not putting anything back. How did Gregor do it? How did he steal Bones's memory?"

Cannelle kept touching herself while staring at me in horror. "Gregor had Marie perform a spell that erases part of a person's memory. He thought you deserved to know how it felt to have the person you love forget about you and whore themselves to others, just as you had done to Gregor."

Oh, how I hated the man. He wasn't content to make me run all over the place with my hands covering my eyes. He had to make sure I did it with my heart ripped out too.

"Why didn't he just kill Crispin?" Ian asked. "If he had him defenseless enough for Marie to bollocks up his mind, why didn't he shove silver through his heart?"

Cannelle's mouth dipped. "The Queen of Orleans wouldn't allow it. She said Gregor could only kill Bones outside her city. She didn't want to participate in the spell or their meeting, either, but Gregor made her."

"He forced her?"

"*Non*, you misunderstand. He *made* her. 'Twas his blood that raised her as a ghoul, and Gregor killed her other sire the night he changed her, so her fealty was to him alone. Gregor agreed to release Marie in exchange, and Marie's wanted free of Gregor for over a hundred years."

"And Bones would trust Marie because she always guarantees safe passage in her meetings." *That clever, dirty schmuck.* "Your part?"

"I was to fuck him, *naturellement*, and once assured that you heard of his infidelity, I was to take him to Gregor." She actually smirked as she spoke.

My anger turned to ice. "Is that all, Cannelle?"

"*Oui.*"

I turned to Ian. "Think she's got more?"

He met my gaze with equal coldness. "No, poppet. I think that's it."

I still had the knife in my hand, slick from Cannelle's blood. "Cannelle," I said, my voice steady. "I'm going to kill you. I'm telling you this so can take a moment to pray if you choose, or to reflect, whichever. You lured my husband around with the full intention of taking him to his slaughter, and that's just not forgivable to me."

"Cat, no," Geri said.

I didn't answer her. Cannelle gave me a look filled with malicious defiance. "But Bones isn't your husband. Gregor is."

"Semantics. You're wasting time. Get right with God. Fast."

"I am a *human*," she hissed. "A living, breathing person. You may have it in you to wound me, but not to kill me."

I ignored that too. "Marie got her freedom for her role. What did Gregor promise? To change you?"

Another hostile glare. "*Oui.* It's my payment for all the years I've served him."

"You backed the wrong horse," I said. "If you would have told Bones what was happening, he'd have turned you himself. He's honorable that way. Instead, you tried to get him killed. You're not going to be a vampire, Cannelle, but I'll let you die like one."

She stood up. "You wouldn't dare. Gregor would kill you."

Then she looked down. The silver knife was buried in her chest. It even vibrated for a few seconds with her last remaining heartbeats. Cannelle watched the handle quiver with astonishment before her eyes glazed and her knees buckled.

I stood over her and felt more of that awful coldness.

"Maybe Gregor will kill me for this, Cannelle. I'm willing to take that chance."

I took my time in the shower, but the scalding water pouring over me didn't make me feel warm. It did clean the blood off, however, and that was a start. Finally I shut it off and grabbed a towel. No more stalling. I had things to do whether I wanted to or not.

The locker room was empty. Geri had left me something to wear, even though she clearly disapproved of what I'd done. Still, she had no recourse since Don just tugged his eyebrow and said it wasn't civilian business. If she stayed long enough at this job, Geri would lose a lot of her current sense of right and wrong. That wasn't necessarily a good thing, but it was a fact all the same.

Geri's clothing donation turned out to be an ankle-length yellow dress with purple flowers. It looked spring-time and happy. I felt wintry and depressed. It seemed like months since I'd worn clothes that were mine. I wouldn't know my own panties if they bit me in the ass.

She'd left her toiletry bag out too. Guess that was a hint. I helped myself to the toothbrush and toothpaste, although I didn't care if Gregor was offended by my breath. The only makeup I bothered with was lipstick because my lips felt like sandpaper. Then I looked into the mirror. Now that I was clean, I looked like death warmed over instead of cold, grim death.

Cannelle's face kept flashing in my mind. *Cold, grim death.* That's what I'd given her.

A knock sounded at the door. "Can I come in?" asked Geri.

I sighed. "Sure."

She came inside the locker room, and from her expression, she was still upset with me.

"Before you say anything," I began, "you should know—"

"I'm not here about that," she interrupted. "Well, yes, but not how you think."

"Oh. Um, if it's about what you did with Bones, I realize—"

"Good Lord, Cat, quit guessing." Geri began to pace. Her ash-blond hair was in its usual bob, and the muscles in her legs flexed with her movements. "It's not about that, though Bones makes out like a demon, doesn't he? I want this off the record before I go any further."

I was intrigued. "All right. Just between you and me."

"I heard you say that you and Bones were finished. Is that true?"

That widened my eyes and raised my hackles. "Why? Now that you know he's single, you want more of what he gave you? Liked what you saw when he pulled his dick out?"

She stopped pacing. "Ease up, Catzilla. I'm not after your man. I was wondering if you'd be after mine."

Huh? "What are you talking about?"

Geri flounced onto a nearby chair. "I'm seeing Tate."

That one I hadn't anticipated. I stared at her for a moment before finding my voice. "How long?"

"A few weeks. Don doesn't know. Neither does the rest of the team, though I think Dave and Juan suspect. I know Tate's still hung up on you, but I've let it slide. You're married and never around, so I just figured he'd get over it. Then last week, he jetted off as soon as he heard that you and Bones were having problems. Now Bones doesn't remember you and you're not going to reintroduce yourself, so I want to know if that opens up the field for Tate."

Professionally, I was annoyed at Tate for fraternizing with a junior officer. On a feminine level, I felt bad for Geri. She clearly had strong feelings for him to be discussing this with me, because we didn't know each other that well.

"I don't see Tate as anything more than a friend, and that's not going to change," was all I ended up saying.

She cocked her head. "You might want to tell him that."

"Believe me." I opened the door, suddenly anxious to leave. "I have."

⚜ ⚜ ⚜

I didn't even make it to the end of the hall before I was grabbed from behind, my senses picking up the inhuman power in the air too late. I let out a yelp, wondering how a vampire could've breached the base's defenses—

"Hallo, Cat," a voice I recognized said.

Spade. I quit kicking, dread washing over me. *If he was here...*

"How in the hell did you get here?" I snapped, looking around as soon as he released me. Thankfully, Bones was nowhere in sight.

"Someone with far more sense than you texted me your location," Spade replied.

"Who?" I began, then stopped as I remembered Vlad texting someone right after arguing that I shouldn't return to Gregor. Damn that meddling Romanian.

"Crispin wants to speak with you," Spade went on. "He's just showering now."

I let out a bitter laugh. "With bleach, I hope, and a strong germicide."

A flicker of remorse shadowed Spade's expression before it hardened. "Good thing you showered as well, else I suspect you'd reek of Vlad."

I was about to correct his false assumption about Vlad and me when I stopped. Why should I? "Could be worse," I settled on saying. "I could have made Bones listen to us."

Spade closed his eyes. "Crispin's incredibly sorry about that. He would never have done such a thing if he'd known who you were."

Even though I wanted away from Spade—and the compound—before Bones got out of the shower, I had to ask. "How much is gone?"

His eyes opened. "Anything to do with you. That has consequences to quite a lot over the past several years. Crispin wasn't aware of his new status as coruler of Mencheres's line. He thought he was still under Ian. It appears his powers have been affected as well. He's not as strong and he can't hear humans' thoughts. In short, he is as he was before he met you."

That only solidified my resolve to return to Gregor. Gregor had been stronger than Bones before the effects of this awful spell. If Bones was back to his power level of seven years ago, he'd be toast against Gregor.

"Is this— Is this permanent?"

"We're not sure. Mencheres doesn't think so, but it will take time. How long, no one knows." Spade cocked his head. I didn't hear anything alarming, but then he grabbed my arm. "Crispin's done. You're coming with me."

"No," I said, tugging hard. I wasn't *nearly* ready to see Bones again.

"He's in the conference room," he went on, not letting go. "Your uncle arranged for the two of you not to be disturbed."

Was *every*one against me? I tried logic next, since attempting to wrest away wasn't working. "Come on, Bones has enough to worry about without adding me to the list—"

"Bollocks," Spade snapped. "Now, shall it be kicking and screaming, or under your own power? Either way, you're going to see him."

I knew Spade well enough to know that he meant what he said, and if I kept resisting, this would turn into a fight that would draw Bones's attention long before I could run away.

I drew my shredded emotions behind a shield that I hoped was strong enough to keep me from falling to pieces. "Fine. You can let go of my arm."

He gave me a jaded look. "Consider me overzealous."

Smart of him not to let me go, because when we came to the door and I could *feel* Bones on the other side, I began to panic. Spade must have sensed that. He whipped the door open, shoved me inside so hard that I almost tripped, and slammed it behind me.

I froze after I regained my balance, then slowly turned around.

Bones stood about a dozen feet away. He wasn't wearing something borrowed—the clothes fit him too well, so Spade must have brought them. His hair was still damp and curled slightly at the edges. Its rich brown color only complemented his brows and dark, almost-black eyes.

"Catherine?" he said.

The blankness in his gaze! He really didn't recognize me, and though I'd expected it, I still felt like I'd been punched in the gut.

I cleared my throat and managed to mutter, "That's me."

Then he did something I didn't anticipate: he laughed. I went from apprehensive to pissed in the time it took to hear it.

"What's so funny?"

Bones sobered, waving an apologetic hand. "You don't know how unsettled I've been, waiting to meet you. For the past few hours, I've heard about this fierce warrior woman I married. Blimey, I half expected you to have bigger biceps than me. Now I see you and you look... like a harmless girl barely out of her teens. It's a bit odd reconciling the two."

As he spoke, he raked me with his gaze. With a surge of self-consciousness, I wished I'd put on more makeup or fixed my hair. Bones was so stunning anyone around him automatically looked a little uglier, and— It didn't matter! With a mental shake, I brought myself back to reality.

"You should know that... we're not really married." There, I said it, even though it clawed to stay in my throat.

A cool appraising look came into his eyes. I'd seen it enough before to know that he was taking stock of me. "Is that what you think, Catherine?"

"It's really weird to hear you call me that," I muttered.

His brow arched. "Did I address you as Cat? Is that your preference?"

"No." It was so hard talking to him as if we were strangers! Part of me wanted to run into his arms while the other part wanted to kick the shit out of him for cheating on me. "You, ah, you used to call me Kitten."

"Did I?" He appeared to mull it over. Then, "It doesn't suit you."

I looked away, blinking. He had no idea how much that hurt. Cannelle wasn't the only one who'd just been stabbed in the heart. Of course, she had helped do this to me. In retrospect, I'd owed her one.

"Call me Catherine then, whatever. Look, Bones, I don't know what Spade told you, but you *left* me. When I told you over the microphone that I was separated, it was true."

"You also told me you were a sixty-year-old, zaftig woman suffering from a malformed spine." He took a step closer. "Clearly untrue, that."

"I was in a bad mood." I kept looking away from him, my gaze flicking from the furniture to the walls to the carpet. Anything but his eyes. He was still staring at me though. I didn't have to see it to feel it.

"An apology is less than worthless for what happened, but nonetheless, I'm truly, deeply sorry."

I drew in a steadying breath. This next part was *really* going to hurt.

"Don't, um, don't worry about it. Like I said, we're separated. Well, not even separated, because technically I'm married to Gregor, all right?" I burst out. "You and I have nothing holding us together, and you had finally realized that and walked out. So do yourself a favor. Keep walking."

If I didn't drive him away now, Bones would stay with me out a sense of obligation, and then he'd get slaughtered. Going back to Gregor was the only way I could keep him safe. Eventually Bones would get stronger, maybe the ghouls wouldn't be so riled since Gregor would no doubt change me into a vampire, and then people would quit getting hurt trying to protect me.

I snuck a glance at him. Bones tapped his finger on his chin, weighing my words while those dark eyes considered me.

"I've heard Charles describe what happened between us, and now you, but it doesn't make sense. If I was finished with our relationship, then why did I fly to New Orleans to lure Gregor into dueling with me? Those are hardly the actions of a man who'd had enough."

I cast around for a response. "You were trying to set me up so that I'd be okay when you left. You see, you did it so you *could* walk out without any guilt or responsibility weighing you down."

He stopped tapping his chin. "Plausible. But then why didn't Gregor take me up on my challenge? Or, if he no longer felt that fighting me was necessary because I'd left you, why did he use witchcraft to tear you from my mind?"

"Because Gregor's an asshole," I snapped. "Um, I mean, I love him and all..." *Time to backpedal, fast!* "In fact, I miss him. With your being gone recently, I, ah, I've come to realize that Gregor's the man for me. So you don't have to feel bad about what happened with Cannelle or, er, anyone else, because I love Gregor."

God help me, that was the best I could manage to say. I even smiled. At least, I felt my face stretch. Hopefully it was a smile.

"I see." His expression was unreadable. Then, after a loaded few seconds, Bones threw me a cheery grin.

"Well, I for one am relieved. When Charles told me I was married and I thought it was permanent, I nearly soiled myself. Limited to only one woman for the rest of my life? Not my style at all. You seem like a nice girl, but we wouldn't have lasted. After all, I hear you don't allow other women in our bed, and how much of *that* would I have been able to stand, hmm? Cinnamon and I went through eleven lasses in the short time we were together, and in truth, I could have gone for more—"

"You *bastard!*" I'd been listening with my jaw dropping progressively lower, but that was the last straw. I threw myself at him, pummeling and kicking while cursing him with every filthy word I knew. Part of me was aware that I was crying, my fury surpassed only by an all-consuming hurt that seemed to boomerang through my emotions. He'd just taken all my worst fears and blown up my heart with them. If that's how he truly felt inside, then we'd never had a chance. Why had he lied and told me that we did? Why had he made me love him so much, when he'd always known he would go back to his old ways?

After several minutes, it dawned on me that Bones wasn't fighting back. He just stood there, absorbing my blows without making a move to defend himself. By the time I'd worked myself into that ugly, hiccupping-crying stage and I couldn't throw another punch, he pulled me into his arms.

"L-let me go, d-d-dammit…"

"Going to tell me more about how you love Gregor?" he asked with heavy irony. "So much that Charles told me you waited for me for days without word, and even when it seemed obvious that I'd abandoned you, you ran off with Vlad Tepesh instead? Was I very witless before? Is that why you thought I'd believe such rubbish now?"

Being in his arms was akin to dragging sandpaper across my raw emotions. I pushed at his chest, but his arms tightened and I'd used up the last of my remaining strength in my fit of wounded rage.

"You don't understand. I have to go back to Gregor—"

"You're not going anywhere near him," he said. "I don't give a rot who you're *technically* married to. All I bother about is that I swore by my blood that you were my wife. That means I will fight until the last drop of blood in me to keep you."

He was speaking clearly and in English, but I was still so upset that I had a hard time understanding. "Then you didn't mean all those awful things you just said?"

He sighed. Since my head was practically wedged in his throat, I both heard and felt it.

"No, I didn't mean any of it... except for the numbers. I won't lie to you, Catherine. Though I didn't wish for more and I'd kill to say there were none, there were eleven other women aside from Cannelle while I was in New Orleans."

That made twelve. In a *week*? Yeah, I knew he'd been promiscuous before we met, but for the love of God! Did he *ever* tuck it away?

He set me back enough to stare into my eyes. "I won't ask you to forgive me, but I would ask that we start again despite this unpardonable offense."

"You don't even know me," I whispered. "Bones... I drove us apart, and Gregor will kill you if we try to stay together again."

He snorted. "Charles told me you'd run to jump on a grenade even if it posed no danger to me, but you don't have to. Gregor's not the first powerful chap to want me shriveled, and he won't be the last. I'll stand or fall as a man, Catherine. You can't protect me from the life I've chosen to live."

"You sure you don't have your memory back?" I muttered. This sounded a lot like what he'd said the day he left me. Okay, I'd have to try harder to make him understand that he needed to get away from me.

"You don't even remember making the choice to be with me, and let me tell you, I am a bitch who's left you no fewer than twice. And *how* can I expect you to honor an oath that I won't honor myself? I was blood-bound to Gregor years before we even met. Why would you risk your life to be with a woman who's going back on the same oath you'd rather die than break yourself?"

His dark gaze didn't waver. "The actions of a frightened, manipulated child don't bear being honorable to. Did Gregor tell you what you were doing when he bound you to him? Did you even know what it meant?"

I wasn't in his arms anymore, but Bones still held my shoulders. For the life of me, I couldn't make myself pull away. "I should have known. I shouldn't have let him intimidate me."

"Do you still love me?"

I squirmed at the abrupt change in topic, let alone the question.

Bones just tightened his grip. "Answer me, and no matter the response, do not dare lie to me."

His tone was the flat, dangerous one I recognized from his dealings with enemies. Shit, maybe he'd coldcock me if I lied. After all, I was a stranger now. There were a thousand reasons why I should take my chances anyway, but when I opened my mouth, only the truth came out.

"Yes."

He pushed the hair from my face with a smile. "I'm glad. Would have been rough forcing you to stay with me if you didn't, but make no mistake, Catherine, I would have. No one's stealing my wife, and that's who you are, so don't argue again. Both of us willingly bound ourselves together, knowing full well the depth of that commitment. You can't say the same about you and Gregor. Now, it seems we've both made mistakes, but those can't be changed. All I'll ask is for your honesty and fidelity from this day forward, and I pledge to you the same. Agreed?"

"You are so going to regret this," I mumbled.

His smile didn't falter. "Agreed? If you don't agree, I'll just knock you upside the head and take you with me anyway."

His tone was light, but he had a glint in his eyes that said he wasn't kidding. It reminded me of the Bones from our early days. Of course, if you counted his current mental state, that's who he was.

"Agreed." *You'll be sorry.*

"And if you try to sneak away, I *will* hunt you down and beat the arse off you."

Oh, yeah. Definitely shades of his old charm. "I get it."

"Good." At last he let me go.

I stepped back in a daze, wondering how all my intricate planning had been demolished so completely.

"Now then, I suspect Charles is still guarding the door. He told me I'd have to brawl with you, and he was right. Strong as a bloody ox, aren't you? Did you just drink vampire blood?"

I gave him a confused look. "No."

He frowned. "I told you that what happened before doesn't matter. You can't be that strong on your own, so you clearly drank from a vampire recently. You promised me honesty, Catherine, and I intend to hold you to it."

A sharp laugh escaped me. "Boy, did Spade forget to mention something important! You don't know what I am, do you?"

His frown deepened. "You're my wife."

I laughed again, this time with real humor. Well, Spade hadn't had much time with Bones before they arrived here. Guess he'd skipped over parts about me that he'd deemed less important.

"I'm half-vampire, Bones."

He still didn't get it. "Being married to one, I suppose you could consider yourself that way—"

"Not consider. I *am.*"

To avoid further argument, I let the light out of my eyes, bathing his face in a soft emerald glow.

His expression was priceless. There were so few times I was able to shock him. Considering all the times that Bones had rendered me speechless with disbelief, it was refreshing to see him that way.

"Look at your eyes," he finally managed.

"That's what you said the first time you saw them. Threw you through a loop then too."

"You breathe, I hear your heart beating—"

"I'll sum it up: my father had sex with my mother right after he was changed. He still had living sperm, and I showed up five months later. You were actually the first vampire I met that I didn't kill, but not for lack of trying."

"You tried to kill me?" His brows went up. "Why?"

"Because you were there. I had a bad attitude about vampires back then. My mom kind of brought me up with a grudge."

"Seven years of my life, replaced with doctored or false memories. You have no idea how livid that makes me."

His frustration was palpable. On a much smaller scale, I knew how he felt, so part of me wanted to hug him and tell him it would be okay. The other part still wanted to beat him for his rampant cheating, unwitting or not, but I did neither. I was a stranger to him now, which meant I didn't have the right to hug him or hit him.

"I can tell you about them, well, part of them. I wasn't there for half. Look, I know what you said, but if this gets to be too much, I'll understand. You've just been slapped with a wife, a memory loss, and an archnemesis, all in the past few hours. I'd pass out if I were you. So despite your best intentions, if over the next few days you realize that you can't do this, feel free to go. Don't worry about me. I'll be all right."

"Thank you for saying that." His features hardened. "Now, don't ever say it again."

He was so damned obstinate. I prayed it wouldn't get him killed.

A knock sounded at the door, and then Spade popped his head in.

"Ah, Crispin, have you convinced your runaway bride to stay? Or shall we have a GPS system implanted in her for easier tracking?"

Bones answered before I could give an ungracious reply. "She's staying."

"Splendid. I'll return this to you then. Cat left it by mistake at my prior residence."

He handed something small to Bones, who gave me a strange look when he took it.

"By mistake, eh?"

Spade smiled. "As it turned out."

Light reflected from my red-diamond wedding ring when Bones opened his palm.

I shifted in a mixture of guilt and defensiveness. "I was angry. Keeping it seemed hypocritical."

Bones studied the ring and then me with equal intensity. "Give me your hand."

Slowly, I stretched it out.

"This stone used to be my most prized possession," he said as he slid the ring onto my finger. "That I gave it to you tells me more about what you used to mean to me than anything Charles has said. I don't expect you to act as though nothing's happened, Catherine. I can handle the consequences of my actions. I only expect you to be honest, as I will be with you."

I looked at the ring on my hand. When I'd thrown it on the floor at Spade's, I never expected to see it again. "This isn't going to be easy."

He released my hand and shrugged. "Nothing important ever is."

Vlad was in the hallway by Don's office. He leaned against the wall as he watched me approach. Bones wasn't with me. Spade had dragged him off for a minute, I assumed to see Ian.

"You texted Spade and told him where we were," I said without preamble.

A half smile flitted across his mouth. "Yes."

"Damn it, Vlad, I thought I could trust you!"

"You can," he replied without a hint of sarcasm. "Gregor would have eventually killed you because he can't control you. I don't think highly of Bones, but at least he'll respect you. He's your best chance for survival, even if you're too emotional to see that at the moment."

"And he might die for it. Since you don't like him, I suppose you'd consider that a bonus?"

Vlad heard the betrayal in my voice, but he only shrugged.

"Who knows what will happen in the future? Now, it's time for us to part and I don't expect to see you again for quite a while, so give me a kiss."

Spitefully, I wanted to say no. He'd tattled on me and didn't deserve one. Then again, without Vlad talking me off a ledge, among many other things, I wouldn't even be here.

I stood on tiptoe gave him a quick, chaste good-bye kiss.

He brushed his knuckles across my face when we parted. "Take care of yourself, Cat."

"Good-bye, Vlad," I replied softly.

"I'm glad to hear you say that, else I'd wonder what the devil you were doing," a biting voice said from behind us.

Oh, shit.

Turning around only confirmed that Bones was on the other end of the hallway. Mentally, I cursed Vlad. My back was to Bones, but Vlad would've seen him.

"Let him believe you have other options," Vlad whispered, too low for Bones to overhear. "Do his arrogance some good." Then louder, "Well, Bones, didn't *you* wake up with more than you went to sleep with? If you don't remember me, let me be of assistance—we don't like each other."

"Oh, I remember that distinctly."

Bones advanced with a glint of green in his eyes. Clearly, he thought the kiss he'd witnessed had been more than platonic. I backed away from Vlad like he was poisonous.

"Um, we really should be going—"

"But, Catherine, I haven't greeted Tepesh yet." His tone held the promise of violence.

I was the only thing standing between the two of them, and it was a precarious position. *Just walk away,* I sent to Vlad. *Now.*

"No," Vlad said mildly.

"No, you won't say hallo?" Bones thought Vlad was talking to him. "Very discourteous."

I turned my back to Vlad and held out a hand toward Bones. "I don't know what you have in mind, but let me remind you that I could pull the territorial card with twelve other women," I said, switching tactics. "We agreed to start over, right? So let's do it."

Bones stared at Vlad for another tense moment before he held out his hand. "Right you are, Catherine. Come with me."

I took his hand and walked away from Vlad without looking back.

We didn't talk for the next several hours. Spade drove and Fabian rode shotgun. Ian had taken another car; thank God for small favors. I sat in the backseat next to Bones and closed my eyes. From his silence, I didn't know if Bones was sleeping or quietly stewing. Occasionally, his leg or shoulder brushed mine from the swaying of the car, but that was it. He'd let go of my hand as soon as we were off the base.

"I'm arranging for some of your personal effects to be waiting when we arrive, Crispin," Spade said, finally breaking the silence. "Pictures, letters, DVDs. Hopefully they should assist with jogging your memory. Cat, it should only be round an hour until we're on a plane. You can open your eyes after that."

I yawned. "Good. I'd like to sleep, but I can't until we're far enough away. Don cleared out the team right after we left, but it gives my uncle more time too."

"Time for what?"

Bones sounded annoyed. He didn't know about the handicap, either. It must feel like we were speaking a different language to him.

"I should find out exactly what Spade told you so I don't assume you know something," I said with a sigh. "Every time I sleep, Gregor sifts through my subconscious and gleans everything I know, like my location, who I'm with, and what we're planning. I've almost gotten everyone killed a bunch of times. Drugging me didn't turn out so well, either. The pills turned me into a psycho bitch with their side effects, and though clocking me must have been enjoyable, that was only temporarily effective."

Bones was silent for such a long moment, I thought, *He's already regretting not walking away when he had the chance.*

"Are you telling me... that I've drugged and *beaten* you?"

His carefully controlled tone told me I'd miscalculated what he was angry about. When put like that, it sounded worse than the reality.

I tried to explain. "You only clocked me once before we got the pills, and what else were you supposed to do? E-mail Gregor with directions to where we'd be?"

"I don't bloody believe this," he said in a hiss.

Spade attempted to soothe him. "Crispin, you were under a great deal of stress, trying to secure her safety and the safety of those around you—"

"Bollocks," he snapped. "Wasn't she also under stress? Bloody hell, you'll never have to explain why you left me,

Catherine, but you might want to clarify why you came back. Gregor must have seemed like a vacation by comparison. Is that why you've been sitting with your eyes closed this entire time? I thought you just didn't wish to speak with me."

"It's not safe for me to know where we are," I continued to insist. "The only time I'm not dangerous is when we fly or I'm out like a light."

"Club you over the head before I shag you, do I?" Bones asked in a conversational tone. "I'm obviously a Neanderthal, so I must whap you a good one and then drag you off for my pleasure, right? This treating you like contaminated waste ends here. Open your eyes."

I almost did out of disbelief. "No."

"Crispin," Spade began.

"She'll not know where we're headed once we reach the plane," he said curtly. "Catherine, open your eyes." His tone rang with pure command.

I almost smiled. "Here's lesson one about me: I don't take orders. Especially when I know they're wrong. My eyes stay shut, Bones, so deal with it."

Instead of getting irate, he let out an amused snort. "Stubborn, are you? Well, pet, here's my response to your lesson—we're traveling north on I-95 in Georgia, just passing the Savannah exit. No need to keep your eyes closed now, is there?"

My lids snapped open with incredulity. "I can't believe you just did that, you shit!"

He clucked his tongue. "Such a foul word coming from such a lovely mouth."

"Don't bother with flattery, buddy, I've heard all your lines," I muttered, still smarting over being outfoxed.

"I expect you have." He smiled slyly. "Still, you married me, so some of them must have worked."

The way he was looking at me made me self-conscious. He was evaluating me as a woman, and with our constant fights the last few times we were together, it had been a while since he'd done that. I didn't even want to remember how far back it was since other things had happened. Maybe Bones had already guessed that, hence the cocky twist to his lips.

Well, deprived I might be. Easy I wasn't.

"Don't even think of it. You're in the doghouse, big-time. It might not be your fault, but a short time ago, I heard another woman swallow your sword. The fact that she's dead now might give you an idea about how much I didn't like that."

His smile didn't waver. "You gave her a more merciful end than I would have. I despise that Cannelle made me a pawn in hurting and humiliating you."

"And she was trying to lure you out to Gregor so he could kill you," I added.

"Oh, that." He made a dismissive motion. "I'd have merely broken her legs if that were her only crime. This isn't an excuse, but you should know that Cannelle encouraged company with us. I thought it was just what she fancied, but now I know it was deliberate."

This was a very painful subject, but ignoring it wasn't going to make it go away. Better to ask now than wonder later. "Were, um, were the others human? I'd like to be prepared if there's a chance that I'll run into one of them later. I'm not asking because I'm sharpening my knives, I just… Never mind. Forget it."

I dropped my gaze, studying the floorboards. Why had I even asked? Maybe one day I'd learn to let well enough alone.

"Humans all, and I'm certain it wasn't accidental," Bones replied. "I suspect Cinnamon was ensuring that no one would ask me any incriminating questions. A vampire or ghoul might have heard of me and therefore made a comment referencing you."

"Fabian did, right?" I still didn't look up. "You must have thought he was crazy."

Bones sighed. "Indeed. I don't pay much attention to ghosts in general—no offense, mate—and he was railing what sounded like insane nonsense to me. I only began to take him seriously after he started singing."

"Singing?"

"That was my idea," Spade interjected. "Had to find a way to get Crispin's attention without attracting others. I had Fabian sing old songs from the *Alexander* that the four of us had made up. No one else would have known them, and at their end, I had him relay messages. Like, *don't leave the city*, or *you're in danger*."

I was torn between admiring Spade's cleverness and fighting the urge to shout, *Couldn't you have added "keep your dick in your pants!"* Fortunately, I held that comment back. Fidelity didn't supersede safety. No matter how much it hurt now, Spade had made the right decision.

"You did great, Fabian," I said, and was rewarded with a smile from the ghost. Of course, his head went through the car seat to do it.

When I returned my attention to Bones, he was staring at me with such intentness that I immediately glanced away. Cool fingers closed around my wrist, bringing my hand to his face before I could snatch it back. When I felt the brush of his mouth on my skin, I tried to yank away. Even that small touch made my heart leap in a way that was almost painful.

His grip didn't loosen as he took in a long, deep breath.

"You smell familiar." His voice was low. "Even though I don't remember meeting you before today, I swear that I recognize your scent."

My heart skipped a beat. Scent was the strongest sense tied to memory. Maybe, just maybe, his memory loss wouldn't be permanent.

Still, it was hard to think with his fingers caressing my hand in feathery touches that belied a grip I couldn't pull away from.

"Can you, um, let go now?" I asked unsteadily.

He inhaled again. "Not yet."

Spade pretended to stroke his eyebrow while in reality, his hand blocked from Bones's view the glare he shot me. *Don't cause a stink*, that single look commanded.

Right. I forced myself to relax. Bones was only holding my hand so he could try to place my scent. No need to let everyone know that such a simple touch hit my emotions with the same force as a sledgehammer.

"Okay, well… you let go whenever you're ready," I managed to reply in a seminormal tone.

A breath hit my knuckles that might have been a muffled laugh.

"I'll do that."

Mencheres, Bones's coruler, was at the residence we arrived at, and for once, I was happy to see him.

"Grandsire."

I wasn't the only one, it seemed. Bones embraced Mencheres with something like relief.

"Can you get this worthless barrier out of my head?" he asked at once.

Mencheres set Bones back and placed his hand on his forehead. After a moment, he shook his head.

"The spell is bound by blood, so only Gregor's blood will lift it."

Bones ground out a curse. Then he cracked his knuckles. "All right. I'll track the sod down and get his blood."

"In your present state, he will kill you," Mencheres said bluntly. "There can be no retribution for it under our laws, and then he will claim Cat as his. Do you condemn her to that, or will you do as I say?"

"I'm not afraid of him," Bones spat, but he glanced over at me.

I had a split second of being torn before logic took over. If believing I was helpless would save him, then helpless I would be!

"If you're determined not to wait until you're stronger before you confront Gregor, then let me go to him now. If Gregor gets me as victory spoils later, I think he'll go a lot rougher on me."

I even manufactured a shiver as if the thought terrified me. It did, but only because the topic was Bones's death. My act worked because this Bones couldn't tell when I was piling it on.

His lips thinned and he returned his attention to Mencheres. "Right, there's more than me to consider now. Very well. What would you have me do?"

"Train with me from morning until dusk to get you ready to face Gregor," Mencheres replied.

Bones gave the Egyptian vampire a self-deprecating smile. "You haven't trained me since I was a lad. Was I much stronger before, or will I need all the strength I can get to defeat Gregor?"

Mencheres cupped his face with open affection, making me remember when he'd said that Bones was like a son to him. "You were starting to realize how very powerful you truly were."

Vagueness. Mencheres was the king of that.

Bones glanced my way again. "Morning till dusk, you say? Then I'll take myself to bed. I remember how you train, so I'll need the rest."

All of a sudden, I was the center of attention. It took me a moment to realize why.

"I snore," I said at once. "Ask anyone, it sounds like trees being chainsawed down. You need, um, some uninterrupted sleep by yourself. I might kick as well."

That last part I said with a glint in my eye. Yeah, I might kick, and if Bones whispered someone else's name in his sleep, I might stab him too.

Bones let out a snort. "Mencheres, if you'll point me in the right direction? I'll stay in my doghouse awaiting Catherine's reprieve."

Spade turned to me and looked like he was about to argue.

Before he could speak, Bones clapped him on the back. "Don't fret, mate. Although I'm not certain, she looks as though she'd steal the covers too. Best all around, really."

Spade laughed, and Bones gave me a cheeky wink as he followed Mencheres up the stairs.

"Sleep well, Catherine."

The house was big. Maybe even a ranch, from the horses I heard outside. The good news was, beyond that, I didn't have a clue as to where we were.

Mencheres put Bones in the room next to mine, so I heard him feed from two people before he went to sleep.

One male, one female, or as I mentally named them, dinner and dessert. That also told me this was a community residence. Either it had a big basement or there was an adjoining cottage, but Mencheres had living snacks close by. Vampire households made me a little uneasy with their throwback to feudalism, not that I had any room to complain. Humans kept their food within easy reach too.

Despite feeling tired, I had a restless sleep, drifting off just to wake up over and over again. It was surreal to be this close to Bones, yet miles apart emotionally. He was still the love of my life; I was only some weird chick he'd found out yesterday that he was stuck with.

The door banged open, revealing a teenage brunette with pigtails in the doorway. "Hello! I'm Heather, and I'm here to get your breakfast. Are you Blood, Body, or Breather?"

She was smiling at me in the friendliest way. Meanwhile, I'd just put my knife back on the dresser.

"What?"

She came in without being invited. Then again, she hadn't been invited to open the door either.

"You must be a Breather," she announced. "The others know right off what I mean. Okay, human food, what'll it be? I guarantee we have it."

Her initial question finally made sense. Yeah, I guess that would be the first issue when determining what someone wanted for breakfast.

"Just point me to the kitchen and I'll take care of it myself."

She laughed like I'd told a joke. "You're House. You can't get your own food. Just tell me what you want and if you want it here or somewhere else."

It was similar to being at Vlad's, only if I were there, she'd have carted the refrigerator in with her.

"You can't just point me to the kitchen?"

A firm shake of her head.

"Right," I sighed. "Eggs and toast, I don't care how they're cooked or what kind of bread. Coffee, cream, and sugar. Where else can I eat aside from this room?"

"Oh, wherever you want, but the balcony's the nicest."

"Where is it?"

"End of the hall to your right," she chirped.

I stopped her on her way out. "Oh, by the way, I'm—"

"Don't tell me your name," she said, the smile wiped from her face. "I'll call you Red, but we don't mention real names. That way we can't repeat what we don't know."

Good God. "Heather, are you okay with being here? You're underage, from my guess, and I could arrange for you to live somewhere else, with your own kind..." My voice trailed off because she suddenly looked ill.

"Please don't. This is the best home I've ever had. They take care of me, I go to school online, and everyone is nice. I don't want to go back to foster care, *ever*. Please don't tell anyone where I am."

I'd tried to be nice and instead I'd scared the hell out of her. "I won't. It's okay. You're doing great. I just... I'm an ass."

She lost that frightened look, but she was still a little cautious. "Don't worry. You're House, so you can say anything. One day I'll be House too."

How could I respond to that? *Keep working hard and it'll happen?*

Finally all I said was, "House doesn't guarantee happiness."

She smiled, bright and sunny once more. "No, but it means someone will be bringing *me* breakfast."

⚜ ⚜ ⚜

The balcony was beautiful, as promised. It overlooked a garden-surrounded swimming pool. Wherever this was, I hoped we were staying a while, despite the oddity of being "House." If I could move around outside, maybe swim or take a walk, I'd be delighted.

"Got some room on that bench?"

My head whipped up. "Denise!"

My best friend staggered back, laughing, when I launched myself at her. I was still babbling out an apology about Vlad burning the house and cars when she shushed me.

"No harm, no foul. Spade billed him, isn't that hilarious? Three days later Vlad sent a check. Oh, but he didn't pay for the ceiling that he'd chucked Tate through, because he considered that Spade's fault for not controlling his guest. Vampires, right?"

I laughed as well, in comic disbelief at the protocol of the undead.

Then Denise tugged on my arm. "I've got something for you. It's one of the reasons why I wasn't here last night. Come with me."

I followed her to a second-floor bedroom, though the bed was almost hidden from all the stuff on it.

"Clothes!" Denise announced. "All your size, all new. You must have felt like a Salvation Army fashion model, always wearing stuff that wasn't yours."

I was overwhelmed by the thoughtful gesture. It didn't seem possible that something as trivial as clothes could make me feel better, but it did. Maybe it was girl DNA.

"I also brought some photos and DVDs, but those are for Bones," she went on. "That's the good news. The bad news is..." She leaned over and whispered something.

"Oh, fuck!" I burst out.

"So much for subtlety." Denise quit trying to keep her voice down. "Spade thought that since she's—ahem—known Bones the longest, he'd feel more comfortable with her here."

"No, Spade's still pissed at me and he's a sly son of a bitch," I muttered, holding up a hand to avoid her arguing. "Point me to Lady Ormsby's room. I don't want to find out her intentions after I'm prying her off Bones's door."

Denise gave me a look that said, *You shouldn't go, but I know you will.* "One floor down, third door on your right."

"I'll be right back."

One floor down and the third entrance on the right later, I banged on the door. "Annette! I need to speak with you. Wake up or stop what you're doing."

Rustling sounds came from within, and then her grumpy reply. "Can't it wait? I'm knackered."

I opened the door. Hey, I'd warned her. "No, it can't."

Annette was sprawled out nude in the bed. A sheet covered one leg that she didn't bother to pull up once she saw me. True, out of everyone, she'd known Bones since the days of their humanity, when he'd been a gigolo and Annette had been his best client.

Her light eyes considered me balefully. "I've flown a considerable amount of time to be here, and I'm returning to my slumber straightaway after you leave."

"Are you going to try to seduce Bones now that he doesn't remember me?" I asked her, ignoring that.

She rolled onto her back. "Always direct, aren't you? Another woman might have invited me to tea, played my friend, and sought to dissuade me with guilt, but not you. Did you bring your knife?"

"It's upstairs, and you're stalling. Answer the question."

"You find me a threat?"

I gave her figure a blunt evaluation. Annette's breasts were full, though without the perfect roundness of youth. Faint stretch marks marred her sides, evidence of when she'd once been pregnant with what was probably Bones's child. Her hips and legs were shapely and generous, exactly the way fashion dictated a woman should look before the past hundred years. She also exuded a sensual decadence, making her flaws somehow more attractive. When she was young, Annette must have been stunning to the point of intimidation, but now she looked gorgeous as well as very accessible.

"Scary as hell, bitch. Flattered?"

A smile curved her mouth. "In fact, I am."

"Flattered? Or going after Bones now that it's your best chance?"

She sat up and let out a sigh. "No, I shan't be scheming after Crispin. Oh, I'd like to. Thought about it the whole bloody flight over, in fact, but I can't. If Crispin's memories return, he'd despise me. Nothing is worth that, darling. I love him too much to risk his hatred."

Any other explanation, I'd have doubted. That one rang true. Faults she might have, and lots of them, but she did love Bones.

"Annette, if I didn't think you'd take it the wrong way, I'd kiss you."

The truth was, she'd be formidable competition. Bones hadn't kept returning to her for hundreds of years because she bored him. Annette one-upped me in many, many ways, so frankly, I was relieved.

"If you kiss me, I *promise* to take it the wrong way," she replied, amusement clear in her tone. "Now let me rest."

"Yeah, happy sleeping." Since I had the answer I wanted, I was in a hurry to leave, especially after her last comment.

Bones came back well after nightfall. Things must have run late, or maybe he was limiting the time he'd have to deal with me. God knows I'd be stalling if I were in his shoes. If Denise hadn't been with me today, I might have climbed the walls.

Instead, I did feminine things. Tried on my new clothes. Took turns with Denise, giving each other manicures and pedicures, then facials. Let her do my hair in different styles. Denise was in girly-girl heaven.

I didn't let on, but I wasn't. Was this what I was supposed to enjoy? Sure, it was nice, and I was so glad that my friend was there, but another day of playing Be a Barbie would send me running for my knives. What was wrong with me? While curls were being put in my hair, I was reminiscing about bloody fights and near-death escapes.

That's why I was relieved to hear Bones return. Hell, I'd almost flung myself down the stairs to see him before I realized he might just want to sleep. Was it rude to greet him if he was really tired or rude not to? Which was worse, to be perceived as a pouncing spider or the aloof wife? There should be a frigging manual for this.

I opted for Chickenshit Plan C: Dash to the upper-floor balcony and see if he sought me out. I wasn't locking myself in a room, but I wasn't wagging my tail by the door either. If only I'd grabbed a book, I could appear legitimately occupied. As it was, I had nothing to do but stare at the night sky.

Downstairs, I heard Bones greet Annette. Spade introduced Denise as his girlfriend since of course Bones didn't remember her. When he asked, "Where's Catherine?" my heart leapt. How pathetic to be so emotional over a simple inquiry.

"She ran away when you came in," Annette said cheerfully.

Bitch, I thought with an inner groan.

"Did she indeed?" Bones replied. "To where?"

"Outer balcony third floor." Again supplied by Annette. She'd better lock her door tonight.

"If you'll excuse me?"

There was a general murmur of acceptance, and then his light, quick footsteps up the stairs, down the hall, and outside the windowed doors closing off the balcony. I stood up and turned around.

"I was just giving you a chance to unwind…," I began, then stopped. The way he looked at me made me more nervous. "What?"

"You told me no flattery, but I can't help it. You're extraordinarily beautiful."

Bones kept staring at me, his eyes flicking from my face to my dress and back again. I sat down because I didn't know what else to do. Jeez, courtship had been easier when we first met. I'd snarled and plotted to kill him; he'd pummeled me and made fun of my training progress.

So how did I handle our strained new circumstances? With babbling. Idiotic, relentless babbling.

"Denise did my hair, nails, and the rest of it. And the clothes are new, which is nice. Don't have to wonder who wore the underwear before me. No matter if you know they're clean, there's something icky about wearing another girl's underwear…."

Good God, are you really talking about under*wear?* the logical part of my mind screeched. *Stop talking now, moron!* But I couldn't seem to shut up.

"…although I never bother with doing all this normally. In fact, most of the time I barely wear makeup, and I only do my hair if I'm going out to kill someone—which, since I quit my job, isn't much anymore. I don't know why I let Denise talk me into this, because when I don't do it again you'll wonder why I only did it in the beginning and everyone will tell you, 'Oh, things change when the girl gets comfortable, that's marriage for you,' and... Aw, hell, I gotta go!"

With that, I bolted from the balcony and went straight to my room, shutting the door. Even that wasn't far enough. I went into the bathroom and turned the shower on, jumping under the spray still fully clothed while I cursed myself for being ten shades of an imbecile. I could just imagine Bones's hushed conversation later tonight with Spade.

Has she ever been treated for schizophrenia? No? Oversight, mate. I'll get right on it.

My head thumped against the tile. A couple of more episodes like that and Bones would be delivering me to Gregor with a big red bow. Maybe I should keep it up. At least then he'd be safer.

In keeping with my new ridiculousness, I stayed in my room and didn't come out. Denise knocked after an hour, but I put her off with a lame excuse about a headache. She didn't press it. After several more useless hours staring at the ceiling, berating myself for behaving like a head case in front of Bones, I fell asleep.

Of course, that's when Gregor showed up.

Water rushed all around me, too thick to swim in. How did I get in the ocean? Why couldn't I swim? Where was everybody?

"Somebody help!"

My cry went unanswered. The water seemed to be pulling me under. I gasped, choked, and felt the burning of it in my lungs. This was how I was going to die. Alone and drowning. Funny, I'd always thought I would die in a fight...

"Take my hand."

Blindly I reached out—and then realization hit me and I yanked my arms back.

"Damn you, Gregor, leave me alone!"

He materialized in front of me, floating right above the water. An invisible wind blew his ash-blond hair, and those smoky green eyes were glowing emerald. The waves lapped at his feet, but they didn't suck him in. That relentless undertow was only for me.

"You're nothing to Bones but an unwanted burden now. How does it feel, knowing what he'd rather be doing and all the women he'd rather be with doing it with?"

"There's one less of those now, isn't there?" I snapped, trying to keep my head above that thick water.

"*Oui*, that was unexpected. You shall regret it, *mon amour*. Come to me now, and you may spare the others my wrath."

"No dice, Gregor. The only way you're getting me is dead."

"Why do you do this," he shouted, giving up his false calm. "I offer you everything, and you'd rather be the whore of a whore!"

Something was in the water with me. It felt like hands wrapped around my ankles, pulling me down. Maybe Gregor could actually kill me in my sleep. After all, Patra nearly had.

"Because I'm happier being a whore's whore than being with you."

After I said it, I quit fighting. I let myself sag and the water closed over my head. In a weird way, it felt like being flushed, because all of a sudden I was moving downward very fast and then—

"Wake up, Catherine!" Bones was shaking me.

Instinctively I coughed, but there was no water in my lungs. I was in bed, and the only thing wet on me was my own sweat.

"I'm awake," I croaked

Bones released me, and that's when I noticed that my cheek stung. Guess he'd been doing more than shaking me.

"You said no more beatings," I joked to take the edge off how rattled Gregor's dream had made me.

Bones let out a relieved laugh.

"Made me break a promise right quickly, didn't you? Charles told me what it would look like if Gregor connected to you in your sleep, but it's the damnedest thing to see it. It's like you're dead, only I can hear your heart beating." Bones leaned closer, brushing away the fine sheen of sweat from my brow. "This *is* Gregor's doing, isn't it? Despicable filth."

"I'm okay." I sat up, pulling the covers over me where I'd kicked them away.

He watched without blinking. "You were crying out that you were drowning. That's very far from okay."

A glance at the clock showed that it was close to five in the morning. "He can't try it again today. It takes a few days before he's strong enough to make another go at me, so I'm fine. Really."

Bones slowly moved away, not taking his eyes off me. It made me flash to how long it had been since we'd been in bed together. Weeks? More? Cowardly, I shut my eyes, hugging the pillow to my cheek as if I were exhausted.

"You can go back to bed, Bones. As I said, I'm fine."

Nothing but loaded silence for a moment, then finally I heard him get up and leave, closing the door behind him.

I opened my eyes and let out a sigh of frustration. Damn Gregor, and damn me for being a fool who'd let him dream-snatch me before. What I wouldn't give to take it all back and not have gone with him that day. Bones—the *old* Bones—had been right. I shouldn't have cared about my lost memories. It wasn't like they'd also stolen my strength and left me dangerously vulnerable as Bones's lost memories had done. Who would have guessed that one day *he'd* need Gregor's blood to unlock what was stolen from his mind? Too bad I hadn't packed an extra vial of Gregor's blood for the road when I drank from him that day...

"That's *it!*"

I vaulted out of bed, my mind racing from a sudden surge of hope. *I'd drunk Gregor's blood.* Was enough of it still in my system to help Bones?

I went straight into Bones's room without knocking. He was just settling himself into bed, and in my excited state, I plowed ahead with no forethought.

"Eat me, quick. It might not be too late!"

Instead of going for my neck, Bones whisked me onto the bed and yanked my pajama bottoms down.

"What is your problem?" I gasped, slapping him. Then I pulled my pants back on. He'd had them off in a blink.

Bones sat on his haunches and touched his face in disbelief. "What's *yours,* luv?"

All of a sudden, I realized his translation. Instead of being apologetic, I was incredulous. "I meant eat me as in *bite* me. Wow, you don't even know me, but you'd just... just dive right in, huh? Come on, a virtual stranger stomps in here and says 'eat me' and you don't even protest? You should've demanded a hand job at least!"

Bones just gazed at me and then dropped his hand from his cheek. "You confuse me, Catherine."

That deflated some off my huffiness. Well, that and the way the sheets barely covered his lap.

"Are you naked?" I asked before catching myself.

He regarded me with suspicion. "Is this another trick question?"

"No, never mind. Look, here's what I meant—*drink my blood*. I had Gregor's blood a couple of weeks ago, so some of it might still be in me. Maybe enough to make a difference. Get it?"

Bones's expression hardened and he gestured to me with an impatient swipe. "Come here."

Oh, *now* he was all business.

"I can't believe you would have let me order you to munch on me," I grumbled, circling the bed to sit by him.

His hand shot out, pulling me closer. "Considering what you overheard the other day, I reckon it's the least I could do."

I didn't have a chance to respond. His mouth went to my throat, I felt his tongue seeking out the right spot, and then he bit.

The warmth hit me almost immediately. Bones's arms supported me, sensing when my spine went to jelly. Deep, steady suctions curled my toes while heat cascaded through me. I knew I was making little gasping sounds, but damned if I could help it. This didn't just feel hot, good, and sensual. It felt *necessary*. Like if he didn't drink me, somehow I'd be the one who was left starving.

I moaned his name, reaching up to touch him. He caught my hands, holding them to my sides while he drew away and closed the punctures with his blood. I swayed without his support, glad I was sitting or I might have fallen over.

"Bones?" I made his name question this time, not an exhalation of enjoyment.

"It didn't do anything, Catherine. Best you leave now."

He looked away when he said it, his shoulders rigid. Everything about him was distant and almost angry.

I got up, cursing myself for not thinking of trying this sooner. What if a couple of more days would have made all the difference?

"I'm sorry," I whispered, and returned to my room as fast as I'd left it.

The next morning, I woke up to find that Bones was already gone. After breakfast, I gave Denise a hug and told her there was something I had to do. Then I marched to the stables and grabbed a shovel.

About fifteen minutes into cleaning the first stall, a teenage boy with freckles and brown hair came running in the stable.

"Stop!"

This I'd expected. "What's your name, kid?"

"Uh, people just call me Pony."

"Pony? Call me Red. I'm House, right? So as House, I get to do certain things. Today I'm going to clean out these stalls and then exercise and rub down the horses. Is that your job?"

"Uh-huh." He chewed his lip nervously.

"Take the day off, Pony. If anyone gives you trouble, send them to me. You can't talk me out of this, so don't bother. Now be a good kid and point me to the feed, okay? Don't worry; I know what I'm doing."

Eight blissful hours of labor later, I felt better. Finally I'd done something productive. The stalls were sparkling although I was covered in dirt, manure, sweat, and straw. Pony had hung around most of the day, trying not to be noticed. Maybe he was afraid I'd screw something up and was preparing for damage control. I gave him a wave when I went into the house, laughing to myself at his dumbfounded expression.

Yeah, kid. Chicks can do the same things boys can.

I took my time in the shower to get the stench of the stalls from me. Then I pulled my damp hair into a ponytail and put on jeans and a comfortable shirt. When I went downstairs, I was in a much better mood. And hungry. Spade and Denise were in the lounge sipping sherry, looking sophisticated even in these rural surroundings.

"Who do I ask to get a burger and some french fries? Oh, and a milkshake."

Spade gave me a mocking grin. "Not going to insist on peeling the potatoes, milking the cow, and churning the ice cream yourself? You *must* be knackered."

"You can take the girl out of the country, but you can't take the country out of the girl," I said tartly, refusing to let him ruin my mood. "Want to check under my fingernails to see if I missed some dirt?"

"I shouldn't wonder if you did." He gestured to a computer across the room. "It's for in-house use. Type what you want and when you want it. They'll send it up."

"Thanks."

Forty minutes later, I was devouring my second burger. Yep, the first one had been that good. Instead of another milkshake, I drank a Coke. Since Denise and Spade probably wanted some time alone together, I let them be and ate on the balcony. I'd just settled back and let out a contented burp when Bones's voice almost made me leap out of my skin.

"Hello, Catherine."

My plate skidded across the floor from my jump. "Holy hell, when did you sneak in here?"

Bones bent for the dish even as I hurried to do the same. His fingers brushed mine when each of us grasped it. I let go first, that cursed awkwardness setting in again.

"Ah, thanks. Don't know why I'm so jumpy. And I guess I should apologize for the truck-driver burp. Charming, huh?"

He set the plate down and his mouth twitched. "Actually, it was. It's the first time I've seen you relaxed. My apologies for startling you. Mencheres and I walked the last few miles back; that's why you didn't hear the car."

I had no idea what to say. After last night's babble fest, then my seriously misinterpreted directive, maybe silence was the best option.

Bones sat down on a nearby chaise lounge. I picked the one across from him and sat.

At that, he vacated his spot and sat next to me, an arched brow daring me to move. "We can do this all night."

I laughed at the idea of playing musical chairs with a vampire about to hit his bicentennial birthday. "Just to see Spade's face, we should."

He laughed as well, an easy chuckle that doused me with nostalgia. His hand found mine and I squeezed back out of habit until reality made me pull away.

Or try to.

His fingers tightened, not letting me go. "We can do this all night too, but really, can't you let me at least hold your hand?"

"God, Bones, I have no idea what I'm doing."

The words escaped in a moment of truthful frustration. Now I really tried to get away, but that made him coil his arms around me.

"Stop. I told you that you smelled familiar. You *feel* familiar as well, and right now, that's all I have to go on."

I stopped squirming. Bones leaned back, maneuvering me until I was cradled by his arms and legs. His chest was my support, and he propped another pillow under him before making a satisfied noise.

"Much better. Are you comfortable?"

I was. My back fit into his chest and his leg dangled off the lounge as it had the many previous times he'd held me like this. The familiarity plus not having to look at him helped quell my awkwardness.

"I'm not making this any easier on you, am I?" I murmured. "You'd be so much better as the spouse of the amnesia sufferer. I'm screwing things up seven ways to Sunday."

"No, you're not, and please quit cataloguing your faults. I don't care if you belch, never wear makeup, chew with your mouth open, or scream profanity in church. Loyalty and honesty, as I told you, are the only two qualities I bother about."

"So it would have been fine if I had been sixty, zaftig, and with a spine like a question mark?"

His snort of laughter tickled my ear. "Yes. Though I would have needed to research the best way to shag you."

I elbowed him. "You probably already know."

Another snort. "A gentleman never tells."

"If I marry one, I'll remember that."

My dry comment only made him laugh again. The way his breath kept hitting my skin sent pleasant shivers through me, and I didn't think it was an accident.

"You're doing that on purpose, aren't you?"

"Of course."

He sounded even more amused. If it were an English term, he probably would have followed it up with *duh*.

"Save your breath, I'm not sleeping with you yet. Getting to know someone *before* you find their G-spot is probably a new experience for you. At least this way I'll be original."

Now his laughter didn't hit my neck, because he threw his head back to let it out without restraint. "Don't fret, Catherine. Even if you weren't my wife, you'd still be an original, but please, tell me all about yourself. I wanted to know everything anyway, but that infinitely lovely 'yet' makes me even more anxious."

"You shouldn't be in such a rush." This topic was starting to make me antsy again. "After all, I might suck in bed."

"Be still my nonbeating heart."

It took me a second, then I elbowed him again. "I'm serious. I suppose we should discuss it though, so, ah, something doesn't come up at a bad time..." I tried to find the right words without blushing.

"I suppose I was very hard to please?" he asked wryly. "Berated you if I wasn't satisfied, did I?"

"No, of course not."

"Then why do you believe I would now?"

Too late, I saw the trap. Aw, hell, how to explain?

"Don't take this the wrong way. You... you loved me. Even the first time, when I didn't know anything, you loved me and it... it meant you were grading on a wide curve, okay?"

"Ah." A pause. "Was I your first?"

This was a *very* personal topic, but it was about him too. Even if he didn't remember.

"My second, but I don't really count the guy before you. He took my 'no' as a 'come and get me!'"

"What was his name?"

"Danny Milton." Wow. Been a while since I'd thought about him.

"One *l* or two?"

His tone was so causal, it took me a second. "One *l*, why... Oh! Are you serious? With everything going on, you'd want to track him down?"

He sat up, jostling me with a little the motion. "With that description, *yes.*"

Since Danny was dead, there was no point in arguing further. "Rest easy then. You already killed him."

"Good."

He leaned back and we sat in silence for a few more minutes. The whole thing felt surreal. Like the past two months hadn't happened and we were back on our own porch just watching the sky together. Every so often, he'd inhale and exhale. Listening to that felt strangely intimate, especially since I felt the rise and fall of his chest against my back. Bones didn't need to breathe, so he was taking my scent into him. Repeatedly.

He was the one who broke the silence. "When I saw you kiss Vlad, I wasn't merely affronted because you were my wife. It... hurt for an instant. Very unexpected, that. And now, instead of learning more about my past with Charles or Mencheres, I'd rather sit here with you. To be frank, it frightens me."

"Why?" My voice was hushed, like the one you'd use if you were sharing secrets in the dark.

His lowered too, until it was soft but not yet a whisper. "I have so much to lose. Overnight, I'm Master of my own line and at war with another Master, but that's not what I'm afraid of. I have experience in leading and in fighting, yet it seems I've already been a shoddy husband. I'm afraid to fail you again, Catherine."

I squeezed his hand. "You don't know how to fail. And before... before our big blowout, you made me very happy, Bones."

He didn't move, but the mood became different. Quiet confessions turned into something else. I felt it in the quickening of his power, the flex of coiling energy beneath me.

"I'd like to make you happy again." His voice thickened. "It doesn't have to be about me. I'll stay within whatever limits you set."

The fact that for a second, a part of me considered it made me fling myself way from him. "No. Believe me; you've already proven yourself in that regard. I-I'm not ready to open that door and I'm not going to crack it, either. You don't deserve to do penance on me while I get off."

Bones watched me while I paced, staying in his reclined position on the chaise longue. Damn him for being so gorgeous, and God help me, I did still want him, no matter that I was dealing with my hurt over everything that had happened, both with and without his memory.

His mouth lifted in his old, knowing smile, and when he inhaled again, that smile widened. "Your desire scents the air, so let me know when you change your mind. It's not penance, I assure you. I simply want you any way I can have you."

I had to leave, now. Before my chastity went up in flames. "Good night."

I left the balcony. Bones didn't follow. As I headed toward my bedroom, I heard him take in another long breath and then let it out in a sigh.

What do you do when you're on a diet and your favorite food is within gobbling distance? I tried more pacing in my bedroom, but that didn't help. Turned on the TV, but that only made it worse. All the local channels were off, leaving just the premiums. No matter what I flipped to, it seemed sex was on every one. Finally, with grim frustration, I ran a bath and settled myself into the tub. Well, it had been a while since I'd done what I was about to do—Bones normally kept me more than sated, so I hadn't needed to self-satisfy—but it had to be like riding a bike, right?

Of course, that didn't turn out as planned either.

First I was too rough. I attacked my flesh like it had done something wrong, which only increased the need while doing nothing to ease it. Great, now I was sore *and* frustrated. Finally I forced myself to go slower and to think happy thoughts. The warm water soothed my previous attempts and my gentleness began to pay off. *At last, progress.* My breath shortened, fantasies and memories intermingling in my mind.

Bones's hands all over me, teasing, seeking, driving me insane. The weight of his body pressing me into the bed. His mouth between my legs, tongue stroking, delving, and flicking, until I couldn't stand it anymore. Then that hard, deep thrust as he'd push himself inside me—

And him flinging open the bathroom door to come toward me. I froze in shock, my hand still jammed between my legs. Then I found my voice. "Get out!"

My demand only slowed him, but it was the conditioner bottle bouncing off his head that brought him to a stop.

"Catherine—"

The shampoo bottle beaned him next. Some of the green left his eyes as the soap followed. Then my razor. Soon I was out of items and just splashing water at him.

"But you called me in here," he exclaimed, backing away at last.

"No, I didn't!"

I yanked the shower curtain off, covering myself, and grasped the iron rod, burning all over with embarrassment.

That backed him all the way out. "It seems there's been a misunderstanding—"

"*Getoutofhere!*"

I couldn't even separate the syllables in my humiliation. He translated, however, and a second later, I heard the door shut. Then worse, Spade's muffled laughter, immediately shushed by Denise.

"For crying out loud," I hissed, the shower curtain still clinging to me. "Can't a person masturbate in peace?"

The next day the adult thing would have been to go downstairs, act as if nothing had happened, and proceed about my business.

Well, who had ever accused me of acting like an adult?

I faked sleep until noon, took lunch in my room, and then watched movies with the fortitude of a professional loaf. Pleaded another headache to anyone who dared to knock and inquire. The only activity I indulged in was a shower, having reassembled mine later the previous night. It was a cold one too, my hands used for hygienic purposes only.

When evening finally came and Bones returned, his question about my whereabouts was met with Spade's instant laughter.

"Headache, mate." Spade didn't bother to suppress his continued chuckles. "You might want to take my word for it. Don't want her injuring herself booting you from her room this time."

"Stuff it, Charles." Bones sounded as amused as I felt. "If anyone needs me, I'll be in my room."

I stayed in bed, not wanting to make my lie more obvious by puttering around upstairs. The small, still-sane part of me argued that I couldn't keep this up. Bones needed support, not hiding. Considering his sexual history, a little rub-in-the-tub probably didn't even register on his dirty meter.

It took three hours of mental berating before I climbed out of bed. Another forty-five minutes of similar scolding in the bathroom, washing my face and brushing my teeth to a ridiculous level. Twenty minutes to rehearse opening lines for our conversation. Another hour of backing out before deciding to go for it. By then, however, I figured it was too late. Bones had to be asleep by now.

That brought me back to staring at the ceiling. I had every speck of knockdown on it memorized. At this hour, couples in the house were starting to get active. Trying to tune out the various noises only highlighted my loneliness. I was so engrossed in my attempts to ignore any grunty, squeaky sounds it took me a few more minutes to realize that some of them came from the next room.

At that, I shot out of bed. Pressed my ear to the wall and strained to listen. Son of a bitch, there it was! Oh, subdued, sure. Very hushed, but unmistakable feminine pants mixed with Bones's moans.

As if in a dream, I saw myself calmly get my knife, walk the short distance to his room, and kick his door right off the hinges.

"What the hell?"

Bones was in bed. Alone, so he or the slut must have heard me coming. His covers were mussed and the TV was on, but I kept my main attention on seeking out my prey.

"Where is she?"

His gaze dropped to the knife in my hand and then the broken door near my feet. "Have you lost your wits altogether?"

"Going to play it that way? Fine."

I darted forward, checking under the bed. Nothing. Then I yanked open the closet doors, tearing one off with my forcefulness. There went another household item, but no one was hiding in the closet. When I headed for the bathroom, Bones had his arms crossed over his chest, watching me with more than a hint of anger.

"Care to play hot or cold? Let me give you a hint: you're freezing."

I threw him a venomous glare and checked the bathroom anyway, keeping a wary eye on the bedroom door. No bitch was going to sneak past me. Had to be a vampire or ghoul. I didn't hear any heartbeat except my own.

No one was in the bathroom either. Or the linen closet, which looked too small, but I checked anyway. I even knocked over the wicker laundry hamper. Only clothes. Then I circled the bed again, seeking any hiding placed I could have missed.

"Getting warmer, pet."

A large wall unit faced the bed and it had closed sections in it. Bones nodded in that direction and I tightened my grip on the knife. *If someone were to scrunch themselves up real small...*

"You're on fire."

For someone who'd just been caught cheating, Bones didn't sound guilty or apologetic. Instead, he sounded pissed and more than a little disgusted.

I marched toward the wall unit. Noises were coming from it. Moans, gasps, groans. Then I glanced at the TV. What—?

"You're watching *porn*?" I turned to him, the beginnings of doubt creeping in.

"Take a closer look," he said with that same harsh edge to his voice.

I gave another cursory glance at the TV screen before zeroing in on the naked male with astonishment. "You're playing old sex tapes of yourself? What kind of a sick—"

"Careful." Bones voice was whiplike now. "Accuse me falsely again, and I'll turn you straight over my knee."

I drew myself up with indignation. "I dare you to try, you porn-reminiscing perv— Ooof!"

Some things time and familiarity had dulled. What should have occurred to me as I made my taunting statement was that Bones never bluffed. Ever.

I was facedown on the bed with my mouth full of blankets before I could even yelp. *Thwack!* went the hard swat right on my ass.

Then Bones flipped me over and grabbed my wrists, moving his face only inches away from mine. "Now, perhaps you'll let me explain. If you had the slightest ounce of trust, you'd have done that earlier. Instead, despite my repeated promises, you thought I was shagging another woman right under your nose, or at best amusing myself with tapes of prior lovers. I've killed people for lesser insults, but since you're my wife, all you'll get is a sore arse. Now look at the girl on the telly, Catherine!"

He used my hair as a handle to tilt my head. Left with few other options, I stared at the screen. Humph, a redhead, figures. Wait a minute…

"That's *me!*"

Bones rolled off the bed with a shake of his head. "*This,* luv, was in the DVDs that Denise gave me, so the only crime I've committed tonight is to ogle my own wife. Off topic, you're absolutely stunning naked. I thought to tell you the same last night, but the many objects hitting me in the face distracted me."

I was still sprawled on the bed, and yes, my ass was sore. He'd whacked it with authority. For a few astounded moments, I couldn't decide if I was angry for him daring to spank me, regretful over falsely accusing him of adultery, or flattered by his last compliment.

My own groans from the tape snapped my attention back to the television. I flushed. After making this on a whim during our boat trip to Paris, I hadn't watched it. Frankly, with everything going on, I'd forgotten about it. Holy hell, this was graphic! We looked like a couple of coke-crazed porn stars.

"I don't want you seeing this," I said, striving to lose my fierce blush.

A single brow arched. "Why not?"

"Because!" I was about to detail my objection in a more reasonable manner when something new on the screen caught my eye. My gaze narrowed. "Wait a minute. *This* isn't supposed to be on here. I told you to turn the camera off. You said you'd turned it off!"

Bones laughed at that, moving over to stand by the TV.

"No, in fact I didn't. I've rewound this part a few times, I confess. You say, 'I won't do that with the camera running,' and I reply, 'I won't let a bloody camera stop us from doing anything.' Then I go to the camera, tap it, come back, and say, 'There. Feel better?' and, ah, you do appear to feel better, luv. But nowhere do I actually *verbalize* that I've shut it off."

My mouth hung open farther.

Bones tapped the screen for emphasis. "We'll rewind it, if you'd like. I don't mind."

It didn't matter that the man laughing at me technically hadn't been the one who tricked me. "You sneaky bastard, you knew I thought it was off!" I sputtered.

"Now, Catherine, I might not remember making that decision, but let me assure you, I'll claim it. And stand by it proudly."

That glint was back in his eyes. The one that said he was contemplating a thousand filthy things, and I'd love them all. Belatedly, it occurred to me he was naked. How could I have missed that? Having my ass whacked and then watching a skin-flick starring myself were my main two reasons.

Unable to help it, I took a good, long look. My God, but he was gorgeous. His creamy skin stretched over his hard muscles like it couldn't get enough of touching them. Then those broad shoulders, rippling arms and chest, flat stomach and of course lower—

"You keep looking at me and licking your lips, and I'm going to get certain impressions," he said, his voice like silk. "Are they the wrong impressions?"

Had I been licking my lips? Well, who could blame me? "Sorry, I didn't mean to eye-hump you. It's, er, just been more weeks than I care to count, so..." *Stop talking!* I groaned inwardly. *It's like you've got verbal diarrhea!*

"Weeks?" That arched his brow higher.

I let out a sigh and tried to keep my gaze above his waist.

"I didn't correct your misassumption before because, well, I was mad. Vlad and I never had sex. We slept together, but as friends, nothing more. So yeah, it's been weeks, and the last time was with you."

Bones shut the television off. Guess I had his full attention now.

"First, thank you for telling me. I'd believed otherwise, of course, from what Charles had said about interrupting the two of you in bed."

"The only thing Spade interrupted was sleep," I said, shrugging. "But of course he didn't come to that conclusion."

"I wouldn't have either," Bones said, sounding almost as if he didn't believe me.

"Yeah, well, I didn't sleep with Vlad because he wasn't you." As soon as I said it, I wanted to take it back. It was too honest, too raw, and in its own way, more exposing than the video he'd just watched. I dashed a hand across my suddenly stinging eyes and tried to shake it off.

"Plus I'm not that easy." Fake, uneven laugh. "I made you wait months before you got me into bed the first time, which was probably a celibacy record for you."

Bones still hadn't said anything. He just stood there. Moonlight peeked through the windows, caressing parts of his body with light while the rest stayed wrapped in shadows.

I had to leave before I said anything else I regretted. I rolled off the bed. "Sorry about your door and your closet and—"

"Get back in bed."

"What?"

He came nearer. "Get back in bed. I'm sick of tossing about, unable to sleep because I hear you, yet you're so far away. It's only been five nights, but it feels like a bloody year. I'm not asking for sex, Catherine. I just want to hold you while I sleep."

I told myself it was the least I could do after smashing into his room like an angry She-Hulk to accuse him of cheating. Plus I'd just admitted to a sleepover with Vlad, so it would look petty if I denied the same request from Bones. None of those reasons were why I nodded and crawled beneath the covers though. Deep down, I needed to feel his arms around me. I'd been through a nonstop emotional ringer the past several weeks that had drained me both physically and mentally. Right now, being held by Bones sounded like the only thing that would get me through the night, let alone whatever else would be thrown at us next.

After I settled myself in bed, I set my knife on the nightstand. It had been in my hand this whole time; what a fruit loop I was. Bones gave it a brief smile and then climbed into bed, grasping me securely from behind. Our bodies were only separated by my pajamas, and feeling him pressed along the back of me filled me with the weirdest blend of comfort, desire, and complete safety. This was nothing like what I'd felt during my sleepover with Vlad. It went deeper in every way.

"I'm glad you didn't argue with me," he said, his deep voice lower as he rested his head next to mine.

He didn't realize it, but this was the same way we'd fallen asleep countless times before, me in his arms with his body curved around the back of mine. My emotions might still be in turmoil, but muscle memory seemed to take over. Contentment stole through my limbs, relaxing my body in a way I would have thought impossible only a few minutes ago.

"I'm tired of fighting with you," I replied, surprised that the words came out with drowsy slowness. When had I closed my eyes? And why was it suddenly impossible to open them?

"Good." Something brushed my neck that was either his fingers or lips. "This is all I want now, but tomorrow night, Catherine, I'm going to seduce you."

I let out a sleepy laugh at his bluntness, not to mention his overconfidence. "Is that a warning?"

Now I was sure it was his lips because he did it again, slower and more deliberately.

"A promise."

❧　❧　❧

Bones was gone when I woke up. I must have really conked out. For a little while I stayed in bed, breathing in the scent of him on the sheets while I wondered what he was doing. Zen forms of meditation or all-out brawling to test his skills? Probably both. Speaking of skills...

His gauntlet from last night shook me from my indolence. If Bones set about to do something, he accomplished it. Add my flagging willpower to the picture and I might as well wait spread-eagled for him. The thought of making love to him inspired mixed emotions. Sure, it had always been great, but as I'd told him, we'd been in love. I didn't want sex with me to be one huge yawn to him, and he'd never admit it if he was disappointed. If only he didn't have so many other women to compare me with.

There were a couple of ways I could handle this. First, worry myself into permanent abstinence. No nookie, no fears about whether it was good for him. That didn't seem feasible, so I discarded it. Second, wait until any sex was great sex. Nothing like a long drought to make the first rain very appreciated. Again, however, that didn't appear to be in the cards. A few more nights of sleeping with Bones while he was naked and I'd be spread-eagling *him*. Plus it wouldn't lead to a closer relationship, and that was the goal.

Okay, that left the third option. This was going to hurt.

I returned to my room, showered, dressed, and then marched downstairs. A funeral march played in my mind because I felt like I was headed for the firing squad.

"Annette."

My too-jovial voice made her raise her head warily. She'd been sipping tea in the parlor with Spade and Denise.

"Cat," she replied.

"You and I never get to chat," I continued with a bright smile. "How about I get some wine and we have a little picnic in the yard, just the two of us, hmm?"

Now she was more than wary. Her gaze darted to Spade in a way that clearly spelled out *help*. However, Annette was anything except a coward.

"I'm sure that would be lovely... if you insist."

"Done!" I flashed another broad, false smile. "Red wine or white?"

A dry laugh escaped her. "Really, dear, what do you think?"

"Red it is. See you in twenty minutes? There's a nice shady tree behind the pool. I'll set up there."

Again she flicked her eyes to Spade, but he just shrugged as if to say *I don't have a bloody clue what she's up to.*

Denise watched this exchange with her forehead wrinkled in disbelief. When I headed to the computer in the other room to punch in my beverage and food requests, she followed me.

"Is everything okay?" she asked.

"You know the first thing you do before planning a mission?" I replied, a brisk mentality setting in. "Field research."

Her hazel gaze widened with comprehension. Then she laughed. "I was going to offer to go with you, but I think I'll stay out of this. My field research days are over."

"Yeah, well. I thought mine were too."

Annette reclined on the quilt like it was a velvet dais. Even the outdoor setting didn't diminish her sophisticated air. She could have been at the poshest restaurant waiting for her next glass of Cristal. Not on the ground with only a blanket between her and the dirt.

"All right, Cat. You've gotten me out in this dreadful heat, what is it that you want?" she said after finishing her first glass.

I took a healthy gulp of my wine before replying. "I'm going to have sex with Bones tonight, and I want to make sure I've got all my bases covered."

Her wineglass almost fell from her hand. "Indeed?"

"You're not invited to join in," I continued pleasantly. "I'd like you to make a magnanimous gesture, Annette. One you get no personal gratification out of."

Both her perfectly shaped brows rose. "You're not making sense, dear."

"Fine, I'll cut to the chase. No one knows more about fucking Bones than you do, and I want him happy. Since he doesn't have love to fall back on if sex with me is mundane, I want to make sure I'm pushing the right buttons with him. So, are you going to help me or not?"

Annette was speechless for a few moments before she laughed, loud and merry. "Oh, Cat! What you don't realize is that right now you are *exactly* like Crispin. This is just what he would do, given similar circumstances."

"Is that a yes?"

She stifled her laughter, but that gleam was still in her eyes. "The most effective method of instruction is demonstration."

"The day I grow balls," I said sweetly. "Verbal only. Yea or nay?"

"Yes." Her lips kept twitching. "You start. Tell me what the two of you normally do, and then I'll tell you what you've been neglecting."

And that's how I ended up detailing my sexual history to Bones's ex-girlfriend, using concise descriptions and leaving nothing out. After fifteen minutes, the amusement had left her and her eyes had started to fleck with emerald.

"Well? What am I missing?"

Annette finished her wine before pouring herself another. She kept giving me sideways glances as she drank, until finally she just stared. "Do you know I've been under the impression that you were straitlaced? You act that way, and while I knew you were passionate—blimey, I have ears— I didn't realize you were such a dirty little vixen!"

She said it accusingly, like I'd been holding out on her. I took another gulp of my own wine and shrugged. "You know Bones. I used to be straitlaced. He got around that."

"So it seems." She shook her head. "Faith, this won't take long. You've no interest in ways to pleasure him with another woman, so I can only suggest three things…"

The items she rattled off almost made me blush. The first I hadn't considered since he was a vampire and I didn't think it pertained, the second was flat-out embarrassing, and the third… well. We'd see.

"Hmmm," was all I said.

She gave me an arch look. "Even so."

We didn't say anything for another minute, both of us drinking our wine.

All of a sudden, I started to laugh. "Can you imagine what he'd say if Bones had his memory back and he came upon the two of *us* discussing the best ways to have sex with him?"

Annette laughed as well. "He'd swear I drugged your wine. He's so bloody protective of you."

Just as quickly, my eyes filled with tears. Yeah, he'd loved me so much that he used to be crazy protective. It had been annoying at times. Now I'd kill to have it again.

She set down her glass and slid across the small blanket. Even as I waved her away, she put her arms around me. "You poor girl," she said softly. "Despite our differences, I know how much you love him. And somewhere deep inside him, past this blockage, he knows it too. There's no spell that can erase that."

Then I did the second most unusual thing I'd ever done with Annette. I let her comfort me as I cried.

The next time Bones came home, I wasn't hiding away upstairs. I was in a chair by the foyer, a half-full glass of gin and tonic next to me. I'd been sipping conservatively, which wasn't what I wanted to do. I'd have downed two bottles of straight gin, left to my own devices, but reeking of liquor didn't lend to a romantic mood.

He saw me as he took off his coat, coming closer with it draped over his arm instead of putting it in the closet. He wore a royal-blue shirt, the deep color setting off his creamy skin. His pants were black, but that was his norm. Years ago, he'd told me he had better things to do than mix and match his tops with trousers.

"Catherine."

Just the way he said my name made my heartbeat speed up. When he leaned down, brushing his lips across my cheek, it sped up even more.

Wherever he and Mencheres went during the day, it had shower facilities. He was freshly washed and smelled like soap, male, and his own natural scent. The combination was better than cologne.

Behind him, Mencheres gave me a quick, approving nod. He'd probably just filched from my mind what my intentions were. Then the Egyptian vampire melted up the stairs without saying a word. Spade and Denise were on the other side of the house, and Annette was out seeing a movie. Who said she couldn't be gracious once in a while?

"I, ah, wanted to talk to you," I said as I stood up and indicated the nearby den.

"Of course."

He laced his fingers in mine as we walked. If only this didn't feel so awkward. Or if I were rip-roaring drunk.

"It's nice to see you," Bones went on. "I've thought of you all day, as usual."

"Stop." I pulled my hand free as I shut the den's door behind us.

"Stop what?"

"You don't have to say that. What I mean is, you don't have to try to seduce me. I've decided to, um, let you out of the doghouse."

Part of me had thought he'd hear that, throw me over his shoulder, and run for the nearest bed. Or, as had happened before, just get busy right where we were. Bones didn't do either.

Instead, a smile tugged at his mouth. "Waving the white flag, are you?"

I threw up my hands. "It just seems fair. You could die for sticking it out with me, and you're very well aware of that. Hell, I'd be demanding some recompense, if I were you. And I know you're not celibate out of preference, so... bar's open."

That drew outright laughter. By the time he reined it in, my foot was tapping in irritation.

"I apologize, luv, but that was priceless. Bar's open? I'll bear that in mind. Are you hungry?"

My foot quit tapping. "Are you being sleazy and metaphorical?"

He didn't burst out laughing again, but from his twitching mouth, it was close. "No, I meant literally. Have you eaten supper yet?"

"Well, no." In all my apprehension, I'd skipped that.

He gave me an appraising look, his tongue tracing inside his bottom lip. "Right, then, let's be off."

He grasped my hand and led me out of the den. When we reached the front door, I stopped.

"What are you doing?"

He gave me a tolerant look. "Can't even remember the last time we went out for fun, can you? No wonder you look so confused. I'm taking you to dinner, Catherine. Alone."

That last word was practically a dare for anyone in the house to try to stop him. So I played the part of Spade and Mencheres.

"We can't, it's not safe. Someone could spot us and tell Gregor, not to mention I can't know where we are. Jeez, if you're not in the mood, just tell me! You don't have to go all crazy."

He laughed again, but this time it was filled with more than humor. Green pinpointed in his eyes and he moved closer until my retreat was blocked by the door.

"My dear, sweet wife, I want you terribly. As to the dangers of going out, you've gotten good at keeping your eyes closed. If there's immediate trouble, I have my mobile and we won't be going far. Besides"—his smile turned wicked—"we haven't even had a proper date yet. What bloke puts out without that? Blimey, I don't know what sort you think I am."

Bones took me to a chain restaurant. Smart, since it would have locations nationwide. Since it was the dinner hour, a long line of people waited to get in, but Bones just flashed his eyes at the hostess and we were given the next table.

I didn't look at the menu. Or the cars in the parking lot, license plates having too much information. I kept my concentration on him, and he made that easy. He sat next to me instead of across from me, touching my arm, back, or hand in casual ways that made me barely able to chew, and he never once let the conversation pause. I'd almost forgotten how charming he could be. It didn't escape the notice of several females in the vicinity either, who kept throwing him interested glances. I reminded myself that there was nothing wrong with looking. Flinging my fork into some chick's forehead for checking him out was undeserved. And too flashy. We'd definitely have to cut our evening short if I did that.

Bones didn't eat since solid food wasn't his preference, so he drank whiskey and encouraged me to eat everything on my plate. Over my objections, he also ordered dessert and goaded me into eating that too. Since it was a brownie with ice cream and chocolate sauce, I didn't require much persuading. When I finally put my fork down, he let out an amused snort.

"Heavy-lidded eyes and a sated smile. Not the way I'd imagined seeing it, but lovely nonetheless. There's one bite left."

I was too stuffed to do more than look at it. "It's good, you should have it."

"All right," he said at once.

Maybe I didn't guess his intention because I was in the mildly dazed state of overeating. Or perhaps I was lulled by his easy charm. What I should have remembered was that this was *Bones*. There was only so long his chasteness would last.

His mouth came down on mine, his hand on the back of my neck keeping me from jerking away in surprise. I gasped at the contact, and he took my parted lips as an invitation. His tongue swept past my lips, deepening the kiss with a skillful sensuality that had me gasping for a different reason. My head tilted back as he explored my mouth with unhurried thoroughness, and when I slid my tongue along his, he sucked on it with erotic hunger.

Sensations hijacked my sensibilities. *The taste of whiskey on his tongue. His hand on my neck, pulling me closer. My nipples hardening when our bodies met. The race of my pulse, increasing with every second. And his throaty moan when my hand moved farther up his thigh—*

I yelped, snatching my hand away as color rushed to my face. I'd been about three inches from feeling him up in a crowded restaurant. What was the *matter* with me?

Bones's eyes snapped open when I broke away, revealing that they'd changed from dark brown to bright green. "What's wrong?"

"What's wrong?" I repeated. "I'm a dirty tramp, that's what's wrong!"

Several heads turned. Oops, said that too loud. I sank lower in my seat, wishing the ground would swallow me.

Bones laughed, low and throaty. "I'm breaking your rule, Catherine, because I'm going to compliment you again. You're even more beautiful when you blush. You'll have me racking my brain thinking up ways to make you do it again."

"Believe me, you already have," I muttered, cursing my heated cheeks.

The waitress stopped by with the check, casting disapproving looks at both of us before hurrying away. First making out at the table, then me howling out my lack of morality. I hoped Bones left her a big tip.

"Let's go, okay? I think I've done enough damage."

His eyes had been marbling back to brown, but at that, they flashed green. "Feeling your response means more to me than anyone in this place, so sod them. I've been afraid that my actions had killed any real desire you had for me. Oh, I knew you fancied the look of me, but that's not the same. I can't decide if I'm more switched on or relieved, and believe me, luv, I have never been so aroused."

He almost whispered the last sentence. Not for propriety, since as stated, he didn't care about that, but because the words were more emphatic softer. All the while, his gaze drilled into mine until I felt stripped both physically and emotionally, and I scrambled to get control of myself.

"Okay, well, we can leave. If you're, ah, ready to go to bed."

Bones leaned back, eying me now with calculation. "Think you'll keep me at bay by shagging me? Wrong. I want you, not just your flesh, though I confess a strong desire for that too. I'll wait to have you until it *is* you. You won't make me settle for anything less."

"Are you sure you don't have your memory back?" I snapped. "Because you sound just like you did the day you left me!"

As soon as the words left me, I clapped a hand over my mouth. I'd just ripped open a wound that had barely scabbed, and from his immediate pounce, he knew it.

"It wasn't only Gregor between us, was it? Did you do this before? Shield yourself away from me?"

"People are waiting for this table." I stalled, looking around to avoid his gaze.

It didn't work. "You don't want to have this conversation back at the house with a dozen eavesdroppers any more than I do. Here and now, Catherine, let's sort this out."

He'd never let it go. Not Bones, king of seeing things through to the end.

"I'll need a gallon of gin for this," I grumbled while trying to move away from him. At least I could get a little physical distance if he was about to rip apart my emotional barriers.

Bones eyed me before slapping money on the table. Then he grasped my hand. "Gallon of gin, you say? I know just the place."

He led me out of the restaurant and I shut my eyes once we reached the parking lot, following the tug on my hand to the car. Once in it, I concentrated on the song playing instead of noises from nearby places. It was an old one, "Under Pressure" by Queen, and I could relate to the lyrics. I was under pressure too, and it was about to get worse.

Bones didn't drive long before we stopped. He opened my door and took my hand again. Even these small touches affected me, bringing out a stinging longing. It was so weird to miss someone when they were right next to you.

"Open your eyes," he said after he led me inside.

The neon *Budweiser* sign was the first thing I saw. We were at a noisy, boisterous bar. At least I didn't feel underdressed as I had at dinner. My button-down shirt and jeans fit right in here.

Bones took us over to the bar. "Gin, top-shelf, the entire bottle."

Money changing hands cleared up the bartender's objection. I was too nervous over our upcoming discussion to be embarrassed by that little scene. When Bones led me to a table at the far end of the bar, I took the bottle from him and began to drink.

Bones waited until my third deep swallow before he spoke. "Did you hold yourself back from me the entire time we were together?"

My hands trembled on the bottle, which I gripped like a lifeline. Still, I refused to lie. "Yeah, pretty much."

"Why?"

Such a simple question. So impossible to answer.

I sighed. "Different reasons for different circumstances. When we first met, it was because I hated vampires and you were one of them. Years later, after you found me, I had fears about my job, my mother, and you wanting me to change over. Then finding out that I was, like, the thirty thousandth woman you'd slept with. Always running into your exes was a little hard to swallow, and—"

"Who told you that number?" he interrupted, astonished.

I took a few more gulps before answering. "You did."

Both his brows went up.

I nodded in confirmation. "I asked, and you said about three to four women a week was your average before me. Multiply that by your age, and there you have it."

"Bugger," he swore. "Don't know what I was thinking, revealing such a thing to my wife." He gave me another appraising sweep of his eyes, as if measuring what had made him tell me that.

I was glad for the switch in topics and plowed ahead. "You also said you considered your virginity lost in stages of four."

His brows went higher. "I told you *that* too? Did you pump me full of truth serum one night? Is that how you got me gabbing like a teenage girl?"

"Some of the things you told me weren't to be believed, but you swore they were true. Like the time you were a whore and after a particularly busy night, you faked a hard-on with a new client by using your fingers to keep your cock straight. Now *that* I could imagine, but you said the woman never knew—"

"Clearly I opened up to you in a very personal way." He cut me off, resolve replacing the disbelief in his expression. "Everyone tells me I was deeply in love with you. The things you know, like my mother's perfume and other stories I've never shared, only solidify that. Yet you admit to holding me at arm's length, and you still haven't said why."

I almost choked on my gin. The spotlight was back on me, with reinforcements.

Bones stared at me, waiting. Around us, people drank and danced and fought and had their own problems. In the grand scheme of things, one wobbly marriage didn't matter except to the two people in it.

"I don't know why," I said at last, very softly. "It seemed like every time I opened up, something bad happened and I'd need my shields to get me through it. I almost jumped off a cliff when I thought you were dead, and Vlad had to talk me down. That's what happens when I let myself go. I can't stand to need you so much, so... I hold back. Just enough. Then if you're gone, I can still function, no matter the reason why you're not there."

A small, twisting smile pulled at his mouth. "Never value something with more than you can afford to lose. Yes, I understand that very well. It's what I've lived by all these years, so it appears I married someone just like me. I suppose it's fitting."

We didn't say anything for a few minutes. I drank while those brown orbs bored into mine whenever I met them, which wasn't often. Finally, he slid his hand across the table, palm up.

"Let's agree to stop, both of us. Take my hand, Catherine. No more safety net, no shields. We'll let each other in, though it will mean living a life as dangerous as it gets. Are you with me?"

My first impulse was to run as far as my legs could take me. Bones's stare promised to hold me to any vow I made, and I didn't think I could handle losing all my defenses. He wasn't offering guarantees either. He couldn't. In life, there were none.

I looked at his pale skin, broad palm, tapered fingers, and short nails. I knew a lot of the history behind that hand, and most of it wasn't pretty. The violence in his past was only exceeded by the licentiousness, and maybe more. Maybe I didn't really want to discover everything about Bones.

And yet in the end, none of my concerns mattered. This was Bones, and I'd never been able to help myself when it came to him.

My hand covered his like steel to a magnet. Even if it destroyed me—and hell, it probably would—I still couldn't do anything else.

Bones drew a knife out with his other hand. I gave him a questioning look as he pressed it to my palm.

"I don't remember doing this before, and until I have my other memories back, I want something of my own."

The knife scored my palm, blood welling up in the cut. He released me and then cut his hand the same way.

"Claim me as yours, Catherine."

An offer and a demand. I met his eyes while taking his hand with mine, feeling his blood start to heal me on contact.

"By my blood, you are my husband," I said softly.

His hand tightened on mine. "By my blood, you are my wife. Forever."

I gave him a small, almost shy smile. "You want to kiss the bride?"

He didn't smile back. Instead, his expression was very serious. "Yes."

This time his kiss was restrained. I was the one who flicked my tongue inside his mouth, craving his taste. Then I was the one who wrapped my arms around him and pulled him closer.

His restraint vanished. He tangled his hand in my hair, tipping my head back and opening my mouth farther while he ravished the inside. I clutched him, suddenly feeling dizzy. His other hand ran down my back, shifting me until our hips lined up. Then he kissed me deeper while the bulge in his pants hit my most sensitive spot.

At the feel of him there, that denied, starved part of me reared up and said, *now.* Not later, not back at the house. Right. Now.

My hands raced down his back, his chest, his stomach—I couldn't stop touching him. Bones let out a harsh moan and lifted me up. My feet made contact with several people as he pushed through the crowd to the exit, but he made it there so fast they probably didn't know what had hit them.

He moved just as swiftly through the parking lot, still kissing me with a hunger that made me oblivious to anything else. Once we reached the car, Bones deposited me on the front seat, but I didn't let go. I pulled him on top of me, barely registering the sound of the car door slamming shut.

He wrestled out of his jacket without breaking his mouth's contact with me. All the while, that bulge continued to rub me in the most inflaming, erotic way. The intimate friction ripped away the last of my control, making me insane with need. He made a rough noise when I wrapped my legs around him, then I felt the seat go all the way back.

His shirt came off with a single, impatient tug, then with a jerk, he split apart my blouse and bra. When my breasts touched him, skin on skin, the contact drove me out of my mind. I twisted against him in mute demand, not caring that I could barely breathe from his ceaseless, devouring kisses. His hands went to my jeans, and after a rip, he pulled them down my legs.

"Don't stop touching me," I gasped, burning to feel his hands on me again. Even the seconds he'd spent taking off my jeans was too long.

"I can't stop," he growled. Then he tore at the front of his pants.

I writhed under him, digging my nails into his back, my whole body thrumming. "Bones—!"

His name ended in a cry as he thrust inside me. My loins clenched at the excruciating pleasure as he moved deeper, stretching me with his length and thickness. I latched my mouth on his neck, straining toward him while my nails raked down his back.

Words spilled out of me, but I didn't know what they were. My heart beat so loudly it deafened me. Those deep, hard thrusts had me sobbing with ecstasy. Every nerve ending sizzled, and my muscles tensed as he increased his pace until I heard myself crying out for more in a voice that broke from passionate sobs.

Bones yanked my hips up, tilting me as he pushed so deeply inside me that I screamed. He leaned forward, increasing the erotic pressure, and rocked hard and rhythmically. Blasts of pleasure shot through me. That boiling tension ruptured all at once, shaking me with the orgasm. He didn't pause, and his continued movements kept me shouting with passion. After a few minutes, his hands clamped on my hips while his whole body tensed. A hoarse cry was followed by a throb deep within as his climax vibrated through me, and I reveled in the feel of it.

After several moments, he shifted to rest his weight on his arms, waiting until I stopped hyperventilating before he kissed me.

"Bloody hell, luv, I'm trembling."

I gasped out a laugh at the surprise in his voice. "You always do."

"No," he whispered. "I don't." Then concern skipped across his features. "Did I hurt you? Didn't mean to lose control like that—"

"Do I feel hurt to you?" I interrupted with another breathless laugh.

He smiled and it melted me to see it. He was still inside me, still hard, and it felt so *right* that I thought I'd cry.

I didn't because in the next instant, red and blue lights flashed behind him. Bones let out a vile curse just a voice boomed out, "Police! Come out with your hands up!"

"Are you out of your bloody mind?" he thundered back.

"What's going on?" I managed to say before he lifted me out from under him, pushing me into the backseat.

"Stay down. Stupid sods just cocked their guns," he muttered.

Guns? "Wait—"

"They're only human, I'll tidy this right up," he said, cutting me off. "There's a bit of a crowd out there, Catherine. Put this shirt on."

I was half sitting on his shirt in the backseat, but my clothes were nowhere in sight, so I grabbed it.

"Coming out, lads, nice and easy," Bones called out.

"With your hands up," the bullish cop reminded him.

Bones opened the door and stretched out his hands. Meanwhile, I scrambled to put on his shirt.

"Nobody move in the car!" came the next bellow.

"It's just my wife, mate, no harm. Come and see for yourself."

Bones was using his vampire voice, raising the hairs on the back of my neck with its timbre. Since I was no longer mindless from lust, I could now hear and see the small crowd hanging out behind the police. Well, what did I expect? Noisy sex in a parking lot was bound to get noticed.

One of the two policemen approached, and I blushed when I saw Bones get out of the car wearing nothing but his shoes. Thank God the other cars blocked most of him from the bar patrons' view.

"Obviously I'm not armed, so let me explain," he said in the same reasonable, echoing tone.

Once the officer was close enough, Bones hit him with his gaze. His eyes gleamed only for an instant, but it was enough.

"Tell your partner that all's well and to come over here," he instructed him quietly.

"Jack, come on over," the cop intoned, lowering his gun. "It's okay, there's no assault in progress."

Inwardly, I ground my teeth. People had called the police because they thought there was an *assault* going on? That's what I got for being a screamer!

"Ed?"

The other cop hadn't lowered his gun. He was still cautious, good for him. But he did come closer. Bones waited until the officer's back was to the crowd before his gaze lit up again.

"Nothing's going on. False alarm, right, mate? We're leaving and you won't even report this."

"Sure," the cop said with the same glazed look as his partner, Ed. He even smiled. "You folks take care now, you hear?"

"Thanks ever so," Bones replied with less graciousness. "Now tell those bloody people to mind their own business and go back inside."

"Folks, there's nothin' going on here." Officer Ed's voice rang out as he waved at the onlookers. "Go on back inside before I start checking licenses and insurance!"

That got results. With grumbles, the people dispersed. There were a few whistles and some lewd comments, but soon only a couple of gawkers remained.

"Right then, gents, off you go."

Bones waited until the police got back in their car before he walked around to the driver's side, totally nonchalant about his nudity. In the interim, I'd gotten his shirt on, grateful that it hung to my thighs since my panties were in tatters and my jeans were ruined. Almost getting arrested postcoitus was definitely a mood kill.

"Here." I handed him his pants when he opened the door. "Zipper's ripped, but they'll cover you."

Bones stepped into them and then got in the car. I crawled back into the front seat and adjusted the lever until the seat was upright once more. We drove off with a spin of tires, me closing my eyes at the whole scene.

"This was my fault, Catherine, I'm sorry," Bones said.

I kept my eyes shut even though it was pointless. "You weren't the one who screamed so loud that someone called the police."

"Perhaps not, but I should have controlled myself until we were back at the house. Even worse, I lost complete awareness of my surroundings. It's a damn good thing only coppers stumbled on us, or I could have gotten you killed."

I let out a watery laugh. "I'm just as much to blame as you are, and if you'd tried to put the brakes on before, there *would* have been an assault in progress."

He chuckled. "This isn't the way I intended things to go tonight, but I'll make it up to you as soon as we get back."

I sighed. "I've got two words that'll make you forget all about that plan."

"Indeed?" He sounded highly skeptical.

"Omaha, Nebraska," I said, and opened my eyes.

"Bugger," Bones said with feeling.

I nodded. "Yup."

While I'd watched the drama with Bones and the police, additional things had caught my attention. License plates. The city's name painted on the cop's car. The radio dispatcher in the background, giving street addresses and codes. In short, my exact location.

Bones pulled his cell out, dialing. The other end picked up on the first ring.

"Hallo, Charles. ... No, we're fine. We're on our way back, but we ran into a spot of trouble. Catherine knows where we are. ... Yes. ... Right. ... See you within the hour."

He hung up. "They'll start preparations. I'll ask you to settle back and close your eyes. You know the city, but there's no need to make it easy for Gregor to find the house. We're going to drive about for a bit to throw you off from the exact distance."

"Can we stop at a gas station?"

"Why? We have petrol... Oh, right." He caught on. "Of course."

I did have to pee, but that wasn't my only reason for wanting to visit a bathroom. The insides of my thighs were wet, and trotting into a house full of vampires like that didn't appeal. Add me wearing only his shirt, and Bones might as well write Got Laid! on his forehead.

Bones went to the nearest service station and got the restroom key for me. I stayed in the car, watching with dark amusement the looks the counter clerk gave him. He was still shirtless and there was a nice big tear along the inseam of his pants. It was a damn good thing Bones healed so fast, or the various scratch marks and hickeys would have been even more incriminating.

After I answered nature's call, I freshened up as best I could with paper towels, water, and liquid soap. A hot shower would have been preferable, but that wasn't in the cards. We'd probably be leaving right after we got back to the house.

Bones materialized next to me when I came out of the bathroom, making me jump. I'd thought he was still waiting in the car.

"You scared me," I said with a little laugh.

He cast a look down the front of me. "Do you regret making love to me?"

I hadn't expected that. "Why would you... What...?"

"Simple yes or no, Catherine," he said, gripping my shoulders and giving me that unblinking gaze.

"No! I mean, I regret what happened afterward with the cops, but... Why, do you?"

"Of course not." He let go. "Then why did you wash as though I'd fouled you?"

He was offended that I'd cleaned up? Okay, that was new.

"Because it's tacky to walk around like that! I know how well vampires can smell, and there's a bunch of them waiting back at the house. Grant me a little dignity, will you?"

391

"Tacky?" Bones appeared to mull the word. "We have a difference of opinion. I'm in no hurry to wash your scent from me. In fact, I can't wait until it's all over every inch of me."

Whoa. Guess Annette had been right about suggestion number two!

A low laugh escaped him. "You're blushing again. I'm finished holding back—you are absolutely stunning. Do you know why I laughed the first time I saw you? Because I still half thought it was a prank. Charles tells me a lurid tale about an archenemy, a forgotten marriage, and a spell to induce amnesia, then in walks this exquisite girl who's supposed to be my wife. It didn't even seem possible."

He kissed me then, quick and fervent. I didn't even have a chance to respond before he ended it.

"Let's go. It seems I don't have any willpower when I kiss you. Later I'll kiss and taste every inch of you. I won't be able to think about anything else until then."

With far more unsteadiness than before, I got into the car. No, it wasn't a good idea for him to kiss me. I wanted more when he did that too, and there were only so many gas stations between here and the house.

Thankfully, no one batted an eye when we arrived in our different attire. Bones gave me his coat to wear, so I was decently covered, at least. He only wore his torn pants and shoes, but there wasn't time for winks and nudges. Mencheres drew him aside as soon as we crossed the threshold, and I went straight to my bedroom to change. Denise and Spade were loading up the car from what I overheard, and Annette was chatting with Fabian, so someone else must be collecting her bags. From the bustle of activity, we'd be leaving soon.

I threw some things into a suitcase that had been laid out on the bed. Already, most of my other things were packed, judging from the empty drawers and the suitcases by the door. A glance in Bones's room showed a freckle-faced teenager hefting some bags toward the door. He smiled at me and told me he'd be back to get mine. Okay, so we were leaving *very* soon.

Spade came to get me ten minutes later. "Come with me, Cat. I'll show you to your car."

"Where's Bones?"

He gave me a jaded smile. "Still with Mencheres, I expect."

That sounded faintly ominous. "It's not his fault," I said at once. "I'm the one who didn't shut my eyes in the parking lot—"

"Quite." Spade interrupted me with a laugh. "Crispin knew when he took you out that you might discover your location. He chose to do it anyway, and now he's being held to task for it. Don't fret. Mencheres is just giving him the rough edge of his opinion."

Spade's demeanor was far friendlier. Ever since Vlad had torched his house, he'd been a little prickly around me.

"Why are you in such a good mood? Happy about a change of scenery?"

"My best friend is happier," he responded instantly. "Come now, Cat. If Denise were the one who'd unwittingly cheated on me and I treated her with cool judgment, how would you respond? Especially if she was truly regretful? You'd be skinning off pieces of my arse and we both know it, so can you blame me for wanting to do likewise?"

Well, that was honest. Put in those terms, he also had a point. I'd julienne him if he hurt Denise. Guess he'd fought similar compulsions.

"If I didn't love him so much, I'd be more logical," I said at last.

Spade smiled. "I know." Then he chuckled and gave my ass a quick smack. "That's why this is still intact, without my boot stuffed up there."

I slapped at his hand, but he'd already moved it away. Then he took my suitcases, using one to gesture with.

"Come along, Reaper. Let's get lost again."

An unknown human was at the wheel of the car Spade led me to. He hadn't bothered to introduce us. That no-name policy, I guessed. As soon as Bones got in, we left. A whole caravan of vehicles was going also, from the sound of it. I had my eyes closed. No need to give Gregor a mental image of things. Wait until he peeked into my mind and found out that I'd had sex with Bones. The thought almost made me smile.

Cool arms settled around me as Bones repositioned me until my head was on his chest. Then something light was placed over me.

"Go on, luv. Open your eyes."

I did and saw a dark sheet covering both of us. It felt like we were kids paying tent, and I bit back the urge to ask if he'd brought a flashlight.

Bones smiled. "Now at least we can look at each other while we speak. We'll be driving round two hours before we switch transportation modes. I know you're tired, but don't sleep until after that."

"I'm not that tired. I usually don't sleep until dawn, anyway."

A dark brow rose. "You've been abed before midnight all week. That's not your normal routine?"

I decided on an honest answer. "I was avoiding you. First it was because I was mad, and then when I was around you, I'd either babble or do something completely embarrassing. Hiding in my room felt like the lesser of two evils."

Bones caught my hand in his. "You're not hiding any longer, right?"

It didn't escape my notice that he held the same hand he'd used for our blood oath.

"No," I said quietly. "Not anymore."

It also didn't escape my notice that the last time we'd been reclined in a car, it had been under very different circumstances. I shifted, finding a more comfortable position, and the movement caused a twinge of soreness down below. Good thing we weren't going over unpaved roads.

Bones stared at me while his other hand slid down until it rested below my navel. "I *was* too rough before. Let me heal you."

His voice was soft, and with the radio blaring, the human driving the car couldn't overhear us. It made our conversation feel private even if our circumstances weren't.

"No," I whispered. "I like feeling you there. You said my scent was comforting? Well, this is to me, and you weren't too rough. I loved it. This is what I usually feel afterward, but it isn't pain, believe me."

I was telling the truth. This was a pleasant sort of ache, and it increased when his eyes began turning green.

"You deserve so much better than a backseat, but I couldn't help myself. I felt so much while touching you that it broke my will. Gregor might have stolen you from my mind, but it's clear you went deeper than that. You're beneath my skin, Catherine, and now I know that no person or spell can take you away from me."

Happiness coursed through me. "Well, if it helps your progress... I guess we'll have to do it every night."

He let out an amused snort. "Believe me, you're not keeping me from your bed any longer. You only succeeded before because I didn't know any better. I'd have been howling outside your door like a mangy dog if I had."

"That would have been the last straw for Spade. He'd have slugged me."

His arms curled around me. The feel of him was like therapy, soothing away my prior hurts.

"Tell me how we met. I want to know everything about it."

I settled back with a contented sigh. "You were on a job, and you'd tracked your mark to a bar in Ohio. I was there too, just itching to kill any vampire I could get alone. I saw you, came over and asked if you wanted to fuck..."

The new house didn't have a barn, horses, or a large, pasture-like backyard. It was in the woods, nothing but trees all around. The interior also wasn't as upscale as the last few places. In fact, it was kind of rustic. Spade wrinkled his nose in mild distaste. I loved it.

We'd flown the past few hours, then switched back to cars for the past forty minutes. It was well after dawn, and I just wanted to shower, brush my teeth, and go to bed wrapped up in Bones's arms. Mencheres, however, had other ideas.

"No, because he's coming with me," was Mencheres's immediate response when I asked Bones if he'd be right up.

"Huh?" I stopped on the stairs, my suitcase still in hand.

"I'm afraid I won't see you until tonight." Bones nearly sighed the words. "Training. We're already a bit late."

"But you haven't slept," I protested, starting back down.

"That does not excuse him," Mencheres stated.

Now I was mad. "Aren't you a little too old for spitefulness by, oh, a few *thousand* years?"

Bones came forward to rest a soothing hand on my arm. "I already knew this was my penalty. Think I'd change my actions because of lost sleep? You just get plenty of rest yourself. After all"—he brushed his lips next to my ear—"you'll need it."

Short of throwing a fit, there didn't seem to be much I could do. I contented myself with mentally informing Mencheres that he was a coldhearted, nasty shit and turned back around. Guess it was just shower, brush my teeth, and go to bed alone for me.

"I'll be waiting for you," I said as I headed back up the stairs.

Bones gave a short laugh. "You'd better be."

I picked the bedroom on the farthest corner of the second floor. Not the largest, but it was farther away from the others. The privacy was an illusion, but it was the best I could do. It would be so nice to have actual privacy again and not just its counterfeit.

After my bath, I slept for a few hours. Not as many as I should have, but I kept waking up and reaching across the empty space. Eventually I gave up and went downstairs.

Annette was watching TV, giving instructions to the actress on the screen. "Don't run up the stairs, fool. The killer's right there!"

Ah, a horror movie. Then I sniffed in confusion. "Are you wearing perfume?"

Annette glanced up and laughed. "Are you blind? Look around, Cat."

At that, I finally took in the rest of my surroundings. Jeez, she was right. If these had been enemy forces, I'd be dead. Roses were on almost every available tabletop. Long-stemmed, gorgeous, crimson roses.

"Bones had these delivered?"

"No, the juice boxes picked them up," she replied, turning her attention back to the movie. "They're in a house up the road."

I wanted to tell her that calling the live-in blood donors juice boxes wasn't polite, but I didn't bother. All I did was mutter, "You'll never be normal," and headed back upstairs.

"Neither will you, darling!" Annette sang out.

Uppity English tart. And yet when she was right, she was right.

Denise set down her cards after Spade nudged her.

"No fair," I protested. "Each player for themselves."

The three of us had been playing poker. Denise was better at bluffing, but her other skills hadn't matured as fast. She and Spade partnered up shamelessly.

"It's not that. We're going out," Spade said, setting down his hand.

"Oh." I dropped my cards. "Well, don't get freaky in a parking lot. Cops don't like that."

Denise burst out laughing. "Is that what happened last night?"

"Let's just say we disturbed the peace and leave it at that."

Spade didn't laugh, but his lips twitched. "It's a wonder Crispin didn't kill them."

I wasn't about to explain more. Should have just zipped it to begin with. "He might have wanted to. I didn't ask."

"Indeed." His mouth quirked again. "Appears he's taking precautions this time. We're going out, Mencheres is leaving, Annette will be staying overnight in the other residence, and Fabian will be floating elsewhere. You'll have the house to yourselves."

A slow flush crept its way up my face. "Bones arranged that?"

Now Spade did laugh. "What do you think?"

Well, what indeed? No fewer than six dozen roses were around the house, plus I'd also gotten a box of new lingerie. That had cracked me up though, because of the note inside: *Now you needn't fret about wearing someone else's knickers.*

Whatever Mencheres had Bones doing, he'd clearly allowed him some time to make arrangements. It shouldn't come as a surprise that Bones had intentions about tonight, lack of sleep or no lack of sleep.

"Um, have a nice time," I said, trying to play it cool.

Spade didn't say, "You too!" with a knowing wink. He only smiled and took Denise by the hand. "We'll be back before dawn."

They left, and shortly after, Annette followed suit. Since it was after dark, Bones would be here soon. I cleaned up the poker debris and then went in my room.

A lot of women have a ritual for a planned sexual encounter. In a way, it was the pre-foreplay foreplay. I took a quick shower and brushed my teeth. I'd already shaved from my earlier bath, so that was done. Then I applied unscented lotion, further smoothing my skin. After a quick blow-dry, I put a few curls into my hair to make it messily full. Finally, I applied a hint of makeup with matte lipstick.

I'd just finished when I heard the car pull up. I went downstairs, wanting to be semi-posed. As the car stopped, I positioned myself on the couch, then thought, *What if he wasn't alone?* I jumped up, starting back up the stairs, but relaxed a second later. I'd only heard one car door shut, so Mencheres must not have returned with Bones.

The key turned in the lock, making it too late for me to repeat my former pose. I only had time to turn around as Bones came in. Instead of the sultry hello I'd prepared, all that came out was a breathy, "Hi."

Bones didn't say anything as his eyes moved over me. I was wearing the long, tonally dyed slip that had come with the new bras and panties. At the top it was the palest pink, with whisper-thin straps and a deep neckline. As it went past my hips, it darkened in color until the bottom was a deep rose. I wasn't wearing anything under it, and since it revealed far more than it hid, his gaze didn't miss an inch.

"Catherine."

His voice, thicker with desire, made warmth course through me.

"Take me to bed." Not very original, but I couldn't seem to say anything else. Really, the last two words were redundant anyway.

In a blink, he was in front of me, his hands on my hips. They massaged me with slow circles as his mouth went to my neck. His tongue at my pulse shivered me, as did the brush of his fangs, then he went past my collarbone, dragging his lips down farther. Finally he settled on my breast, licking the peak before sucking it through the material.

The chafe of silk and his mouth grew while his hands explored my curves. He didn't raise the slip but used the fabric to his advantage as he dragged it along my body. I gripped his head, feeling dangerously weak when his mouth descended on my other breast.

"Take me to bed *now*," I managed to say, glad it hadn't come out as another, more explicit demand.

A strong suction had me arching my back to press closer to him. My nipples throbbed when he lifted his head. His eyes met mine, and they were scalding green.

His arms coiled around me, lifting me though his head stayed near my breasts, kissing the valley between them. The staircase didn't even creak with his quick steps, and he went straight to my bedroom. He could probably smell which one I'd slept in.

Bones set me on the bed, but I pushed him back when he began to stretch out next to me.

"Take off your clothes."

He stopped me when I began to undo his buttons. "Not yet."

"Yes. I want to touch you."

A groan came out of him. "Later, luv. I'm barely clinging to my control as it is, and I have plans for you."

That wasn't what I wanted, no matter how great it would feel. "Forget your control. I want you, not your willpower."

"Willpower?" He chuckled, smoothing the nightgown up my leg. "You're very wrong. I don't have any with you."

I stopped his hand. "If your clothes stay on, so do mine."

He began unbuttoning his shirt. I slid my palms along his chest when it was revealed. His skin felt incredible, so sleek and tight. When his shirt came off, he started on his pants. I slid closer to him, kissing his neck. His other hand climbed higher up my thigh.

My breath caught at the intimate stroke of his fingers. His touch was gentle, finding and then teasing the most sensitive parts of me. I opened my legs, gasping, and he began to suck on my throat. Not breaking the skin, just capturing my pulse in his mouth and tonguing it.

I pushed his pants down his legs. Two small thuds on the floor were his shoes, then finally he was naked. I couldn't stop touching him, reveling in the hum of power under his skin, his muscles, and all the familiar ridges and valleys of his body. Feeling them again aroused me almost as much as his seeking fingers. When I reached down to close my hand around him, he caught it.

"Let me look at you." Lust deepened his voice. His fangs were also out and his eyes were green fire. He dragged my nightgown up and over my head before letting it fall to the side. When he spoke again, his voice was throatier. "Sometimes I think I've dreamt you. Or that I've died and you're my heaven."

I stroked his cheek. "Or your hell, but I don't want to debate. I want you inside me."

"Yes." It was a hiss.

His body covered mine, pressing me back. My legs cradled his hips as he took my hands, stretching my arms over my head. Then the hard, thick feel of him grazed me.

I strained against him, impatient, wanting to grab him and feel him cleave into me. "Now, Bones."

His eyes glowed brighter at my panted words. "Not... yet."

He slid down, his mouth settling between my legs. A long, slow lick tore a cry from me, then additional, sensual delves left me burning with need.

"So sweet," he growled. "You taste like crushed flowers, and I must have more."

His tongue went deeper, almost convulsing me. Bands of pleasure yanked together in my belly, my heart thumped, and every inch of me felt on fire.

"Bones, *now!*"

A high-pitched demand he responded to by pulling my thighs over his shoulders, continuing his erotic assault. I clutched his head, all my words replaced by moans. He tasted every millimeter of me until I rocked against him in ecstasy. Everything inside me tensed when he began to suck on my clitoris, his fangs rubbing instead of piercing. Those strong pulls detonated the fireball in me, that inner throb erupting so fast I didn't even have time to scream. Bones moaned, caressing my thighs as I shuddered from my climax.

Then languorous warmth filled me, making me sound drowsy though I was far, far from sleepy. "Your mouth is deadly, you know that?"

A laugh tickled me and he gave a last lick before answering. "I enjoyed that so much I almost came with you."

I kissed him when he slid up, winding my arms around his neck. "Not yet," I breathed as he grasped my hips and moved between them.

"No?" he asked, stilling. "Too soon afterward?"

I pushed him away enough to maneuver. "No, but first…"

My head was at his stomach when he stopped me with a steel grip.

"Don't."

The flat refusal in his voice surprised me. "Why not?"

Something lurked in his eyes, gone in an instant, but I still caught it. If I hadn't known him so well, I wouldn't have.

"Not now." He moved me up and smiled. "My control is thin, and I want to take my time. Not be disgracefully quick like in the car."

"Bones." I held his gaze. "I'm not asking, and *don't* stop me again."

I slid lower on the bed, and he held himself absolutely still. It pierced me, because I'd seen in that glimpse what the real problem was. Raw, guilty shame had flashed in his eyes. The memory of what I'd overheard with Cannelle bothered him as much as it did me, it seemed.

I rubbed my cheek on his stomach while handling him with soft touches. "I love your skin. It's like a drug. I have to feel you when I'm near you, and when I'm near you, I want to taste you…"

I flicked my tongue into the crease of his thigh and his tenseness eased a notch. He couldn't see it, but I smiled. In this, I was confident. Long ago he had taught me all his weaknesses.

I licked along both creases of his thighs, only letting my breath fall on the hard length that throbbed against my cheek. Then my tongue grazed the sensitive skin of his sack, and he shuddered.

He sat up, reaching for me. "Catherine, let me—"

"No." I batted his hands away. "Just you."

He laughed somewhat unsteadily. "Why do I feel as though I'm in trouble?"

I met his eyes, giving a single, long lick along the length of his shaft. "Because you are."

Several minutes later, he came with a shout that would have caused someone to call the police if we'd been back in that bar parking lot.

"You think that my mouth is deadly?" His voice was strained as he pulled me up to him. "You've shown me to be a rank amateur."

My laugh was throaty. "If you're just being polite, you have only yourself to blame. You taught me what to do."

"Then well done to me." Bones captured my mouth with a long, deep kiss that excited me almost as much as hearing his shout of pleasure.

I slid on top of him, straddling him. "Too soon afterward?" I teased.

Hard flesh pierced me, replacing my laughter with an extended moan. Oh, the feel of him! Moving slowly but powerfully, swaying me to his pace. I balanced with my hands on his shoulders until he sat up, gripping me close. Then his mouth went to my breast, sucking with erotic intensity before his fangs penetrated the tip.

It wasn't a deep bite. Just enough to send throbs of pleasure through me from the juice in his fangs. My nipple felt seared, and when he sucked and bit the other one, all my defenses fell away.

"I love you." It was a gasp I couldn't hold back even though logic said it was too soon. My reason had just flatlined, however, leaving only my emotions in control.

Bones's mouth left my breasts and he froze like I'd flipped a switch.

Suddenly, I was nervous. "I meant, I love *this*—"

"Don't you dare." His hands left my body to hold my face. "Say that again."

"I don't want you to… to feel obligated—"

"Never say *that* to me again."

He was still inside me but not moving anymore. Back at the compound, I'd admitted to Bones that I loved him but hadn't said it since. Now, however, the intimacy of our joined bodies was too powerful, forcing out the words that fear wanted to hold back.

"I love you, Bones. I love you so much. God, so very, very much."

"Do you know how that makes me feel?" he whispered. "I've been many things these past two centuries, but I haven't known real happiness until this moment. I don't know if these are old emotions or new ones, and I don't care anymore. Please, Catherine. *Please.* Say that again."

He kissed me with the longing of someone starved, then began making love to me with an intensity that had tears coursing down my cheeks. I forgot that he was running on no sleep. Forgot Annette's advice on what tricks to try. I forgot everything except his last request, and I told him that I loved him with almost every gasping breath.

Author's note: *This is the end of the deleted alternate "middle" of* Destined for an Early Grave. *The rest of the story would have gone on pretty much as the published version, with Cat turning into a vampire and Gregor kidnapping and then forcibly changing over her mother. I had planned to have Bones regain his memory during the climactic fight scene with Gregor at the end. In that, Gregor would have used a knife secretly filled with his blood, intending to kill Bones in those vulnerable moments when his memories came crashing back. Cat's reaction would have been the same: blowing Gregor's head off when she realized that Bones was about to die. Cat would have gotten away with interfering in their duel the same way she did in the published version: Veritas would have examined the knife and found the secret device on it, confirming that Gregor had cheated. Cat's confirmation that Bones's memory had returned would have come right afterward, the first time he called her Kitten again.*

THANK YOU FOR READING

I hope that you enjoyed *Outtakes from the Grave!* Continue reading for a peek into Jeaniene's other best-selling series.

The Night Prince series:
    Once Burned
    Twice Tempted
    Bound By Flames
    Into The Fire

She's a mortal cursed with dark power. He's the prince of night…

After a tragic accident left Leila with a terrifying ability to channel electricity and to see a person's darkest secrets through a single touch, she is doomed to a life of solitude. Then creatures of the night kidnap Leila, forcing her to reach out to the world's most infamous vampire. Vlad Tepesh inspired the greatest vampire legend of all, and his ability to control fire makes him one of the most feared vampires in existence, but whatever you do, *don't* call him Dracula.

Teaser for *Once Burned*, book one in the Night Prince series:

"Why didn't you tell me there was a catch to drinking your blood? Maximus said that doing it made me, ah…"

"Mine." Vlad finished my sentence without hesitation.

My temper rose at his complete self-assuredness. "I didn't agree to that, so forget it."

He sat on the edge of the bed and leaned down, setting his arms on either side of my face. "You think my blood is the only tie between us?"

His voice was low, yet edged with palpable hunger. It seemed to rub me in places I'd only ever touched before, making my anger fade under a flash of desire. Vlad was so close that his hair was a shadowy veil all around me, and when he began to caress my face with light, sure strokes, it was all I could do not to close my eyes in bliss.

"This is our true tie," he whispered, his breath falling hotly onto my lips. "You're meant for me, and I *will* have you."

Praise for the Night Prince series:

"There are many Draculas out there, but only one Vlad, and you owe it to yourself to meet him."—#1 *New York Times* best-selling author Ilona Andrews

"I always open a Frost book with happy anticipation."—#1 *New York Times* best-selling author Charlaine Harris.

"I loved this book! A must-read for Jeaniene Frost fans."—*Fresh Fiction*

"One of the most riveting books that I have read this year."—*Romance Junkies*

"A taut, intriguing paranormal romantic suspense that keeps the pages turning from the very first paragraph."— *Kirkus Reviews*

To learn more, watch the book trailer, and read the first twenty percent, go here: http://jeanienefrost.com/night-prince-books/

The Broken Destiny series:
The Beautiful Ashes
The Sweetest Burn
The Brightest Embers

Sometimes falling in love really is the end of the world…

Ivy has always seen things she cannot explain. But when her sister goes missing, Ivy discovers that the truth is worse—her hallucinations are real, and the one person who can help her is the dangerously attractive guy bound by an ancient legacy to betray her.

The fate Adrian fought to escape is here, but he never expected the desire he feels for Ivy. Adrian knows what Ivy doesn't—the truth about her destiny and a war that could doom the world.

Teaser from *The Beautiful Ashes*, book one in the Broken Destiny series:

"I'm warning you, Ivy. Don't push me."

"Or what?" I flared. "You have nothing to threaten me with! The only reason I can stand to keep going is because I don't have anything to lose, so pushing you doesn't scare me—"

I didn't see Adrian's hands flash out, but suddenly they were in my hair as he yanked me to him, his mouth scorching mine.

My shock vanished. So did my questions. Desire hijacked my emotions, leaving nothing except a surge of need. Hints of alcohol flavored his kiss, but beneath that was his taste, infinitely more intoxicating, and I responded as if it was my drug of choice. I moaned as my head tilted back. Then he pulled me across the seats until I was on top of him.

"This is why I stayed away." Growled against my mouth as his hands started to rove over me with knowing, ruthless passion. "Can't be near you without wanting you. Can't stop myself anymore—"

His words cut off as his kiss deepened, until I could hardly breathe from the erotic thrusts and delves of his tongue. I'd been kissed before, but never like this. He wasn't exploring my mouth. He was claiming it.

Praise for the Broken Destiny series:

"A pure stunner. Frost skillfully balances passion and peril in an attention-grabbing story that's exciting from page one."—*Publishers Weekly*, starred review

"Jeaniene Frost brings her signature wit, sizzle, and extraordinary imagination to this epic new series."—#1 *New York Times* best-selling author Jennifer L. Armentrout

"Jeaniene Frost is blessed with a creative soul."—#1 *New York Times* best-selling author Sherrilyn Kenyon

"A fast-moving tale that refuses to let up until the end. Books don't get more fun or action-packed than this!"—*Romantic Times*

"If you prefer nail-biting, otherworldly suspense and adventure with your love story, this one's for you."—*Book Page*

To learn more, watch the book trailer, and read additional excerpts, go here: http://jeanienefrost.com/brokendestiny/

About the Author

Jeaniene Frost is the *New York Times*, *USA Today*, and international bestselling author of the Night Huntress series, the Night Prince series and the Broken Destiny series. To date, foreign rights for her novels have sold to twenty different countries. Jeaniene splits her time between North Carolina and Florida with her husband Matthew, who long ago accepted that she rarely cooks and always sleeps in on the weekends. Aside from writing, Jeaniene enjoys reading, poetry, watching movies, exploring old cemeteries, spelunking and traveling – by car. Airplanes, children, and cookbooks frighten her.

Find Jeaniene on:
www.jeanienefrost.com
www.goodreads.com/author/show/669810.Jeaniene_Frost
www.frost-light.livejournal.com
www. twitter.com/Jeaniene_Frost
www.facebook.com/JeanieneFrost
www.youtube.com/user/JeanieneFrost

Made in the USA
Columbia, SC
20 July 2021